PRAISE FOR *FURYBORN*

"Legrand's epic feminist fantasy is scary, sexy, and intense, set in a world made rich with magic, history, and a gorgeously imagined literary tradition."

—Melissa Albert, author of *The Hazel Wood*

"*Furyborn* is an addictive, fascinating fantasy. Truly not to be missed, this story…will have you on the edge of your seat."

—Kendare Blake, #1 *New York Times* bestselling author of the Three Dark Crowns series

"A veritable feast of magic: mystical beings, ruthless power struggles, and gorgeously cinematic writing that will sweep you off your feet."

—Traci Chee, *New York Times* bestselling author of the Sea of Ink and Gold series

"Immersive and intricate, *Furyborn* is a kick-you-in-the-teeth and grab-you-by-the-heart tale of two queens."

—Roshani Chokshi, *New York Times* bestselling author of *The Star-Touched Queen* and *A Crown of Wishes*

"Lush, riveting, and full of intrigue, *Furyborn* is a gripping read that grapples with questions of power, fate, and our abilities to change the world."

—S. Jae-Jones, *New York Times* bestselling author of *Wintersong*

"Epic in scope, endless in imagination, this book will grab hold of you and refuse to let go."

—Amie Kaufman, *New York Times* bestselling author of the Illuminae Files series and the Starbound trilogy

"A captivatingly imaginative world filled with intrigue and deception. *Furyborn* will leave you breathless and aching for more."

—Lisa Maxwell, *New York Times* bestselling
author of *The Last Magician*

"Legrand has created magic on every page. Flawed, smart, and fierce heroines kept me dazzled and breathless. Explosive and stunning."

—Mary E. Pearson, *New York Times* bestselling author of
The Remnant Chronicles and The Jenna Fox Chronicles

"Captivating and lovely, volatile and deadly. *Furyborn* is a sexy, luscious shiver of a book."

—Sara Raasch, *New York Times* bestselling
author of the Snow Like Ashes trilogy

"Two very different and fascinating young women, a delicious villain, nonstop action, and heart-pounding romance. A fantastic read!"

—Morgan Rhodes, *New York Times* bestselling
author of the Falling Kingdoms series

"Beautiful, brutal, heart-stopping, and epic, *Furyborn* is a world to lose yourself in—just bring weapons. It's dangerous there."

—Laini Taylor, *New York Times* bestselling author of *Strange the Dreamer* and the Daughter of Smoke and Bone trilogy

"Epic and unforgettable. I was captivated by the story of two powerful young women fighting to survive in this vivid, unique fantasy world. A must-read!"

—Amy Tintera, *New York Times* bestselling
author of the Ruined trilogy

FURYBORN

FURYBORN

THE EMPIRIUM TRILOGY • BOOK 1

CLAIRE LEGRAND

sourcebooks
fire

Published by Sourcebooks Fire, an imprint of Sourcebooks, Inc.
P.O. Box 4410, Naperville, Illinois 60567-4410
(630) 961-3900
Fax: (630) 961-2168
sourcebooks.com

The Library of Congress has cataloged the hardcover edition as follows:

Names: Legrand, Claire, 1986- author.
Title: Furyborn / Claire Legrand.
Description: Naperville, Illinois : Sourcebooks Fire, [2018] | Series:
    Empirium trilogy ; 1 | Summary: Rielle may prove to be one of the
    Prophesized Queens, if she survives the trials, and a thousand years later
    bounty hunter Eliana helps a girl who could be the answer to the prophecy.
Identifiers: LCCN 2017034431 | (13 : alk. paper)
Subjects: | CYAC: Fantasy.
Classification: LCC PZ7.L521297 Ash 2018 | DDC [Fic]--dc23 LC record
available at https://lccn.loc.gov/2017034431

Printed and bound in the United States of America.
VP 10 9 8 7 6 5 4 3 2 1

For Brittany,
who knew Celdaria first

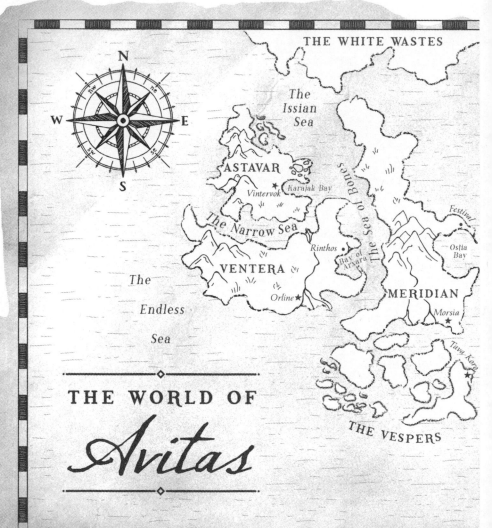

THE WHITE WASTES

The
Issian
Sea

ASTAVAR

Vintervok   Karajak Bay

The Sea of Bones

Festival

The Narrow Sea

Rinthos •

Ostia
Bay

Bay of
Arxara

VENTERA

Orline ★

MERIDIAN

Morsia
★

The

Endless

Sea

Tava Kore

THE VESPERS

THE WORLD OF

Avitas

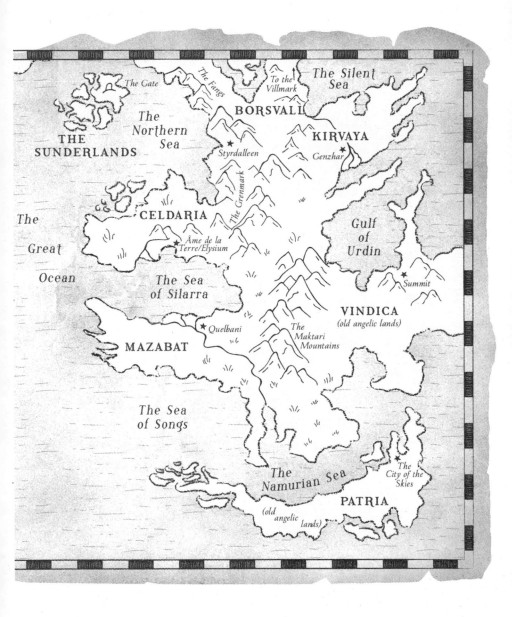

An End and a Beginning

"Some say the Queen was frightened in her last moments. But I like to think that she was angry."

—*The Word of the Prophet*

The queen stopped screaming just after midnight.

Simon had been hiding in her closet, fingers jammed into his ears to block out the noise. For hours, he had crouched there, knees drawn to chest, head bowed.

For hours, the queen's rooms had shuddered in tandem with her screams.

Now, there was silence. Simon held his breath and measured the seconds, like counting after a lightning strike until the thunder rolls: Is the storm fading, or is it coming closer?

One. Two. Three.

He reached twenty and dared to lower his hands.

A baby cried out into the silence. Simon grinned and scrambled to his feet, a wave of relief crashing through him.

The queen's child was born—*finally*. Now he and his father could flee this city and never look back.

Simon pushed past the queen's gowns and stumbled out into her bedroom.

"Father?" he asked, breathless.

Garver Randell, Simon's father, turned to face him, his eyes weary but his smile broad. And behind him lay Queen Rielle, her wild, dark hair plastered to her pale skin, her bedsheets and white nightgown stained red. She held a fussing bundle in her arms.

Simon crept closer to the bed in wonder, even as the sight of the queen made angry heat bloom in his chest. His kingdom's new princess was a small thing—scrunched red face, skin slightly darker than her mother's, wide brown eyes, a mop of wet black hair.

Simon's breath caught in his throat.

The baby looked very much like her late father.

Rielle stared at the child, then gazed up at Simon's father in bewilderment.

"I thought I would kill her," said the queen. She laughed, wiping her face with shaking fingers. "I dreamed I would. And yet here she is after all." She fumbled to adjust the baby in her arms. She didn't seem to be very good at holding babies.

It was strange to see the queen like this—small in her nest of pillows, looking hardly more than a girl though she was twenty years old. This queen who had allied with the angels and helped them kill thousands of humans.

This queen who had murdered her husband.

"Audric would have loved her," Rielle whispered, her face crumpling.

Simon's small fists clenched at his sides. How dare she talk about King Audric when she was the one who had killed him?

He had learned only a few things about the night the capital fell. King Audric had fought Queen Rielle on the broad veranda attached to the castle's fourth floor. The king's sword had blazed with the light of the sun, his diamond- and mirror-studded armor shining brighter than the stars.

But not even King Audric the Lightbringer, the most powerful sunspinner in centuries, had been strong enough to defeat Queen Rielle.

The queen had carved a sword out of the air, a blinding weapon forged from the empirium itself. Rielle and Audric had fought blade to blade, but the fight had been brief.

And when Rielle plunged her glowing hand into Audric's chest to tear out his heart, there had been nothing but bloodlust in her eyes as she watched her husband fall to ashes at her feet.

Simon wasn't a violent child, but all the same, he thought that if he looked at the queen for one more second, he might strike her.

So he uttered the Sun Queen's prayer in Audric's honor—*May the Queen's light guide him home*—and turned to his father instead.

That's when Garver Randell went rigid and whispered, "He knows," then fell gasping to his knees.

Simon rushed to his side. "Father? What is it? What's wrong?"

Garver clutched his head, his body jerking. "He knows, God help us, he *knows*," he moaned, and when he looked up, it was with eyes gone gray and cloudy.

Simon's heart sank to his feet. He knew those eyes, and what they meant.

An angel had found its way inside his father's mind at last.

And from the terror on his father's face, Simon knew it must be Corien.

"Father, listen to me! I'm right here!" Simon grabbed his father's arm. "Let's go. We can leave now! Please, hurry!"

Simon heard the queen behind him, singing softly to herself: "This is how you hold your child. This is how you murder your husband." Her laughter was thick with tears.

"He knows what I am," Garver rasped.

Simon's growing dread turned his body to stone.

Corien knew—that his father was a marque, and Simon was too. Neither angel nor human, but with the blood of both inside them.

Suddenly, the markings hidden on Simon's back beneath his tunic felt like flares that would alert everyone in the conquered city to where he was hiding. For years, he and his father had lived secretly in

Celdaria's capital, concealing their marked backs and their forbidden magic. They had been healers, honest and hard-working, sought out by commoners and temple magisters and even the royal family.

And now...now, Corien *knew*.

Simon shoved his father toward the door. "Father, move, please!"

Garver choked out, "Get away from me! He'll find you!" He seized Simon by the collar and shoved him away.

Simon's head smacked against the queen's four-poster bed, and he slumped to the floor, dazed. He watched his father turn, laugh a little, clutch his head. He watched him mutter angry, foreign words in a voice that was half his and half Coriens and then run, limping, to the terrace window.

Then, with a strangled cry, Garver Randell threw himself off the queen's tower.

Simon lurched up, grabbed the bed-curtains for support, stumbled forward, and fell. Head throbbing, fighting back the urge to be sick, he crawled across the floor to the terrace. At the railing, the mountain wind slapping his cheeks, he couldn't bear to look down. He pressed his face against the cool stone, wrapped his arms around two posts. Someone or something was making an awful choking noise.

"Simon," said a voice behind him.

He realized, then, that the awful noise was coming from him.

He jumped to his feet, rounding on Queen Rielle.

"You did this," he cried. "You killed us all! You're a monster! You're evil!"

He tried to say more: She had betrayed everyone in the kingdom of Celdaria, everyone in the world. She was supposed to be the Sun Queen, their savior and protector. And yet she had become the Blood Queen. The Kingsbane. The Lady of Death.

But Simon's tears blocked his voice. The wind whipping down along the mountainsides carved shivers from his skin. His small body heaved; he could hardly breathe.

He folded his arms tightly around himself, squeezing his eyes shut as the world tilted. He could not stop seeing the image of his father running out onto the terrace and flinging himself over the railing.

"Father," he whispered, "come back, please."

The queen settled gingerly on the settee across from him, her baby still in her arms. Her feet were bare and bloody, her nightgown soaked through with sweat.

"You're right, you know," said Rielle. "I did do this."

Simon was glad the queen didn't try to apologize. Nothing she could say would make anything better.

"I think," Rielle continued slowly, "that he will kill her."

Simon sniffed, wiped his mouth. His teeth chattered; he could not stop crying. "What do you mean?"

Rielle turned to look at him, her lips chapped and cracked. Once, Simon remembered, he had thought the queen beautiful.

"My daughter." Rielle's voice was hollow. "I think Corien will kill her. Or he'll try to."

Simon bit out, "He should kill you instead."

Rielle laughed at that—and kept laughing hysterically. Simon could only stare at her in rage and horror until she brought her child to her face, nuzzled her cheek against its own. The baby cooed and sighed.

"This is how," Rielle whispered, "you hold your child." She made a soft, sad noise. "Audric would have loved her."

Then the queen's face contorted, and she cried out in pain. She clutched her baby to her stomach and doubled over, gasping.

The stone shuddered beneath Simon's feet. The walls of the queen's rooms shifted in and out, like they were breathing along with her.

Rielle's skin glowed, changing, and for a terrible moment, Simon thought he could see through her flesh to the blood and bone beneath— and to the light beneath even that. She was outlined in shimmering flecks of gold, a luminous creature of sparks and embers.

Then the light faded, and Rielle was dim and human once more.

Simon's blood roared with fear. "What was that?"

"It won't be long now." Rielle turned her glittering gaze up to him, and Simon recoiled. The skin around her eyes was dark and thin. "I can't hold myself together for much longer."

"Do you mean…you're dying?"

"I've tried so hard for so long," Rielle muttered, and then she screamed once more, went rigid. Blazing bolts of light shot out from her fingers and streaked into the night, arcing over the dark city. The light left behind charred streaks, jagged across the terrace floor.

Rielle looked up, her face slick with sweat. Light moved in shimmering waves beneath her skin. Simon could not look away; she was at once the loveliest and most terrifying thing he had ever seen.

"Are you…hurting?" Simon asked.

Rielle laughed, a surprised little gasp. "I'm always hurting."

"Good," Simon replied, but not without a twinge of shame in his chest. She was a monster, yes, but a barefoot, exhausted monster with a child held tenderly in her arms.

The queen, his father had always told him whenever Simon stewed in his hatred, *was once just a girl. Remember that. Remember her.*

Then Rielle went very still.

"Oh, God," she whispered. "He's coming."

Simon backed away, alarm ringing in his ears. "Corien?"

Rielle used the wall to pull herself up, her shifting face tight with pain. "I cannot allow him to find you. Garver hid you well, but if he realizes you're here now and what you are…"

Simon touched his back, as if that could hide the markings there. "You…you know about us?"

Rielle's face flickered with something Simon couldn't read. "A friend told me. Just in case…well. In case I needed to know."

"I don't understand—"

"And I don't have time to explain. Hide with her; stay out here. I'll distract him."

And with that, Rielle pressed her daughter into Simon's arms and hurried back into her rooms.

Simon stared down at the baby. Her dark, serious eyes locked onto his face as if he were the most interesting thing in the world. Despite his aching head and the horrible hollow pain in his gut, Simon allowed her a small smile.

"Hello," he said and touched her cheek. "I'm Simon."

"Here, take this." Rielle reappeared, holding in her hand a necklace—a flat, gold pendant with a winged horse in flight carved onto its surface. On the horse sat a woman with streaming dark hair and a sword raised victoriously. Rays of sunlight fanned out behind her.

It was an image that had taken over Celdaria during the last two years, since the Church had declared Rielle to be the foretold Sun Queen.

How they had all loved her, once.

As the queen tucked the necklace into her baby's blanket, Simon watched her quietly. "Are you sorry for what you did?"

"Would it make you feel better if I was?"

Simon had no answer.

The queen kissed her daughter's brow. "He won't have you," she whispered. "Not you, my precious one."

Then she turned to Simon and, before he could protest, brushed aside his ash-blond hair and pressed a kiss to his forehead. His skin smarted where her lips had touched; tears gathered behind his eyes. He felt like he stood on the edge of a swaying cliff, like a terrible thing was about to happen and he could do nothing to stop it.

"Go to Borsvall," Rielle told him. "Find King Ilmaire and Commander Ingrid. Show them this necklace. They'll hide you."

The doors to Rielle's outer rooms slammed open.

"Rielle?" Corien roared.

Rielle cupped Simon's cheek and met his eyes. "Whatever happens, don't let him see you."

As she turned to go, Simon grabbed Rielle's hand. Without her, he would be alone with this child, and he suddenly wanted nothing more than to hide his face in Rielle's arms. Monster or no, she was now a parent, and that was a thing he craved more than anything.

"Please don't go," he whispered.

She gave him a tight smile. "You're strong, Simon. I know you can do this."

Then she hurried back inside and met Corien in the middle of her bedroom.

"Where is it?" came Corien's voice, low and dangerous.

Simon shifted slightly, peeking through a small sliver between the terrace curtains. His heart jumped in fear to see the leader of the angels—a beautiful man, pale and chiseled, hair gleaming black, lips full and cruel.

"She," Rielle corrected him. "I have a daughter."

Corien's gaze was deadly still. "And where is *she?*"

"I've sent her far away. With someone so powerful you'll never find her."

Simon's heart lifted. Was someone coming to help them?

Corien laughed unkindly. "Oh yes? And who might that be?"

"You can try and find the truth," said Rielle, "but you'll soon discover you're no longer welcome inside me."

With a snarl, Corien struck her hard across the mouth. Rielle stumbled, her lip bloodied, and Simon's gaze found hers. Her flaming-gold eyes were hard, triumphant. There was a strength on her tired face that he'd never seen before.

I've sent her far away. With someone so powerful you'll never find her. You're strong, Simon. You can do this.

And suddenly Simon understood: no one was coming to help them.

He was the powerful someone.

And it was up to him alone to save the princess.

He would have to use his magic—his half-blood marque magic, the traveling magic that had doomed nearly all of his kind—to send them both hundreds of miles away, to Borsvall and to safety.

Rielle turned back to Corien.

"You shouldn't get so angry," she told him. "You make mistakes when you're angry. If you hadn't been so blinded with it, you'd have stayed with me, grabbed her the moment she was born, and slit her throat right then and there."

Corien smiled coldly at her. "You might have killed me for that."

The queen shrugged. "Perhaps I'll kill you now anyway."

Simon turned away, his chest tight with fear. How could he possibly do this? He was only eight years old. He had read his traveling books over and over, of course, but he still didn't understand everything inside them. And from what his father had taught him about the old days, before the marques were hunted down by both humans and angels, most of their kind didn't attempt traveling until adulthood.

You can do this, Simon, came a voice. A woman's voice—but not the queen's. Familiar, but...

He whirled, searching the darkness, and found no one.

You must *do it*, said the voice. *You and the child, Simon, are the only ones who can save us. Quickly, now. Before he discovers you. Your father hid you well, but I can't protect you any longer.*

A thick, fleshy sound came from inside the queen's bedroom. Glass crashed to the floor. The queen cried out, and Corien muttered something hateful.

The castle groaned. The wall against which Simon hid rumbled like something deep underground was awakening. A hot burst of air erupted from inside the bedroom, shattering the windows. Simon ducked low over the baby. She squirmed against his chest with a muted, angry cry.

"Hush, please," Simon whispered. The air vibrated around him; the terrace rocked beneath his feet. Sweat rolled down his back. A thrumming bright light from within the bedroom swelled, growing ever more brilliant.

He closed his eyes, tried to forget the strange woman's voice and concentrate. He searched his mind for the words in his forbidden books, now abandoned beneath the floorboards of his father's shop:

The empirium lies within every living thing, and every living thing is of the empirium.

Its power connects not only flesh to bone, root to earth, stars to sky, but also road to road, city to city.

Moment to moment.

Only marques, Simon knew, had this mighty gift. The gift of traveling. The ability to cross vast distances in an instant and walk through time as easily as others walk down the road.

Simon had often fantasized about what it would be like to travel back to the time before the Gate was made—before the old wars, when angels still walked the earth and dragons darkened the skies.

But he couldn't think about time, not just then. Time was a dangerous, slippery thing. He must think only about distance: Celdaria to Borsvall.

"No, Rielle!" Corien was screaming. "No! Don't do this!"

Simon looked back inside to see Queen Rielle on her knees with her face turned to the sky, struggling to stay upright as a brilliant shell of light swelled around her. Corien pounded on the light, burning his fists, but he couldn't touch her. He clawed and shouted, cursed at her, pleaded with her.

But all his screams were no use. Rielle's body was unfurling in long streams of light, her skin flaking away like ash on the wind.

Simon turned away and whispered to the princess, "Don't worry, I won't let go. I've got you."

He closed his eyes, bit his lip, ignored the desperate shouts of Corien and the queen's blinding light. He directed his mind northeast, toward Borsvall. As his books had instructed, he guided his breath along every line of his body, every sinew, every bone.

Now.

His eyes snapped open.

Twisting strands of light, thin and smoky, floated through the air before him.

Heart racing, Simon held the princess close with one arm and reached out with the other. He listened to his blood, for it knew the way just as it knew to step, to swallow, to breathe. He felt through the night for the correct threads of *here* and *there*. Somewhere before him lay a road, hidden to his eyes but known, unquestionably, by the power that thrummed in his veins, and if he could just find the right thread, tug it free, lay it out before his feet like a winding carpet—

There.

A single thread, brighter than the others, danced at his fingertips.

Simon hardly dared to reach for it. If he moved too slowly or too quickly, if his mind wandered, the thread could slip away from him.

Behind him, the queen screamed at Corien, her voice thick with fury: "I am no longer yours!"

There was no time for doubt. Simon reached for the brightest thread, cautiously guided it around his fingers like a lock of shining hair.

Take a moment, his books had said, *to get to know your thread. The more familiar you are with it, the more likely it is to take you where you want to go.*

As Simon stared at the thread hovering in his hand, others brightened and drifted closer, pulled by the force of his concentration.

Though they scorched the tender skin of his palms, he gathered up the threads in his hands, guiding them through the chill night air. Soon he had maneuvered the threads into a quivering ring, and past the ring stretched a passage into darkness.

The first thread, the brightest, crept to Simon's chest and clung there like a briar, tugging him gently forward.

Simon felt silly about it but thought to the thread nevertheless, *Hello.*

The pressure of its touch lightened.

Simon saw faint shapes through the shifting, sharpening passage:

A winding path of black stone, a tall, narrow gate. Ice-capped mountains. Soldiers pointing in awe, shouting in the harsh Borsvallic tongue.

Every muscle in Simon's young body snapped rigid. With each breath, the world dimmed. And yet laughter bubbled up inside him even so. He could not imagine ever being happier. It was not easy, this power, but it was right, and it was *his*.

Then, behind him, Queen Rielle cried out something Simon couldn't understand. Her voice shattered.

Corien's frantic screams were hoarse with anguish.

Simon swallowed hard, fear crowding him like a swarm of insects.

A great, sudden stillness swallowed away all sound—the infant's cries, the humming threads. The world fell silent.

Simon looked back just as a column of light shot up from the queen's bedroom and into the night, turning the sky white as the dawn. Simon hid his face, bowing his head over the infant in his arms. His traveling hand shook as he worked. An instant later, the silence erupted into a shattering boom that shook the mountains and nearly knocked Simon off his feet.

The castle pitched beneath him. The air popped with the smell of fire. One of the mountains surrounding the capital collapsed, followed by another—and another.

Hold on to her, said the woman's voice once more, high and clear in his mind. *Don't ever let her go.*

The threads were slipping in the grip of Simon's thoughts. He felt stretched between where his feet stood and where the thread at his chest tugged.

Go, Simon! the woman's voice cried. *Now!*

Simon stepped toward the ring of light that led east just as a blazing heat bloomed at his heels.

The last things Simon knew came at him slowly:

A bright wall of fire rushing at him from all sides, crackling like a thousand storms. The air shifting around him as he stepped through the threads' passage, like cold water sliding over his skin. The princess screaming in his arms.

The sight of the Borsvall mountains fading.

The thread attached to his heart changing. Twisting.

Darkening.

Breaking, with a snap like thunder.

A force slamming into him, snatching him forward by his bones.

The baby being ripped from his arms, no matter how hard he tried to hold on to her.

A piece of fabric, ripping in his hands.

And then, nothing.

— 1 —

RIELLE

*"Lord Commander Dardenne came to me in the middle
of the night, his daughter in his arms. They smelled of
fire; their clothes were singed. He could hardly speak.
I had never seen the man afraid before. He thrust Rielle
into my arms and said, 'Help us. Help her. Don't let
them take her from me.'"*

—Testimony of Grand Magister Taliesin Belounnon,
on Lady Rielle Dardenne's involvement
in the Boon Chase massacre
April 29, Year 998 of the Second Age

TWO YEARS EARLIER

Rielle Dardenne hurried into Tal's office and dropped the sparrow's message onto his desk.

"Princess Runa is dead," she announced.

She wouldn't describe her mood as *excited* exactly, but her own kingdom, Celdaria, and their northeastern neighbor, Borsvall, had lived in a state of tension for so many decades that it was hardly noteworthy when, say, a Celdarian merchant ship sank off Borsvall's coast or patrols came to blows near the border.

But a murdered Borsvall princess? That was news. And Rielle wanted to dissect every piece of it.

Tal let out a sigh, set down his pen, and dragged his ink-smudged hands through his messy blond hair. The polished golden flame pinned to his lapel winked in the sunlight.

"Perhaps," Tal suggested, turning a look on Rielle that was not quite disapproval and not quite amusement, "you should consider looking less thrilled about a princess's murder?"

She slid into the chair across from him. "I'm not happy about it or anything. I'm simply intrigued." Rielle pulled the slip of paper back across the desk and read over the inked words once more. "So you do think it was assassination? Audric thinks so."

"Promise me you won't do anything stupid today, Rielle."

She smiled sweetly at him. "When have I ever done anything stupid?"

He quirked an eyebrow. "The city guard is on high alert. I want you here, safe in the temple, in case anything happens." He took the message from her, scanning its contents. "How did you get this, anyway? No, wait. I know. Audric gave it to you."

Rielle stiffened. "Audric keeps me informed. He's a good friend. Where's the harm in that?"

Tal didn't answer, but he didn't have to.

"If you have something to say to me," she snapped, color climbing up her cheeks, "then just say it. Or else let's begin our lesson."

Tal watched her a moment longer, then turned to pick up four enormous books sitting on the shelf behind him.

"Here," he said, ignoring the mutinous expression on her face. "I've marked some passages for you to read. Today will be devoted to quiet study. And I'll test you later, so don't even think about skimming."

Rielle narrowed her eyes at the book on the top of the stack. "*A Concise History of the Second Age, Volume I: The Aftermath of the Angelic Wars.*" She made a face. "This hardly looks concise."

"It's all a matter of perspective," he said, returning to the papers on his desk.

Rielle's favorite place in Tal's office was the window seat

overlooking the main temple courtyard. It was piled high with scarlet cushions lined in gold piping, and when she sat there, dangling her legs out into the sun, she could almost forget that there was an enormous world beyond the temple and her city—a world she would never see.

She settled by the window, kicked off her boots, hiked up her heavy lace-trimmed skirts, and rested her bare feet on the sill. The spring sunlight washed her legs in warmth, and soon she was thinking of how Audric blossomed on bright, sun-filled days like this one. How his skin seemed to glow and crackle, begging to be touched.

Tal cleared his throat, breaking her focus.

Tal knew her far too well.

She cracked open *A Concise History*, took one look at the tiny, faded text, and imagined tossing the book out the window and into the temple courtyard, where citizens were filing in for morning prayers—to pray that the riders they had wagered upon in today's race would win, no doubt. Every temple in the capital would be full of such eager souls, not just there in the Pyre—Tal's temple, where citizens worshipped Saint Marzana the firebrand—but in the House of Light and the House of Night as well and the Baths and the Firmament, the Forge and the Holdfast. Whispered prayers in all seven temples, to all seven saints and their elements.

Wasted prayers, thought Rielle with a slight, sharp thrill. *The other racers will look like children on ponies compared to me.*

She flipped through a few pages, biting the inside of her lip until she felt calm enough to speak. "I've heard many in the Borsvall court are blaming Celdaria for Runa's death. We wouldn't do such a thing, would we?"

Tal's pen scratched across his paper. "Certainly not."

"But it doesn't matter if it's true or not, does it? If King Hallvard's councils convince him that we killed his daughter, he will declare war at last."

Tal dropped his pen with a huff of annoyance. "I'm not going to get any work done today, am I?"

Rielle swallowed her grin. *If only you knew how true that is, dearest Tal.*

"I'm sorry if I have questions about the political climate of our country," she said. "Does that fall under the category of things we're not allowed to discuss, lest my poor vulnerable brain shatter from the stress?"

A smile twitched at the corner of Tal's mouth. "Borsvall might declare war, yes."

"You don't seem concerned about this possibility."

"I find it unlikely. We've been on the edge of war with Borsvall for decades, and yet it has never happened. And it *will* never happen, because the Borsvall people may be warmongers, but King Hallvard is neither healthy nor stupid. We would flatten his army. He can't afford a war with anyone, much less with Celdaria."

"Audric said..." Rielle hesitated. A twist of unease slipped down her throat. "Audric said he thinks Princess Runa's death, and the slave rebellion in Kirvaya, means it's time. That the Queens are coming."

Silence fell over the room like a shroud.

"Audric has always been fascinated with the prophecy," Tal said, his voice deceptively calm. "He's been looking for signs of the Queens' coming for years."

"He sounds rather convinced this time."

"A slave rebellion and a dead princess are hardly enough to—"

"But I heard Grand Magister Duval talking about how there have been storms across the ocean in Meridian," she pressed on, searching his face. "Even as far as Ventera and Astavar. Strange storms, out of season."

Tal blinked. *Ah*, thought Rielle. *You didn't know that, did you?*

"Storms do occur out of season from time to time," Tal said. "The empirium works in mysterious ways."

Rielle curled her fingers in her skirts, taking comfort in the fact that soon she would be in her riding trousers and boots, her collar open to the breeze.

She would be on the starting line.

"The report I read," she continued, "said that a dust storm in southern Meridian had shut down the entire port of Morsia for days."

"Audric needs to stop showing you every report that comes across his desk."

"Audric didn't show me anything. I found this one myself."

Tal raised an eyebrow. "You mean you snuck into his office when he wasn't there and went through his papers."

Rielle's cheeks grew hot. "I was looking for a book I'd left behind."

"Indeed. And what would Audric say if he knew you'd been in his office without his permission?"

"He wouldn't care. I'm free to come and go as I please."

Tal closed his eyes. "Lady Rielle, you can't just visit the crown prince's private rooms day and night as though it's nothing. You're not children anymore. And you are not his fiancée."

Rielle lost her breath for an instant. "I'm well aware of that."

Tal waved a hand and rose from his chair, effectively ending all talk of the prophecy and its Queens.

"The city is crowded today—and unpredictable," he said, walking across the room to pour himself another cup of tea. "Word is spreading about Princess Runa's death. In such a climate, the empirium can behave in similarly unpredictable ways. Perhaps we should begin a round of prayers to steady our minds. Amid the chaos of the world, the burning flame serves as an anchor, binding us in peace to the empirium and to God."

Rielle glared at him. "Don't use your magister voice, Tal. It makes you sound old."

He sighed, took a sip of his tea. "I am old. And grumpy, thanks to you."

"Thirty-two is hardly old, especially to already be Grand Magister of the Pyre." She paused. She would need to proceed carefully. "I wouldn't be surprised if you were appointed as the next Archon. Surely, with someone as talented as you beside me, I could safely watch the Chase from your box—"

"Don't try to flatter me, Lady Rielle." His eyes sparked at her. There was the Tal she liked—the ferocious firebrand, not the pious teacher. "It isn't safe for you out there right now, not to mention dangerous for everyone else if something set you off and you lost control."

Rielle slammed shut *A Concise History* and rose from the window seat. "Damn you, Tal."

"Not in the temple, please," Tal admonished over the rim of his cup.

"I'm not a child. Do you really think I don't know better by now?" Her voice turned mocking. "'Rielle, let's say a prayer together to calm you.' 'Rielle, let's sing a song about Saint Katell the Magnificent to take your mind off things.' 'No, Rielle, you can't go to the masque. You might forget yourself. You might have fun, God forbid.' If Father had his way, I'd stay locked up for the rest of my life with my nose buried in a book or on my knees in prayer, whipping myself every time I had a stray angry thought. Is that the kind of life you would like for me too?"

Tal watched her, unmoved. "If it meant you were safe and that others were safe as well? Yes, I would."

"Kept under lock and key like some criminal." A familiar, frustrated feeling rose within her; she pushed it back down with a vengeance. She would not lose control, not today of all days.

"Do you know," she said, her voice falsely bright, "that when it storms, Father takes me down to the servants' quarters and gives me dumbwort? It puts me to sleep, and he locks me up and leaves me there."

After a pause, Tal answered, "Yes."

"I used to fight him. He would hold me down and slap me, pinch my nose shut until I couldn't breathe and had to open my mouth. Then he would shove the vial between my lips and make me drink, and I would spit it up, but he would keep forcing me to drink, whispering to me everything I'd ever done wrong, and right in the middle of yelling how much I hated him, I would fall asleep. And when I would wake up, the storm would be over."

A longer pause. "Yes," Tal answered softly. "I know."

"He thinks storms are too provocative for me. They give me *ideas*, he says."

Tal cleared his throat. "That was my fault."

"I know."

"But the medicine, that was his suggestion."

She gave him a withering look. "And did you try to talk him out of it?"

He did not answer, and the patience on his face left her seething.

"I don't fight him anymore," she said. "I hear a crack of thunder and go below without him even asking me to. How pathetic I've become."

"Rielle..." Tal sighed, shook his head. "Everything I could say to you, I've said before."

She approached him, letting the loneliness she typically hid from him—from everyone—soften her face. *Come, good Magister Belounnon. Pity your sweet Rielle.* He broke first, looking away from her. Something like sorrow shifted across his face, and his jaw tightened.

Good.

"He'd let me sleep through life if he could," she said.

"He loves you, Rielle. He worries for you."

Heat snapped at Rielle's fingertips, growing along with her anger. With a stubborn stab of fury, she let it come. She knew she shouldn't, that an outburst would only make it more difficult to sneak away, but suddenly she could not bring herself to care.

He loves you, Rielle.

A father who loved his daughter would not make her his prisoner.

She seized one of the candles from Tal's desk and watched with grim satisfaction as the wick burst into a spitting, unruly flame. As she stared at it, she imagined her fury as a flooding river, steadily spilling over its banks and feeding the flame in her hands.

The flame grew—the size of a pen, a dagger, a sword. Then every candle followed suit, a forest of fiery blades.

Tal rose from his desk and picked up the handsome polished shield from its stand in the corner of the room. Every elemental who had ever lived—every waterworker and windsinger, every shadowcaster and every firebrand like Tal—had to use a casting, a physical object uniquely forged by their own hands, to access their power. Their singular power, the one element they could control.

But not Rielle.

She needed no casting, and fire was not the only element that obeyed her.

All of them did.

Tal stood behind her, one hand holding his shield, the other hand resting gently on her own. As a child, back when she had still thought she loved Tal, such touches had thrilled her.

Now she seriously considered punching him.

"In the name of Saint Marzana the Brilliant," Tal murmured, "we offer this prayer to the flames, that the empirium might hear our plea and grant us strength: Fleet-footed fire, blaze not with fury or abandon. Burn steady and true, burn clean and burn bright."

Rielle bit down on harsh words. How she hated praying. Every familiar word felt like a new bar being added to the cage her father and Tal had crafted for her.

The room began to shake—the inkwell on Tal's desk, the panes of glass in the open window, Tal's half-finished cup of tea.

"Rielle?" Tal prompted, shifting his shield. In his body behind her, she felt a rising hot tension as he prepared to douse her fire with his own power. Despite her best efforts, the concern in his voice caused her a twinge of remorse. He meant well, she knew. He wanted, desperately, for her to be happy.

Unlike her father.

So Rielle bowed her head and swallowed her anger. After all, what she was about to do might turn Tal against her forever. She could allow him this small victory.

"Blaze not with fury or abandon," she repeated, closing her eyes. She imagined setting aside every scrap of emotion, every sound, every thought, until her mind was a vast field of darkness—except for the tiny spot of light that was the flame in her hands.

Then she allowed the darkness to seep across the flame as well and was left alone in the cool, still void of her mind.

The room calmed.

Tal's hand fell away.

Rielle listened as he returned his shield to its stand. The prayer had scraped her clean, and in the wake of her anger she felt...nothing. A hollow heart and an empty head.

When she opened her eyes, they were dry and tired. She wondered bitterly what it would be like to live without a constant refrain of prayers in her thoughts, warning her against her own feelings.

The temple bells chimed eleven times; Rielle's pulse jumped. Any moment now, she would hear Ludivine's signal.

She turned toward the window. No more prayers, no more reading. Every muscle in her body surged with energy. She wanted to *ride*.

"I'd rather be dead than live as my father's prisoner," she said at last, unable to resist that last petulant stab.

"Dead like your mother?"

Rielle froze. When she faced Tal, he did not look away. She had not expected that cruelty. From her father, yes, but never from Tal.

The memory of long-ago flames blazed across her vision.

"Did Father instruct you to bring that up if I got out of hand?" she asked, keeping her voice flat and cool. "What with the Chase and all."

"Yes," Tal answered, unflinching.

"Well, I'm happy to tell you I've only killed the one time. You needn't worry yourself."

After a moment, Tal turned to straighten the books on his desk. "This is as much for your safety as it is for everyone else's. If the king discovered we'd been hiding the truth of your power all these years...

You know what could happen. Especially to your father. And yet he does it because he loves you more than you'll ever understand."

Rielle laughed sharply. "That isn't reason enough to treat me like this. I'll never forgive him for it. Someday, I'll stop forgiving you too."

"I know," Tal said, and at the sadness in his voice, Rielle nearly took pity on him.

Nearly.

But then a great crash sounded from downstairs, and an unmistakable cry of alarm.

Ludivine.

Tal gave Rielle that familiar look he so often had—when she had, at seven, overflowed their pool at the Baths; when he had found her, at fifteen, the first time she snuck out to Odo's tavern. That look of *What did I do to deserve such trials?*

Rielle gazed innocently back at him.

"Stay here," he ordered. "I mean it, Rielle. I appreciate your frustration—truly, I do—but this is about more than the injustice of you feeling bored."

Rielle returned to the window seat, hoping her expression appeared suitably abashed.

"I love you, Tal," she said, and the truth of that was enough to make her hate herself a little.

"I know," he replied. Then he threw on his magisterial robe and swept out the door.

"Magister, it's Lady Ludivine," came a panicked voice from the hallway—one of Tal's young acolytes. "She'd only just arrived in the chapel, my lord, when she turned pale and collapsed. I don't know what happened!"

"Summon my healer," Tal instructed, "and send a message to the queen. She'll be in her box at the starting line. Tell her that her niece has taken ill and will not be joining her there."

Once they had gone, Rielle smiled and yanked on her boots.

Stay here?

Not a chance.

She hurried through the sitting room outside Tal's office and into the temple's red-veined marble hallways, where embroidered flourishes of shimmering flames lined the plush carpets. The temple entryway, its parquet floor polished to a sheen of gold, was a flurry of activity as worshippers, acolytes, and servants hurried across to the peaked chapel doors.

"It's Lady Ludivine," a young acolyte whispered to her companion as Rielle passed. "Apparently she's taken ill."

Rielle grinned, imagining everyone fussing over poor Ludivine, tragically lovely and faint on the temple floor. Ludivine would enjoy the attention—and the reminder that she had the entire capital held like a puppet on its master's strings.

Even so, Rielle would owe her a tremendous favor after this.

Whatever it was, it would be more than worth it.

Ludivine's horse stood next to her own just outside the temple, held by a young stable hand who seemed on the verge of panic. He recognized Rielle and sagged with relief.

"Pardon me, Lady Rielle, but is Lady Ludivine all right?" he asked.

"Haven't the faintest," Rielle replied, swinging up into the saddle. Then she snapped the reins, and her mare bolted down the main road that led from the Pyre into the heart of the city, hooves clattering against the cobblestones. A tumbled array of apartments and temple buildings rose around them—gray stone walls engraved with scenes of the capital city's creation, rounded roofs of burnished copper, slender columns wrapped in flowering ivy, white fountains crowned with likenesses of the seven saints in prayer. So many visitors had come from all over the world to Âme de la Terre for the Chase that the cool spring air now pressed thick and close. The city smelled of sweat and spices, hot horse and hot coin.

As Rielle tore down the road, the crowd parted in alarm on either side of her, shouting angry curses until they realized who she was and fell silent. She guided her mare through the twisting streets and made for the main city gates, her body pulled tight with nerves.

But she would not give in to her power today.

She would compete in the Boon Chase, as any citizen was free to do, and prove to her father that she could control herself, even when her life was in danger and the eyes of the entire city were upon her.

She would prove to him, and to Tal, that she deserved to live a normal life.

⭠ 2 ⭢

ELIANA

*"Eliana says that on the day the Empire took our city,
you couldn't breathe without choking on the taste of
blood. She said I should be glad I was only a baby,
but I wish I could remember it. Maybe then I would be
stronger. I would be a warrior. Like her."*

—Journal of Remy Ferracora, citizen of Orline
February 3, Year 1018 of the Third Age

1,020 YEARS LATER

Eliana was on the hunt when she heard the first scream.

Screams weren't so unusual in the city of Orline, especially in the Barrens, where slums sprawled across the river docks in a dark plain of misery.

This one, though, was high, piercing—a young girl's scream—and fell silent so abruptly Eliana thought she might have been imagining things.

"Did you hear that?" she whispered to Harkan, who stood beside her with his back against the wall.

Harkan tensed. "Hear what?"

"That scream. A girl."

"I heard no scream."

Eliana glanced at the nearby darkened window, adjusted her new velvet mask, admired the lean lines of her body. "Well, we all know your hearing's shit."

"My hearing is not shit," Harkan muttered.

"It's not as good as mine."

"We can't all be as marvelous as the Dread of Orline."

Eliana sighed. "Sad, but true."

"I think even I, with my shit ears, would hear a scream. Maybe you imagined it."

But Eliana didn't think so.

In the city of Orline, girls and women had been disappearing of late—not shipped off to an Empire work camp nor taken to the Lord of Orline's palace to be trained in the maidensfold. Those things left behind gossip, trails of evidence.

These recent girls were simply being taken. One moment they were there; the next they were gone.

At first, Eliana hadn't let herself care. No one in her neighborhood had been taken, and she didn't think the Empire would start abducting its own favored citizens. Her family was safe. It therefore wasn't her problem.

But the more girls disappeared, the more stories she heard of vanished women, the harder it became for her to ignore the situation. So many sisters gone, and so many mothers—snatched from their loved ones, taken as they slept. Not criminals, not Red Crown rebels.

And then there were the rumors that persisted in some circles, despite their absurdity, of a hole in the sky on the other side of the world. Possibly in Celdaria. Possibly in the Sunderlands. Every rumor told a different tale. Some thought everything was connected—the hole in the sky, the vanished girls.

Eliana was not one of them. Hole in the sky? More like fear run amok. People were becoming hysterical enough to look to archaic legends for comfort and truth.

Eliana refused to join them.

Then she heard it again: a second scream. Closer.

A sour feeling drifted through her body, raking violent chills across her skin. The world tilted, froze, then righted itself. The sweet odor of the white gemma tree flowers overhead turned rancid.

Beside her, Harkan shifted. "Are you all right?"

"Don't you feel that?"

"Feel *what*? What's going on with you tonight?"

"I feel…" The edges of her vision shimmered like a heat mirage. "I don't know what I feel. Like an adatrox is nearby, but worse."

At the mention of the Empire soldiers, Harkan tensed. "I don't see any adatrox. Are you sure?"

A third scream—more desperate this time and quickly stifled.

"Whoever it is," Eliana muttered, her voice tight and angry, "they're close."

"What? *Who*?"

"Arabeth's next meal." Eliana flashed Harkan a grin, then unsheathed Arabeth—the long, jagged-bladed dagger she kept at her hip. "Time to play."

With one last peek at her reflection, she darted out from the shadows and into the cramped, grime-slicked alleyways of lower Orline. Harkan called after her; she ignored him. If he wanted to stop her, he could try, but she'd have him flat on his back in two seconds.

She smirked. The last time she'd pinned him like that, it had been to his bed.

She honestly couldn't decide which context she preferred.

All the same, she didn't want to start a fight just yet. Not when she had a girl-snatcher to hunt.

She entered the Barrens, slipping between patched tents and sagging wooden shacks dotted with dying fires. Beyond the Barrens crawled the wide Bruvian river, its banks clogged with piles of festering white moss.

Her first time in these slums, aged ten, she had nearly gagged from the smell. That had earned her a hard glare from her mother.

Now, eight years later, the stench hardly registered.

She scanned the night: A beggar picking the pockets of an unconscious drunkard. A gaunt young man, coifed and powdered, coaxing a woman through a painted door.

Another scream. Fainter. They were heading for the river.

The feeling crawling up her spine magnified. It felt—she knew no other way to describe it—as though it had a *will*.

She placed her hands on her knees, squeezed her eyes shut. Spots of color danced behind her eyelids. On the battered wooden support beam beside her, someone had scrawled a childish drawing of a masked woman in black, leaping through the air with a knife in each hand.

Despite the ill feeling blotting her vision, Eliana couldn't help but grin.

"El, for the love of the saints, what are you doing?" Harkan came up beside her, put a hand on her shoulder. "What's wrong? Are you hurt?"

"Me? Hurt?" She swallowed hard against the sick feeling tightening her throat. "Dearest Harkan." She gestured grandly at the drawing of herself. "How could you think such a thing of the Dread of Orline?"

She sprinted away and jumped off the top level of the docks onto another level about one hundred feet below. The impact jolted her with only a slight pain. She was up and running again in an instant. Such a fall would break Harkan's legs; he'd have to take the long way down.

If Remy were there, he would tell her not to be so obvious.

"People have started to notice," he had told her just the other day. "I hear talk at the bakery."

Eliana, stretching on the floor of her bedroom, had asked innocently, "What kind of talk?"

"When a girl falls three stories and then jumps right back to her feet in the middle of the Garden Square, people tend to notice. Especially when she's wearing a cape."

Eliana had smiled at the thought of their gaping, awestruck faces. "And what if I want them to notice?"

Remy had been quiet for a long moment. Then: "Do you *want* Invictus to come and take you away from me?"

That had silenced her. She'd looked up at her little brother's pale, pinched face and felt her stomach turn over.

"I'm sorry," she'd told him quietly. "I'm such an ass."

"I don't care if you're an ass," he'd replied. "Just don't be a show-off."

He was right, she knew. The problem was, she *liked* showing off. If she was going to be a freak with a miraculous body that no fall could kill, then she might as well have fun with it.

If she was busy having fun, then she didn't have time to wonder why her body could do what it did.

And what that meant.

Running through the docks, she followed the trail of wrongness in the air like tracking the scent of prey. The docks' lowest level was quiet, the summer air still and damp. She ran around one corner and then another—and stopped. The scent, the *feeling*, roiled at the edge of this rickety pier. She forced her way forward, even though her churning stomach and every roaring ounce of her blood screamed at her to stay away.

Two figures—masked and wearing dark traveling clothes—waited in a long, sleek boat at the pier's edge. Their tall, blunt builds suggested they were men. A third figure carried a small girl with golden-brown skin like Harkan's. The girl struggled, a gag stuffed in her mouth, her wrists and ankles bound.

Red Crown? Unlikely. What would the rebels want with stolen children? And if Red Crown were involved in the abductions, Eliana would have heard whispers from the underground by now.

They could be bounty hunters like herself, but why would the Undying Empire pay for what it could simply take? And working in a group? *Very* unlikely.

One of the figures in the boat held out its arms for the girl. Lumps crowded the boat's floor—other women, other girls, bound and unconscious.

Eliana's anger ignited.

She pulled long, thin Whistler from her left boot.

"Going somewhere, gentlemen?" she called and ran at them.

The figure on the dock turned just as Eliana reached him. She whirled, caught him with her boot under his chin. He fell, choking.

One of the figures from the boat jumped onto the dock. She swiped him across the throat with Arabeth, pushed him into the water after his comrade.

She spun around, triumphant, beckoned at the abductor still waiting in the boat.

"Come on, love," she crooned. "You're not afraid of me, are you?"

Once, she had flinched at killing. Her first had been six years ago, at the age of twelve. Rozen Ferracora, Eliana's mother, had brought her along on a job—the last Rozen had taken before her injury—and someone had ratted them out. The rebels had known they were coming. It had been an ambush.

Rozen had felled two of them, and Eliana had hidden in the shadows. That had always been her mother's instruction: *I'll keep you from killing as long as I can, sweet girl. For now, watch. Learn. Practice. What my father taught me, I will teach you.*

Then one of the rebels had pinned Rozen to the ground, and Eliana had known nothing but rage.

She flew at the rebel woman, thrust her little blade deep into the woman's back. Then she stood, staring, as the woman gasped away her life in a pool of blood.

Rozen had taken Eliana's hand, hurried her away. Back home in their kitchen, her brother, Remy—then only five—had stared wide-eyed as Eliana's shock gave way to panic. Hands red with blood, she had sobbed herself hoarse in her mother's arms.

Luckily, the killing had grown much easier.

Two masked figures darted forward out of the shadows, small bundles in their arms. More girls? They tossed the bundles to their last remaining comrade in the boat, then spun to meet her. She ducked one blow, then another, then took a hard one to the stomach and a sharp hook to the jaw.

She stumbled, shook it off. The pain vanished as quickly as it had come. She whirled and stabbed another of the brutes. He toppled into the filthy water.

Then a wave of nausea slammed into her, mean as a boot to the gut. She dropped to her knees, gasping for air. A weight settled on her shoulders, fogged her vision, pressed her down hard against the river-slicked dock.

Five seconds. Ten. Then the pressure vanished. The air no longer felt misaligned around her body; her skin no longer crawled. She raised her head, forced open her eyes. The boat was gliding away.

Wild with anger, head still spinning, Eliana staggered to her feet. A strong arm came around her middle, pulling her backward just as she prepared to dive.

"Get off me," she said tightly, "or I'll get nasty." She elbowed Harkan in his ribs.

He swore, but didn't let go. "El, have you lost your mind? This isn't the job."

"They took her." She stomped on his instep, twisted out of his grip, ran back to the dock's edge.

He followed and caught her arm, spun her around to face him. "It doesn't matter. This isn't the job."

Her grin emerged hard as glass. "When has restraining me ever worked out in your favor? Oh, wait." She sidled closer, softened her smile. "I can think of a time or two—"

"Stop it, El. What have you always told me?" His dark eyes found hers, locked on. "If it isn't the job, it isn't our problem."

Her smile faded. She yanked her arm away from him. "They keep taking us. Why? And who are they? Why only the girls? And what was that...that *feeling*? I've never felt anything like that before."

He looked dubious. "Maybe you need to sleep."

She hesitated, despair creeping slowly in. "You felt nothing at all?"

"Sorry, no."

She glared at him, ignoring the unsettled feeling in her gut. "Well, even so, that girl was no rebel. She was a child. Why would they bother taking her?"

"Whatever the reason, it's not our problem," Harkan repeated. He took a long, slow breath, perhaps convincing himself. "Not tonight. We have work to do."

Eliana stared out at the river for a long time. She imagined carving a face into a slab of flawless stone—no sweat, no scars. Only a hard smile that would come when called, and eyes like knives at night. By the time she had finished, her anger had faded and the unfeeling face was her own.

She turned to Harkan, brought out the cheeky little grin he despised. "Shall we, then? Those bastards worked up my appetite."

The Red Crown rebel smuggler known as Quill snuck both people and information out of Orline. He was good at it too—one of the best.

It had taken weeks for Eliana and Harkan to track him down.

Now, they crouched on a roof overlooking a tiny courtyard in the Old Quarter, where Quill was supposed to meet a group of rebel sympathizers trying to flee the city. The courtyard reeked sweetly from the roses lining the walls.

Beside her, Harkan shifted, alert.

Eliana watched dark shapes enter the courtyard and crowd together in the corner below a climbing rosebush. Waiting.

Not long after, a hooded figure entered from the opposite corner and approached them. Eliana curled her fingers around her dagger, her blood racing.

The clouds shifted; moonlight washed the yard clean.

Eliana's heart stuttered and sank.

Quill. It had to be him. There was the faint limp in his gait, from a wound sustained during the invasion.

And there, waiting for him, were a woman and three small children.

Harkan swore under his breath. He pointed at the children, signed with his hand. He and Eliana had engineered a silent code years ago, when she first started hunting alone after Rozen's injury. He had insisted she not go by herself, and so he had learned to hunt and track, to kill, to turn on their own people and serve the Empire instead—all for her.

No, came his message. *Abort.*

She knew what he meant. The children weren't part of this job. Quill was one thing, but the idea of handing innocent children over to the Lord of Orline… It wouldn't sit well with Harkan.

Honestly, it didn't with Eliana either.

But three rebels waited at the courtyard's shadowed entrance: Quill's escort and protectors. There was no time, and it was too big a risk to spare the family. She and Harkan had to move quickly.

She shook her head. *Take them*, she signed back.

Harkan drew a too-loud breath; she heard the furious sadness in it.

Below, Quill's head whipped toward them.

Eliana jumped off the roof, landed lightly, rolled her feet. Thought, briefly, how it was a terrible shame that she couldn't sit back and watch herself fight. Surely it looked as good as it felt.

Quill drew a dagger; the mother fell to her knees, begging for mercy. Quill pushed his hood back. Middle-aged, ruddy-faced, and intelligent in the eyes, he had a serenity to him that said, *I fear not death, but surrender.*

Four seconds later, Eliana had kicked his bad leg out from under him, relieved him of his knife, struck the back of his head with the hilt. He did not rise again.

She heard Harkan land behind her, followed by rapid footsteps as the other rebels rushed into the courtyard. Together she and Harkan had them down in moments. She whirled and flung her dagger. It hit the wooden courtyard door, trapping the eldest child in place by his cloak.

The others froze and burst into tears.

Their mother lay glassy-eyed on the ground in a bed of rotting petals. One of the rebel's daggers protruded from her heart.

Eliana yanked it free—another blade for her arsenal. She wondered why the rebels had killed the woman. To protect themselves?

Or to grant her mercy they knew she would not otherwise receive.

"Fetch the guard," Eliana ordered, searching the mother for valuables. She found nothing except for a small idol of the Emperor, crafted from mud and sticks, no doubt kept on her person in case an adatrox patrol stopped her for a search. The idol's beady black eyes glittered in the moonlight. She tossed it aside. The children's sobs grew louder. "I'll stay with them."

Harkan paused, that sad, tired look on his face that made her hackles rise because she knew he hoped it would change her, one of these days. Make her better. Make her *good* again.

She lifted an eyebrow. *Sorry, Harkan. Good girls don't live long.*

Then he left.

The eldest child watched Eliana, arms around his siblings. Some impulse stirring deep inside her urged her to let them go, just this once. It wouldn't hurt anything. They were children; they were nothing.

But children couldn't keep their mouths shut. And if anyone ever found out that the Dread of Orline, Lord Arkelion's pet huntress, had let traitors run free…

"We were afraid the bad men would take her too," the boy said simply. "That's why we wanted to leave."

The bad men. A tiny chill skipped up Eliana's neck. The masked men from the docks?

But the boy said no more than that. He did not even try to run.

Smart boy, Eliana thought.

He knew he would not get far.

The next afternoon, Eliana stood on a balcony overlooking the gallows.

Lord Arkelion lounged at the east end of the square, the high back of his throne carved to resemble wings.

Eliana, watching him, folded her arms across her chest. Shifted her weight to one hip. Tried to ignore the figure standing in a red-and-black Invictus uniform beside His Lordship's throne.

From this height, Eliana couldn't tell who it was, but it didn't matter. The mere sight of that familiar silhouette was enough to turn her stomach.

Invictus: a company of assassins that traveled the world and carried out the Emperor's bidding. The most dangerous jobs, the bloodiest jobs.

It was only a matter of time before they recruited her. She imagined it daily, just to see if the idea would ever stop terrifying her.

So far, it hadn't.

Probably Rahzavel would be the one to come for her. Eliana had seen him at a handful of His Lordship's parties over the years. Each time, he had requested a dance with her. Each time, his flat gray gaze had dared her to refuse him.

Oh, how she'd wished she could have.

"An invincible bounty hunter," he had crooned in her ear during their last dance together the previous summer. "How curious." He had threaded his cold fingers through hers. "You'll make a fine addition to our family someday."

When Rahzavel came for her, he probably wouldn't even let her say goodbye to her loved ones before escorting her overseas to Celdaria, the heart of the Undying Empire—and to the Emperor himself.

Welcome, Eliana Ferracora, the Emperor said in her most awful dreams, his smile not reaching his black eyes. *I've heard so much about you.*

And that would be the end of life as she now knew it. She would become one of the elite—a soldier of Invictus.

She would become, like Rahzavel, a new breed of monster.

Today, however, was not that day.

So Eliana watched, tapping her fingers against her arm, wishing His Lordship would get it over with. She was hungry and tired, and Harkan was beside himself with shame. And the longer they stood there, the more desperately he would expect something from her that she couldn't give him:

Regret.

The Empire guard marched Quill and the eldest child up to the gallows. It been constructed in the ruins of the temple of Saint Marzana, the revered firebrand of the Old World—the world before the Blood Queen Rielle had died. Before the rise of the Empire.

Empire soldiers had almost entirely demolished the temple when they seized Orline. Once, the temple had been a grand array of domed halls, classrooms and sanctuaries open to the river breeze, and courtyards draped in blossoming vines. Now, only a few crumbling pillars remained. Saint Marzana's statue, standing guard at the temple entrance, had been destroyed. A likeness of the Emperor now loomed there instead—his features masked, his body cloaked. Gold, black, and crimson banners flanked his head.

The plaza beneath him was crowded but quiet. The citizens of Orline were used to executions, but Quill was popular in certain circles, and not even His Lordship often slaughtered children.

When Eliana and Harkan had presented the captive children to him, Lord Arkelion had smiled kindly, inspected the younger ones' teeth, and sent them off with one of his mistresses. The children had reached back for their brother, wailing all the way down the throne room until someone had, blessedly, shut the doors.

But the eldest child had not cried. And he was not crying today, not even as he watched the executioner raise his sword.

"The Empire will burn!" shouted Quill, his hair plastered to his scalp with sweat.

The sword fell; Quill's head rolled. An uneasy wave of sound swept through the crowd.

Only then, his face splattered with fresh blood, did the boy start to cry.

"El," Harkan choked out. He took Eliana's hand in his sweaty one, rubbed his thumb along her palm. His voice came out frayed. He had not slept.

She had slept like the dead. Sleep was important. One could not hunt without a good night's sleep.

"We don't have to watch," she told him as patiently as she could manage. "We can go."

He released her hand. "You can go if you want. I have to watch."

There it was again—that same exhausted tone, like a sad-eyed hound resigned to its next beating.

To keep from snapping at him, Eliana fiddled with the battered gold pendant under her cloak. She wore it on a chain around her neck every day and knew the scratched, worn lines of it by heart: The arch of the horse's neck. The intricate details of its wings. The figure riding astride it, sword raised, face blackened from time: Audric the Lightbringer. One of the dead Old World kings her brother obsessed over for reasons Eliana couldn't fathom. Her parents told her they had found the trinket on the street when Eliana was still a baby and given it to her to calm her crying one sleepless night. She had worn it for as long as she could remember, though not out of love for the Lightbringer. She cared nothing for dead kings.

No, she wore it because, some days, she felt like the familiar weight of the necklace at her throat was the only thing that kept her from flying apart.

"I'll stay," she told Harkan lightly. Too lightly? Probably. "I've got the time."

He didn't even scold her. The executioner lifted his sword. At the last moment, the child raised his hand in a salute—a fist at his heart and then held up in the air. The sign of allegiance to the rebellion, to Red Crown. His arm shook, but he stared at the sun with unblinking eyes.

He began reciting the Sun Queen's prayer: "May the Queen's light guide me—"

The sword fell.

Eliana's tears surprised her. She blinked them away before they could fall. Harkan covered his mouth with one hand.

"God help us," he whispered. "El, what are we doing?"

She grasped his hand, made him face her.

"Surviving," she told him. "And that's nothing to be ashamed of." She swallowed—and swallowed again. Her jaw ached. Pretending boredom was hard work, but so was war. And if she fell to pieces, Harkan would crumble even faster.

The Lord of Orline raised one hand.

The citizens packed into the plaza below chanted the words that constantly circled through Eliana's mind like carrion birds:

"Glory to the Empire. Glory to the Empire. Glory to the Empire."

⇥ 3 ⇤

RIELLE

*"After the breaking of the Sunderlands, the Seven
returned to the mainland, and still they could not rest.
Their people had been at war for decades, and they
craved a safe place to call home. So the saints began
in Katell's homeland and used their power to carve out
of the alpine mountains a paradise. Sheltered by high
peaks, verdant with forests and farmlands, this haven
was named Âme de la Terre and became the capital of
Celdaria. They built the queen's city in the foothills of
the highest mountain and surrounded it with a crystal
lake that seemed carved out of the clearest sky."*

—A Concise History of the Second Age, Volume I:
The Aftermath of the Angelic Wars
by Daniel Riveret and Jeannette d'Archambeau
of the First Guild of Scholars

The starting line was chaos.

Some riders competed in the name of the Church temples.
Those from the Pyre, Tal's temple, wore scarlet and gold. Black and
deep blue for the House of Night, the temple of shadowcasters and
Tal's sister, Sloane. Umber and light green for the Holdfast, the earthshaker temple.

The great Celdarian houses had also sent representatives. Rielle passed riders in lilac and sage for House Riveret, russet and steel for House Sauvillier. Riders had even traveled from the distant kingdoms of Ventera and Astavar, which lay across the Great Ocean.

Many riders, like Rielle, had been hired by merchants eager for the winning purse—though none of them were as wealthy as her sponsor, Odo Laroche.

And none of the other riders had had the privilege of training with the king's finest horsemasters since they were old enough to sit in a saddle.

Grinning, Rielle guided her mare beneath the maze of stilted spectator boxes. Her ears rang from the noise—gamblers shouting their bets, children racing through the crowd and shrieking with delight. Smoke from market vendors selling roasted pork sandwiches and blackened fowl skewers stung her eyes.

She finally reached the tent set aside for Odo's riders. The gown she wore was a favorite—forest green to match her eyes, iridescent vines sewn at the hem, a swooping neckline that showed off her collarbones—but the midday sun made her itch to rip it off. Leaving her horse with the paid swords guarding the door, she slipped inside to change.

And froze.

Audric was already there, clad in only his riding trousers and boots. His fine emerald tunic and embroidered jacket hung neatly from the back of a chair. In his hands, he held a plain linen riding shirt.

He grinned at her. "Took you long enough," he said and threw her a shirt of her own.

She caught it, barely. "The crowds are larger than I had anticipated," she said, though her throat was suddenly dry, and it astonished her that she could manage a word.

It had been a long time since she had seen her kingdom's prince so unclothed.

Growing up together, it would have meant nothing. She had spent hours playing with him and Ludivine in the gardens behind the castle. They had swum together in the lake surrounding the city, worshipped together at the Baths.

But that had been before.

Before Audric and Ludivine's betrothal, an arrangement that bound the houses of Courverie and Sauvillier even closer together. Before Audric had transformed from her shy, gangly, awkward friend into Prince Audric the Lightbringer, the most powerful sunspinner in centuries.

Before Rielle had realized she loved Audric. And that he would never be hers.

She drank in the sight of him—the lean muscles of his arms, his broad chest, his narrow waist. He was not as dark as his father, not as pale as his mother, the queen. Dark-brown curls, damp from the heat, loosely framed his face. Dappled sunlight fell through the tent's netting and painted his skin radiant.

When he looked up at her, she flushed at the warmth of his gaze. "Lu's all right?" he asked.

"And enjoying the attention, I'm sure. And your mother?"

"I told her I'd take care of Lu, and that she should relax and enjoy the race." He shook his head ruefully. "She thinks I'm a dutiful son—"

"And instead you're sneaking off to risk life and limb." Rielle threw him a sly smile. "Your lie was a kindness. She'd be frantic if she knew where you really were."

Audric laughed. "Mother could use a fright now and then. Otherwise she gets bored, and when she gets bored, she starts to meddle, and when she meddles, she starts pestering me and Lu."

About when we will be wed. The unsaid words lingered, and Rielle could no longer look at him.

She stepped behind the dressing screen Odo had provided, undid her gown, stepped out of it. Clothed in only her shift, she reached for the trousers Audric tossed over to her.

"If I didn't know better," she said, keeping her voice light, "I'd say you're sounding rather rebellious. And here I thought you weren't one for breaking rules."

He laughed again. "You bring it out of me."

This was, she began to realize, a terrible idea. She should have asked Odo for a separate tent. Undressing five feet away from Audric was the sort of delicious madness for which she could never have prepared herself.

God help her, she could hear the fabric of his riding tunic sliding against his torso. She could almost *feel* it, as if he were there beside her, drawing her gown up over her head, freeing her of the last remaining barrier between them.

As she tried to wriggle into her own black tunic, cursing herself and her unhelpfully vivid imagination, she got her arm stuck through the heavy embroidered collar.

"Rielle?" came Audric's voice. "Hurry, they've started announcing the racers."

Damn, damn, damn. Rielle twisted and squirmed, tugging at her shirt.

On the other side of the screen, the tent flap opened. "The race is starting, and it seems my two riders are nowhere to be found," came Odo's smooth baritone, with only a touch of irritation. "May I remind you that I'm wagering quite a bit of coin on both of you, as well as my own head, should either of you be stupid enough to be discovered? Or worse, break your necks?"

"We'll be right there," Rielle called. "Have I ever given you reason to doubt me?"

"On numerous occasions, in fact," Odo replied. There was a pause. "Shall I enumerate them for you?"

"One moment, please, Odo," Audric said, laughter in his voice.

The tent flap closed.

"Can I come around?" Audric called.

"Yes, but...oh, hang on." With a violent twist, Rielle managed to free herself. She jerked down the tunic, fumbling with the gold ribbons at the neckline. "Yes, all right, I'm decent."

Audric rounded the screen, her leather riding jacket and cap in hand. "Could it be that we're about to sneak into this life-threatening race, and *you're* the flustered one?"

"Never mind that you tried to get out of doing this a dozen times." Rielle yanked her cap from his hand. "Never mind that you haven't broken a rule in your life before now."

"But what an inaugural defiance it is, don't you agree?" He moved closer to help her fasten the tunic's clasp between her shoulders. His fingers grazed the nape of her neck. "I mean, I could have begun my rebellious streak with something simple. Being late to morning court, skipping my prayers, bedding a servant girl—"

She burst out laughing. It sounded shriller than she would have liked. "You? Bed a servant girl? You don't know the first thing about courting a woman."

"So you think."

"I don't believe it."

"Am I that hopeless a case to you?"

"To start, you'd have to put down your books every now and then."

"Lady Rielle," came his teasing voice, "are you offering to educate me in the art of seducing a woman?"

A terrible silence fell. Rielle felt Audric tense behind her. A blush crept up her cheeks. Why had she let herself get drawn into this, of all conversations? She knew nothing about courting anyone.

Her father had made sure of that.

Once, at thirteen, Rielle had come home after watching fifteen-year-old Audric practice his swordwork in the barracks yard, feeling on edge and ready to burst out of her skin.

Her father and his lieutenants had run Audric through many drills that day. Magister Guillory sat nearby, offering advice whenever she saw fit. As Grand Magister of the House of Light, the ferocious old woman had overseen Audric's sunspinner studies for years. She and Rielle's father had helped Audric focus the sometimes overwhelming call of his power into the physical, reliable work of fighting with a sword.

Rielle had watched many of Audric's practices, but that particular one had been different. She had not been able to get him out of her head afterward—how he'd moved in the afternoon light, every motion steady and sure, brow furrowed in concentration as his sword scattered flares of sunlight across his skin. She had brought her father his customary drink after dinner that night and been so rattled that she dropped the cup.

Her father had raised an eyebrow. "You're not yourself tonight."

She had said nothing, unsure of how to answer him.

"I noticed you in the yard today," he observed mildly. "You've been coming around often of late."

Rielle crouched to sweep up the mess, her hair hiding her hot face.

Then her father had pulled her to her feet, hard enough to hurt her wrist.

"I know what you're thinking," he had told her, "and I forbid it. You might lose control one day and hurt him. He has a rare gift, do you understand? The most power anyone has had in half an age. It's important for the realm to see that he is master of it, not the other way around. The last thing Audric needs is someone like you hovering about."

Rielle's eyes had filled with tears. "Someone like me?"

Her father had released her, impassive. "A murderer."

Lord Commander Dardenne had not allowed his daughter to attend Audric's practices after that.

Now, at eighteen, Rielle had not kissed a soul, nor come close to it. Certainly she had imagined it, and often. She knew she was beautiful—if not in the conventional sense, then in the way that at least made people look, and look hard. *Striking* was the word Ludivine often used. Or *arresting*.

Her father had only once commented on her looks: "You have the face of a liar. I can see all the machinations of the world in your eyes."

Nevertheless, Rielle cultivated this beauty however she could, dressing in the most outlandish fashions she could get away with—bold and just shy of revealing, crafted from exotic fabrics that Ludivine secretly ordered for her and that made her stand out at court like a peacock among pigeons. Every time she had dared to show herself in such a garment, she had sensed hungry gazes upon her and felt her own secret hunger rear up inside her belly, hot and eager.

But even then, her father's words hung about her neck like a yoke of thorns, and she tamped down every voracious instinct she possessed.

Besides, she didn't want just anyone, not enough to take the risk.

So she kept herself apart, her frustrations manifesting in slick and frantic dreams, sometimes of Audric, sometimes of Ludivine or Tal—mostly of Audric. After those nights, when Dream Audric had drawn her into his bed, she would wake to find the mirrors in her room cracked, once-extinguished candles freshly lit and sputtering.

Her father was not wrong; there was a danger to her, an unpredictability. She would not bring that to someone else's bed.

Especially not someone who had been promised to her friend.

Rielle made the mistake of looking at Audric over her shoulder, and his dark gaze locked onto hers for a brief moment before they both looked away.

"We should go," she said. She grabbed her jacket from his hands, twisted her hair up into her riding cap, and went outside to mount her horse. She wrapped her cap's veil about her neck and face, tucked the end of it into her collar. When Audric joined her, wearing his own protective coverings, they did not speak, and she was glad.

This race would not be kind to her if she remained distracted.

Together, they followed the other riders to the starting line.

Audric rode one of Odo's horses, a chestnut Celdarian mare from the southern riverlands. Rielle's own mount, another from Odo's stables, was smaller—a gray Kirvayan mare named Maliya who held her banner tail high.

Rielle took her place at the starting line, five slots to the left and two behind Audric. The herald, high overhead, announced each racer through a small round amplifier engineered at the Forge.

When Rielle heard her own false name announced, she waved to the crowd, to generous applause. Though her and Audric's assumed identities meant nothing to these people, the name of their sponsor—the wealthy merchant Odo Laroche, who owned half the city's businesses—carried tremendous weight.

High overhead, King Bastien took his place before the amplifier to begin the opening remarks.

"To celebrate another year of peace in our kingdom," the king's voice boomed, "and in hopes for a bountiful harvest—and a joyous festival—and to give thanks to God who has blessed Celdaria with such gifts, I welcome all of you to this year's Boon Chase!"

King Bastien returned to his seat, and the drummers began. The lines of racers shifted; the air crackled against Rielle's skin.

The race heralds blew on their horns once. Twice.

Rielle curled her gloved fingers around Maliya's reins, every inch of her body thrumming.

The final racers took their place—twelve masked arbiters in the royal colors of plum, emerald, and gold. They would run the course and watch for foul play.

The drumbeats accelerated, matching Rielle's pounding heart.

The heralds blew their horns a third time.

With a deafening roar from the crowd, the racers plunged forward onto the Flats, the wide stretch of grasslands outside the city gates.

The Chase had begun.

The first few minutes were a blinding frenzy of sound and color. The hooves of five dozen horses kicked up clouds of dust.

To Rielle's right, a man with a metal guard over his teeth yanked on a spiked glove and knocked another racer off his mount with the thrust of one meaty arm. The other racers trampled him, cutting off his screams, and his horse left the course with its reins trailing.

Rielle drove Maliya forward, looking around wildly. An arbiter should have disqualified the man for that. But in the storm of dust, she couldn't pick out the arbiters' colors. It was as though they had vanished.

She crossed the Flats, guiding Maliya through a throng of shoving elbows and flying whips, racers shouting at their mounts to move and yelling threats in a dozen languages. When she reached the foothills of Mount Taléa, she slowed her pace and directed Maliya up the steeper forested climb. She saw a flash of familiar color through the trees ahead. Black and gold. Odo's colors.

Audric.

She lowered herself against Maliya's neck, urged her mare up the foothills, and emerged out of the trees into the first mountain pass. A broad stretch of grass shivered in the wind before her. Walls of rock towered on either side.

Rielle's heart lifted. She murmured the Kirvayan words Odo had told her the mare would respond to: "Ride the wind, falcon of my blood, wings of my heart!"

Maliya shot forward.

The wind whipped past them, ripping tears from Rielle's eyes. She caught up to Audric and crowed with triumph.

He glanced her way, his scarf falling loose. He grinned at her, and her heart leapt. Despite the danger of the race, she couldn't help but wish they could stay out here—away from court, away from everyone else—forever.

Seconds later, Audric veered away, taking the shortest path around the mountain. His Celdarian mare was bred for such steep, rocky trails.

But Maliya was built for speed. Rielle pushed her on across the pass, and Maliya obeyed. The wind howled in Rielle's ears. She could hardly hear herself breathe. The shapes of the other riders, fanning out across the pass, were blurs of color. They were catching up to her.

She turned Maliya right, onto a narrow cliffside trail. Not her first choice, but it would give her better time. She told herself not to look and yet couldn't help it, peering over the edge into the chasm below. She broke out in sick chills; her vision tilted. One wrong shift of her weight, one misstep from her horse, and she'd fly to her death.

Behind her came a clatter of hooves and rock. When the cliff trail widened, sloping down into the wooded foothills, she looked back.

One racer zipped by her, and then three more, so close she could smell their sweat. Behind them, a racer rammed his horse into the side of another, knocking both horse and rider off the cliff Rielle had just traveled. The fallen horse let out a terrible scream, then fell silent.

Rielle turned away, heart pounding, eyes stinging from the dust clogging the air. She exited the woods near the trail to the second pass that would bring her around Mount Taléa and back toward the city.

There, she found arbiters at last: seven of them, some distance ahead of her. They had thrown off their masks, letting their blond, braided hair fly free. They were letting out shrill war cries that Rielle recognized at once from one of Audric's interminable lectures about Borsvall.

They were closing in on the rider nearest them—a man in black and gold, his cap and scarf fallen free, the wind ripping through his dark curls.

The world distilled to this single, terrible moment. Dread knocked the wind from Rielle's lungs.

The arbiters, whoever they were, were no soldiers of her father's. They were from Borsvall.

And they were surrounding Audric with their swords raised to kill.

~ 4 ~
ELIANA

"But when the Empire forces came to Orline, the capital of Ventera, they were struck blind by a brilliant light. It was the Sun Queen, glittering and vengeful. She led the charge with King Maximilian at her side, and everyone she touched felt their long-forgotten magic awaken. They were sunspinners once more, firebrands and earthshakers. And the river that morning ran red with Empire blood."

—The Sun Queen's Triumph (Being an Alternative History of the Kingdom of Ventera)
As written in the journal of Remy Ferracora
June 14, Year 1018 of the Third Age

After the executions, Eliana saw Harkan home to his tiny apartment on the top floor of the building next to her own.

As she turned to go, he said softly, "El?"

She hesitated. If she stayed, they would share his bed, as they often did. His touch would be absolution—his strong, brown arms, the tender way he held her after and stroked her hair. For a little while, she would forget who she was and what she had done.

But then, Harkan would want to talk. He would look into her eyes and search for the girl she had once been.

The thought exhausted her.

"Please, El," Harkan said, his voice strained. "I need you."

He could hardly look at her. Was he embarrassed that he didn't want to be alone? Or ashamed to crave the touch of a monster?

Unbidden, a memory surfaced: the boy's defiant, tear-streaked face, just before the executioner's sword fell.

Eliana's stomach clenched. She squeezed Harkan's hand. "All right, but I just want to sleep."

His voice came gently: "Me too."

They climbed through the terrace window and into his room—plain and small, strewn with rumpled clothes. The rest of his family's apartment remained silent and shuttered. Since his mother and older brothers had died at the wall the day the Empire invaded ten years earlier, Harkan had not touched any of their things or sat in furniture they had sat in or used his mother's pots and pans. The apartment was a tomb, and Eliana dared not enter it for fear of breathing ghosts into her body.

But Harkan's bedroom was a familiar, untidy place. Over the years, Eliana had spent as many nights there as she had in her own.

She climbed into his bed, waiting. He pulled the drapes nearly shut, leaving the window open behind them. He lit the four squat candles he kept on a side table—one for each member of his lost family. When he had pulled off his shirt and boots, he climbed in beside her and drew her down into the warm nest of his arms.

"Thank you," he murmured against her cheek.

She smiled, wriggling closer. "I always sleep better when I'm with you."

He laughed softly. Then the room filled with silence. He worried the ends of her braid between his fingers. "Someday, we'll have enough money to leave this place."

Eliana closed her eyes. It was the beginning of Harkan's favorite story, one he had told her countless times. She didn't have the heart to tell him she couldn't stand listening to it, not today. That this story had been a comfort when they were young and didn't know any better but was simply cruel and pointless now.

So she waited until she could speak instead of yelling at him, and asked, as she always did, "Where will we go?"

"North across the Narrow Sea, to Astavar."

Astavar. Eliana used to dream about what it would look like— white-capped mountains, lush green valleys, a world of ice and snow and night skies filled with twisting strands of colored light.

Now it was simply a place on a map. Ventera's northern neighbor and the last free country left in the world.

"No one gets in or out of Astavar," Eliana countered, falling into the rhythm of their practiced back-and-forth.

"We'll find a smuggler," Harkan continued. "A good one. We'll pay whatever we need to pay."

"Astavar will fall one of these days. Everyone falls to the Empire. Look what happened to us."

"Perhaps. But in the meantime, we could have a few years of peace. You, me, your mother, Remy." He squeezed her hand. "A proper family."

Just like the one Eliana had destroyed mere hours ago. Suddenly she found it difficult to swallow. Suddenly her eyes felt hot and full.

Damn it. This was what came of trying to be a good friend.

"I don't know that I could ever be proper," she teased. It sounded unconvincing even to her.

"Think of it, El." Harkan's thumb smoothed circles against the crook of her arm. "The sea isn't large. We could be in Astavar in an hour, maybe two. We could find a small place, maybe by a lake. I could farm. Remy could bake. Your mother could continue with her mending. And you—"

"And me?" Eliana sat up. She couldn't play this game any longer. "If we could get past the Empire troops at our border, and if we could find a smuggler who wouldn't betray us to the Empire, and if we could convince the Astavaris to let us cross their border…if we managed to do all that, with money we don't have, what would I do, then, in this fantasy of yours?"

Harkan ignored the harsh edge to her voice. He kissed her wrist. "Anything. You can hunt game. I'll teach you how to grow tomatoes. You can wear a straw hat." He pressed his lips to her shoulder. "I suppose you don't have to wear a hat. Although I'm not ashamed to say I've been daydreaming about it for so long that my heart might break if you didn't."

"It won't work," she said at last.

"The hat?" Harkan's gaze was soft. "On the contrary, I think it would flatter you nicely."

In that moment, she hated him almost as much as she hated herself.

She moved out of his arms, drew her tunic over her head, and gently pinned his wrists to his pillow.

"There's no place for a girl like me in your dream world, love," she explained with a coy smile. "All I know how to do is kill, remember?"

"And this," Harkan said, his eyes dark and his voice low.

"And this," she agreed and then kissed him deeply enough that he had nothing else to say.

That evening, she returned home at dusk to prepare dinner.

"Darling Mother!" She dropped a kiss on her mother's cheek.

"What happened today?" asked Rozen Ferracora. She sat at the table, parts from her latest tinkering job scattered across the worn wood. Nuts and bolts. Nails and knives. "I heard about the boy—and Quill."

"Oh, did you?" Eliana shrugged, started chopping carrots. She felt her mother's eyes upon her and chopped faster. "Well. What do you expect? Another banner day in the glorious kingdom of Ventera."

Later, Remy came in and sat at the table, watching Eliana lay out their dinner—a loaf of fresh bread, vegetable stew, a block of hard cheese—all of it high quality, freshly bought in the Garden Quarter.

Eliana had never been more aware of their lovely little home, their stock of food, the relative safety of their neighborhood.

All of it bought with the blood on her hands.

She filled her mother's bowl and set it before her with a flourish.

Remy broke the silence, his voice shaking. His blue eyes were brilliant with unshed tears. "You're a coward."

Eliana had expected that. Still, the vitriol in his voice was a gut punch. She almost dropped her plate.

Rozen hissed at him, "Stop it, Remy."

"I heard a child was executed today, and that rebel, Quill. The one who smuggles people out of the city."

Eliana's throat tightened painfully. She had never seen such an expression on Remy's face. Like he didn't recognize her—and didn't want to.

With relish, she bit off a chunk of bread. "All true!"

"You did that," he whispered.

"Did what?"

"You killed them."

She swallowed, knocked back a gulp of water, wiped her mouth. "As I've said before, my *cowardice* keeps us warm and fed and alive. So, dearest brother, unless you'd prefer to starve…"

Remy shoved his plate away. "I hate you."

Rozen sat rigid in her chair. "You don't. Don't say that."

"Let him hate me." Eliana glanced at Remy and then quickly away. He was looking right at the soft hole in her middle, the hollow place she let no one but him see. It ached from the bruise of his words. "If it helps him sleep at night, he can hate me until the end of his days."

Remy's eyes flicked to her neck, where the chain of her necklace was visible. His expression darkened.

"You wear King Audric the Lightbringer around your neck, but you don't deserve to." His gaze traveled back to her face. "He'd be ashamed of you if the Blood Queen hadn't killed him. He'd be ashamed of anyone who helps the Empire."

"If the Blood Queen hadn't killed him," Eliana said evenly, "then it wouldn't matter, would it? Maybe the Empire would never have risen. Maybe we'd all be living in a world full of magic and flying horses and beautiful castles built by the saints themselves."

She clasped her hands, regarded him with exaggerated patience. "But Queen Rielle did kill him. And so here we are. And I wear his image around my neck to remind myself that we don't live in that world. We live in a world where good kings die and those foolish enough to hope for something better are killed where they stand."

She ignored them both after that and devoured her stew in silence.

Her mother found her later that night, when Eliana was cleaning her blades in her room.

"Eliana," said Rozen, panting slightly, "you should rest." Even with her prosthetic leg, it took her some effort to get upstairs unassisted. She leaned hard on her cane.

"Mother, what are you doing?" Eliana rose, helped her to sit. Her daggers and smoke grenades lay across the floor, a tapestry of death. "You should be the one resting."

Rozen stared at the floor for a long moment. Then her face crumpled, and she turned into Eliana's shoulder.

"I hate seeing you like this," she whispered. "I'm sorry for this. I'm sorry I taught you... I'm sorry for everything."

Eliana held on to her, stroking her messy knot of dark hair. She listened to Rozen whisper too many apologies to count.

"Sorry about what?" Eliana said at last. "That Grandfather taught you how to kill? That you taught me?"

Rozen cupped Eliana's cheek in one weathered hand, searched her face with wet eyes that reminded Eliana of Remy's—inquisitive, tireless. "You'd tell me if you needed a rest? We can ask Lord Arkelion for time—"

"Time for what? To bake cookies and paint the walls a fresh color?" Eliana smiled, squeezed her mother's hand. "I wouldn't know what to do with myself."

Rozen's mouth thinned. "Eliana, don't play coy with me. I can see right through that smile of yours. I *taught* you that smile."

"Then don't apologize for teaching me how to keep us alive, all right? I'm fine."

Eliana rose, stretched, then helped Rozen to her own bed. She made her a cup of tea, kissed her cheek, helped unstrap her leg for the night—a finely crafted, wooden apparatus that had cost Eliana the wages from two jobs.

Two executions. Two slaughtered souls.

When Eliana returned to her room, she found Remy waiting for her, hugging his knees to his chest.

She crawled into bed beside him, struggling to breathe through a sudden tightness in her chest. Grief crashed upon her in waves. Dry-eyed, she let them pull her under.

Remy said quietly, "I don't hate you," and allowed her to hold on to him. She closed her eyes and tried to focus on only him—the twin scents of flour on his clothes and ink on his hands. The sound of his voice singing her "A Song for the Golden King." It had been Eliana's favorite lullaby as a child—a lament for Audric the Lightbringer.

Remy's small hands stroked her hair. She could crush him if she wanted to. And yet, given the chance, her bony bird of a brother would face off against the Emperor. Even if it killed him.

And I have a warrior's strength, she thought, *but the heart of a coward.*

A cruel joke. The world was full of them.

"I can't bear it," she whispered, her voice muffled against Remy's shirt.

"Can't bear what?" Remy asked quietly.

"You know what."

He said nothing. He was going to make her say it.

She sighed. "Killing people. Hunting people. Being good at it."

"You like being good at it," he pointed out.

She didn't argue. "It's getting worse out there. And I still have no answers."

"The missing women?"

"Who's taking them? And where? And *why?*" Her fingers curled around his wrists. She imagined pulling him down into the safe, dark world under her bed and never letting him leave.

"You're afraid we might be next," he said.

"I'm afraid we could be. Anyone could be."

"You're right." Remy lay down beside her, his eyes close and bright. "But all that matters right now is that you're here, and so am I."

Eliana held his hands to her heart and let him sing her into a fitful sleep.

The next job arrived several days later on Eliana's doorstep.

Packaged in a brown paper parcel, it was marked with the address of the city's most expensive tailor.

Eliana took the package and gave the messenger three silver coins. The pale-skinned man wore the plain brown tunic of an apprentice, and at first glance looked as ordinary as anyone. But Eliana knew at once that this man was no tailor's apprentice.

She thanked him with a silent nod and returned to her bedroom. From her window, she watched him walk down the street, crowded with Garden Quarter shoppers.

He walked almost perfectly. But Eliana had learned to watch for a certain stiffness in the way adatrox moved—every so often, a tiny, unnatural tic accompanying shifts in direction. A slight dimness in the eyes, delayed movements of the mouth, the brow. The subtler parts of the face that told you what the person inside was thinking.

It was as though the Empire's soldiers moved not by their own will, but by someone else's.

She hoped she never found out why the adatrox could seem normal one moment—laughing, talking, yawning—and then, without warning, fall perfectly quiet and still. Statue still. A shadow falling over the face, clouding the eyes. It could last an instant or for hours.

Whatever the Empire did to its legions of soldiers, she hoped it had not been done to her father, wherever he was. If he was still alive.

She placed the parcel on her bed and paused for a moment, readying herself.

She often heard of potential jobs when visiting Remy at the bakery or while attending one of His Lordship's parties with Harkan. She would allow some favored son or daughter of the Empire to kiss her in a curtained corner, whisper secrets to her. Then, later, she and Harkan would fall together into bed until they no longer felt so unclean.

But sometimes jobs came as messages, especially for Eliana.

These, she did not share with Harkan.

They often arrived folded between powdered fritters wrapped in thin paper, to remind Eliana of Remy—and how close he had been to this note and its messenger with the blank-slate eyes. She would read those orders with shaking hands.

Today, the job came tucked beneath folds of silk—a wine-colored whisper of a dress with long slits up each leg, shimmering as though it had been dipped in diamonds. The back was entirely bare, save for three thin, beaded strands. It was a flattering color for her, and the measurements seemed right. It would drape nicely over her body.

She swallowed past the sick knot in her chest. Lord Arkelion paid too close attention to her—and had for some time now. Eliana unfolded the message and read the encoded instructions three times over:

The Wolf rides on the full moon.
I want him alive.
Glory to the Empire.
Long live His Holy Majesty the Undying Emperor.

She stared at the exquisite penmanship.

Though the message bore Lord Arkelion's seal, the writing was not his.

It was Rahzavel's.

This writing, then, was a message within a message: Rahzavel was on his way to Orline. He was after the Wolf, and he wanted Eliana's help.

She didn't blame him.

Unlike Quill, the Wolf was not some Red Crown lackey. He was the right hand of the Prophet, lieutenant to the mysterious leader of Red Crown himself. The Wolf had evaded the Empire for years, and now he was here in her city.

Eliana's eyes found the figure written across the bottom of the note in that same meticulous hand:

20,000 gold

Her heart raced.

A payment of 20,000 in Empire gold?

Money like that was a small fortune—and, coming from Rahzavel, the invitation Eliana had long feared: *Deliver the Wolf. Take our money.*
Join Invictus.
Serve the Emperor.

She had never told Harkan how she had, over the past two years, accepted even more jobs than he knew and saved as much as she could.

She had never told him just how deeply she had come to long for his fantasy of living in some quiet corner of Astavar with goats and fresh bread and tomato plants.

Instead she had saved and killed and hunted and saved. And now, with 20,000 gold in addition to her savings…

She heard the bell ring downstairs. Remy was home; his laughter lit up their house. How miraculous, that he could still laugh so easily.

Eliana threw the note into the fire and watched Rahzavel's words burn. Once the note was ashes, she glanced out her window at the darkening sky. It was the first night of the full moon.

If Invictus wanted her, they could have her—but they would never touch her family.

She would deliver the Wolf as ordered.

She would accept her reward and ensure that Remy, Harkan, and her mother could safely leave the country.

And she would begin the hunt that very night.

5

RIELLE

"Fleet-footed fire, blaze not with fury or abandon
Burn steady and true, burn clean and burn bright"

—The Fire Rite
As first uttered by Saint Marzana the Brilliant,
patron saint of Kirvaya and firebrands

Rielle saw the seven false arbiters converging on Audric, their swords gleaming. Borsvall men.

Other racers veered out of the way as they continued through the pass, eyes fixed on the course and the coin waiting at the end.

Audric looked over his shoulder, the enemy soldiers forming a *V* behind him. One carried a sword that drew long spirals of blackness from the air—a shadowcaster, flinging darkness ahead of him and clouding Audric in fog.

Rielle saw these things, and she saw none of them.

There was only Audric. Never mind the betrothal, never mind Ludivine, and damn the entire royal court to the Deep.

He was hers, and these men wanted to kill him.

A knife-sharp rage crested within her.

How *dare* they?

She snapped Maliya's reins and let out a sharp cry. The mare took her racing after them.

There was no way even Audric could defeat them all, not

unarmed—and Rielle knew he was unarmed today. When she had suggested he keep at least his secondary, less powerful castings hidden somewhere on his person, he had protested. *Weapons are against the rules, Rielle. Even my daggers. You know that.*

If he had Illumenor, his sword, there would be no question. But Audric could not bring down sunlight without his castings. Not even the saints had been able to do that.

No one could, Rielle knew, but her.

In an instant, years of lessons teaching her to stifle every instinct she possessed fell away. A locked door wedged shut in her heart flew open.

She flung out her hand as though she could stop the assassins with her fury alone. A blast of heat flooded her body. Her fingertips were ten points of fire.

Flames erupted on either side of her, shooting toward the pass in twin blazing paths.

The world shook. A hot hiss rent the air in two. She ducked flying clods of earth. Maliya lurched beneath her, let out a shrill cry. Rielle barely managed to keep her seat.

She heard a shout of panic and looked back the way she had come. The blackened land behind her looked as if it had been raked open by monstrous claws. Other racers were bringing their horses up short, steering them away from the shredded ground.

Beneath Rielle, Maliya's glistening sides heaved. She was pushing her horse too hard. They should not be running so quickly.

But Rielle refused to stop.

There, in front of them—the Borsvall assassins. They were entering the pass and tearing back through the mountains to the city, trying to intercept Audric before he could reach it. Enormous boulders rolled down the mountains on either side of the pass and crashed into one another, sending dirt and rocks flying. The other racers tried to dodge the debris; only some succeeded. Several bodies fell and did not rise again.

Rielle considered stopping to help the nearest one, but then saw an assassin's spear flash, flinging sticky knots of fire at Audric. A firebrand. The flames clung to Audric's cloak and boots. He ducked a streak of fire arcing over his head and turned his horse right. The air around him shimmered and popped. His sunspinner power, itching to erupt?

Rielle kicked Maliya hard. Faster, *faster*.

If anything happened to him, if he died before she could tell him—

The ground burst open on either side of her. Fresh flames spewed from the earth she'd ripped open, blasting her face with heat. Rocks went flying; one slammed into the shoulder of another racer as he struggled to get out of her way, and he fell.

Guilt spiked through her, but then Maliya shrieked, disoriented. Something was wrong. Her gait was uneven.

Rielle slipped, nearly tumbling off. She yanked herself back up, hard, and inhaled a mouthful of smoke.

Maliya made another terrible sound. She was wheezing; Rielle's legs were burning. Everything was too hot.

Up ahead, Audric had made it to the pass.

Rielle pushed Maliya harder, and they followed him in. The air was full of smoke, flames, the roar of falling rock. The dizzy euphoria of power sweeping through Rielle's body was so overwhelming she could hardly stay in the saddle, hardly think, hardly *breathe*.

And something, very near, was burning.

Beyond the assassins, a flash of color, a man's cry: Audric, just out of his attackers' reach, urging his horse faster. But the Borsvall men were almost upon him.

Rielle licked her lips, tasted sweat.

She had not brought any weapons. Why hadn't she brought any *weapons*?

The Borsvall rider nearest her turned in his saddle and cried out in horror. He thrust his ax into the air, yanked it back. Rielle's horse surged forward beneath her, let out a sharp cry, and stumbled. The man was a metalmaster; his power flew out from his body through his casting and jerked Maliya's bit left, right, and left again. A sour metallic tang in the air made Rielle want to gag. She reached down into the air and threw everything she felt at him.

Heat ripped through her, belly to fingers. A knot of sizzling white flew at the Borsvall rider and enveloped him in gold. For a moment he seized, outlined in light. Then he was writhing on the ground, his ax dissolving into ash beside him.

Rielle flew past him. She gagged at the smell of him, at the sight of the charred mess that had once been a body.

Just like her mother.

They had been at home that day, surrounded by candles. An evening prayer, a simple argument—and an explosion.

Rielle glanced down at her hands. Her riding gloves were singed through; streaks of blood slicked her palms. She turned one hand to the left, to the right. A white-gold shimmer winked just under her skin, then faded.

Sunlight.

Wouldn't Magister Guillory be proud of her? A true sunspinner, one who could bring down the sun with her bare hands.

She laughed, a torn sound. What was happening to her? Her body was a bonfire, spreading out and out, and she couldn't stop it.

She dropped the reins, instinct screaming at her to reach for a weapon, and though she found only empty air, her palms crackled with heat. Blind and desperate, she threw her hands at the Borsvall attackers. An invisible force flung them to the ground. Their horses ran free, crazed with fear.

Rielle looked around, dazed. The quaking world behind her, fanning out along Maliya's path, was a spiderweb of fissures. Her mind felt similarly ruptured, like her power had knocked loose all her edges.

Where was Audric? She searched wildly through the smoke and dust.

"Rielle!" A familiar voice.

Audric, on foot. She must have knocked him off his horse as well, and now he was limping. She kicked Maliya into action. Audric stepped back from her approach. Something terrible fell across his face.

What did he see?

A thick black arrow zipped past her.

Rielle yanked Maliya around, turning her so hard she could feel the cut of the bit in her own mouth. She bore down on the man who had shot at her. He faced her, reaching for another arrow.

He nocked it. He took aim not at her, but at Audric.

Rielle cried out for Audric to move, urged Maliya forward to get between him and the archer.

Maliya took a few faltering steps, and then something beneath Rielle gave way. She looked down. Her horse was a raw, pulpy mess—drenched with blood, patches of her gray coat charred black and smoking.

The horror of it struck Rielle in the gut. She dropped the reins and leaned back in her saddle. She had to get away from this terrible thing beneath her. Where had it come from?

Maliya's hindquarters sagged and buckled; Rielle fell hard on her side. She crawled, frantic, clawing at the dirt to get out of the way.

Another arrow from the Borsvall assassin—but not aimed at Rielle, nor at Audric. The arrow pierced Maliya between the eyes; her screams fell silent. The wreck of her lay there, steaming.

Rielle huddled on the ground, the scent of Maliya's burned flesh thick in her nose. A distant part of her mind still searched for Audric, but when she tried to rise to her feet, her body wouldn't cooperate. Heaving, she pushed herself up and retched. She was covered in dirt and blood—her own and Maliya's.

The clang of metal against metal crashed through the air. Swords.

Audric.

Frantic, Rielle searched through her dimming vision for a weapon of her own, something one of the Borsvall men had dropped. Even a rock would do.

Oh, God help her, her poor horse.

What had she done?

She wiped her bleeding palms on her shirt. The earth still vibrated, as though an army ten thousand strong was marching on the capital.

"Stop it," she whispered, for she knew it was all her doing—the horse, the falling rocks, the rifts in the earth.

She had lost control, after everything Tal and her father had tried to teach her. She'd only wanted to show them she could be trusted, that she deserved a life outside the temple and her own lonely rooms.

And now her father would hate her even more deeply than he already did.

Everyone on the course had seen.

What *was* she?

She slammed her hands into the ground, heedless of pain. "Stop it!"

A roar, a swift burst of wind. Suddenly everything was hot.

She heard the distant sounds of screams from the race grounds. Someone was speaking over the amplifier.

She looked up.

Her crawling had brought her to the highest point of the pass. In front of her lay a downward slope, then the Flats. The finish line, spectator boxes clustered around it. The capital—the roofs of the seven temples and of Baingarde, the king's castle, gleaming in the sun.

Twin trails of fire stretched from her hands down toward the city like long, hungry tongues.

Rielle staggered to her feet, exhaustion rocking her. Audric shouted in warning. Rielle turned to see one of the remaining Borsvall men approaching, his sword raised, fire crackling along the blade. His eyes were wide and white, his face drawn. This assassin, this firebrand with his flaming sword, was afraid of *her*.

She dropped again and rolled; his sword whistled through the air where she had been standing. Fire singed her hair. Smoke stung her nostrils.

Audric leapt in front of her, a glowing dagger in each hand.

Rielle felt faint with relief. He'd snuck in weapons after all.

Audric's face was hard with rage. When the assassin's fiery sword crashed into his sunlit daggers, the blow hurt Rielle's teeth. Sparks flew. Flames spit near Audric's face as the firebrand's sword bore down on him. But he did not waver. He stood strong before Rielle, the daggers throwing sunlight across the ground. He roared and lunged at the assassin, dislodging his sword. Twin orbs of sunlight burst from his crossed daggers and knocked the assassin to the ground. The assassin pushed himself back to his feet, his face and arms burned, and raced at Audric with a desperate, guttural cry.

Rielle's head rang with each clash of their blades; she clamped her hands around her skull. She had to hold herself together. If she couldn't stop her fire, the city would burn.

Audric met each of the other man's strikes with his own. His daggers sang; the air shuddered with heat. He wove back and forth, evading a killing thrust. Spun around, hurled a shield of light from his daggers, ran the blinded man through in the gut. The assassin fell, his sword abruptly snuffed out. Another assassin approached. Audric whirled, caught the second man's blade between his own. This one was a windsinger, the wind gusting and howling around him. It spiraled off his sword like an army of storms and nearly knocked Audric off his feet.

Their swords flashed, but even Audric had his limits. This second assassin was a boar of a man. If only Audric had Illumenor—

"Run, Rielle!" Audric shouted, curls plastered to his brow. He shoved his attacker, ducked a wild thrust of the man's sword.

Rielle looked around, saw a glint of metal in the dirt: a fallen dagger, its hilt engraved with the crest of the Borsvall royal family—a dragon flying over a mountain.

Gathering her last strength, Rielle grabbed the dagger and lurched to her feet. Her legs nearly buckled; her vision dimmed. She pushed past the pain careening through her body and leapt, and the blade found its way home in the Borsvall man's throat.

Rielle watched the man drop, felt his summoned wind disappear as he drew his last breath. The world was a faint buzz around her.

She watched the wildfire race down the slope toward the city, igniting every blade of grass it touched.

Stop, she thought. *Please, stop it. Don't hurt them.* She reached for the fire with what remained of her ravaged control, tried to pull the inferno back to her, but darkness flooded her vision.

Maybe she hadn't caused the fire after all. Maybe this was a terrible dream. She would wake on the morning of the race. Ludivine would help her sneak away from Tal's office. They had it all planned out.

She would win the race, and Audric would sweep her into his arms, laughing. He would congratulate her, beaming with pride, and then leave her to dine privately with Ludivine, and a part of Rielle would die, as it always did when she was reminded of the simple, terrible truth of their engagement.

Rielle caught a scent on the wind—singed hair, scorched horseflesh. It had been no dream.

How could she have done this?

How had she done this?

Her father was right. Tal was right. She should spend the rest of her life in a quiet room, dulled with poison. She could not be trusted.

She fell to her knees, her head spinning, and strong arms caught her. She felt a hand in her hair and lips hot against her forehead.

"Rielle," Audric cried. "Rielle, God, you're hurt. Stay with me. Look at me, please."

Before blackness took her, she heard another voice—male and lovely and soft as shadow.

I think it's time I said hello, said the voice. It felt something like a kiss, and it came from both far away and very near.

Then she knew nothing.

6

ELIANA

"The Venteran capital, Orline, is a well-situated port city on the southeastern coast. Despite the sweltering heat and the occasional stench from the swamplands on the western border, I am forced to admit it boasts a certain unique beauty—a luxurious city of stone terraces, hidden courtyards, and hanging moss, hugged by a broad, brown river that begins two thousand miles north in the Venteran highlands."

—Initial report of Lord Arkelion to His Holy Majesty, the Emperor of the Undying, upon successful seizure of Orline February 13, Year 1010 of the Third Age

On the first night of the full moon, Eliana did not sleep. She donned her new mask, painted her lips crimson, and flung her favorite cloak about her shoulders—a little theatricality never hurt anyone—and disappeared into the night.

She took to the rooftops, to the hop shops that reeked of lachryma, to the red rooms owned by friendly madams. She spent a night drifting through the Barrens.

She watched, and she listened.

She sought out her usual informants—frightened rebels willing to betray Red Crown or useful opportunists who would play double agent for coin.

She asked questions and demanded answers. She threatened and coaxed.

Mostly, she threatened.

But she found nothing of the Wolf. Not a glimpse, not a whisper.

On the second night of the full moon, Eliana came home with a fist-size knot in her stomach and a dozen frantic questions in her mind.

Did the Wolf know she was tracking him? Was that why everything had gone quiet?

Was Rahzavel watching her?

Was this some sort of test?

Was she failing?

She sat on the terrace outside her room and watched the sunrise bleed the world red. Part of her longed to cross the gap between rooftops, sneak into Harkan's room, wake him up with her mouth, and let him love her into oblivion.

But instead she sat still as a gargoyle, hood up and gloves on, and waited—and wondered.

If she didn't find the Wolf, what would Rahzavel do?

And if she was hunting the Wolf, was he in turn hunting her?

On the last night of the full moon, Eliana came home with panic humming beneath her skin to find that someone had broken into her house.

When working, Eliana preferred to enter and exit the house via the tiny stone terrace outside her third-floor window. That way, the front entrance on the road remained undisturbed.

Tonight, though, her window was open. A thin strip of wood

marked where the paint had been scraped off; someone had forced open the lock. There was a crack in the pane of glass.

As she stood frozen, she caught a scent on the air, just as she had the night of Quill's capture—that same unbalanced sensation that had left her feeling thrown out of alignment with the world around her. A sour pressure sat heavy against her tongue and shoulders.

Someone was here. *They* were here, those masked girl-snatchers from the docks. She knew it with a gut certainty. The only times she had ever felt such a sensation were that night and this one.

Which mean that now her mother…

And Remy?

They only take women, Eliana told herself, her heart kicking frantically. *They only take girls.*

Sweat beaded along her hairline. She could get Harkan to help her, but by then it might be too late.

She dropped down to the second-floor terrace outside her mother's room. The flowers of Rozen's rooftop garden perfumed the air and turned Eliana's stomach.

She found the window unlocked, which was odd. Her mother always locked the window before bed. She eased open the pane and slipped inside…and stopped.

Her mother was gone.

The room reeked with the trail of whatever phantom *thing* the abductors carried with them. The sheets had been pulled half off the mattress. A shattered teacup lay in pieces on the floor.

And her mother's prosthetic leg stood propped in the corner.

Terror rooted Eliana to the spot.

You're afraid we might be next, Remy had said the night of Quill's execution.

No. *No.* Not her mother. It wasn't possible.

Whoever was behind the abductions did not take women from the Garden Quarter. They were protected in this neighborhood.

But if the abductions were part of something bigger than Lord Arkelion's whims, maybe beyond his control altogether—

Footsteps sounded from the third floor. Her own room. Nearly silent but not quite. Their house was old; the floors creaked.

Remy, she thought, *please stay asleep. Please still be safe in your bed.*

She unsheathed her dagger, slipped out the door to her mother's bedroom. She crept past Remy's closed door and up the stairs to the third-floor landing.

Pressed flat against the wall beside her bedroom door, she waited. The door opened, and a tall figure stepped out into the shadows. Paused. Moved toward the stairs.

A man.

In the moonlight spilling out from her bedroom, she saw his mask of mesh and metal.

Fear punched through her.

The Wolf.

Supposedly, he never showed his face, choosing to always wear a mask. But a madam Eliana knew swore she had once seen the Wolf take it off. He was scarred, she said, as if from the rake of claws.

She said he had eyes like winter—icy cold and pitiless.

Well, then, Eliana thought. *We'll be well matched.*

She ran at him, kicked him hard in the small of his back. She expected him to fall down the stairs.

He did not.

He turned, caught her leg, flung her to the landing floor. With her free leg, she kicked his shin, twisted free, and jumped to her feet. He let his gloved fist fly; she ducked, and he hit the wall instead.

That slowed him a bit. She kicked the back of his knee. His leg buckled, but he was fast. He turned and shoved her, hard. She lost her footing and fell down the stairs to the second-floor landing.

The Wolf followed, seized her upper arms, and pushed her over the banister.

She fell two floors to the foyer, landing hard on her back. Her head cracked against the tiled floor, and for a fleeting moment she saw stars. But then she gritted her teeth and jumped to her feet.

The Wolf had hurried down after her, still poised to strike. He'd known that such a fall wouldn't seriously hurt her—or even kill her— as it might have someone else.

Fresh terror fluttered at the back of her throat. Her skin suddenly felt ill-fitting over her unbreakable bones.

He'd been following her, then. He'd seen her work. Or he had at least heard the rumors of the invincible Dread of Orline and believed them—no matter how ridiculous they seemed. Either way, he was here. He'd caught her out.

Interesting. And worrying.

She dodged his punch at the base of the stairs, whirled and kicked. He grabbed her cloak and yanked her back against him. She elbowed him in the gut, heard him grunt. Pulled Arabeth from her hip, turned, aimed for his heart—

But he was too quick; her dagger hit nothing but air. She staggered, thrown off-balance. He shoved her back against the wall beside the kitchen door. Her head hit brick, and the room dipped and swayed around her.

He grabbed her wrist and twisted, forcing her to drop Arabeth. He kicked the blade down the hallway, shoved his arm against her neck, pinned her. She grabbed Whistler from her thigh and swiped at him. Not a fatal cut, but he still cursed and released her.

She ripped Tempest from her boot and looked up, ready to strike—

The Wolf held a revolver, its muzzle pointed at her face.

Everything went still.

"Drop the knives." His voice was low, refined, and cut like ice. "Against the wall. Slowly."

"That's cheating," she fumed. "You brought a gun." But she obeyed, backing away from him until her shoulders brushed the wooden boards of the wall.

The Wolf followed, his body towering over her. He ripped Nox and Tuora from her belt and pressed Tuora's blade against her throat, then dropped his gun and kicked it away.

She stared at the blank metal face looming over her, searching for eyes beyond the mesh and finding none.

"Take off your mask," he ordered.

She did, then fixed him with the hardest smile she could muster.

"Dread," he murmured, his breath caressing her cheek, "is only a feeling, easily squashed. But wolves, my dear, have teeth."

~ 7 ~

RIELLE

"Beware, beware the Sauvillier smile—
A beautiful moon on a night most vile
It'll cut you to your bones, it'll fog the sharpest eyes
So says a man from the river who never tells lies"

—Celdarian traveling song

Rielle surged upright, yanked out of fire-edged dreams into a world of sudden panic.

"Audric," she croaked. The word scraped her raw throat. He had to be near. If he had died, *if he had died—*

"Hush." Cool hands brought a cup of water to her lips, helped her drink. "He's alive and well."

Rielle blinked, and Ludivine's face came into focus. She wore her long, golden hair in loose waves. Her pale blue eyes were bright, the only chink in an armor of serenity. With her hair down, her face clean and scrubbed, she could have passed for a girl much younger than nineteen. Nevertheless, she was a high lord's daughter, a lady of the House Sauvillier, the cousin and betrothed of the crown prince, and Celdaria's future queen. And even in her dressing gown, she looked every inch the part.

"There you are," she said, smiling. "For two days you've been fading in and out. We've only managed to feed you bites, sips of water." Ludivine's pale brow furrowed. She gathered Rielle's hands in her own. "You terrified me, darling."

"Tell me what happened," Rielle said, trying to sit up.

Ludivine hesitated. "You should rest."

But then Rielle remembered how Maliya had collapsed and felt suddenly, violently sick. Ludivine held back the unruly dark mass of her hair and rubbed between her shoulders as she emptied her stomach onto the floor.

One of Ludivine's maids scurried over to clean the mess, then glanced fearfully up at Rielle. The maid finished cleaning and fled to the sitting room with as much haste as decorum allowed.

Rielle watched her leave. Once she and Ludivine were once again alone, Rielle said, "Tell me."

"The assassins are dead," Ludivine said softly. "Fifteen of the racers are dead. We are…uncertain how each of them died, but we are blaming their deaths on the assassins and the circumstances of the race itself."

Rielle couldn't meet Ludivine's eyes. She could hardly stand feeling the reality of her own body's existence. Fifteen racers dead. *Fifteen.*

Her blood hummed with the memory of it—the crashing boulders and flaming earth, the fallen racers and their horses' screams.

She clenched her fists, shut her eyes, counted her breaths. "Lu, I'm sorry."

"Everyone else is safe," Ludivine continued. "Tal and his acolytes managed to control the fire before it could spread to the race boxes and the farmlands."

The fire. *Her* fire.

Rielle couldn't even remember how it had started. The entire affair, since seeing the assassins surround Audric, was nothing but a fog of confusion.

Shame gripped her like a hot fist. "I see. I shall have to thank them personally."

"At the very least," Ludivine said, but her voice was gentle. "Your horse…"

Rielle made a small, choked sound. She could still feel the poor animal's flesh blistering at her touch. The assassins had deserved their deaths, but not Maliya, and not the fifteen racers.

She closed her eyes. "Odo will be furious."

"He is simply glad you're alive."

"And Audric?"

Ludivine laid her hand over Rielle's. "Audric is fine."

"He's not hurt?"

"Truly, Rielle. He's perfectly fine. I should send for him soon. He's been rather impatient to speak with you."

Rielle heard the prim note in her friend's voice. Sometimes she could have sworn Ludivine knew every in and out of her true feelings. "Not yet." *If I see him, I will say something unforgivable. I will say too much.* "There's a lot to explain, and I—"

"Yes, indeed there is. I didn't know you were an earthshaker, Rielle. And a firebrand as well?"

Rielle stiffened at the deceptive sweetness in Ludivine's voice. It was a tone rarely used on her. "I am neither of those things."

"You're certainly something. The capital is in an uproar. Bodies, we can explain away. But altered mountainsides, scorched and shattered earth? Many people have questions."

"And the king wants answers."

"Yes."

"Well, he will have to torture them out of me."

"That isn't funny."

"I'm not—"

"Stop *lying* to me." Ludivine rose to pace across the room. When she turned back, her face was flushed, her eyes bright. "How could you have kept this from me? We trust each other. I would never have let anything happen to you."

"It was not your truth to know," Rielle said tightly.

"And what truth is that? What happened out there? What are you?"

That was a blow. Rielle's voice unraveled. "I wish I knew."

"The prophecy says…" Ludivine paused, gathering herself. "'They will carry the power of the Seven.' The two Queens are foretold to be able to control all the elements, not just one."

Rielle let out a harsh, tired laugh. "Are you really explaining the prophecy to me?"

"People will think you are one of them."

"I'm well aware of that, Lu."

"Rumors are already circulating. The city—"

"Is terrified?" Rielle rubbed shaky hands across her face. "They're not alone."

"I thought we had no secrets between us."

"I can make it go away. I just…need more time."

"Make it go away? What, as though this power you have is a bad mood? Those are your father's words."

Rielle closed her eyes. "Father. God help me."

"He is with the king now."

Rielle quailed at that, but she forced up her chin. "I won't let them kill me."

Ludivine's expression softened. "Rielle…"

"They can try, and I'm sure they will. But I won't let them." She stood, her head throbbing.

Ludivine gently caught Rielle's wrist, then cradled Rielle's face in her hands. Rielle let her eyes fall closed. Ludivine's scent—lavender oil and clean skin—enveloped her in memory: Morning walks in the gardens, their arms linked. Childhood nights curled up between Ludivine and Audric by the wide hearth in his rooms.

"I won't let them hurt you either," Ludivine repeated, her voice firm and clear. "Never. Do you hear me?"

Rielle tried for lightness. "Oh, and what will you do? Sweet Lady Ludivine would not hurt even a fly, I've been told."

Ludivine smiled. She opened her mouth to speak, but Rielle stopped her. The moment of calm had brought forth a memory.

"Someone spoke to me," she said abruptly.

Ludivine frowned, blinking. "What?"

"Before. I saw the fire, and I couldn't stand up. Audric caught me, and...then I heard someone speak to me."

"You mean, Audric spoke to you?"

"No. Someone else. It was..." Rielle paused, trying to recall the exact feeling, and her skin thrilled as though someone had drawn a feather across her belly. "It came from inside me."

Ludivine arched an eyebrow. "Audric's healer did say you might have a slight fever."

"No, Lu, I'm telling you—"

Someone pounded on the outer door of Ludivine's apartment, prompting the maid from before to hurry in a moment later, her eyes wide. She glanced over her shoulder. "Begging your pardon, my lady, but you have a visitor..."

Ludivine kept Rielle's hand in hers. "Lady Rielle is not ready to receive visitors just yet."

"Apologies, my lady, I tried to tell them—"

"It's the king," Rielle said. "Isn't it?"

The maid would not meet her eyes. "We were ordered to send word as soon as you'd awoken, my lady."

"His Majesty has many questions, Rielle," came a voice she knew well.

Lord Commander Armand Dardenne strode in from the sitting room, pushing open the door to Ludivine's bedroom without bothering to knock. He was steel and iron, every inch of him impeccable. He regarded his daughter with all the warmth of a statue.

She started forward. "Is Tal—?"

"Grand Magister Belounnon has already been questioned by the councils," he continued, "as have I. You're next. Make yourself presentable."

Without another word, Ludivine and her maids helped Rielle behind the dressing screen and into a muted dress of dusky blue and ivory, with a high collar and ribboned sleeves. It was pretty enough to charm, demure enough not to offend.

"Should I be angry that you sent your maids to root through my wardrobe without my permission?" Rielle murmured with half a laugh.

"I couldn't care less if you're angry or not," Ludivine said, straightening Rielle's skirts. "All these years of my guidance, and I still don't trust you to pick the appropriate gown for any occasion."

"Some would say my fashion sense is unique and forward-thinking."

"Yes, and such a sense is not one to parade about during a royal questioning." Ludivine raised an eyebrow at one of her maids. "I need the jeweled combs on the table there."

Once Ludivine had pinned back her long, dark hair, Rielle checked her reflection in the mirror. She looked small and strange, the softness of her dress in stark contrast to the red scratches on her face, the shadows under her sharp green eyes.

"If you're finished," came her father's voice.

Rielle closed her eyes and drew a deep breath, but before she could move, Ludivine drew her into a warm embrace and kissed her on the cheek.

"Remember," Ludivine whispered, "if anyone wants to hurt you, they'll have to go through me. And Audric. And Tal. And many, many others. The king will not act rashly. Trust him. Trust us."

Rielle held Ludivine to her for another moment, then stepped out from the dressing screen. Her father offered her his arm; reluctantly, she took it.

"Father," she began, "before we go down—"

He ignored her. "Everyone in this castle is starving for gossip at the moment. Do not speak of anything important while they bring us downstairs."

"They?" she asked, but once they stepped into the sitting room, she understood.

Twenty soldiers of the royal guard waited for them, lining the path out of Ludivine's apartment with their swords drawn.

Rielle faltered only for a moment as the guards escorted them out into the windowed hallway, where morning sunlight bathed the polished stone in gold.

She lifted her chin, set her jaw. Audric was still alive. She did not regret what she had done.

Good, came the voice, pleased. *You should regret nothing. It was past time.*

She was feverish. She was exhausted, hearing things.

Nevertheless...

Who are you? she thought.

There was no answer.

The silence unnerved her, and though it was childish, she couldn't help but say quietly to her father, "I am not afraid."

"My daughter," he replied, something new and haggard in his voice, "you should be."

⇥ 8 ⇤

ELIANA

"They call him the Wolf. He's the Prophet's favorite, our informants tell us. They say he cannot be captured, but rest assured, my lord: we will find this Wolf, carve every secret from his body, and leave him to bleed dry."

—Report written by Lord Arkelion of Ventera to His Holy Majesty, the Emperor of the Undying June 21, Year 1018 of the Third Age

The Wolf bound her hands to the stair banister and ordered her to sit on the bottom step. Then, to her surprise, he took off his own mask and lowered his hood.

Eliana's madam acquaintance had greatly exaggerated.

His scars were silvered streaks across his forehead, nose, and cheeks. There were patches of marred skin, worn from fire or wind, but the face itself, framed by tousled ash-blond hair, was stern, sharp. Handsome.

But the madam had been right about his eyes: winter blue and diamond cold.

"See something you like?" Eliana glanced up at him through her lashes. Shifted her body toward him, arched her back just enough to make a point.

The Wolf knelt before her. "You're good."

Grinning, she looked him up and down—lean and tall, slim-fitting trousers and vest and cuffed sleeves, weapon holsters on a sash around his torso and a low-slung belt around his hips. "So are you, Wolf. It's a shame I'll have to kill you. Were our circumstances different, I'd ask to see your sword."

"A bitter disappointment, to be sure." Now he was the one to let his gaze roam over her. "You're much more fun than I had imagined."

"Fun?" She laughed low in her throat. "You've no idea just how fun I can be." She leaned back as best she could with her hands bound, feigning boredom. "So. You exist after all. The mighty Wolf. Fearsome Red Crown captain, unstoppable soldier. Right hand of the Prophet himself. More like a dog than a wolf if you ask me. You rebels are all the same."

"Are we, now?" His easy smile chilled her.

"Tell me," she pushed on, "when you report back to the Prophet, do you crawl on your belly to him? Kiss his boots? Does he whip you for not having managed to overthrow the Emperor yet? You'd better get on with things, you know. More rebels are dying every day." Smiling, she leaned closer, willing her pounding heart quiet. "I make sure of it."

He shifted closer to meet her. Even kneeling, he was tall. "If you're trying to make me angry," he murmured, their mouths mere inches apart, "I'm afraid it won't work."

With every moment he crouched there staring at her, his eyes wandering over each plane and curve of her body, Eliana felt closer to outright terror. There was a stillness about him—a sense of something horrible lying in wait, tightly coiled—that pressed against her skin like the memory of a bad dream.

For a moment, she lost her nerve.

"What do you want?" she asked.

His smile spread slowly. "Why, Madam Dread, I want you."

The strange tenderness in his voice sent ice up her spine. "Where is my mother?"

"I haven't the faintest."

She scoffed, rolled her eyes. "I didn't realize Red Crown was in the habit of snatching defenseless women from their beds. Aren't you people supposed to be heroes? Fighting our oppressors, saving the world from tyranny?"

"Red Crown is not responsible for those abductions."

"Then who is?"

"A good question. I have my guesses."

It was pointless to accuse him further. She had long ago ruled out Red Crown's involvement in the disappearances.

But she could not stop imagining her mother held captive somewhere, alone and afraid, wondering when her daughter would come for her.

Eliana's eyes grew hot. Her fingers itched for her daggers. "Either kill me," she said cheerfully, "or untie me so I can cut out your lying tongue."

"I've no interest in doing either of those things." A smile pulled at his mouth. "I have a proposal for you, but I'd rather not talk about it here, in case whoever took your mother decides to return. What say we take our secrets elsewhere, little Dread?"

Little? The moment she had the chance, she would knock him on his ass.

"Are you mad?" she snapped.

"Many have wondered." He curled two fingers under her chin, made her look at him. His touch jolted her; she forced herself to lean into his hand.

"I hunt people like you," she told him with a slight, hard smirk.

"Yes, and you do a fine job of it." All humor in his voice died. "Tell me, Madam Dread: If I pledge that I will help you find your mother, in exchange for your assistance, will you join me?"

Eliana tried to read him and could find nothing to go on. Join him? A ludicrous thought. She could not possibly trust him.

And yet, if she refused him, if he fled the city and she went to Lord Arkelion empty-handed, what then?

She longed to shut her eyes and have a moment alone to think. *Mother, I'm sorry. God, I'm so sorry. I'm coming as soon as I can. I'll find you. I swear it.*

"I leave this city tomorrow," the Wolf continued, "and you might just get the shit kicked out of you for letting me slip through your fingers. So you can join me or not, but either way, you won't catch me." A small smile. "You want to find your mother, yes? Wouldn't it be smarter to do it with help?"

Her thoughts scrambled and raced. "Goodness me, what a night. The famous Wolf, needing help from a girl—"

"My mission begins tomorrow evening. Do we have a bargain or not?"

"Tomorrow is His Lordship's naming day. There's a fete at the palace."

"What a happy coincidence."

She narrowed her eyes. "Only tomorrow night?"

"No. Our mission will be longer."

"How much longer?"

"I cannot say."

"Or you will not."

"Those are my terms. Do you accept?"

Her wound-up nerves felt ready to detonate. She managed a disinterested sort of sneer. "Why me?"

"You know the palace. You'll make it easier to get inside."

"And after that? Why bring me with you?"

"Because I need to move fast, and I need another killer on my side. Someone as good as I am."

"Or better."

"She says, bound on the floor."

"You pulled a gun on me. I would have beaten you, otherwise."

"Perhaps."

"Must be quite an important mission," she continued mockingly, "and yet you would risk trusting me."

"I'm gambling that you won't risk losing your mother," he replied.

The Wolf had her there. And judging by the look on his face, he knew it.

"And if I don't accept this bargain?"

"Then I will leave and never see you again, and you'll go on about your life here, if you can call it that. Unless they kill you for failing to capture me."

Eliana stayed silent to see what he would do.

After a moment, he untied her wrists, discarded the bindings, and stood. "Well?"

She calculated how long it would take to kick him, send him staggering, grab his revolver, and shoot. She'd never used a gun—they were rare, expensive, and she never let herself spend the money on them—but pulling a trigger seemed simple enough.

Five seconds. Perhaps six.

She could do it. She rose.

And then she saw Harkan.

He was coming in from the kitchen, his body dipped in shadow, his favorite dagger in hand. Behind him, Remy watched tensely from the kitchen.

Harkan's gaze found hers, held firm. *I've got you.*

"I'll help you," she told the Wolf slowly, "but only if I can take my brother with me."

Remy's eyes widened.

"The little baker's boy?" The Wolf frowned. "You can't be serious."

Eliana kept her face blank. Just how much did he know about her? "I assume we're stealing something from the palace, then delivering it somewhere. Some piece of intelligence? Wherever we're taking it afterward, Remy will come. You'll get him safe passage to Astavar and do nothing to harm him. Or we've no deal."

He glared at her. "That wasn't my offer."

"Yes or no, Wolf."

He tilted his head. His eyes caught the moonlight and made him look like something from one of Remy's more fanciful tales—a night creature, made of secrets and sharp edges. An Empire monster for the Sun Queen to slay. "Only those who are frightened of me call me that. And you aren't frightened of me. Are you?"

Harkan approached through the shadows—one step, two steps.

"Not even a little bit," she lied. "So what shall I call you instead?"

He inclined his head. "You can call me Simon."

"Fine. *Simon*. And one more thing: my friend, Harkan, will come with us as well."

Behind Simon, Harkan raised his dagger to strike.

Eliana flexed her fingers.

Simon's mouth thinned, the only warning. A turn, a shove, and then Harkan was flat on his back on the floor, Simon's boot pressing into his throat, his weapon in Simon's hand.

"Him?" Simon pointed at Harkan with the dagger. The look he threw Eliana was one of profound disgust. "Your lover?"

Eliana shot Simon a rakish smile. "Jealous already? Let him go."

"El," rasped Harkan, struggling to breathe, "we can't trust him."

"No," she agreed. "But he can't trust us either." She held out her hand for Tuora. "Release him, or no deal."

Simon paused, then returned Tuora to her and stepped away.

Eliana slipped the dagger into the holster at her belt, knelt at Harkan's side, and helped him sit up. "Tell me more about this mission of yours, Wolf."

"Information only as you need to know it, little Dread," Simon said. "Until then, do as I tell you, and I'll help you find your mother. You have my word."

"The word of a rebel doesn't count for much."

"And what about the word of a fellow killer?" He took off his glove and held out his hand. "Have we a bargain?"

Eliana hesitated. If she accepted his offer, her life here would be forfeit. Lord Arkelion did not deal with defectors lightly, and Rahzavel would not allow her to disappear into the night. By doing this she would be endangering not only herself, but Remy and Harkan as well.

But if anyone could help her find her mother, and get all of them to Astavar and to safety, it would be the Wolf, with all of Red Crown—the very people she had spent so long hunting—at his disposal.

If she played this right, she could keep Harkan and Remy out of the Empire's grasp for a few more years. She could elude Invictus, stay with her loved ones, find her mother, and keep them all safe.

She searched Simon's eyes for lies and found only cold steel.

"Eliana, don't agree to this," Harkan rasped, glaring up at Simon. "We'll find Rozen another way."

But there was no other way. Eliana stood and clasped Simon's hand.

"We have a bargain," she said and tried to ignore the way her skin shivered at Simon's touch—like the sensation of being watched from the shadows or the simmering charge of a storm she could not outrun.

9

RIELLE

*"The seven saints combined their powers and opened
a doorway into the Deep with wind and water, with
metal and fire, with shadow and earth. And when Saint
Katell, last of all, let fly her blazing, sunlit sword, the
angels fell screaming into eternal darkness."*

—*The Book of the Saints*

The Hall of Saints was the largest, most sacred room in Baingarde.
White stone pillars supported soaring vaulted ceilings ribboned with elaborate carvings of suns and moons, trees and flames.
The ceilings themselves boasted a map of the world of Avitas: Celdaria
and the other four nations of the sprawling eastern continent. North
of Celdaria lay the Sunderlands and the Gate. And across the Great
Ocean were the western kingdoms of Ventera, Astavar, and Meridian.

On a tall, white marble dais at the front of the room sat the High
Court's bench; grand, high-backed chairs for the king and queen; an
ornate, wide-seated chair for the Archon, the head of the Church; and
a multilevel gallery large enough to seat the members of every temple
and royal council.

Above the dais towered Saint Katell, the patron saint of Celdaria
and all sunspinners in the world. Her right arm held up her sword—
her casting—which was now hidden somewhere in Celdaria.

Katell's other hand clutched a fistful of ragged stone feathers.

Angels, miniature and pathetic, their faces contorted in agony, crawled up the legs of her white mare, pleading to no avail.

Around her head shone a halo of light, plated in gold, kept burnished and flawless.

Saint Katell the Magnificent—a sunspinner and, after the Angelic Wars, a queen. The unifier of Celdaria. Loved by an angel but strong enough to resist the temptation of the enemy.

And, in the thousand years since, the children of her line had sat on the throne.

The other six saints lined the vast hall, three on each side. Gigantic and solemn, stone and bronze, they each carried their own casting and were framed by an element: Saint Nerida, waterworker and the patron saint of Meridian, brandishing her trident as waves crested at her back, her kraken coiled at her bare feet. Saint Grimvald, metalmaster and the patron saint of Borsvall, striking his way on dragonback through a storm of iron shards, his hammer in hand.

And Saint Katell, riding her shining white mare.

Twenty armored guards stood at the foot of the dais, facing Rielle. They were her father's men and women, people she knew by name. She felt their eyes on her—concerned, curious. Afraid.

They are right to be afraid, came the voice, without warning. *But not you.*

Rielle stiffened. In this environment, it was impossible to hear the voice without remembering the truth: mind-speaking was something the angels once did.

Her skin crawled at the thought. So many people were staring at her that she could hardly remain still. Her father stood surrounded by a contingent of armed guards. Queen Genoveve, King Bastien, Ludivine. The Archon, serene in his robes. The councils—with the obvious, alarming exception of Tal.

And Audric.

He sat beside his parents, on the edge of his seat as if prepared to launch himself off the dais in case of disaster. When Rielle's eyes met his, he sent her a small smile, thin with worry.

Rielle relaxed slightly.

Audric is here, she told herself. *He won't let them hurt me.*

She found the king, above. The expression on his face made him look more troubled than she had ever seen him. King Bastien was a man of good humor. Rielle had grown up to the sound of his laughter booming through the halls of Baingarde, had screamed gleefully while he chased her, Audric, and Ludivine through their childhood play-room in countless games of go-find-the-mouse.

There was no trace of that man today.

Rielle resisted the urge to wipe away the sweat gathering at her hairline. She curtsied low, her skirts pooling on the spotless floor. "Your Majesty."

"Lady Rielle Dardenne," King Bastien began, "you have been brought here today to answer inquiries about the incident that occurred during the Boon Chase two days past. I will ask you a series of questions, and you will answer them truthfully in the eyes of the saints."

"I understand, my king." The massive room swallowed Rielle's voice.

King Bastien nodded, paused. The gray threading through his black beard and the laugh lines across his brown face made him look older than Rielle had ever thought him before.

Then his gaze hardened. Rielle resisted the urge to take a step back from the new, dangerous charge in the air.

"How long," he asked, his voice cool and matter-of-fact, "have you known yourself to possess elemental magic?"

Somehow, Rielle had thought this would begin with something less direct. A question or two, or five, that would give her time to find her voice.

But at least, perhaps, they thought she was only an elemental and not…whatever she truly was. Maybe her punishment, then—and Tal's and her father's—would not be as severe as she had feared.

The prophecy's words ran through her mind: *They will carry the power of the Seven.*

"Since I was five years old," she answered.

"And how did you come to this conclusion?"

He asked it so casually, as though they did not already know the answer.

A chair creaked as someone shifted their weight. Rielle glanced over and found Tal's sister, Sloane Belounnon, with the rest of the Magisterial Council surrounding the Archon. She sat rigid in her seat, her dark, chin-length hair looking unusually severe against her wan skin. She looked as though she had not slept.

How must Sloane feel, to know that her brother had kept such a secret from her?

"When…when I was five," Rielle continued, "I set fire to our home."

"How?"

"I was angry. My mother and I had had an argument."

"About what?"

It sounded ridiculous, horribly small. "I didn't want to go to sleep. I wanted to sit up with Father and read."

"So," the king said calmly, "you set your house on fire."

"It was an accident. I was angry, and the anger built up until I could no longer contain it. I ran outside because the feeling frightened me. It felt like something inside me was burning. And then… when I turned around," she said, the memory clawing at her, "I saw fire consuming our house. One moment it had not been there, and the next, it was."

"And you had caused this."

"Yes."

"How did you know?"

How did you see your own hand moving and know it was attached to your arm and your shoulder and your blood and your bones? Like that.

"I knew because it looked and sounded and felt like me," she explained. "It felt the same as my anger had felt. The same scent, the same flavor. I felt connected to it." She hesitated. "Grand Magister Belounnon has since helped me understand that what I sensed in that moment was the empirium. The connection between myself and the fire was the power that connects all things, and I had accessed it."

Rielle dared to look at the Archon, sitting beside the Magisterial Council. He stared back at her, his small bright eyes unblinking. The torchlight made his pale skin and smooth head gleam.

"And was your mother able to escape?" the king continued.

Rielle's throat tightened, and for a moment she could not speak. "No. She was trapped inside. Father ran in to get her and brought her out. She was alive, but then…"

Say it, child. The voice returned, compassionate. *Tell them. They cannot hurt you.*

With the stone saints staring down at her, their unfeeling eyes cold and grave, the strange voice should not have been a comfort. But hearing it nevertheless settled her churning stomach.

"I was afraid," she continued, "when I saw my mother. I had never seen burns before. She was screaming, and I yelled at her to stop, but she wouldn't, and then…all I could think was how I needed her to stop screaming." She hurried through the story, as if trying to outrace the memory of those climbing flames. "Then she stopped. Father laid her on the ground, begged her to wake up. But she was dead."

The room shifted, murmuring.

"And you have hidden this murder from us for thirteen years," King Bastien declared.

"It was not a murder," Rielle said, wishing desperately to sit. Her body still felt bruised from the fight in the mountains. "I did not mean to kill my mother. I was a child, and it was an accident."

"We are concerned with facts here, not intentions. The facts of the matter are that you killed Marise Dardenne, and you have—with the help of your father and Grand Magister Belounnon—lied about it for thirteen years."

"If someone had asked me if I had killed my mother, and I had denied it," Rielle replied, looking straight up at the king, "then that would be a lie, Your Majesty. Keeping a secret is not lying."

"Lady Rielle, I am not interested in semantics. You concealed the damage you were capable of doing while you ate at my table, while you were schooled with my son and niece, and thereby placed them and all those around you in danger. Some might consider such a deception treasonous."

Treason. Rielle kept her eyes on King Bastien and her hands flat against her thighs. If he had meant to frighten her, he had succeeded.

"And on the day of the race," said the king, "not only did you start a fire when you attacked those men—"

Anger bloomed inside her. If she was to be found guilty of treason, then she might as well earn her punishment. "When I saved Prince Audric's life, you mean."

A louder murmuring rose from the gallery, but King Bastien simply inclined his head. Rielle knew it was the only thanks she might receive, but it was enough to give her a bit of courage.

"When you attacked those men," the king continued, "you not only started a fire. You ripped open the earth. You carved sheets of rock from the mountains. One of the surviving racers has described you gathering sunlight from the air using only your hands. Another claims you threw the assassins from their horses by no visible means she could detect. Even though the assassins themselves were elementals, you easily overpowered them." The king looked up from his notes. "Does that align with your own recollection?"

Then they did know what she had done, that she was no mere elemental. Her jaw ached from clenching it. "It does, Your Majesty."

"So then, you are not only a firebrand but an earthshaker, a

sunspinner, and also, perhaps, other things. I think you will understand our alarm as we contemplate what this means. No human who
has ever lived has been able to control more than one element. Not
even the saints."

A tiny spark of pride lit inside Rielle.

"Lady Rielle," he went on, "if you had been near a body of water
during this race, would you have caused it to flood?"

"It is impossible to say if I would have or not, Your Majesty."

"Could you have, then?"

A flood. Years of lessons with Tal had shown her only hints of such
power, and though she'd never been as strong with water as she'd
been with fire—

You know you could do it, the voice murmured. *You could flood the
world. That kind of power hums beneath your skin. Doesn't it?*

A cautious delight unfurled within her. *Who are you?* she asked the
voice.

It did not answer.

She lifted her chin. "Yes, I believe I could have."

A new voice spoke up: "Did you like it?"

It was such a perfectly astute, perfectly terrible question that Rielle
did not immediately answer. She found the speaker—severely handsome, fair-haired, an elegant jawline. Lord Dervin Sauvillier. The
queen's brother and Ludivine's father.

Beside him, Ludivine sat poised and clear-eyed in her gown of
luminous rose, lace spilling out her sleeves.

"Lord Sauvillier," said the king sternly, "while I appreciate your
interest in these events, I have not given you leave to speak."

Queen Genoveve—auburn-haired, pale as her niece Ludivine—
touched her husband's arm. "However, it is a reasonable question if
we are to determine how best to proceed."

Rielle looked to the queen and was rewarded with a small smile
that reminded Rielle of Ludivine—a Ludivine who had grown up not

alongside Audric in the airy, sunlit rooms of Baingarde, but rather in the cold mountain halls of Belbrion, the seat of House Sauvillier.

Queen Genoveve's gaze slid over Rielle and moved away.

"I am not certain," Rielle replied, "that I entirely understand Lord Sauvillier's question."

Ludivine's father raised a deferent eyebrow to the king, who nodded once.

"Well, Lady Rielle, if you'll forgive me my bluntness," said Dervin Sauvillier, "I wonder if you enjoyed what you did on the racecourse. If you enjoyed hurting the assassins." He paused. "If you enjoyed hurting your mother."

"If I enjoyed it?" Rielle repeated, stalling.

For of course she had enjoyed it. Not the pain she had caused and not her poor mother's death.

But the relief of it... That, she craved. The rush of release through every muscle in her body. Those forbidden, blazing moments—practicing with Tal, running the Chase—when she had known nothing but her power and what it could do. The shining clarity of understanding that this was her true, entire self.

Sometimes she couldn't sleep for wanting to feel that way again.

"Your hesitation is alarming, Lady Rielle," said Lord Sauvillier.

"I...did not enjoy the pain I caused others," Rielle answered slowly. "For that, I feel nothing but shame and remorse. In fact, I am appalled that anyone might think I could enjoy doing such things to any living person, let alone my own mother. But...do the teachings of our saints not tell us that we should take pleasure in the use of the power that has been granted to us by God?"

Out of the corner of her eyes, Rielle saw the Archon shift at last, leaning forward slightly.

It was as if Audric had been waiting for a signal from her, and he did not disappoint. "My lord, may I answer her question?" he asked his father.

King Bastien did not look happy, but he nodded.

"The saints' teachings do indeed tell us that, my lady," said Audric, looking straight at her as if they were the only two in the room, "and they also tell us that power is not something elementals should deny or ignore. Even when that power is dangerous, and perhaps even especially then. I of all people know the truth of that."

Rielle said nothing, though she felt weightless with relief. With those words, Audric had shown her that he understood. He forgave her. The steady belief shining in his eyes warmed her down to her toes.

"With all respect, Your Majesty," Lord Sauvillier said, and now he simply sounded exasperated, "we cannot possibly compare this woman and her careless destruction of her surroundings with your son, who has consistently demonstrated unimpeachable discipline and has not once let his power get the better of him."

A swift rage crested in Rielle. "Perhaps the challenge facing me is greater, as it seems I am more powerful than our prince."

The silence that followed was so complete it felt alive. Lord Sauvillier recoiled in disgust, his mouth thin and angry. The king might have been carved from stone, like one of the watching saints.

Rielle waited, heart thundering. She wanted to look to Audric but resisted.

Finally, King Bastien spoke. "Lady Rielle, you are familiar with the prophecy, as spoken by the angel Aryava and translated by Queen Katell."

Of course she was. Everyone was.

"I am, Your Majesty," Rielle answered.

"The Gate will fall," the king recited. "The angels will return and bring ruin to the world. You will know this time by the rise of two human Queens—one of blood, and one of light. One with the power to save the world. One with the power to destroy it. Two Queens will rise. They will carry the power of the Seven. They will carry your fate in their hands. Two Queens will rise."

The king paused. In the wake of the prophecy's words, the hall felt chilled.

"The most popular interpretation being, of course," King Bastien continued, "that the coming of the two Queens will portend the fall of the Gate and the angels' vengeance. And that those two Queens will be able to control not only one element, but all of them."

Yes, of course, and everyone knew that too. Not that most people gave much thought to the different interpretations in modern times—if they gave the prophecy any thought at all.

Rielle was one of the exceptions. Often, she had found herself reading the prophecy's words over and over, running her fingers across the scripted letters in Tal's books.

A Queen made of blood and a Queen made of light. The Blood Queen and the Sun Queen they had come to be called over the centuries.

And now, after so many years, they hardly felt real. The Gate stood strong in the Sunderlands, far in the northern sea, guarded and quiet, with the angels locked safely away on the other side. Queens from a prophecy might as well have been characters in a tale. Children chose sides, assembled play armies, staged wars in the streets.

The bad queen against the good queen. Blood warring with light.

Am I one of them? Rielle had wondered, though she had never found the courage to ask Tal or her father outright. *And…which one?*

"You see, Lady Rielle," said the king, "my charge is not to decide whether what you have done is a crime and whether—or how—you should be punished. It is that you seem to be neither firebrand nor sunspinner nor earthshaker, but all of those things, and more, which is unprecedented. You performed magic more powerful than there has been in half an age, even after spending thirteen years being taught to suppress your abilities in the hope that they would disappear. And you did so without the aid of a casting, which is something not even the saints could manage at the height of their glory.

"My sacred duty," said the king, his face grave, "is to determine what, exactly, you are. I must decide if you are one of these Queens—and if so, which one."

Rielle heard the unsaid words plainly: *And what that will mean for you.*

She clenched her fists in her skirts and curtsied before the king, the shadow of Saint Katell falling like a sword across her neck.

10

ELIANA

"When darkest is the night
When lost is the fight
When blood is all in sight
Look to the rising dawn"

—Venteran folk song

Whenever Eliana dressed for one of Lord Arkelion's parties, she thought about her father.

Ioseph Ferracora had spent most of her childhood fighting on the eastern front as the Empire wore down the last of Ventera's resistance.

"Every night he's gone, we'll leave lights in the windows for him," her mother had decided. In those golden days before the invasion, before Remy, the distant war had felt no more real to Eliana than a ghost story.

"But what will the lights do?" Eliana asked.

"They belong to the Sun Queen," Rozen explained, "and will help bring your father safely back to us."

So every night before bed, Eliana had lit the candle in her window and whispered the Sun Queen's prayer: "May the Queen's light guide him home."

As she grew older, she came to dread her father's visits, for they became shorter, and they would always end. But she never stopped looking forward to the summer solstice, when Ioseph would return for the annual festival—and most importantly, for the Sun Queen pageant.

Before the Fall, before the Blood Queen Rielle died and left everything in ruins, the world was full of magic. So said the stories, and as a child, Eliana had believed in them with all her heart. They said people of the Old World used shields and swords to summon wind and fire. They worshipped mighty saints who had banished the race of angels into oblivion, and they believed that a queen would someday save the world from evil. She was called the Sun Queen, for she would bring light into darkness.

Even long after the age of the Old World had ended, and it was understood that angels and magic did not exist, had never existed—that the legends of the Old World were simply that—many people still visited temples to pray to the saints, and the myth of the Sun Queen remained.

And every summer, Ioseph Ferracora returned home to his daughter, bringing with him some new ornament for her costume—a gilded hairpiece from Rinthos, a white mink pelt smuggled in from Astavar.

Together, Eliana and her parents would join the parades crowding the city. Children with gold-dusted cheeks climbed up the crumbling statues of Saint Katell the sunspinner to leave garlands of gemma flowers around her neck. Musicians beat their drums and plucked their harps. White-robed storytellers performed tales of the Sun Queen's long-awaited coming.

The parade ended at the high turn of the river, in the easternmost hills, where the statue of Audric the Lightbringer stood. He sat on his winged horse, sword in hand and somber eyes fixed on the eastern horizon. It was Eliana's favorite statue in the city, for the doomed king's face looked both brave and tired. Looking at him made her heart twist with pity.

"I'm sorry, Lightbringer," she whispered to him, that last year. She kissed his weathered stone boot, clutched her necklace bearing his ruined likeness in the other. As always, she searched for his face in the necklace's layers of wear, but while the winged horse was clear, the person riding it had been buried beneath the darkness of time, no matter how diligently Eliana tried to clean it.

"Watch the horizon," Rozen had whispered to her daughter, an infant Remy asleep in her arms. "Do you see her? Do you see the Sun Queen?"

"Will she come this year, Papa?" seven-year-old Eliana had asked, elated even after the long night.

"Keep looking, sweet girl," Ioseph had answered, his arms trembling around her. "Keep watching for the light."

He had left again for war the next day, and he had never returned.

Ten years later, Eliana sat before the mirror in her bedroom as Remy finished twisting her wavy brown hair into a low knot. Her cheeks— not so pale as Remy's, closer to the warm olive tones of her mother— shimmered with silver powder. Dark kohl rimmed her eyes; diamonds glinted in each ear.

She finished applying a rich red dye to her lips and smiled at her reflection.

"I look good," she declared.

Remy rolled his eyes. "You always look good."

"Yes, but tonight it's really something, isn't it?"

"I'm just going to keep rolling my eyes until you stop talking."

She grinned at him in the mirror. "So. Tell me once more."

Remy sulked on her bed. "I'm supposed to stay with Harkan, no matter what, and do exactly as he tells me, no matter what, and not even think of asking you again about what you'll be doing tonight. No matter what."

Eliana stood, the wine-colored gown Lord Arkelion sent her falling in sparkling folds about her legs. "And if something happens to Harkan?"

"I wait for you at the east bridge, by the Admiral's statue."

"But nothing will happen to Harkan," said the man himself, entering from the hallway. He wore tall brown boots, dark trousers, a long coat that hugged his trim torso, and a hooded cloak. He set down a small bag of supplies and ruffled Remy's hair. "Harkan's altogether too impressive for that."

Normally Remy would have rolled his eyes and told Harkan that the only impressive thing he could do was belch like a drunk old grandfather.

But Remy sat silent and pale, his lips chapped from biting them. Since their mother's disappearance, he had not let anyone see him cry, had even bravely tried to match Eliana's jokes, but she knew better.

If something went wrong, if anything happened to him or Harkan because of the deal she had made with Simon…

She tucked her necklace into her dress, the pendant rough against her skin, and smoothed her features into a glittering mask.

"Remy," Harkan said, "why don't you go collect your things?"

"I'm not stupid," Remy muttered. "Just tell me to leave so you can talk."

"Fine. Leave so we can talk."

When Remy had gone, Harkan took Eliana's hand.

"Tell me you're not making a terrible mistake, trusting this man," he said quietly.

A thrill of nervousness rippled through her at the grave expression on his face. "You know I can't tell you that."

"Good. Because then I'd know you were lying."

Despite herself, she smiled, and when Harkan finally grinned back at her, she cupped his face in her hands and brought him down gently for a kiss. With his hands warm against her bare back, Eliana could almost believe this was just another night—going to a party with Harkan, dancing and flirting and coming home with a job.

"We will find her, El." Harkan kissed her temple and let her go, his eyes soft on her face. "But first—"

"First," she said, trying on a smile, "I have a party to attend."

In the Evening Ballroom of Lord Arkelion's palace, only a handful of small candles dotted the room, and the shivering floor spun with dancers. Large windows opened into the night, letting in the river breeze.

Eliana pretended to sip her wine and scanned the room, counting the motionless figures around the perimeter—adatrox. Twenty of them.

Her mouth thinned. On a normal night, upward of five hundred adatrox patrolled the enormous palace and its sprawling grounds. But tonight there would be close to a thousand.

She continued counting. Thirty. Thirty-five. Mostly men, a few women. Dark and pale. Black cloaks and gray surcoats and blank-eyed stares that could turn murderous in an instant.

An idol to the Emperor towered in a corner of the ballroom. Eliana, glaring at it, sent a quick prayer to Saint Tameryn of the Old World, the legendary shadowcaster and the patron saint of Astavar. The Empire could raze their temples to the ground and tear down their statues, but they could not police the prayers inside her head.

Hide me, Tameryn, she prayed, *lady of swiftness and illicit deeds.*

If, that is, you ever actually existed.

Chiming tones floated in from the city's central plaza—the clock tower, striking midnight.

Eliana waited five minutes before drifting across the ballroom, smiling and making excuses whenever someone asked her for a dance. She made her way through the maze of candlelit sitting rooms surrounding the ballroom, keeping one eye on the adatrox patrolling the hallways. Then she slipped into a narrow servants' passage and followed the winding stone stairs to the palace's lower levels—the infirmary, the servants' quarters, the kitchens.

Any servants she passed knew her well enough to look the other way.

As she rounded the corner into a hallway stacked with crates of vegetables and sacks of flour, a tingle of nerves climbed up her spine.

If this was all some elaborate trap of Simon's, if he betrayed her at the last minute and abandoned Remy and Harkan to certain death... well. She wouldn't be beaten without taking him down with her.

She paused, listened to the bustle of the kitchens to make sure no one was approaching, then opened a heavy, locked door that led to a small stone supply yard.

Simon slipped inside, wearing the adatrox uniform Eliana had stolen for him. In the fitted surcoat, with the winged shield of the Empire emblazoned on his chest, he could have passed for one of the silent soldiers—except for that sharp light in his eyes and the way he moved. Sinuous and graceful, with none of the adatrox's stiffness.

"At last," he said dryly. "I was beginning to worry."

"I find that unlikely." She shut the door and swept past him, noticing with savage delight how his eyes trailed down her body. That could be useful later. "Let's move."

She led him through the cramped servants' passages up to the third floor, where they emerged into the palace proper. The deep-piled carpets muffled their steps. Music drifted through windows open to the vast gardens below.

In the north wing, the walls turned red, the moldings ornate. Gas lamps burned in jeweled casings; the air smelled of perfume. They turned a corner into a portrait gallery of black-eyed generals. At one end of the corridor hung a painting of the Emperor himself.

Eliana's heart pounded. She had never been in the north wing before. She couldn't shake the childish fear that the Emperor's painted black eyes were following her every step.

"Well," she said, "we're here. Now it's your turn."

Simon slipped past her. "Watch and learn, little Dread."

"Call me 'little' again and I'll punch you."

A smile twitched at his mouth. "You know just how to entice me."

"Have you forgotten? My punches hurt."

"Forgotten? In fact, I relish the memory."

She scowled, but then they reached a set of wooden doors marked by an engraving of a naked woman, her cascading waves of hair masking her face, and Eliana froze.

"The maidensfold?" She shot a look at Simon. Female concubines lived in this tower, their male counterparts in the south wing. "Why?"

"There's a girl inside," Simon explained, taking hold of Eliana's arm. "Cover me while I retrieve her. Try not to get hurt. I won't have you slowing me down."

Eliana bristled. As though he stood a chance of navigating back down through the castle without her.

"Follow my lead," said Simon, knocking on the door.

Eliana nodded, ready to grab Arabeth from the slit in her skirt.

The doors opened, revealing two adatrox. Men. One pale, one dark.

Their brows furrowed to see Simon. He shoved Eliana into the foyer. She kept her eyes obediently on the floor, her heart pounding.

"What's this?" asked one of the adatrox.

"Special delivery," Simon answered smoothly, before pulling his sword from his belt and gutting both of them. They dropped to the floor. Simon kicked the door shut behind him.

A girl passing by the foyer, clad in gauzy silks, ran off shouting warnings.

More adatrox rounded the corner. Simon ran at them, Eliana right on his heels. He took out one of the adatrox with a swift punch and a swipe of his blade.

Eliana leapt at the other. The adatrox lunged at her, sword in hand. She sidestepped his thrust, stabbed him in the throat. He thudded to the floor, choking. Then his clouded gaze fell on her face—and darkened. Sharpened.

A sick feeling swept over her. She staggered, unbalanced. She felt... *seen*. As if the shadows around her cloaked secret eyes that had come awake to stare.

The adatrox went still, his gaze blank and unseeing as he bled out on the floor. Whatever darkness had touched his eyes, it was now gone. Or maybe had never been there at all?

She turned and raced after Simon, following the sound of metal on metal down a wide hallway lined with embroidered drapes. She found him in a softly lit bathing room that smelled of jasmine and roses. Three adatrox surrounded him.

She took care of one by opening his throat, then evaded the fists of another before sweeping his feet out from under him and kicking him in the head with the heel of her beaded sandal. A girl fled past her and the bleeding adatrox, then out the door, clutching a shawl to her chest and leaving a trail of red footprints behind her.

Across the room, Simon struggled with another adatrox. A group of girls was backed into the far corner, trapped with her and Simon between them and escape. One of them let out a sharp sob.

Eliana scanned the frightened face of each girl. Which was the one Simon needed to retrieve? And why? What use was a concubine to the second-highest ranking member of Red Crown?

Eliana felt the adatrox in the doorway behind her before she saw him, barely turned in time to dodge his sword. She slipped in a pool of water on the floor and went down hard, banging her knee.

Before Eliana could regain her balance, the adatrox swung his sword in her direction once more—only to stumble back as a string of sapphires and diamonds landed around his neck. The person behind him pulled on the necklace, hard, and the adatrox dropped his sword to claw at his throat, gagging.

Eliana picked up his sword and ran it through his heart. He collapsed.

She looked up and met the gaze of a girl holding the necklace, at the end of which dangled an enormous opal. The girl's skin was a warm brown, her hair black, her eyes a pale hazel. Though she wore nothing but a blood-spattered sheer blue slip and dark-gold maidens-marks on her wrists, she had the bearing of a queen.

"You're welcome," the girl said, breathless.

Simon stormed over. "Good, you've met." He took the girl by the arm and moved toward the door. "This way."

Eliana sheathed Arabeth and followed them.

"My name is Navi," the girl said, smiling back at Eliana as Simon hurried her out of the room.

But Eliana did not reply, for when she glanced back at the open windows of the bathing room, she saw a figure drop down from the roof to land on the terrace outside.

Tall and thin, with creamy, pale skin and fair hair tied back in one long braid, dressed all in black save for a bloodred dress cloak that swept the ground:

Rahzavel.

11

RIELLE

*"Of Aryava's prophecy, there are many interpreta-
tions. Some dismiss his dying words as the nonsense
ramblings of a great angelic mind gone to ruin. But
all scholars do agree on this: despite the war divid-
ing their people, the blood of both humans and angels
that stained their hands, the angel Aryava loved Saint
Katell the sunspinner—and that love saved us all."*

—"A Discourse on the Prophecy of Aryava"
As translated by Grand Magister Isabeau Bazinet
of the Holdfast
Transcribed on October 6, Year 12 of the Second Age

After two hours, the king declared a recess, and Rielle's guards
escorted her into one of the hall's antechambers.

She sank into the first chair she saw, so tired she felt ill. The councils had attacked her with questions—what it felt like to manipulate
so many elements at once, and all with the same body. If singing the
wind felt different than controlling fire or shaking the earth, or was it
all the same to her?

What sort of lessons had Tal given her over the years?

Oh, he had tried to kill her, on occasion, to test her restraint?

How had he done that, and how many times?

How had she fought the instinctive desire to save herself? What a marvelous testament to her control. And where, they asked, had that control been, out on the racecourse?

They had let her sit for at least some of the questioning, but she still felt as exhausted as if she had ridden the entire Chase all over again. Twice.

Just as her eyes started drifting shut, the doors flew open, and Audric entered the room.

"Leave us," he told the guards.

The guards did not move. There was a beat of silence in which everything hung suspended.

"I think if Lady Rielle wanted to kill me," Audric snapped, "she would have done it years ago. Leave us."

The guards left at once.

Rielle was now entirely awake. She stood, her heart thundering. Where to even begin with him?

"Audric," she said, her voice coming out frayed, "I'm sorry I didn't tell you."

"I understand why you didn't. God, Rielle, I... Please, don't apologize. Are you all right?"

She let out a soft huff of laughter. "Not entirely."

Audric came to her, cradled her hands in his. His thumb brushed against her wrist like a kiss. "I cannot forgive them for doing this to you."

Every gentle press of his fingers made Rielle's stomach twist. "Father and Tal?"

"They should be ashamed of their cowardice."

"Well, I'm sure Tal is, anyway."

"Good."

"They thought they were doing what was best."

Audric frowned. "For the kingdom."

"Of course."

"And for you?"

She hesitated. How many times had she asked this question of her father, only to be shamed into silence? "My happiness is unimportant compared to the safety of those around me."

"Unimportant!" Audric released her, dragging a hand through his dark curls. "That's what they've been telling you all these years."

Suddenly the air around them felt charged; Rielle's fingers prickled from the nearness of magic. The air bloomed with heat. Rielle caught the slightly singed scent of sunspinner magic—a blazing noon sky, a hot summer's day. Audric's eyes snapped to hers before he turned away, his shoulders high and tense. He moved to the window, placed his palm against the sun-warmed glass.

When he looked back to her, his face was not quite so furious, and the air had calmed.

"Your happiness is important, Rielle," he said softly. "And I'm sorry I didn't see what was happening this entire time, right before my eyes. If I'd known, I would never have let them…"

He trailed off, his jaw clenched. She wanted so badly to touch him.

"I know," she told him instead.

"You were marvelous out there, during the race. I've never seen that kind of power. Rielle, it was beautiful."

She could not help but flush with pleasure, despite everything. "They were going to kill you. I couldn't let that happen."

He raised an eyebrow. "And I cannot take care of myself?"

"You can, and you did. But—" She fell silent, swallowing her voice. *But if you had died, I couldn't have borne it.*

If you had died, I don't know what would have happened next. What I would have done to avenge you.

Audric cleared his throat. He seemed to choose his words carefully. "When I saw you riding toward me, I didn't know that the blood was from your horse. I thought it was yours. You were covered in it, and I thought…" He walked toward her, his gaze lingering on her face, and then looked away.

His presence was like a touch hovering just above her skin. Rielle wanted desperately to lean into it. Bask in it. Claim it.

"You could say thank you," she finally managed to say. "At the very least."

"If you promise you won't terrify me like that again. Or at least give me warning so I can prepare myself."

"Of course," she agreed, "if you warn me the next time you plan on getting yourself attacked by assassins."

He grinned at her. "We did fight well together. I wouldn't mind doing it again." Then his expression softened. "Thank you, Rielle."

She hoped he could not read her face. "What happens now?"

"That's what I've come to tell you," Audric began, and then the door opened, admitting Ludivine and the guards.

"Did you tell her?" she asked, looking troubled.

"What is it?" Rielle said. "What have they decided?"

"They're requesting you come back inside at once, Lady Rielle," said one of the guards.

"Tell my uncle the king that she will attend him momentarily," Ludivine said, her sweet smile not reaching her eyes. "And if he protests, then you may tell him to bite his tongue or else his niece will hate him for the rest of his days."

The guard flushed and bowed his head, then retreated into the hall.

"Many in the councils are afraid," Ludivine told Rielle quickly, "and the king is under tremendous pressure to act before rumors start spiraling out of control and spark a panic. Before..." She paused. "Before anything else happens."

Before I lose control again, Rielle thought grimly.

"He would not have agreed to this unless he had no other choice," Ludivine continued.

Rielle's stomach dropped. "Agreed to what?"

"Seven trials," Ludivine explained. "One for each element."

"Tests of your power," Audric added, "engineered by the Magisterial

Council. To ensure you can control your abilities." He looked away, his mouth twisting bitterly.

Ludivine placed a gentle hand on his arm. "They will not only be testing your control. They will also be testing your loyalty. You must not waver in this, Rielle. One hint of defiance, one glimmer of treachery—"

"What is it, exactly, that they think I'm going to do?" Rielle burst out, an edge of incredulous laughter in her voice. "Defect to Borsvall? Turn around in the middle of a trial and murder the king where he stands?"

"We don't know what the Blood Queen will do, when she arrives," Ludivine continued gently. "One with the power to save the world. One with the power to destroy it. One of blood. One of light."

"I'm already tired of hearing that damned prophecy," Rielle muttered, and was gratified to see Audric's tiny smile.

"The point is," Ludivine pressed on, "that the councils believe you to be one of the Queens. And if they can ensure that you are loyal, that you want only to protect Celdaria, and not destroy it—"

Rielle threw up her hands. "But why in God's name would I ever want to?"

"Then this will signify to them," Ludivine said, talking over her, "that whatever the prophecy says, you have made a choice. To protect and not harm. To serve and not betray."

"And if I choose not to participate in these trials?" Rielle asked, once she had found her voice again.

"Then," said Ludivine quietly, "they will have no choice but to consider you a threat."

Rielle stepped back. A cold, sick feeling wound its way through her. "They will kill me."

"Not as long as I draw breath," Audric said, his fists clenched.

"I beg your pardon, my lord," the first guard muttered, uneasily entering the room, "but I delivered Lady Ludivine's message to the king, and he requests—"

The look Audric threw him was murder. "I know very well what the king requests." When he at last turned back to Rielle, his gaze was steady. "I won't allow anyone to harm you. You'll conquer these trials, and once you've convinced everyone—"

"Then I will serve the crown," Rielle finished for him. Everyone knew the Sun Queen, if she ever arrived, would serve at the pleasure of Celdaria's rulers. She would lead the kingdom's armies into battle. Using her power, she would protect the country, protect the Gate.

Protect the king.

"Then you will serve the crown," Audric agreed.

Someday, he meant, she would serve *him*—and his queen. She looked to Ludivine and then away.

"My lord," urged the guard from the door.

"I'm ready," Rielle said, before Audric could threaten the man further, and led the way back into the hall.

She stood once again before the dais as the councils shifted and settled above her. Her mind danced around the question: *How am I feeling right now? I have just been threatened with death.*

She recognized she should probably be more upset, but it was all such a wild shift from what her life had been only two days before that she simply felt numb.

I will be tested, she thought.

It will...probably hurt.

Then, slowly trying out the idea: *I will show them what I can do.*

She considered it. To be sought after instead of hidden away, to protect her country instead of living in fear that she was capable of nothing but hurting people, to be loved instead of hated...

Tears stung her eyes.

I will be loved.

She found her father, surrounded by guards, standing expressionlessly beneath the statue of Saint Grimvald—a metalmaster, just as he was. She wondered what he was thinking. All his and Tal's careful work, brought to ruin. And now the future—hers and theirs—lay in her hands alone.

She made herself stand tall.

They will love me. All of them will.

Rielle listened as King Bastien repeated what Ludivine and Audric had told her: seven trials, one for each of the seven elements, to be designed by the Magisterial Council and administered to her over the next seven weeks.

If, by the end of that time, she had proven her abilities and her control to a satisfactory degree—if she had throughout the trials consistently demonstrated loyalty and devotion to the crown, and neither defiance nor volatility—then she would be deemed the Sun Queen, the most holy symbol of the Church and the prophesied protector of the crown, and would be accorded all due privileges and tributes.

If not...

"Then, Lady Rielle," said the king, his voice heavy, "I will have no choice but to order your execution."

Rielle allowed the hall's silence to grow. Lord Dervin Sauvillier watched her, his eyes keen. Across the gallery from him, the Archon sat, sedate, with his hands folded in his lap.

"I do not decree this lightly," added the king. "I have known you all your life, and your father has served me for twice that long. But I cannot allow that to affect my duty to protect my people. We must be certain you are not the danger we have feared for a thousand years."

Oh, Rielle, said the voice, returning with a swift jolt of anger, *please tell me you won't let them trap you like this.*

But she had already stepped forward to speak. She felt as bright and sure as the sun.

The Magisterial Council believed it to be a choice, Ludivine had said—to protect and not harm. To serve and not betray.

It was a choice, and she had made hers.

She would be a symbol of light and not of death.

"I understand your fear, my king," said Rielle, "and I will happily endure these trials to prove my worth and my strength to you, my people, and my country." She made herself look around the room. No one would be able to accuse her of cowardice. She found Audric and Ludivine, drew strength from the sight of their faces. "I am not afraid to test my power."

Whispers moved through the assembled councils. Rielle lifted her chin to stare up at the king.

I will show you what I can do.

I will show you who I truly am.

"Then, Lady Rielle," said the king at last, his expression torn, "let the trials begin."

⇀ 12 ⇀

ELIANA

"You will hear things about the Emperor's assassins, things designed to terrify you. That their loyalty to him gives them extraordinary strength. That, like him, they cannot be killed. But I tell you, the butchers of Invictus are as flesh and blood as you are. It is a battle of beliefs. Can your faith outlast theirs?"

—*The Word of the Prophet*

Y ou don't look surprised to see me," said Rahzavel. He approached through the bathing room with a dancer's grace. "So you're a fool, but you're not stupid."

Every instinct screamed at Eliana to run out of the maidensfold after Simon and Navi, but to where? And then what? Rahzavel would chase her to the ends of the earth. He and Invictus and the Emperor himself would view her defection as a personal insult.

She had time for two fleeting hopes—that Simon and Navi would get out of the palace safely. And that Simon would find a spark of mercy in his heart and protect Remy and Harkan.

Then Rahzavel attacked.

He was fast, through the bathing room and upon her before she had the chance to strategize. He raised his sword, and with that pale face smiling coldly at her, everything Eliana knew abandoned her in an instant.

She turned and ran.

Rahzavel chased her through the scented labyrinth of the maidensfold. He caught up with her, let his sword fly. Eliana swung the adatrox sword, its heavy hilt slick with blood, and parried. Rahzavel advanced; Eliana barely blocked each of his cuts.

Their blades caught. Eliana stepped back and quickly turned her sword, dislodging him. She swiped wildly at his torso, but he was too quick. He advanced again. Eliana stumbled back, found a carving of a scantily clad woman on a tabletop, threw it at him, and ran.

She heard the carving hit the floor. Rahzavel's quick footsteps followed her through a series of narrow carpeted rooms.

Her strikes became desperate; Rahzavel was too fast, too meticulous. She gasped for breath; he hardly seemed to break a sweat. She ducked his sword, the blade hissing past her neck. She flung aside the adatrox sword, used her free hand to grab whatever she could find—vases, goblets, gilded plates—and fling them back at him.

He laughed at her, dodging it all.

They emerged once more into the bathing room, the tile slick from water and blood.

A lone girl huddled in the corner, whimpering.

Rahzavel's smile unfolded. "You're frightening the whores, Eliana."

She thrust at his belly with Arabeth; he blocked her easily.

They circled each other, Eliana blinking back sweat. Her hair had fallen loose from its knot.

"You should never have turned," said Rahzavel, every syllable pristine. "You could have been one of the Emperor's favored. Your family would have wanted for nothing."

Then, without warning, someone shoved Eliana from behind. She lost her footing on the slick tile, and Rahzavel used his sword to knock Arabeth away.

He lobbed a hard backhand across her face. She fell, her head knocking against a low table.

Dazed, she saw movement and color—one of Lord Arkelion's concubines, scurrying away. The girl had pushed her.

"It seems the bonds of sisterhood do not extend to traitors." Rahzavel's voice floated above her. He straddled her hips, his face inches from her own—clean-shaven jaw, straight nose, gray eyes flat and distant.

She felt a sharp pain below her throat and glanced down, too dazed to fight.

He was cutting her.

A new panic seized her, shocking her awake. She needed to get away from him, *now*, before he saw the truth.

"Many would kill their dearest loved ones," Rahzavel murmured, "for the chance to serve the Emperor as we do in Invictus. And yet you have thrown in your lot with the Prophet's lapdog?"

Another cut, a shallow X between her collarbones.

She twisted in his grip. He cut into the soft flesh of her upper arm.

God, no, he'll see—

"I suppose I shall have to find the Emperor a more grateful recruit," he mused softly, "and keep you for myself."

He swirled one long finger in her fresh blood and dragged it down her arm to her elbow.

He glanced down—and froze.

Eliana followed his gaze. The world slowed and stilled.

Together they watched the cut on her arm close.

An instant later, the skin was as good as new.

Rahzavel's gaze shot back to hers, and for the first time since she had known him, she saw a spark of something other than bloodlust in his eyes.

Wonder. Confusion.

Fear.

Eliana could hardly breathe. Her blood raced hot beneath her skin.

"What are you?" Rahzavel whispered.

A sudden movement, just beyond Rahzavel's shoulder. A tall, dark shape; a shift in the air.

Eliana flashed Rahzavel a smile. "I am your doom."

Rahzavel leapt up, turned, and met Simon's sword with his own.

Eliana rolled away, retrieved Arabeth, and pushed herself to her feet, ready to jump in after Simon and help, but the sight of them stopped her in her tracks.

Rahzavel and Simon whirled, stabbed, struck, their blades cutting the air. They swerved and ducked and parried and thrust. Whoever the Prophet was, he had obviously made sure Simon was well trained enough to fight even the Emperor's own assassins.

She followed them into the expansive sitting room at the rear of the maidensfold, unsure how to help. Her vision had cleared, but Simon and Rahzavel were moving so quickly it seemed to her simply elegant chaos—daggers and swords, crimson and silver, the blood on the floor and the bloodred wings of Rahzavel's cloak.

Their fight took them onto the terrace surrounding the maidensfold. Eliana hurried after them, the warm coastal breeze washing over her. Below, one of the river's tributaries crawled slowly to the sea.

Rahzavel's blade caught Simon's, pinning him against the stone railing. They were locked together, Simon's eyes full of cold fury, Rahzavel's empty and deadly. Simon's knees were buckling.

Eliana saw her opportunity, dove for Rahzavel's back with her dagger. He whirled at the last moment, knocked both her weapon and then Simon's out of their hands. Eliana grabbed a porcelain urn from a nearby table, brought it crashing down on Rahzavel's shoulders. He barely stumbled, but it was enough.

Simon kicked Rahzavel's elbow, and the assassin dropped his sword. Then Simon shoved him across the terrace railing.

Kicking and clawing, Rahzavel jabbed Simon in the throat, but Simon held on, gasping for air. Eliana hurried to his side, helped him push.

Rahzavel tumbled over the railing and fell into the blackness below.

Eliana gazed over the edge, trying to see if he hit the river, but the night was too dark. She wiped blood from her face, breathing hard.

Simon joined her, coughing from Rahzavel's last blow to the throat. He spat over the railing, his lip curled with disgust.

"Do you think the fall was enough to kill him?" the girl—Navi—asked, joining them at the railing.

Then the bells of the watch towers along the palace walls began to ring.

Navi hissed a curse. "Razia. She disappeared shortly after you arrived. She must have reported you."

Eliana's eyes met Simon's. "Follow me. We'll have to do this the hard way."

She led him and Navi back through the palace, down a different network of narrow servants' passages. They met three adatrox coming up from the ballrooms. Navi flattened herself against the curving stone wall while Eliana and Simon punched and stabbed their way free.

They dashed inside a suite of rooms in the palace's east wing, where party guests occupying the bedrooms shouted in protest, then raced out onto another wide terrace, this one lit with rose-glass lamps and fragrant from heaps of flowers. Below, Lord Arkelion's gardens were a sea of light and color.

Eliana led the way, jumping off the terrace into a row of shrubs. She landed hard, branches cracking beneath her, and rolled to her feet. She heard Simon and Navi land behind her, heard Navi's soft cry of pain.

Partygoers leapt back, alarmed. Someone screamed.

Eliana whirled, searching. A squadron of adatrox burst out of the Morning Ballroom, swords in hand. Two held rifles. They crouched on the steps, aimed, prepared to fire.

Two shots rang out; Eliana ducked. A nearby stone urn shattered. A group of dancers in silks and bangles fled, screaming.

Eliana led Simon and Navi through the gardens, knocking past the stunned guests, trying to ignore the sounds of the pursuing adatrox. She could not think of Rahzavel, of how lucky it was that he would have no chance to tell anyone about the impossible thing he had seen.

She would think only of Harkan, of her mother, of Remy.

Remy, I'm coming. Don't be afraid.

More adatrox waited for them at the gardens' perimeter, where a guarded tunnel led into the outer yards. Simon barreled into the adatrox, cut down two. Eliana saw a revolver flash and shoved Simon out of the way just as a shot rang out, then spun around and sliced open the shooter's throat.

They made it into the outer yards, then through the Lord's Gate and into the city itself. The Old Quarter was in a panic, citizens scrambling to return to their homes. Limp naming day garlands scattered the uneven cobbled streets. Fireworks exploded overhead in a shower of red.

Eliana looked back to see the palace looming some distance away— and a dozen adatrox in close pursuit.

Finally, they emerged from the Old Quarter and barreled through the bedlam of the common markets on the city's edge, where vendors and shoppers, having planned for a night of revelry, now scrambled for safety.

Eliana looked ahead to the east bridge. Signal fires flared to life in the towers flanking the water. Soon every soldier in the city would know exactly where they were.

They hurried past the towering Admiral's statue, where Harkan stood waiting. He lit a bombardier and hurled it past them toward the approaching adatrox. An explosion, screams of shock and pain—then a ringing silence.

The market grounds lay in ruins. The bombardier had bought them a moment or two.

A small weight slammed into Eliana, throwing its arms around her. *Remy.*

She kissed the top of his head. "It's all right. I've got you. I'm here."

Harkan stood behind him, looking past Eliana. More adatrox were coming, pouring down from the city's upper levels. He threw back his hood, loaded the revolver Simon had given him.

"El, take him and go," he told her.

Eliana stared at him, Remy in hand. "You're coming with us."

"Simon can't spare more grenades. I can hold them off."

"Are you mad? You can't shoot worth a damn." She grabbed Harkan's arm. "And there are too many of them. They'll kill you!"

Simon yanked Remy from her grip, roared, "Eliana, now!" and hurried across the bridge, sheltering Navi and Remy against his body. The two halves of the bridge, lowered to bring in supplies for the fete, had begun to raise. Remy looked back frantically for Eliana, but arrow fire from the city's inner wall rained down upon them, and soon he was lost to the night.

Eliana grabbed Harkan's hand. "Come *on*—"

But he stood firm, pulled her in to his body for a clumsy, hard kiss.

"I've always loved you," he whispered against her mouth.

"You tell me this now?" She wanted to smack him. A sob burst out as shaky laughter. "You idiot—"

A nearby explosion nearly threw them off their feet. The adatrox had detonated one of their own bombardiers. Behind Eliana, the bridge shifted and groaned.

"I can handle this." Harkan shoved her toward the bridge. "Go!"

She stared at him for a helpless, frozen moment, drinking up the sight of him—the dark fall of his hair, the beautiful square line of his jaw. Her throat filled up with all the things she had never said, and all the things she had.

None of it was enough.

She turned and fled across the bridge, not looking back even as she heard Harkan open fire. He cried out, and her chest seized around her heart. She ran blindly across the shaking bridge, jumped across the gap at the top, and stumbled down the other side. She joined Simon as he fought through the tower guards, Navi and Remy close behind them.

With each step she took, each swipe of her blades, grief struck her. Tears and smoke left her half blind.

First her mother, now Harkan. Her best friend. Her light on dark days.

She had left him. She had *left* him.

She listened for his gunfire and heard only chaos. The adatrox archers on the city wall shouted commands to one another. Simon hissed at her to move faster. He grabbed a bombardier from a fallen adatrox, triggered it, threw it back at the guard tower.

The explosion threw them off their feet. Eliana's chin hit the ground. A shock of pain jolted her skull. But they had destroyed the tower, collapsed the bridge. It would give them a few minutes. She pushed herself up.

Past the bridge, they hurried into one of the scattershot encampments that had formed outside the city—refugees fleeing the dangerous countryside, hoping for a chance to get in the city. The camps were pandemonium. People bolted away from the city walls, trampling the slow and sick. Bleating animals ran crazed from their pens.

Still holding Remy close by the arm, Simon tossed Navi his adatrox cloak. She caught it and drew the hood up over her face. Two soldiers in threadbare cloaks found them with a pair of saddled horses. Others raced past them toward the city wall. Red Crown rebels, Eliana assumed, all ready to die to protect them.

Good, she thought. *Their deaths will buy us time.*

"Take the boy," Simon ordered. Navi nodded, her face hidden. One of the rebels gave her a leg up, and then helped Remy before running toward the wall with the others. The last rebel turned to face Simon, her battered face lit with some inner fire.

She put a fist to her heart and then to the air—the Red Crown salute. "The Empire will burn," she said.

Simon inclined his head. "May the Queen's light guide you."

Then the woman was gone.

"Wrap your arms around my waist," Navi murmured to Remy, "and hold on tight. What's your name?"

"Remy," he answered, glancing fearfully over at Eliana. "Where are we going?"

"No." Eliana emerged from her numb shock, backed away from Simon. "I ride with Remy."

"Sorry," Simon replied. "Can't have you tearing off into the countryside before you fulfill your end of our bargain."

Only days before, she had been the Dread—queen of her own bloody world. Unstoppable and unchallenged.

Now, she was in danger of losing everyone she loved, and she could do nothing to stop it. Nothing but leave the only home she had ever known and trust her brother's life to a stranger who would not answer her questions.

Her unraveling patience snapped.

She accepted Simon's outstretched hand, climbed up behind him, and brought Arabeth to his throat.

"Tell me where we're going, Wolf, and why," Eliana murmured, "or this ends right now."

Navi urged her horse slowly toward them. "My friend," she said to Eliana, "I swear to you, he is not our enemy."

"Navana is a princess of Astavar," Simon answered, "and we are taking her home."

"The Empire's invasion is coming much sooner than we had thought, and in greater numbers." Navi looked out from her hood, her gaze grave and earnest. "I must warn my people in time, or Astavar will fall. This is not information we can trust to the underground."

Eliana stared at the girl. It was impossible: a princess, posing as one of His Lordship's concubines. An invasion.

Astavar will fall.

And if it did, so would the world's last free kingdom. The Undying Empire would rule all.

"Will you please lower your damned dagger?" Simon snapped. "We're wasting time."

Eliana did, and Simon threw her a murderous glare over his shoulder before adding, "Try not to fall off."

As they fled through the eastern hills, leaving the city of Orline behind them, they passed the crest of land where the statue of Audric the Lightbringer had once stood. Now there was only bare land, scorched and gray from war.

Still, as they passed the spot, Eliana felt the old pang in her heart for the dead king and thought a prayer she had not allowed herself to say in years:

May the Queen's light guide us home.

~13~

RIELLE

"From sky to sky
From sea to sea
Steady do I stand
And never will I flee"

—The Earth Rite
As first uttered by Saint Tokazi the Steadfast,
patron saint of Mazabat and earthshakers

The mountain was falling down around her.

Rielle hoped it was a dream. Maybe the last few days entirely had been a nightmare, and now she would wake up, and everything would be as it once was.

Open your eyes, Rielle.

Yes. She knew she needed to open her eyes, to move, to *run*, but the dumbwort coursing through her veins made movement feel impossible.

They'd drugged her.

The damned Archon had decided on it, so that when she awoke at the site of her trial, she wouldn't know where she was or how she'd gotten there. As though throwing her into these trials the day after her testimony, with no time to train with her father or study with Tal, wasn't enough of a punishment for her many lies.

Indeed it was not, according to the Archon.

"Perhaps, Lady Dardenne," he had told her blandly, his watery dark eyes fixed unblinkingly on her face, "if you had chosen to reveal yourself immediately following your mother's murder all those years ago, things would be different now."

"And as a five-year-old child," she had snapped, unable to keep quiet, "such a choice had been solely my responsibility, I suppose?"

The Archon had folded his hands in his lap, seven rings glittering on his soft white hands. "Even children," he had said, "know it is wrong to kill."

Open your eyes, Rielle. Her brain was screaming at her, or perhaps someone else was nearby. Maybe one of the council members overseeing the trial. Maybe Tal.

Maybe that strange voice had returned.

Open your eyes!

She forced herself upright, her limbs clumsy and leaden. Her vision rocked violently back and forth. She placed a gloved hand on either side of her throbbing head.

Then she sensed the heavy press of something rising high above her, cold and unrelenting.

Stone.

Be prepared to move as soon as you awaken. Tal's instructions from earlier that morning drifted through her mind like sticky fragments of a dream. *They won't give you time to recover.*

He had refused to look her in the eye, and she had refused to beg him for it.

A rumbling from behind and above snapped her head around. Like a series of gut punches, her senses crashed back into place:

The clean bite of ice.

The air, thin and freezing.

Her fingers, mostly numb. Cold seeped in through her leather boots and the thickest trousers she owned, neither of which were warm enough for such an environment. But the Archon had decided she had given up the right to proper clothing, that she could only use whatever she already had in her closet, and she would not be allowed any other aid. And so, twelve hours later, here she was, thrown out into—

The mountain.

It was falling down around her.

Not one of the little mountains from the Chase route, but one of the monstrous peaks that formed an angry, snowy spine heading east from the capital.

Move, Rielle!

She stepped back, looked up, stumbled over chunks of ice, caught herself on a snow-crusted boulder.

As she watched, sheets of stone slid off the nearest peak, crashing into the snow piled on their slopes and sending up glittering sprays of ice. Suddenly she was back on the Chase course, watching the mountain pass crumble and not caring—because how was she supposed to care about falling mountains with Audric in danger?

But Audric was not here. Rielle was alone.

Twelve tiny lights glinted high above, surrounding her.

Her sluggish mind caught up with her rapidly awakening body.

No. She was not alone.

Those lights belonged to elementals: Grand Magister Florimond and her earthshaker acolytes from the Holdfast. A dozen of them formed a perimeter, castings in hand, ordered by the Archon to bring down the mountain and flatten her.

This was the earth trial, the first of seven that would decide her fate.

They'd rushed things—angry with her, possibly afraid of her. This was sloppy and uncharacteristic of the Church, done without witnesses, pomp, or ceremony.

But that hardly mattered. If she didn't run, she'd be crushed.

Rielle, run!

Down the mountain she bolted, darting past trees, leaping over veins of frigid rock. She jumped over a fallen tree half buried in snow and dropped into a drift three feet deep. Lost her balance, lurched forward, sank into the snow, and inhaled it, coughing. She fumbled for a grip on the ice, pushed herself to her feet, looked back over her shoulder.

The wide snow sea was now a churning wave cresting hundreds of feet high, devouring everything in its path. Black pines snapped in two; fleeing foxes and deer disappeared, sucked beneath the furious white rush. Great slabs of rock rode the wave, tossed and tumbling.

Terror shot through Rielle's body, drowning out everything else she knew.

She looked ahead once more. The pass sloped slightly upward before her. If she could make it to higher ground, she could perhaps escape the avalanche's path.

Or, said the voice, abruptly returning, *you could—*

But Rielle couldn't hear the rest over the roar of the thundering mountain. Pine branches and fistfuls of ice rained down upon her. Her lungs burned, each frigid breath searing her throat as she fought her way through the snow. She clawed against trees to propel herself forward and scraped her gloved fingers raw.

There: a slight rise of rock, dotted with stumps of trees whose spindly roots cascaded down the rocks like snakes slithering for their holes.

Rielle leapt for the rise of rock—and missed.

No, she didn't miss.

The earth was opening, her path falling away beneath her feet.

She reached out blindly, desperate for a handhold. Caught a lip of frozen rock with one hand, crashed into the rock front-first. Hung there, dizzy, gasping for breath.

A light winked at the corner of her left eye.

The earthshakers weren't going to let her escape so easily.

Her feet dangling over the widening chasm, she flung up her other hand, grabbing for a better hold. She tried to pull herself up, every muscle straining.

When she made it home, she would have to ask her father for help strengthening her body.

If she made it home.

Would this be it, then? Would she die in this first trial, hastily slapped together as if it were nothing of importance? As if her life, and the fates of Tal and her father, meant nothing?

No, she damn well would not.

That, said the voice, *is what I like to hear.*

With a ragged scream, Rielle pulled herself up, her body burning in protest. She wondered if her arms would snap off, then scraped her knees against rock and scrambled to the top of the rise.

She ran to the left, her breath punching in and out of her lungs in ice-cold fists. Stone rose ahead of her in pillared clusters, ribboned with snow and mud. The path was solid. Hope swelled in her chest.

Then, with a great echoing groan, like the plates of the earth had been shoved out of alignment, the path before her cracked open. Tiny chasms snaked across the ground, widening like the swarming mouths of subterranean creatures eager for a kill.

Rielle's stomach plunged to her toes. But there was no time to waste. She closed her eyes and jumped.

Her feet slammed to ground.

She opened her eyes. Still alive, still breathing.

She jumped and jumped again across the shifting patches of rock. The chasms widened; the ground quaked and jerked, trying to buck her off. A violent shudder threw her to the side. She fell—scraping her arm and knees raw—pushed herself up, and ran.

The air churned with shards of ice and rock. The avalanche blocked out the sun and sucked the air from the sky. The world above her was white and roaring; the world beneath her was coming apart like it must have done when God first breathed life into the universe.

I will not die here, she thought.

She pushed herself faster, her entire body on fire. Past the trees ahead there had to be a path to safety, ground too high for the avalanche to touch. If she could just make it a bit farther—

Then she saw the truth:

Beyond the trees, there was no path.

It was a sheer drop. A canyon—and no way across.

Her mind screamed that this was the end.

Her body decided to disagree.

"No," she whispered.

No, agreed the voice. *Not today. Not ever.*

Rielle whirled around to face the roaring white snow-sea, planted her frozen legs on the cliff's edge. She thrust her hands into the air and squeezed her eyes shut. Didn't think anything, didn't even think *stop*.

She threw up her hands, the solid heat inside her screaming *No!* more loudly than any voice or word ever could.

A narrow wall of rock, wide enough to shelter her, burst out of the ground before her and shot up into the air mere seconds before the avalanche slammed into it.

Rielle stood, head bowed and eyes closed, her hands pressed flat against the fast-rising rock, palms sparking against the stone like flint. The avalanche broke with a roaring howl on either side of her. The churning snow and rock scraped against her arms and feet, threatened to lift her up off the ground and fling her into the canyon.

Hold fast to the rock, said Rielle's blood.

Hold fast.

And the narrow slab of rock seemed to listen. It stood tall, shaking against the force of the crashing avalanche. The air tasted sour, damp tendrils of mud-scented earthshaker magic straining to their limit as they whipped through the air.

A tiny flame of triumph unfurled between Rielle's burning lungs.

They had tried to kill her, and they had failed.

They had crashed a mountain down atop her, and she had lived.

She stood trembling on the cliff's edge, the same mountain that had tried to kill her now shielding her from itself.

"Please stop," she whispered to the mountain. She didn't blame it for being angry at such abuse. She pressed her cheek against the hot wall of stone, which now stood rigid like an ancient thing that had always existed on that spot—a queer pillar of rock, lonely and stubborn.

The tips of her fingers were aflame. If she kept this going much longer, her chest would crack open, her heart would burst, her lungs would give out.

"Please," she whispered, each word an effort, "stop." Exhausted tears leaked down her cheeks.

Then, whether it was a response to her plea or simply the moment Grand Magister Florimond decided enough was enough, the mountain eased itself back whole. The avalanche subsided; boulders dropped abruptly from the sky.

It was chaos to stillness in the span of five seconds.

A bird called out forlornly.

Rielle let herself fall, slumping at the foot of her rock. The snow was a cool pillow under her flaming cheek.

"Only six more," she whispered, a watery smile playing at her lips, and then pain hit her all at once.

I'll be here when you wake, said the voice, and some dim, spinning part of her tired mind whispered back, *Thank you.*

⫸ 14 ⫷

ELIANA

"Since our war with the humans began, I have had only
one dream. Every night, the fog surrounding it lifts,
and I understand more of what I see: a woman, made
of gold brighter than the sun. She stands in a river of
blood, and light falls from the ends of her hair. Is she
friend or foe? This my dreams have not made clear to
me. But I know this: she will come. In this war, or the
next, she will come."

—Lost writings of the angel Aryava

"I hear you're a storyteller," said Navi.

Eliana waited for Remy's response.

Nothing.

For two days they'd been driving the horses north by night, hiding in tense silence when they heard signs of pursuing adatrox patrols, and then, from sunup to sundown, waiting in the trees for nightfall.

The moment they'd had a chance to rest, hiding in a ditch lined with reeking mud as the sun shone dangerously bright above, Remy had whispered, "What happened to Harkan?"

"He stayed behind to give us time to escape," Eliana had told him, her voice carefully careless and her heart in shreds. "I left him instructions. He'll catch up with us later—"

"Don't lie to me. He's dead, isn't he?"

She couldn't look at him. "Harkan? Come on, you know it takes more than a few adatrox to—"

"Shut up."

"Truly, Remy. We can't know for certain." Even as she said the words, she couldn't bring herself to believe them. "He could still be alive—"

"Please." Remy had drawn his knees to his chest and turned away from her. "Just shut up."

He had said nothing since.

Now, however, Navi seemed determined to make him speak.

"What kind of stories do you like to tell?" she asked.

Eliana, on first watch, leaned against a nearby silver oak, Arabeth in one hand and Whistler in the other. She glared into the forest. Slender silver oaks with faintly gleaming bark surrounded them, as did waxy-leaved, white-flowered gemma trees. Stout watchtowers, branchless save for frazzled-looking clusters at the top, stood lopsided throughout. They were popular along Orline's outer wall, traditionally planted to ward off invaders, which Eliana found hysterical. She'd always thought they resembled old men with soft bellies and wild hair.

When she'd first told Remy that, he'd considered the tree nearest them, then put his nose in the air, bowed, and said to the tree, "Well met, good sir. Might I offer you a comb?"

Eliana had laughed so hard she'd actually squeaked.

Her hand tightened around Whistler. *God, it'd be nice to fight something.*

Instead of standing here, feeling sorry for myself.

And angry.

Mostly angry.

No. She drew a long, slow breath. *Mostly missing Harkan.*

And Mother.

And Father.

For a moment she allowed herself to imagine Harkan there beside her, on watch with her, distrusting Simon with her, worrying about her mother with her—and her throat tightened so painfully that she lost her breath.

Pay attention, Eliana. You're on watch.

She glared at the trees until her eyes dried, then glanced sidelong at Simon, who had settled down to rest. He sat in the shadow of another oak, scanning the dawn-lit forest.

She considered him. Grief and worry nettled her insides. This stillness was maddening.

What would he do if she lunged at him with blades drawn? He'd bested her back home, but only because of his gun. If she could gut him before he could reach the holster—

And then what? The whole point of this mad venture was to use him, not kill him.

Eliana thumped her head against the tree at her back and glared at the sky.

"Talking to me might make you feel better," Navi insisted, her voice kind.

Eliana rolled her eyes.

But then Remy surprised her. "I like to write stories about magic," he replied hoarsely.

Eliana's breath caught. She hadn't realized until that moment how deeply she'd missed the sound of his voice.

"Magic?" Navi sounded intrigued. "You mean the Old World?"

"I like writing about the elementals. Especially earthshakers."

"Why earthshakers?"

"Sometimes I wish an army of earthshakers would come to Orline. Crack open the ground, let it swallow the city whole."

"I see," said Navi evenly.

"Sorry," Remy muttered. "Eliana says I shouldn't talk about things like that. It isn't kind."

That seemed to amuse Navi. "And your sister is?"

Bitch. Eliana flashed her the smile she usually reserved for marks she wanted to coax into bed. "When I want to be," she replied.

Remy threw her an irritated look.

Navi put her arm around his shoulders. "I do understand wanting to tear down your city," she said. "Sometimes I think life would be easier if the oceans would rise up and drown Astavar. Then I wouldn't have to spend every moment of my life in an agony of worry for it."

Remy nodded. "Waterworkers could do that."

"Indeed they could, if there were any left. And they'd have to be quite powerful, even then, to sink an entire country."

A beat of silence. Then Remy said, hushed, "Queen Rielle could have done it."

"*Ah.*" Navi let out a little sigh. "The Blood Queen herself. Yes, I'm sure she could have plunged every mountain standing to the depths if she had lived long enough to do it. Do you ever write stories about her?"

"I wrote a story once about what would have happened if she hadn't died. If she'd lived forever with the angels, and the world still had magic in it. Do you think the angels would have made her one of them? That's what I wrote, in my story. She led them to the sky, and they searched for God in the stars."

"I think," said Navi slowly, "that if the Blood Queen had lived, she would have become something more powerful than even the angels, with all their millennia of knowledge, could have comprehended."

Eliana pushed herself off the tree, no longer able to stand there and listen to Remy's voice grow more and more excited, as if this Princess Navana were some dear friend of his, as if he didn't care that Eliana waited in the shadows, ready to slit any strange throats that might happen by.

And would he rather I stand idly and watch him get torn to pieces the next time we're attacked?

She knew what he would say: Yes.

The fool.

Because at least then I wouldn't be killing. Is that right, dearest brother?

"Do you like writing stories?" Remy asked.

"I like telling stories others have written," Navi answered. "Stories about Astavar most of all."

Remy hesitated. Then, shyly, "Will you tell me one?"

Eliana dared to look back at them. Remy had wedged himself against Navi's side in the bracken, their backs against a felled watch-tower tree, his head tucked under hers. The girl was stroking his shaggy hair, slow and soft, and when she caught Eliana staring, the expression she wore was one of such compassion that Eliana fantasized, for an immensely satisfying moment, about stalking over and striking her square in the jaw.

She turned away, toward Simon—

But he was gone.

She froze. Fear carved her chest into ribbons.

"I certainly will share a story with you, and I'm honored that a wordsmith like you would ask," Navi replied. "You know, of course, that the patron saint of Astavar is—"

"Tameryn the Cunning," Remy said, his voice lighting up. "She was a shadowcaster. I read that she slept under the stars with her black leopard for a pillow."

"And did you also read," Navi said, "that shadows grew out of her scalp instead of hair? Her favorite comb was coated in crushed black pearls and carved from the bones of a wolf who died saving her life when she was a girl."

"I don't know that story," Remy whispered, awestruck.

Eliana crept away from them, their murmured voices following her into the morning air like an unfamiliar lullaby. Daggers out, she circled the tree under which Simon had been standing. Gone.

She supposed he could be relieving himself somewhere, but the unease inching up her torso said otherwise.

Ducking underneath a drooping oak branch, using Whistler's blade to part a curtain of hanging moss, Eliana knew she was moving too far away from camp, that she shouldn't leave Navi, Remy, and the horses untended, but without Simon, they were all lost. They'd get turned around in these swamp-riddled forests faster than—

A shift in the air, slight but undeniable.

Someone was near.

Eliana crouched in the shadow of a gemma tree, searching the forest.

Then something cold pricked the side of her neck.

"Give me a reason to kill you," came a woman's voice, vicious and made of gravel, "and I'll do it."

Eliana pressed her neck harder against the woman's knife, felt the blade's tip sink into her flesh. The pain thrilled her. *I am here*, it said, *and I do not run from death.*

I seek it out.

She laughed. "You'd die trying, I'm afraid."

The woman made a scornful noise. "Unlikely," she spat out, and then brought the hilt of her knife down hard against Eliana's head.

⭢ 15 ⭠

RIELLE

*"I no longer have a name. I relinquish my casting to
its destruction and forsake the magic with which I was
born. I dedicate my mind and body to the guidance of
the Church and the study of the empirium. I no longer
have a name. I am only the Archon."*

—Traditional induction vow of the Archon,
leader of the Church of Celdaria

The voice followed Rielle back into the waking world, companionable and silent.

Strange, that a voice could be silent. If it wasn't speaking, yet Rielle could sense it beside her, then it wasn't merely a voice.

It belonged to someone—a body, a *person*—and whoever it was, they were close.

Who are you? She hoped the voice could hear—and that it couldn't. Had she gone mad?

Gently teasing, the voice answered, *I suppose I'll tell you now. You deserve it, Rielle. You escaped the mountain after all.*

A smile crept across her lips. Before, the voice had sounded vague, undecipherable. But now…

You're a man.

Mmm. An affirmative, soft and playful. Almost purring.

Rielle's smile grew, heat climbing up her cheeks.

Do you have a name? she asked.

Of course.

And then Rielle felt eyes upon her, though she could see nothing but the churning velvet black of her awakening mind.

Cool fingers touched her wrist.

Rielle stirred. Shifted.

Tell me? Her voice held an unfamiliar coy lilt. She had spent her childhood cautiously flirting with Tal, with Ludivine, even daring to with Audric from time to time, but this felt different. New—and immense.

Please?

The voice took a slow breath in, then blew an even slower breath out—a content, sated sound. Not quite a groan; not quite a sigh.

Rielle's skin prickled, warming.

My name, said the voice, lips grazing the curve of her ear, *is Corien.*

"Lady Rielle, you're awake. And quite pleased with yourself, it seems."

Rielle's eyes flew open.

A wall of windows framed with drapes in the colors of House Courverie admitted afternoon light. The painted ceiling above her, bordered with gilded molding, displayed Queen Katell in all her glory. First as a young acolyte in the Celdarian heartlands; then as Saint Katell, driving the angels through the Gate; and lastly, crowned and robed, the first queen of Celdaria.

Across from Rielle sat the Archon. His eyes fixed on Rielle, mildly curious.

Behind him stood ten members of the holy guard. The seven temple sigils decorated their gleaming gold armor, echoing the sigils sewn into the Archon's robes. The holy guard owed no sense of allegiance to Lord Commander Dardenne, the kingsguard, the city guard; they belonged only to the Archon and the Church.

Ignoring the anxiety nipping up her arms, Rielle sat up and fixed the Archon with a look she hoped was as infuriatingly untroubled as his own.

"I am indeed pleased, Your Holiness," she said, smiling, "for it seems I've successfully completed the first of my trials. If you had stopped an avalanche using only your two hands and the determination of your will, surely you would be proud of yourself as well?"

She paused. Would this be too much?

She couldn't resist.

"But then," she said, watching the Archon's face, "it would be difficult for you to imagine such a thing, since you've given up all rights to your magic. And, even before you did, you had to use a casting to access your power. I am burdened by no such constraints."

The Archon sat unblinking, his smile small and tight.

Rielle did not break her stare.

Good, said Corien. *Make him sweat.*

A door in the wall to Rielle's right opened, admitting one of King Bastien's pages. "His Majesty is ready for you, Your Holiness."

"Excellent." The Archon rose. "Lady Dardenne, follow me."

Rielle obeyed, the holy guard forming a loose circle around her as she walked.

Do they really think I'll lose all sense of reason and kill everyone in my sight? she thought darkly.

Some do, said Corien.

Something about his tone of voice—of thought?—startled Rielle. *You're not just saying that. You know what they think.*

Silence, then.

Corien? Suddenly her heart was a rolling drum in her chest. The impossibility of what was happening felt abruptly, terribly clear. She was talking to a voice in her head, as if this were a normal thing, and had so easily fallen into doing so that already it felt like a long-formed habit.

That was…not good.

The truth returned to her: mind-speak was something the angels once did.

Repulsed—by herself or by the idea of Corien, Rielle couldn't decide—she imagined stepping away from him, shutting herself behind a door, and turning the key.

What are you not telling me? she whispered against the lock.

Corien's voice came thin and cold: *Pay attention, Rielle. Your jailers await.*

"Lady Rielle," came the voice of King Bastien, pleasantly enough. "You look well, all things considered."

Rielle blinked twice, coming back to herself. She stood before a long rectangular table of polished wood. Framed portraits of kings and queens of the Courverie line adorned the far wall. To her right, a wide spread of windows opened to a sun-soaked veranda.

This was the king's Council Hall, where his Privy Council met.

And there was the king himself, with his closest advisers: Queen Genoveve beside him, staring at Rielle over the rim of her wine goblet. The Lady of Coin and the Lord of Letters. The judges of the High Court, appointed by the king.

Grand Magister Florimond, the most powerful earthshaker in Celdaria. The woman who had engineered the avalanche.

And Rielle's father, his face drawn and unreadable.

She had not embraced him for years, yet now, oddly, she found herself craving it.

But only for a moment.

She raised a cool eyebrow at him and bowed. She caught sight of her ruined boots and realized she was still wearing the clothes from the mountain. Her body chose that moment to make itself known— every scrape and sprain, every bruise. Her wounds sparked equal parts pain and triumphant pleasure.

She had fought the mountain and won.

She straightened once more, pain blooming in her sore shoulders.

"Thank you for saying so, Your Majesty," she said. "My queen. My lord father. Grand Magister. I am glad to see you all well."

"And we are glad to see you well, Lady Dardenne," King Bastien replied.

"Are you?"

Her father's head snapped around to glare at her.

A throaty chuckle sounded in Rielle's mind. *Darling girl.*

Rielle bit the inside of her lower lip. "Forgive me, my king. That was insolent of me."

"And was it not also insolent," murmured Queen Genoveve, "to spend your days endangering my son and niece, without a care as to their safety?"

Rielle stepped forward, outrage spiking in her chest. As one, the kingsguard surrounding the room and the holy guard at the Archon's side shifted, hands at their swords.

She set her jaw and stood her ground. "My queen, I love your son and niece more than anyone in this world. If you think I've spent one moment of my life without thinking of their safety, you are gravely—"

The slam of a door cut her off. Rielle turned to see Audric striding toward her, dark curls falling over his forehead in disarray and Ludivine just behind him.

A wave of such relief washed over Rielle that she had to touch the king's table for support.

Then Audric was there, gathering her into his arms. Against her matted, mud-crusted hair, he whispered, "Rielle, they wouldn't let us see you."

Tucked safely beneath Audric's chin, Rielle let her eyes fall closed and breathed in his familiar sunspinner scent—the steady warmth of sunbaked stone. "And yet here you are."

"You're all right?" Audric pulled away, searching her face. "What happened?"

"I successfully completed the earth trial," Rielle answered, unable to stifle a broad smile as she looked up at him. "Only six more remain."

At Audric's elbow, Ludivine beamed. "Oh, Rielle, that's wonderful."

"Yes, Grand Magister Florimond and her acolytes created an avalanche," added the Archon, "intended to kill Lady Rielle. Obviously it did not. To our great relief." He paused. "And to your even greater relief, it seems, my prince."

Rielle's cheeks burned, but when she looked past Audric to meet Ludivine's gaze, she saw nothing but love and a warm smile.

Audric stepped away from Rielle. "My lord Archon, you mock the life and safety of our Sun Queen? Please, help me understand that. It seems disrespectful at best and blasphemous at worst."

"May I remind you, my son," said Queen Genoveve, "that Lady Rielle has completed only one of seven trials. And it is not for you to determine whether or not she is the Sun Queen."

Audric's eyes shone, his shoulders square. "She will not merely complete the trials; she will transcend them."

The Archon sniffed. "On what do you base this faith?"

"I've known her all my life—"

"You have known a lie."

"That's enough." King Bastien clasped his hands on the table. "We're not here to argue about the past. We're here to discuss the future."

"You're right, Father," said Audric, approaching him. "Don't make Lady Rielle complete the rest of these trials alone and unprepared." He looked back at Rielle, his expression alight with conviction and belief. Belief in *her*. "She should complete the trials in front of as many people as possible."

"It should be a spectacle," Grand Magister Florimond agreed, leaning forward to face the king. She was a stout, short woman with ruddy skin and thick brown hair in a crown of braids on her head. "The things Lady Rielle accomplished on that mountain…" She shook her head, glanced at Rielle. "These are things the people need to see."

Rielle felt a flutter of delight at Magister Florimond's awed expression. "Why?"

Magister Florimond opened her mouth to speak, then hesitated and glanced at Audric instead.

"Because," Audric said, watching his father, "when the Gate falls and the angels return, the Sun Queen will need the support of the Celdarian people at her back. They need to see her work. They need to love her."

The judges, the Lord of Letters and the Lady of Coin, even the queen, shifted uneasily, as did some of the guards stationed around the room.

Rielle looked to her father. At last, he returned her gaze. She wondered if he was remembering the same thing she was: secret evenings in Tal's office after a day of lessons, Rielle on her father's knee and slowly reading the words of Aryava's prophecy aloud:

Two Queens will rise.

One of blood.

One of light.

She had been young enough then, and perhaps not yet frightening enough, that her father still touched her with something like affection.

"Audric," said King Bastien tightly, "I would ask you not to speak of such things right now."

"But it's precisely now that we must speak of these things." Audric's voice was taking on that earnest, gruff quality it had whenever he went off on one of what Rielle and Ludivine called his scholarly fits.

Despite everything, Rielle glanced sidelong at Ludivine, who was stifling her own smile.

"Princess Runa's death," Audric continued. "The slave uprisings in Kirvaya. The unprecedented storms across the ocean, in Meridian and Ventera. The shifting mountains in the old angelic lands, displacing entire villages overnight. And now," he said, looking back at Rielle, "there's Lady Rielle. Maybe those assassins knew something we didn't, and their attempt to kill me was really an attempt to draw out her power for all to see. Or maybe it was simply coincidence. Either way, we cannot ignore the timing of these events."

Audric returned his impassioned gaze to the king. "The angel Aryava knew, centuries ago. He warned us of this time, and now it is upon us."

King Bastien's normally open expression was a barred door. "That's enough, Audric."

"Father, we ignore the signs at our peril—"

The king rose to his feet. "That's enough!"

Audric stepped back, meeting his father's glare for one searing moment before looking at the floor.

The Archon cleared his throat. "Perhaps there is some wisdom to the prince's suggestions. Whether or not the prophecy's events are unfolding before us, if Lady Rielle is forced to complete the trials in plain view of the Celdarian people—"

"Then the challenge will be even greater for me," Rielle interrupted. "And you will know I am not to be feared." She took Audric's place before his father, her heart pounding fast and sure. "For I'll be not only fighting for my life, but for theirs as well."

"That," said King Bastien, "is a terrible risk."

Queen Genoveve set down her goblet with some force. "A risk we cannot take. My love, this is nonsense."

"The city guard," Rielle insisted, "the royal guard, the holy guard, every acolyte from the temples. All of them can be on alert, ready in case I falter." She took a deep breath. "But I won't falter. I've been taught well by my father and by Tal."

"Taught while hidden within secrets and lies," the Archon added.

Rielle ignored him. "They can continue my lessons, with the help of everyone on the Magisterial Council."

She glanced at Grand Magister Florimond. The woman inclined her head. "I, for one, will be glad to help Lady Rielle in this."

Rielle gave her a small smile. "Word will get out, my king, about the trials. About me. Too many people know what's happening for rumors not to escape. Think about how our people will react if they find you've been keeping such a secret from them. Enough lies have been told, enough secrets kept. I had a part in that, and I don't wish to any longer."

King Bastien returned to his seat, considering her in silence.

"If we tell the people everything…" Audric added, coming to stand beside her.

"And if they can see Rielle's power and control for themselves…" said Ludivine, on Rielle's other side.

"Then that will show them you trust her."

"And they, in turn, will trust her," Ludivine added. "And you as well, Uncle."

"And," finished Rielle, "if there are dark turnings elsewhere in the world, perhaps they will then think twice about setting their sights on Celdaria, if they know we are united. If there are no secrets to exploit."

"If," King Bastien said slowly, "they see that we have the most powerful human to ever live as our guardian?"

Corien, at last, returned. *He's not wrong*, came his low voice. *There has never been a human like you, Rielle. And there never will be.*

Rielle fought to keep her smile hidden. That, she sensed, would not help her case.

Finally, King Bastien took a deep breath and reclined in his chair. "You three," he said, looking at Rielle, Audric, and Ludivine in turn, "have had far too much practice concocting schemes together. It is difficult to argue with such a front."

"My love…" began Queen Genoveve urgently.

"It's settled, then." King Bastien placed his palms flat on the table. "The remaining six trials will be public events, open to all. What did you call it, Brydia? A spectacle?"

Grand Magister Florimond inclined her head. "Perhaps too flippant a word."

"No, it is a good word. A celebratory word. And that's what this will be: a celebration of Celdaria's might and the power of its citizens."

King Bastien looked to his son. "A clear sign to every soul living that Celdaria is not afraid of strange storms or shifting lands. Or old tales of death and doom that have no bearing on our future."

For a moment Rielle feared Audric would say something else, further invite his father's anger, but then King Bastien left the room, his kingsguard flanking him. The others followed shortly after, Audric hurrying out after his mother, and Rielle's own father disappearing before she had the chance to speak to him.

"Well," Ludivine said brightly. She grabbed Rielle's hands and grinned. "I don't know about you, but after that? I could use a drink."

16

ELIANA

"Lift your eyes to the eastern skies
Wait for the sun, and with it—rise
We will march down the roads gone black with the dead
We will tear down their walls and paint their crowns red"

—A rowing song composed by suspected Red Crown
ally Ioseph Ferracora during the siege of Arxara Bay

E liana awoke beneath a threadbare quilt, in a small dark room, to
the unwelcome sight of Simon sitting near her.

He reclined on a wooden chair, one long leg resting on the other,
and held a glass of reeking alcohol.

Eliana sat up, remembering to grit her teeth as if the pain from the
blow to her head had lingered.

"You have five seconds to tell me where we are and where Remy
is," she said smoothly, "and who knocked me on the head, and where
I can find them, before I disembowel you."

"And good morning to you, dearest Dread," said Simon, with a
salute of his glass. "I must say, you are looking particularly, well,
dreadful, if you'll forgive the joke."

"Where are my knives?" She realized, with a jolt of shock, that
she was no longer wearing her ruined party gown. In fact, she was no
longer wearing anything, except for the pendant around her neck.

"You piece of shit," she said quietly. "Where are my clothes, where are my knives, and where is my brother?"

"Remy is safe and sleeping. Navi as well if you're curious. Though I'm sure you're not." Simon tossed her a heap of clothes. "Aster wanted to tend to your wounds and get that blood-soaked gown off you. Maybe to make up for her sister knocking you on the head and then, it seems, drugging you? I scolded Marigold roundly for wasting quality goods on you, but she was unrepentant."

Eliana picked up the tunic he had tossed her, grimacing at the frayed hems and patched sleeves. "Who is Marigold?"

"Aster's sister. Try to keep up." He knocked back the rest of his drink and set down the glass. "Anyway, every time Aster tried to dress you, you kicked her. But worry not, she's a tough one."

She glared at him until he said, "Ah," and turned around to face the wall.

"Interestingly," he continued, "you had no wounds that Aster could see."

Eliana's pulse quickened. She tugged on underwear, undershirt, and trousers—too baggy for her, not to mention fusty and faded, but at least they were clean.

"Disappointed that I was lucky enough to emerge unscathed from our valiant escape?" She pulled on the stained linen tunic. "I bet you'd love to have seen my body marked head to toe with scars to match your own, wouldn't you?"

"Actually," Simon replied, "I wouldn't."

She waited for elaboration, and when none came, she examined the jacket he'd brought her—a moth-eaten, bell-sleeved affair with a dull embroidered collar that had once certainly been gaudy and now looked simply pathetic.

"Decent clothes aren't something you rebels care much about finding, I suppose?" she muttered, nevertheless shrugging on the jacket.

"If you're finished."

She made quick work of her wild hair, braiding it into submission. "Give me my knives, and I'll refrain from hitting you for at least five minutes."

"Have you always been this unspeakably irritating?"

"Has your face always looked so temptingly carvable?"

"You wanted to know where we are," Simon said, gesturing toward the door. She pushed past him into a dim stone hallway. A path of wooden planks lined the earthen floor. Following the distant sound of conversation, she turned a corner, passed two doors set clumsily into the wall, and emerged onto a wooden platform overlooking an underground pit. The walls glistened from the slow drip of water.

The pit's floor was covered in people: refugees, clothed in rags. Faces dark and pale, grown and young, all marked with dirt, ash, and blood.

And around the perimeter—standing watch on platforms, moving through the gathered refugees with supplies and stretchers—were rebels. Some wore rifles strapped to their backs; others carried daggers at their waists.

Suddenly Eliana felt neither tired nor irritated.

Simon had brought her to a Red Crown encampment.

Immediately, she leaned against the platform's railing, as if overwhelmed by the sight laid out before her. She let out a sigh of pity just loud enough for Simon to hear.

And she began counting:

Two rebel soldiers patrolling the pit's floor. Six more distributing supplies. Five platforms around the room, one soldier stationed at each. An open crate of potatoes against a nearby stretch of wall; a dozen more, similarly marked, stacked beneath that.

Simon came to stand beside her. His scarred hands rested on the railing next to her own.

The pit's size? She measured quickly. Maybe one thousand square feet, and twenty feet deep.

The number of refugees inside it? Three hundred, give or take.

"Speechless, Dread?" said Simon. "Allow me a moment of shock."

She stepped away from him. "What is this place?"

She let her words carry a small tremor, enough for Simon to maybe wonder: Has the Dread's heart been touched by the sight of such sprawling misery?

Ah, she thought, *but the Dread has no heart.*

"Crown's Hollow." Simon moved toward a set of stairs at the side of their platform. "Come. I'll show you."

She didn't follow him, let some fear rise into her eyes so he'd think her nervous. "Tell me here."

"This is not Orline, Dread. Follow me, or Red Crown will make your life as miserable as you've made theirs."

Her laugh was shrill, unconvincing. *Underestimate me, Wolf. I dare you to do it.* "That would take some doing."

"You've made this war a game for yourself, but here it is not a game, not for these people. And if you flaunt your kills in front of them, I will show you no mercy."

The ferocity in his voice startled her. For a moment Eliana could find nothing to say.

Then she said scornfully, "You think you know me," and moved to join him. "But you're wrong."

"And you don't know this war," Simon countered. "You will, though, and soon. Consider this an introduction."

He said nothing else, and she was glad, for as they descended into the crowd of people, she could think only of the stench, and the low buzz of too many living, breathing humans crammed into too small a space. Children huddled in makeshift tents. A woman sharpened her knives as a tiny girl at her knee watched, wide-eyed. A young man read to his dozing companion by the light of a dying fire.

The air was a sea of sweat and filthy clothes and sewage. Worse than that, though, was the unifying expression the refugees wore.

There was a hollowness to their faces—a hunger, an exhaustion—that pushed at Eliana's ribs and turned her throat sour.

She couldn't imagine what they had seen, and she didn't care to. She had her own past of horrors to contend with, her own sleepless nights.

"How can you live with it?" Harkan had asked her, when they were both twelve years old. He had recently learned what Eliana was training to do and seemed to be struggling with how to talk around her, now that he knew what she could do with a knife.

"With what?" she had asked, concentrating on cleaning the set of blades her mother had purchased for her. *First they must be cleaned*, Rozen had told her. *Take your time. Get to know them. They will need names.*

Names? Eliana had asked, giggling.

Yes, Rozen had answered, her gaze the tiniest bit sad. *They will be the truest friends you ever have.*

"How can you live with knowing that you'll kill people?" Harkan had nervously watched her work. "Good people."

"It's easy," Eliana had replied. Back then, the gravity of what she was doing had sat heavy in her stomach like a stone in a never-ending sea, but her mother had instructed her that if she didn't learn to tuck away that sick feeling, it would consume her. So Eliana tried on the face she had been practicing in the mirror every morning—thoughtless, bored, sly—and said to Harkan, "It's the only way to stay alive."

Harkan had shaken his head and looked away, as if the sight of her was something he could no longer bear.

"I don't know what's happening to you," he had whispered, but he had stayed nonetheless, helped her clean her blades and name them. "Arabeth," he'd suggested for the wicked, jagged one, even allowing a ghost of a smile when Eliana approved. Once that was done, he'd crawled into bed and held her until falling asleep.

But Eliana had not slept that night. She'd lain there beside Harkan, her eyes squeezed shut, wishing she would wake up in the morning and all would be as it should. Her father would return home, the Empire would be gone, and King Maximilian would still be alive.

Harkan would look at her like she was his friend again and not something terrible and new.

Saint Katell, Eliana had prayed, *hear my prayer. Send us the warmth of your wisdom. Light the dark path before me.*

Find the Sun Queen. Tell her we're waiting. Tell her we need her.

She had turned her face into her pillow, tears coursing silently down her cheeks. *Tell her I need her.*

In the dim light of Crown's Hollow, Eliana focused on the back of Simon's head.

How can you live with knowing that you'll kill people?

Good people.

She ignored the murmuring refugees at her feet and told herself, *Don't look at them.*

Don't look.

Don't.

Instead she listened to the rebels bustling through the crowd. Passing out food, standing bored on the platforms, squeezing through the narrow spaces between the pit walls and high stacks of crated supplies, they began to drop whispered treasures.

"...Lord Morbrae arrives tomorrow..."

"The raid...two miles northeast..."

Lord Morbrae. Eliana knew the name: one of the Empire's roaming royalty, he moved from village to village, outpost to outpost.

Something brushed Eliana's wrist. She flinched away and looked down.

A refugee woman with a black scarf tied around her wrinkled, pale head reached for Eliana with a watery smile. Her arm was mottled with burn scars, skin shining taut in the spotty firelight.

Eliana barely resisted the urge to slap her.

Don't look at them.

Don't look.

Don't.

Simon, however, gently grasped the woman's hand and knelt down to speak to her.

Eliana looked away, arms folded tightly across her chest. A hot wave of anger rose up her throat—that the woman had dared to touch her, that Eliana had wanted to slap her, that Eliana *hadn't* slapped her.

That this room was crowded with people too weak to make a life for themselves in the Empire's world.

And that Simon was forcing her to walk among them.

She stepped away to lean against a column of rock, gazing about the room with practiced disinterest while her mind kept counting: four doors up above, by the platforms, and four more on the floor level. One stood maybe twenty feet away. Where did they lead? Tunnels?

A pair of rebels exited the nearest door, arms packed with folded bandages.

Eliana lowered her head as they approached, hunched her shoulders, closed her eyes. A dozing refugee, tired and alone, that's all she was.

"...Monday morning," whispered one of them, hurrying by, "we'll blow them all to the Deep—"

"Let the angels wrestle with His Lordship for a while." The second rebel guffawed. Nobody talked about angels without it being a joke. Not unless you were mad or a child who believed the old stories.

Like Remy.

Eliana listened closely as the rebels passed.

"Not sure even the angels deserve Lord Morbrae among them..." said the first, and then they had passed out of hearing range.

So. She would need to give Simon the slip and roam about until she found someone willing to confirm the scattered bits of information, but if it was true, tomorrow morning, Lord Morbrae would arrive at an Empire outpost two miles northeast of Crown's Hollow.

And the day after, the rebels would raid the facility, taking down one of the Empire's strongholds.

What to do with that knowledge, if anything, Eliana didn't know. But she filed it away with a smug twinge of satisfaction.

"Contemplating your vile past?"

Eliana opened her eyes and shot Simon a nasty smile. "Finished chatting with your girlfriend?"

Simon gestured toward the nearby door, which stood slightly ajar. "After you."

She pushed off the wall. "So where do they come from, these refugees of yours?"

"They come from everywhere. Ventera. Meridian. Even from as far south as the Vespers if they have a strong enough boat."

"And you feed and house them? Treat their wounds and illnesses?"

At the door, Simon stopped her with a touch on her arm. She turned back to him with a coy grin, but the innuendo on her lips died at the look on his face. He considered her in silence, like he was trying not only to read her face, but to look even past that and find a deeper truth.

Look all you want, she thought savagely. *You'll find nothing good.*

"Yes," he said at last. "We treat their wounds and illnesses."

Eliana ignored the disquiet in her belly, gave him a slight hard smirk. "There are many such Red Crown camps throughout the country, I assume?"

"Yes."

"Your rebellion might be more successful if you didn't spend so much time nursing the damned."

The door before them opened.

"Revolutions mean nothing if their soldiers forget to care for the people they're fighting to save," said a new voice. Two men stood there, and a woman. The man who had spoken was short, slight, pale-skinned with wild copper hair, and when Eliana's gaze dropped to his waist, where a smallsword hung in plain view, the man clucked his tongue.

"Ah-ah," he said, wagging his finger at her. "There will be no violence tonight."

"Give me my knives and my brother, or I'm afraid I'll be forced to disobey." Eliana clucked her tongue. "And I was so hoping we could be friends."

The other man, tall and muscular, with dark skin and black hair cropped close to his head, moved his hand to the revolver at his belt.

"Don't bother," said the first man, placing a hand on the other's arm. "She's afraid and lashing out."

Eliana burst out laughing. "You think I'm afraid?"

"Everyone's afraid. You're just better at hiding it than most." The man's eyes flicked to Simon. "So Simon says, at least."

Eliana's laughter died, but a deadly smile remained. "I don't believe we've been introduced."

"Ah! Of course. How rude of me. I am Patrik, and I oversee Crown's Hollow. This is Hob," he said, gesturing to the other man. "My lieutenant and also my husband. And I believe you've already met Marigold," he added, gesturing to the woman on his left.

She was older, with weathered brown skin and gray braids, and a malicious gleam in her eye. "I hit you on the head."

Eliana grinned. "And I'll soon return the favor."

Patrik clasped Eliana's hand, gave it a firm shake. "And of course I know *you*, Eliana Ferracora. Yes, I know exactly who you are." When he smiled at her, it was not without kindness, but Eliana knew the glint of a killer when she saw one.

"Cause trouble in my home," he said cheerfully, "and I will cut you from skull to navel, no matter how much I like your brother. And no matter how much Simon likes you."

Simon gave a dismissive scoff, but Patrik was already guiding Eliana through the door. "Now then," he announced, with a clap of his hands, "who's hungry?"

17

RIELLE

"I worry about Rielle. All children have tempers, but hers comes with a certain look I've not seen on the faces of others her age, or even much older. Her rage holds a delight, a hunger, that I'll confess sometimes keeps me awake through the night. I haven't talked to my husband about it. Sometimes I think I'm jumping at shadows. I should not be writing this. In fact, I think I will burn it."

—Journal of Marise Dardenne
Confiscated by the Church of Celdaria
in the Year 998 of the Second Age

Again!"

Rielle exhaled sharply, blowing a sweaty dark curl out of her eyes, pushed hard off the ground, and jumped—first over a boulder, then over a pile of wooden rails. Then she scrambled up the rocky slope past the rails and down the steeper other side.

Don't lose the pole, she told herself. *Don't. Lose. The pole.*

She made it to the bottom, dropped to her belly, and slid under the net into the mud pit. If she touched the wide-weave net stretching above her, she'd have to start over at the beginning of the course, and her father would add another stone to her pack.

She'd made it halfway through before her hands slipped and she fell chin-first into the mud. Inhaling a mouthful, she choked and gagged.

"Up!" barked a voice from above.

She bit back a curse. Of course he would choose that moment for a fight. She found an opening in the net and crawled up through it, maneuvering her long wooden pole free just in time for her father's attack.

His own pole flew fast at her shoulders. She ducked, raised her pole, and swung it around to strike. The poles met with a sharp wooden crash that hurt Rielle's teeth. She swayed, lost her footing, caught herself on the net.

"Get up!" Her father's pole swung again, rapped hard against her knuckles.

"Damn it!" She bit back smarting tears of pain and lunged to her feet, swinging wildly. "I was down!" But her feet got caught in the netting, and she tripped and fell hard on her tailbone.

"And you're down again." Her father made a soft sound of disgust and flung his pole to the grass outside the pit. "You didn't even make it to the wall climb that time. Get up, and go back to the beginning."

Rielle rose to her feet, shaking with exhaustion and rage. She kept her eyes to the ground, ignoring her ever-present guard, which stood silently around the obstacle course her father had engineered. If they thought she looked ridiculous, well, they weren't wrong.

The course Rielle had described to Audric and Ludivine as her "woodland torture chamber" lay in a secluded area of the foothills of Cibelline, the highest mountain in Celdaria. The saints had constructed Katell's castle, Baingarde, upon its slopes centuries before. Every day for six days straight, in preparation for the next trial, Rielle had met her father here—to strengthen her body, he'd said, and improve her agility.

So far, all it had done was make her sore. And angry as the darkest corner of the Deep.

"I'm not an athlete," she spat at her father, picking her way out of the mud pit and tossing her pole away. "Nor am I a warrior."

He let out a sharp laugh. "Never has anything been so clear as that."

"And yet you insist on putting me through this for hours!" She marched across the grass, peeling off her mud-soaked gloves, gauntlets, shin guards, and at last the cursed, heavy pack of stones.

"We've been out here since dawn," she muttered. "I should be studying with Tal by now, practicing with Grand Magister Rosier. Water's always been my weakest element. Or I could be working on my costume with Ludivine."

"A costume." Her father scoffed. "Yes, a wise use of your time, that."

"Ludivine's idea, and a good one. If I want our people to love me—"

He laughed again, soft and unkind.

"—and show them I'm not afraid—"

"Even you're not that good a liar."

"Stop interrupting me!"

He fell silent, glaring at her. She glared right back, heat climbing up the back of her neck, up her arms, coiling in her belly.

Her father glanced at her hands, but she kept them clenched tight. She knew what he was looking for—wild sparks, the birth of a fire that would rage out of control and consume everything in its path.

As she fought back tears, fists clenched at her sides, she wished, not for the first time, that her father had been the parent she had killed—and that her mother had lived.

"If you are to have any chance of surviving these trials," he said at last, "if you want to have more than raw power and dumb luck on your side, then you will need to become stronger, and quickly."

"I've been studying for years, working on my control with Tal—"

"And that may not be enough!"

Rielle stood her ground even as he advanced upon her. She could feel her braid slipping, sense how sloppy and small and foolish she appeared next to Lord Commander Dardenne. The man somehow looked unruffled even in his muddy training uniform. She bit down hard on her tongue.

"This is no joke, Rielle," her father continued. He re-knotted the ties holding the thin leather padding in place around her torso, straightened her collar, tucked loose hairs back into her braid so roughly that it hurt her scalp. "The earth trial was nothing compared to what the Magisterial Council will engineer for you next. This is only the beginning of a long, hard path. Your life as you knew it is now over. You understand this."

Rielle's cheeks flamed. What must her guard think of him scolding her as he would a small child? "Yes, Father," she said quietly. "I understand."

"If you fail, they will kill you. They might kill me and Tal as well."

Rielle looked at her boots through a film of tears. "I've thought of that."

"Have you? We can't know the council's mind, nor the king's. These are extraordinary circumstances."

"Yes, Father."

He removed one of his gloves, used his bare hand to turn up her chin. She stared at him, eyes full, until his mouth twisted and he walked away. He sat on the ground by the mud pit, found his canteen in the grass, and took a swig of water.

"Sit," he said, handing the canteen to her. "Drink."

She obeyed, saying nothing. As she drank, she stole glances at her father, noting the gray at his temples and peppering his thick, dark hair, the lines around his stern mouth. She realized, with a swift turn of sorrow, that she couldn't remember what he used to look like, before her mother's death had stolen his smile.

"Do you remember," she asked, "that lullaby Mama sang to me?"

Her father was gazing out at the mud-spattered obstacle course, the unsmiling ring of soldiers around it, the dense pine forest beyond that. Rielle watched him, examining his profile. She ached, suddenly, to hold his hand and ask him if he was as afraid as she was.

She curled her fingers through the grass instead.

"I don't remember any lullaby," he answered tonelessly.

Rielle couldn't be sure if that was a lie or not, but she nodded anyway and looked out into the forest just as he did. She drew in a deep breath and began to sing.

By the moon, by the moon
That's where you'll find me
By the moon, by the moon
We'll hold hands, just you and me
We'll pray to the stars
And ask them to set us free
By the moon, by the moon
That's where you'll find me

When a few moments of unbearable silence had passed, she added, "I can't always remember things about her. How she smelled. The feel of her hands. But I remember her voice, and I remember that song."

As soon as the words left her lips, her father rose to his feet, dusted off his trousers, retrieved her pack of stones, and handed it to her. She could read nothing on his face except for the same quiet resolve it always wore—the certainty of Rielle's wrongness and of his own long suffering at her hands.

"Again," he said. "Back to the beginning."

Rielle didn't know how many people were outside waiting to watch her battle the ocean, but from the sound of them, it must have been a lot.

She shifted in her new boots and fought the urge to fiddle with the hem of her heavy cloak, the cords of which she had tied around her throat and torso, to keep her costume hidden until the last minute.

The costume had been Ludivine's idea; keeping it hidden had been Audric's.

Ludivine had tugged Audric proudly into her rooms late last night once her tailors had completed their final fitting and proclaimed, beaming, "Isn't she stunning, Audric?"

Rielle had made herself look right at him. Why wouldn't she? There was nothing strange about showing off her fancy new trial costume to one of her oldest friends. Was there?

But her cheeks had burned, her heart pounding so fast she thought she might choke on it, and then he'd suggested, "I don't think you should show your costume until the very last moment."

Surprised, she had managed to ask, "Why?"

He'd smiled softly at her. "Because then they'll spend the whole trial hoping desperately that you survive, if only so they'll have the chance to see you again."

Rielle shivered now to think of his soft words.

Outside, Grand Magister Rosier's voice boomed over the Forged amplifier:

"My brothers and sisters, citizens of Celdaria, a few words before the trial begins…"

As he described the trial and its rules and reminded everyone that there was no need to worry for their safety—every acolyte from his temple was in attendance, ready to harness the waves should the candidate lose control—Rielle closed her eyes and recited the Water Rite under her breath: "O seas and rivers! O rain and snow! Quench us our thirst, cleanse us our evil—"

The flap of her holding tent opened. "And here I thought you hated praying."

"Tal!" She turned into his arms without a second thought, blinking back a rush of tears. "I thought you said the Archon wouldn't let you see me alone."

"Sloane's just outside." He stroked her hair, kissed her brow. "In her endless generosity, she's allowed us two minutes to talk."

"I heard that," came Sloane's dry voice from outside.

Rielle closed her eyes, breathing deeply. Tal smelled of firebrand smoke and temple incense, a welcome contrast to the briny salt stench of the ocean outside. She could almost pretend they were back in his office, ready for a lesson.

"I do hate praying," she said, pulling back with a tight smile, "but right now? I'll try anything."

Tal carefully searched her face. "You're frightened."

"Frightened? Me?" She shrugged, trying not to let her teeth chatter. Why did the ocean make everything feel so damned *cold*? "It's just that some stuffy old magister once told me praying helps my concentration."

Tal smiled sadly, then scrubbed a hand over his stubbled cheeks. "I can't believe this is happening. I keep waiting to wake up."

"Don't start moaning to me. I'm the one about to do this, not you."

"You're right." He folded her hands into his own, bent down to look her in the eye. "I'm sorry, love. I just wish we'd had more time."

A horn blasted outside, reminding Rielle of the Boon Chase starting line. That day already seemed ages past. The thought that she had been scared of a horse race was enough to make her want to laugh—or maybe cry.

"Lady Rielle?" The head of her personal guard, assigned to her by the king, opened the tent flap. She was a solid, broad-shouldered woman named Evyline, whose pale face wore a permanent stern frown. "They're ready for you."

Rielle stole one last glance at Tal. She knew what he was thinking. She was remembering the same thing:

Let's go over here, Rielle! Here, under the willow tree, where the water is warm and quiet.

Tal's hands tight around her throat, holding her under.

She shuddered, swallowing hard.

"Don't hesitate to fight this time," Tal said softly. His hands flexed at his sides, as if he longed to reach for her. "This is not about proving yourself. This is about staying alive."

"No one knows that better than I do," she replied.

"Lady Rielle?"

Without another word, she stepped past Tal and stone-faced Sloane, who surprised her by grabbing her hand and gently pressing her palm.

"Be safe," Sloane murmured.

Then Rielle emerged into the sun.

Spectators sat in hastily erected wooden stands surrounding the bay, the nearest ones close enough that Rielle could clearly see the curiosity and suspicion on their faces. There must have been hundreds of them, thousands—practically the entire capital and anyone who'd heard about the trials and was able to travel to the coastal city of Luxitaine in time.

They were all watching her in silence.

Her guard following close behind, she walked to the edge of the pier and forced her head high beneath the hood of her cloak. A lonely gull cried out overhead. At the edge of the pier stood two acolytes, their castings in hand—a broadsword and a metal disk engraved with waves.

The horn sounded a second time.

One more and she would begin.

She gazed out over the water—a wide bay encircled by low black cliffs. The water was calm as glass.

But it would not be calm for long.

Well, said Corien, *here we are.*

She almost jumped out of her skin. *Corien! I haven't heard from you since*— She set her jaw against the sudden, wild hope that he could somehow provide her with an exit from this horrible day.

I can't stop this. You've played right into their hands.

I don't want you to stop this.

He chuckled lightly. *You can't lie to me.*

She loosened the ties of her cloak. *I'm showing them they have no reason to fear me. They will love me for it.*

They will kill you for it.

If all you're going to do is try to make me afraid, she told him icily, *then stay away from me.*

I'm trying to help you see the truth.

She stepped forward and let her cloak fall to the ground.

The crowd gasped. Murmurs broke out like waves cresting across the shore.

Rielle couldn't help a small, genuine smile.

She knew the costume was a good one, a form-fitting suit made from a stylish, brightly colored new fabric Ludivine had ordered from Mazabat. It would keep her warm in the water but was flexible enough for her to swim with ease. Waves embroidered with glittering thread swirled across the fabric in the temple colors of the Baths—slate blue and seafoam—and the fabric itself clung to her curves like a second skin. Mesh boots, light as air and with slightly elongated toes, rose to her knees. The suit's collar was high in the back and low in the front. Ludivine had dusted her skin with shimmering paint, and with her hair piled on top of her head and held in place by shell combs and pearl-tipped pins, Rielle knew she looked like Saint Nerida herself.

The horn blasted for a third time.

The water began to churn.

Rielle took a deep breath—and dove under.

~ 18 ~

ELIANA

"My story is the same as all the others. Everyone I love has died; all my nightmares have come to life. Our world is lost, and so are we. There. Will that make a good story for your collection?"

—Collection of stories written by refugees
in occupied Ventera
Curated by Hob Cavaserra

After dinner, Eliana claimed a seat in one of the busier common areas of Crown's Hollow and cleaned her knives.

From her stool by the fire, she could see everything in the low-ceilinged room: Red Crown soldiers switching watch shifts, supplies being tallied, refugees being carried into the sick wing on makeshift stretchers.

According to Simon, they would leave Crown's Hollow in the morning, once fresh horses had arrived. Until then, her spot by the fire was the perfect place to settle and notice everything worth noticing. Most of the passing rebels didn't look twice at her. Maybe Simon had decided it was best to keep word of her identity from spreading.

A pity, that.

Her blades were hungry.

Remy lay beside her, head resting on his folded jacket as he read the latest entry in his notebook. Patrik had loaned him a pen; fresh ink smudged his fingers.

"Can we go to bed yet?" he asked with a yawn.

"No."

"Why not?"

"Too much work to do." She held up Nox, her crescent-shaped blade, and rubbed at smudges that didn't exist.

Remy set his notebook aside. "You're lying."

She smiled at him. "Am not."

"You're not telling the whole truth, then."

Eliana glanced up as Navi sat down beside them.

"Eliana," Navi said in greeting.

"Your Highness." Eliana gave her a mocking bow.

Navi ignored her, looked instead to Remy. "Hello there, my friend. Did you like your supper?"

Remy nodded and passed Navi his notebook. "I wrote down the story you told me about Saint Tameryn and the wolf. I changed some things."

"For the better, I'd wager." Navi scooted closer to him and settled his notebook in her lap. "I didn't do the story justice."

Remy flushed pink. "*I* liked it."

"You know, I think I'm ready for bed after all." Eliana folded her knives into a rag she'd snatched off a crate. "Remy, let's go."

He frowned at her. "But Navi's going to read my story!"

"I don't care."

"Oh, Eliana." Navi touched Eliana's hand. "I was hoping we could get to know each other a little."

A taut humming cord inside Eliana gave way. Her surveillance efforts seemed unimportant in the face of a sudden, roaring fury.

"All right. Fine." She faced Navi, legs crossed, as though they were friends exchanging secrets. "Remy and I are risking our lives to get you to Astavar. What intelligence are you carrying that's so important?"

Navi's smile was as patient as Eliana's was brittle. "You know I can't tell you that."

"Where was my mother taken? What's happened to her?"

Remy sat up. "El…"

"I don't know the answer to that."

"And where was Astavar when Ventera fell?"

Navi's eyes narrowed. "I'm sorry?"

"Where was Astavar when the Empire stormed our borders? Raped our men, women, and children? Burned our libraries and farmlands? Executed our king and queen and their children on the steps of Saint Ghovan's temple in Orline?"

Her body vibrated with anger. She pressed her palms flat to the floor. "Where was Astavar when my father was killed?"

All activity in the room had fallen tensely quiet. Eliana felt the eyes of a dozen rebels upon her.

"You were hiding," Eliana continued, her voice soft. "Hoarding your food and your weapons. Fortifying your borders. You watched us bleed. You heard us scream for help. And did nothing."

"I won't apologize for my people doing whatever was necessary to keep themselves alive," Navi said at last. "Just as you won't apologize for what you've done to protect your family. And I wouldn't ask you to."

For a moment Eliana couldn't speak. The truth of Navi's words knocked her in the gut.

How can you live with it?

She ignored the memory of Harkan's voice, held out a hand for Remy, and felt a cruel thrill when he obeyed.

"Don't talk to me about my family," she said. "And stay away from my brother."

She spat on the floor by Navi's feet. Then she turned, Remy in hand, pushed past the staring rebels, and left the room.

"Ah, Eliana!" Patrik looked up from his table in the common room. "How lovely to see you up and about at this hour."

Hob, seated beside him, glanced up at her, then scowled at the notebook he was writing in.

Eliana hadn't been able to sleep. She'd been lying on the tiny, lumpy pallet she shared with Remy, tensely staring at the ceiling with an iron fist in her stomach and knots turning in her shoulders. She'd borne it for a good hour before giving up.

Now, she was...what? She didn't know. Looking for information? Maybe these rebel saps knew something about the people who'd taken her mother.

Looking for a fight? Her body melted a little at the thought. *God*, yes, a fight would do the trick. She longed to punch something until the skin broke on her indestructible fists. Maybe she could wake up Simon, piss him off. He'd try to hit her, and she'd make him pay for it.

"Patrik." She stepped into the room and nodded at him—a little sheepish, a little soft. The apologetic bounty hunter, finally starting to see the error of her ways. It was almost a funny enough thought to make her laugh right there in front of them. "Hob. I was hoping someone would be awake."

Patrik beckoned her over. "Someone's always awake here. We're peeling potatoes. Well, *I'm* peeling potatoes. Hob's writing." Patrik let out an aggrieved sigh. "I'm used to it though. Doing all the work around here, I mean."

"You poor, overworked darling," said Hob, his voice a deep monotone.

Eliana chuckled and took her earlier seat at the hearth.

"And will you not say hello to me?"

Eliana jumped to hear Simon's low voice from the shadows. She hadn't noticed him there, slouched in a stained, high-backed chair, long legs propped up on an overturned crate. He gazed at her over the rim of his glass, blue eyes gleaming in the firelight.

Irritated with herself for having missed him, Eliana snapped, "Are you ever *not* drinking?"

With a tiny grin, he mumbled into his glass, "Helps me sleep. Keeps me sharp. Keeps the voices at bay."

"Which is it, then?"

"All. Or none." He leaned his head back against the chair, closed his eyes, and let out a long, animal groan of satisfaction. "What about you, Eliana? What voices do you hear in the deep dark of night?"

The sound of her name on his lips lingered in the crackling hot air by the fire. Eliana tore her gaze away from his bared throat; long silver lines of scar tissue shifted as he swallowed.

Then, from the nearest door, a soft voice broke the silence: "Patrik?"

Patrik turned, a smile spreading across his face. "Linnet! Shouldn't you be in bed, little one?"

A small child, maybe eight or nine years old, crept forward from the shadows, a ratty doll clutched in her hands. Bandaged cuts and purple bruises marred her pale skin.

"I don't like sleeping," said Linnet. She climbed into Patrik's lap and stared gravely at Hob's notebook. "I think I'm ready now."

Hob looked up at her. "You don't have to, Linnet, if you don't want to."

The girl's fingers were white around her doll, her thin lips cracked. "I want to. I promise."

Eliana's throat clenched at the girl's haunted expression. "What are you going to do to her?" she asked sharply.

Linnet peered at Eliana through the shadows. "Who're you?"

"Just a monster who likes to wear masks," Simon mumbled into his glass.

Linnet's eyes widened in alarm.

"Linnet's going to tell us her story for Hob's collection." Patrik fixed first Simon, then Eliana, with a cutting glare. "And no one's going to interrupt her, are they?"

Hob opened his notebook to a fresh page. "You're nine years old, aren't you, love?"

Linnet kept glancing over at Eliana with something like awe on her face. Her gaze dropped to the knives at Eliana's belt. "Yes."

Hob began writing. "Can you tell me your family name?"

Linnet rested her chin on her doll's head and said nothing.

"What about where you lived?" Patrik asked softly.

Linnet squeezed her eyes shut and shook her head a little.

"That's all right." Hob smiled. "You don't have to tell me that."

"I don't remember," Linnet whispered.

"I can't remember what I ate for breakfast this morning," Patrik said. "An apple, maybe? A hat? A belt buckle? No, that can't be right…"

Linnet smiled shyly. She stroked her doll's snarled hair ten times before she began to speak.

"The bad men found us in the morning," she said at last.

Hob's pen scratched across the page.

"Mama said to be quiet," Linnet continued, "so I was, like playing fox-and-rabbit, but then Will sneezed right when the bad men were walking outside our door."

"Can you tell me who Will is?" Patrik asked.

Linnet's mouth screwed up into a mean little bow. For a long moment, she didn't speak.

Then, "My brother," she said.

The words hit Eliana like a punch to the jaw. Suddenly Linnet wasn't Linnet; she was Remy, frail and tiny, telling a story he should never have had to tell.

The skin on Eliana's wrist began to itch, right where the old refugee woman had touched her.

Don't look at them.

Don't look.

She shot out of her chair, ready to storm for the door. She didn't have to listen to this. She *wouldn't* listen to this.

But Simon grabbed her arm, held her fast. He said nothing; the icy look on his face was enough to stop her in her tracks.

She glared at him, fuming. She could start a fight, kick herself free, put a stop to story time and give this poor girl a show.

Instead she settled back onto the hearth beside Simon. He wanted her to listen, for whatever malicious reason he'd concocted? Fine. She would listen. And, later, she'd make him regret it.

"The door was already smashed," Linnet was saying, "because we had a party with Mama. She said, *Let's have a mess party.*"

"A mess party?" Patrik whistled low. "That sounds fun. What is that?"

"That's when you make your house dirty instead of clean," Linnet explained.

"That sounds like the best kind of party I could possibly imagine."

Linnet bit her lip. "We set fire to the garden and let our animals go loose, and then Mama... She smashed the windows with an ax. It made her cry, doing it, because Papa loved those windows."

Hob glanced up, his face soft. "Why did he love them?"

Linnet shook her head slowly—back and forth, back and forth. "Because," she whispered after a moment, "I painted them."

Eliana looked away, toward the dying fire. The air in this place was stale, sour. Too many people with unwashed bodies and rotting hurts. She breathed in and tasted death on her tongue. An ill knot was expanding in her belly, forcing its way up through her chest.

Her mother's words returned to her: *If you don't learn to tuck away that sick feeling, it will consume you.*

She closed her eyes, clenched her fists. The fire was too near, too hot. Her skin crawled from it; the heat siphoned all the air from her lungs.

She should never have left her bed.

"Why are you making me stay for this?" she asked, her voice tight and low.

"Because I can," Simon replied and then downed the rest of his drink.

"We tore up our beds and our pillows." Linnet was whispering faster now. "We made red dye from berries and painted the walls. Mama said…Mama said…"

Patrik glanced at Hob. "Maybe we should stop for now—"

"No!" Linnet flung away her doll. It hit the wall and dropped to the floor. "Mama said it had to look real." She gasped a little, like her own words were choking her. With nothing now to hold on to, she clutched the table's edge, stared fiercely at it. "Mama said it had to look like people died there. We were hiding, and the bad men came, and Will sneezed, because he sneezes when he gets excited, and I was crying. I couldn't help it. Mama said…*hush*. She held her hands…over my mouth—"

The girl was having trouble breathing. She looked around, wild-eyed, and then, before Eliana had time to prepare herself, Linnet scrambled off Patrik's lap and ran to her.

She slammed into Eliana's front, threw her arms around her neck, and buried her face in Eliana's braid. She clung there, her little bird's body trembling like it was ready to crack. Her breath came in frantic gasps against Eliana's ear.

"Mama said…" Linnet whispered, over and over. "Mama said *hush*. Mama said *please be quiet*…"

Eliana couldn't move, could hardly *breathe* with this weight she didn't ask for hanging from her neck. She wanted to shove the girl off her, then rip Hob's notebook from his hands and throw it into the fire.

It will consume you.

Breathing thinly through her nose, she tamped down the rising panic winging hard up her throat.

She didn't think of Remy, probably tossing with nightmares down the hall. He'd never slept away from home, not once in his life.

Didn't think of her dead father, her vanished mother, the soft way they'd looked at each other before war ripped them apart.

Didn't think of Harkan and his warm bed, the scent of him like coming home.

A girl couldn't think of these things, couldn't think about teary-eyed children and their tragic stories—not if she was also a killer.

I am the Dread of Orline.

"Then what happened?" Eliana asked. Her voice came out thick, not the hollow, flat thing she'd tried for, and she hated herself for it. She needed to get out of this room before it ate her alive.

I will not be consumed.

"They marched inside," Linnet whispered. "I saw wings on their chests. That's the Empire's sign." She turned her face into Eliana's neck. "Did you know that?"

"Yes." Eliana's collar grew wet beneath Linnet's chin. The heat of the fire licked up her back. What was the old prayer? For Saint Marzana, the firebrand. Remy would know. "I did know that."

Ah, yes. She remembered the prayer now: *Burn steady and burn true. Burn clean and burn bright.*

She stared across the room at Hob and Patrik, hoped her unblinking bright glare made them squirm.

"They took Mama by her hair," Linnet said, "and dragged her into the back room. She was screaming so loud it hurt my ears, and Will, he's big, he beat the bad men, had one of his fits when he starts spitting and hollering, and he looked at me, and...and..."

She didn't say anything after that. She pressed her face tight against Eliana's neck, shivering.

"He told you to run," Eliana finished for her. "He gave you time to run."

Then she unfolded the girl from her body, lowered her to the floor. Patrik was there immediately with the abandoned doll and a quiet endearment.

Eliana pushed past them both to Hob's table. Rage snapped up her body like the lash of a whip.

"Why did you do this?" She jerked her head at Linnet, now cradled in Patrik's arms. "Why make her relive it?"

Hob watched her calmly. "She wanted me to write it down, so she wouldn't forget."

"How many do you have?"

"One thousand three hundred and twenty-five. I've filled twelve books so far. People come through here, they have stories to tell. Some of them want me to write them down. Some write them down for me." Hob took a deep breath. "I think someone ought to know about them. About everyone. Even if it's only me and Patrik."

Eliana eyed the notebook and its gnarled pages with disdain. "It's a waste of time," she spat, "writing stories for the living dead."

Then she left them, Linnet calling faintly after her. The girl didn't even know her name: "Mama?"

Eliana stormed out into the cramped, dark corridor and around the first corner, then subsided against the wall, her heart drumming for an escape and her hands shaking. She fisted them in her jacket, bit down hard on her tongue.

It had been a mistake—to leave Orline, to strike her bargain with Simon, to drag Remy along with them. Reckless and sloppy.

She should have gone from her mother's empty bed straight to Lord Arkelion's door and demanded he help bring her home.

I will not be consumed.

She'd been a loyal servant of the Empire for years, hadn't she?

I will not be consumed.

Maybe that would be enough for them to accept her back.

That, and the map of Crown's Hollow now living in her brain.

"It seems the Dread has a heart after all," said Simon, appearing around the corner so silently that she startled.

She managed a tiny laugh, thinking fast. He could not suspect, or he'd shoot her on the spot. "Is it such a shocking thing to imagine?"

Simon lightly touched the crook of her arm, and there was a fragility to the movement that surprised her. The fire-warmed heat of his body suffused her own.

"Come," he murmured. "I'll walk you to your room."

It was a quiet walk, and by the time they reached her door, Eliana had coaxed the proper fall of tears from her eyes. She turned her face up to Simon, gave him a good view.

Her mother had told her that her beauty would make working for the Empire both easier and harder.

This time it made things easier. She saw the shift on his face as he looked at her—tiny but obvious. A softening and a craving.

A thread of triumph unspooled in her belly.

Farewell, Wolf. May death find you at your greatest moment of joy.

"Remy always says there's hope for me yet, even after everything I've done," she said quietly. *Forlorn* was the word. "I'm not sure he's right." She laughed, her eyes full.

Simon shifted, hesitated, then cupped her face in one large, callused hand. His touch was so delicate it sent a chill down Eliana's front, despite her new resolve to end him.

"People like us don't fight for our own hope," he said quietly. "We fight for everyone else's."

Then he opened her door a crack and stepped aside. "Good night, Eliana," he said, then swiftly moved past her and was gone.

Eliana entered the room and shut the door behind her. Once inside, her face hardened to stone, and her heart along with it.

She wiped her cheeks dry and gave Remy a gentle shake. "Remy, wake up."

He turned, grunting. "El? What is it?"

"Stay quiet. Get out of bed and put on your boots."

"Why?"

"We're leaving." In the dark, her smile was vicious, but she kept her voice kind. "Simon needs our help on a very important mission."

— 19 —

RIELLE

"O seas and rivers! O rain and snow!
Quench us our thirst, cleanse us our evil
Grow us the fruit of our fields
Drown us the cries of our enemies!"

—The Water Rite
As first uttered by Saint Nerida the Radiant,
patron saint of Meridian and waterworkers

The trial's rules were simple:

Hidden in the bay were three items. When assembled, they would form a trident—a replica of Saint Nerida's casting. Rielle was to retrieve and assemble the trident and present it for all to see before the ocean ate her alive.

Simple.

Except the water was damned cold.

And Grand Magister Rosier and his acolytes were making it angry.

Rielle kicked up to the surface to gain her bearings and was promptly pulled back under by a black wave twenty feet tall. Swimming hard, she pushed herself up and gasped for air before another wave knocked her back into the water.

This would get her nowhere.

She remembered Tal's words: *Don't be afraid to fight.*

In fact, though, she was afraid.

When Rielle was a child, and Tal had held her under the water in the Baths, she'd at first fought him. She'd known at once that he was testing her, but with her lungs burning, her panic so desperate she thought she might die from it, she had been ready to do anything for the chance to breathe again.

Looking up through the clear, soft water, she'd seen Tal's blurry figure hunched over her. She had imagined his voice, guiding her through her lessons:

The empirium is in all living things. Think of it like tiny crystals, forming the basis of everything that is.

The goal, then, is to reach with your power beyond the visible, beyond the surface of things.

To take hold of the empirium itself—the grains of life, finer than sand—and change it.

Lungs burning just as they had that day years ago, Rielle closed her eyes in the swirling dark sea and recited the Water Rite. Her body cried out for air, and she ignored it.

"I'm sorry, Rielle," Tal had sobbed after releasing her. He'd held her small, choking body, breathed into her mouth to help her recover her air, tucked her soaked head under his chin. "Forgive me. Please, forgive me."

"I did well, didn't I?" She'd smiled up at him, coughing up water. "Tal, I didn't lose control! I saw the water! The bits of water, they were small and pretty, and I saw them, and I wasn't afraid!"

Tossed about beneath the waves, her body burning and her vision fading, Rielle remembered Tal's stricken, confused face. After, in his office, as she sat sipping a cup of tea beneath a blanket, he'd combed her hair smooth, then held her until she finally stopped shivering.

"You saw it, didn't you?" he'd whispered, awestruck.

Cozy in his arms, she'd mumbled sleepily, "Saw what?"

"The empirium."

She'd wrinkled her nose and looked up at him. "Didn't you see it too?"

But, no. He hadn't, and he wouldn't. Seeing the empirium with one's own eyes was not a thing others enjoyed. Rielle had seen the truth of that in Tal's marveling gaze, felt it in how reverently he helped her back home and into her own bed.

In the water, remembering that day, Rielle's mind cleared and settled. *You saw it, didn't you?*

Yes. She had.

Her power itched to surface, and she let it rise.

I must breathe in this water.

So I will.

Rielle opened her eyes and saw the water of the bay strewn through with countless flecks of golden light, so tiny that when she focused on them, they melded into a solid, brilliant sheen.

The empirium.

She blinked. The gold faded.

But she was not alone here. The empirium was all around her—brushing against her mind like tendrils, reaching for her, calling to her.

Her mind focused and clear, her lungs burning, she pushed out with her thoughts, moving the water away from her body until she was surrounded by a hair-thin shell of air.

It held, but it wouldn't forever. Already she could feel the shell cracking, the weight of the waves pressing down on it as though against a thin pane of glass. A dull ache pulsed through her muscles. Her mind stretched and shifted like someone had reached into her skull and was reshaping the deep, dark place behind her eyes.

Your power is a miracle, Rielle, said Corien, his voice tinged with awe. *I don't understand it. Help me understand.*

Rielle kicked hard and dove deeper.

—◆—

The first item was easy:

A three-pronged trident head, sharp-tipped and silver, lying in a cluster of seaweed on the ocean floor.

Rielle kicked her way down, the pressure of the storming water making her ears throb. She grabbed the middle prong, and her palm lit up with pain. Her blood clouded the water; the shell around her body wavered.

Rielle recalled the story of Saint Nerida in the final battle at the Gate—how she had used her trident to impale the angel Razerak through his gut. His scream was loud enough that the sea birds along the northern Celdarian coast had dropped dead from the skies.

Focus, Rielle, she told herself, furious that she'd grabbed the prong without thinking. But then the sight of her own hand grasping the trident head gave her a burst of inspiration.

The people above, waiting for her to drown, would remember the stories of Saint Nerida too.

Rielle pushed herself off the seabed, kicking hard until she burst out of the water and thrust the trident head high into the air. Sheets of rain, thrown from a sky churning with clouds, slapped her cheeks.

Light shone down upon where Rielle bobbed in the waves. Acolytes from the House of Light cast bright beams of sunlight from the cliff tops.

Rielle turned her face up to the warmth, and once the crowd saw her—triumphantly holding the first piece of the trident, her sliced hand bleeding down her arm—a roar of cheers exploded. And though her protective shell of air muffled the sound, Rielle heard enough to know the truth:

They hadn't expected her to emerge after so long underwater. But now she had, and now...now anything was possible.

Rielle grinned and dove back down. Once underwater, her air shell constricted, twisting about her body like a rag being wrung out. She choked, her throat tightening. She closed her eyes and fought for enough calm to pray.

Grow us the fruit of our fields.

She opened her eyes, glared at the angry black depths.

Drown us the cries of our enemies.

She reached for the empirium.

Follow me.

Obey me.

Warmth snapped at her fingers and toes.

Was the empirium listening?

Her focus renewed, she swam, searching the murky water for clues. But she saw only churning silt and salt, the occasional flitting shape of a swimming creature.

Then a hulking darkness solidified in the watery shadows—a sunken ship, half submerged in shifting sand and glowing faintly from within.

It was worth a try.

Rielle swam closer. The dense current of the water moved ever faster, flinging her wildly through swirling eddies one moment and pushing against her as a solid wall the next.

Inside the ship's cracked hull was an eerie, half-lit land. Luminescent pink barnacles clung to the walls and ceiling. She swam through the captain's quarters, the galley, a storeroom choked with fish that darted away at her approach…

There. A twinkling light caught her eye.

A gemstone, fist-sized and an inky blue in the darkness, winked at her from the floor of the ship. Saint Nerida's sapphire. It would fasten to the end of the trident's staff.

Rielle grabbed the sapphire, slipped it into her pocket, then froze.

The shimmering, rose-colored light suffusing the ship was suddenly brighter than it had been a few moments before.

Slowly, Rielle turned, and her stomach clenched in horror.

The luminescent barnacles that had carpeted the walls, lighting her way, weren't barnacles at all. They were jellyfish—a swarm of them, cat-sized and glowing pink with bright bruise-purple centers. Sizzling light zapped between the fuzzy ends of their tentacles.

Panicking, Rielle kicked to push herself away from them.

Something sharp jabbed her leg from behind; she whirled around in the water.

They were surrounding her. Drifting closer, inexorably, as if attracted to her rising terror. One of them bumped against her arm; a piercing hot sting jolted her. Another found her temple, her bleeding hand. They swarmed, reaching. Knots of glowing tentacles blocked her view of the ship and the sea beyond it.

She forgot all her prayers and lessons and screamed.

The scream broke her shell of air; the water closed in around her, cruel and cold.

She realized the change too late and gasped, choking on the sea.

Desperation forced her to move. She swam, wild, clumsy, swiped the trident head through the jellyfish, felt the prongs pierce something thick and gelatinous. A tentacle wrapped around her ankle, her unhurt arm. She reached back with the trident and sliced through them, tugged herself free.

She pushed and clawed, the swarm's angry lights cutting across her vision. She hoped her suit was offering her some protection, but already her vision was dimming.

Air. Air. *Air.*

She made it out of the boat, reaching desperately for the surface. Her feet were numb, clumsy. She couldn't tell what her body was doing, just knew she had to get up, get up, *get out*—

She burst out of the water, coughing hard. A wave pushed her under. She flailed, flipped over, found a burst of strength, climbed back up. Sweet *saints*, the air was glorious, pure and cold in her aching lungs. The rain beat down on her. Another wave pushed her under, and another right after. She emerged again and looked around wildly. Where were the cliffs? Where were the sunspinner acolytes with their beams of light?

She saw blackness, shifting and growing all around her—no sky, no clouds.

The blackness, she realized with a burst of fear, was waves.

She dove, groped her pocket until she felt the hard gemstone, safely tucked away. She swam, searched the water, surfaced, and dove again. Were they watching her up above? Could they see her? She must have looked absurd—soaked and bleeding, suit torn, skin raised in angry welts.

You can do this, came Corien's voice. His presence was calm and still. *You can do so much more than this.*

Can I? She wanted to sink to the seabed and cry. *Unless you're going to help me, leave me be.*

His voice vanished; she was alone.

She couldn't possibly find the focus to re-create her precious shell, so she resurfaced and dove, resurfaced and dove. Her eyes were on fire from the salt; she could see *nothing* in this churning black water.

And then—how long had it been? Minutes? Days? Her body was one massive, searing throb of pain—she saw it. It was chance, really: an overhead swing of one of the sunspinner's light beams. Something long and thin glinted, then vanished.

Thrust into a rise in the seabed, closer to the surface than the other pieces had been, stood the trident's shaft.

She dove for it, all her focus narrowing in on this one spot. A force rose up within her, something eager and hot and familiar. And as it raced up through her body, firing her blood alive, the ocean around her flashed gold once more.

She understood now; it was easy, with the empirium lighting the way. Move the water, create a path.

The next thing she knew, she was no longer swimming. She was running, her mind clear and blazing hot. Water shot up on either side of her; she was carving a path through it. She reached the trident's shaft and stood panting on the ocean floor. Around her, the water was a narrow, roaring tunnel, spewing water into the air above like a geyser.

But here on the seabed, everything was quiet, softly floating, softly black and blue and gold. Rielle stood in the tranquility of it, assembled the trident with shaking hands. Attach the prongs to the shaft, the gemstone to the end. She grasped it and looked up.

A column of water led straight up into the air, a path she had carved in that last desperate swim without even realizing she was doing it.

A savage pleasure swelled within her.

I did this.

Me and no one else.

And how does it feel? Corien asked quietly. His presence hovered at the door to her mind.

I feel...

She couldn't articulate it. Standing there, looking up at the chaos of the water gripped by her power, she could only gape and revel in it and exist.

I feel...

A small fear twisted in her breast, but she couldn't listen to that now, when everything felt so...so...

She closed her eyes, shivering. The air around her vibrated with warmth. Beyond that, the sea churned, relentless and cold. Sprays of water kissed her cheeks.

Corien's voice was as gentle as her father's long-ago embrace: *Tell me, Rielle.*

I feel...alive.

And you are. You are more alive than anyone.

But then the small fear grew. It reared up and shouted: What might this display have done, up on the surface?

Terror crashed through her body.

Her triumph faded; her focus shattered. The water followed soon after.

It slammed down upon her like the force of a thousand fists, and flung her to the ocean floor. She floated there, stunned, her head ringing.

Rise up, Rielle, Corien urged her.

I...I can't.

You did it. You're almost finished.

Rielle watched the trident sink beside her. Her eyes closed.

With no small amount of irritation, Corien said, *Your friends are worried sick for you, Rielle. Especially that boy.*

Audric. Rielle groped for the trident. *Ludivine.*

Yes, Corien said, nastily now. *Go to them, ease their pain. They love you so.*

Rielle forced her eyes open. Lungs burning. Vision dimming. She pushed herself up. She kicked and fought, clawing through cold water, and when she burst up above the waves, she remembered to hold the completed trident above her head.

The sunspinners' beams shone down upon her. Her arm shook under the trident's weight, but she held it fast.

This time, the crowd's roar was deafening.

In an instant, the rain stopped. The waves flattened and calmed, clouds rolling away to reveal a mild blue sky.

Rielle saw through her burning eyes the nearby pier, crowded with figures. One dove into the water, swiftly heading her way. Those still on the pier shouted after whoever it was.

Rielle could hardly swim, the trident slowing her. She'd only gone a few feet when a strong arm gathered her up against a body that radiated so much warmth it could only belong to one person.

"Audric," Rielle whispered, clinging to him, her limbs trembling from exhaustion. "You feel nice."

He let out shaky laughter. "We need to get you to my healer. You're cold as ice."

"Thank God you're here." She squinted up at him as he awkwardly swam back to shore with one arm, her body tucked against him with the other. "I'm tired of swimming."

"What's all over you?"

Rielle looked blearily at her hands. "Oh. Jellyfish attacked me. The waterworkers made them angry, maybe."

"God, Rielle…" Audric's voice broke. "I'm so sorry."

"Don't worry. I stabbed them. The jellyfish, not the waterworkers." She glared wearily at the pier, where the acolytes waited. "Though that's still a possibility."

He laughed again, then said quietly, "Rielle?"

"Yes?"

"Were you frightened?"

She closed her eyes and whispered, "Yes."

His arms tightened sweetly around her, his mouth warm against her temple. "I wish I could—"

"Your Highness!" A waterworker acolyte knelt on the edge of the pier and extended his hand. He stared at Rielle like she was Saint Nerida risen from the dead.

Audric ignored the man, gently detaching himself from Rielle. "Here, I'll help you up."

"No." Rielle grabbed the edge of the pier and turned in the water to face him. "They need to see me stand on my own."

He smiled and handed her the trident. "Your prize, my lady."

She squeezed his hand, then shakily climbed up the pier, refusing the assistance offered her by Grand Magister Rosier, his acolytes, even Tal.

On her own two feet, she stood, swaying slightly, and looked up at the thousands of people lining the cliffs—waving their arms, pumping their fists, shouting her name. When she raised the trident in both hands, their cheers became thunderous.

She turned to face the Magisterial Council, who had gathered on the pier. Tal beamed, his eyes alight with pride. Sloane stood at his side with her arms crossed, a thoughtful frown on her face, her short, dark hair plastered to her pale cheeks.

And beside her stood the Archon, beads of rainwater sliding down his implacable face.

Rielle handed him the trident with a grin she knew was gracelessly cocky. But she didn't care one bit.

"Your move," she said with a slight bow. "Your Holiness."

ELIANA

"Dark-hearted Tameryn had never seen anything good come by daylight. With her daggers, she carved shadows from every corner and hollow. She breathed life into their gasping mouths, twined them around her limbs and neck, tied their newborn fingers into the ends of her hair. There the shadows whispered secrets to her, in gratitude, and so she was never alone and always safe in the shroud of night."

—*The Book of the Saints*

S neaking out of Crown's Hollow during the perimeter guard's shift change had been dispiritingly easy.

Even the tense two-mile trek through the wild, thinking that every rustle of leaves was a Red Crown scout—or worse, Simon—had gone more quickly than Eliana had hoped. Remy believed her story. Simon, she'd told him, had gone on a mission for the nearest Empire outpost, to retrieve an important piece of information for Navi. He had left Eliana instructions: If he hadn't returned within two hours, they were to come to his aid.

"Even me?" Remy had asked.

"Especially you."

His eyes had narrowed. "Why?"

"Because you're sweet-looking, and no one will suspect you of lies.

You can sneak around in very small spaces. And you're a storyteller. You can improvise as I need you to."

"And we can't tell the others?"

"No."

"Why?"

"Simon said not to. Don't ask me to explain his choices. I couldn't possibly begin to."

Remy didn't look convinced, but at least he wasn't arguing. So far, so good.

But getting an audience with Lord Morbrae without being killed for betraying the Empire? That would be a challenge, even for the Dread.

Maybe they don't really mind that much that I helped the rebellion's most notorious soldier push one of the Emperor's personal assassins out of a tower?

It was a nice thought.

Eliana scanned the moonlit forest, shifting her weight from one foot to the other. Her muscles burned from the sustained crouch, but it was a good burn. It reminded her: no more rebels; no more sad stories or lost princesses.

No more Simon.

"Is that him?" Remy whispered beside her.

They'd been waiting outside the Empire outpost for two hours, watching for the arrival of Lord Morbrae as the trees around them shivered in mist and the night sky inched toward a gray dawn. And now, as Eliana looked back at the outpost through a net of wet branches, she saw what Remy had seen.

A convoy approached the perimeter wall. Ten mounted adatrox. A coach pulled by four horses.

A door in the wall opened, admitting torchlight from within.

So. The Red Crown intelligence had been accurate.

She hoped.

"Looks like a general's escort to me," Eliana whispered.

Remy stared up at her from within the hood of his cloak, shivering even with the thick night steaming around them. "Maybe we should go back."

Eliana turned to him, bracing herself. "Listen carefully. We're not here to help Simon."

Remy blinked. "What?"

"I'm going to negotiate with Lord Morbrae for information about Mother and for amnesty for all of us. At least until I can get you to Astavar. Then I don't care what they do to me."

"You...*what?*" Remy's face clouded over. He stepped back from her. "You lied to me."

Eliana sighed, glanced quickly at the outpost. "Yes, and you'd think you'd be used to that by now."

"You're going to give them information about Crown's Hollow."

"Remy—"

She reached for him, and he slapped her hand away.

"What's wrong with you?" he whispered. "All those people—"

"The refugees? They'd do the same thing in my position. They'd do whatever it took to keep their family alive and safe."

Remy shook his head, took another two steps away from her. "You're wrong. Some would. Not all. I wouldn't."

A call from the outpost distracted her; she turned, squinting through the shadows.

Then Remy grabbed Arabeth from her belt and ran.

"Remy!" she called after him as loudly as she dared.

Behind her, one of the horses pulling the coach whickered and stamped its foot.

She looked to the outpost, then back out at the swamp. Remy's small form disappeared into the gloom, running toward Crown's Hollow. She had to chase him down. None of this was worth it if they were separated.

She stood, heard a twig snap behind her, and froze.

A male voice asked mildly, "What's this?"

Slowly, Eliana turned. A uniformed man stood a few paces away, silhouetted by the torchlight of the outpost's perimeter wall. Behind him stood a dozen adatrox, rifles aimed at her heart.

Eliana put her hands in the air.

"My name is Eliana Ferracora," she called out. "I am the Dread of Orline. I was taken captive by Red Crown soldiers and escaped. I have intelligence you'll want."

Silence, then. The tree bugs hovering above her head rattled and droned. Sweat itched along her brow.

"And what," said the man, "will you want in exchange for this intelligence?"

"Safe passage for myself and my brother back to Orline. A guarantee of amnesty. And the return of my mother as well. She was abducted from her bed two weeks ago. I want her back. Alive and whole."

The man stood in silence for another moment, then approached her. As he moved closer, the shadows shivered away to reveal a reedy, clean-shaven man, with light-brown skin and short dark hair. Like all the Empire's generals—like the Emperor himself—his eyes shone as black as a deep hollow in the ground.

Whatever drugs the Emperor fed his dogs to alter their appearance so drastically must have been truly monstrous.

Eliana met his gaze without flinching. "Lord Morbrae."

He smiled, held out one leather-gloved hand. The gathered adatrox lowered their weapons.

"Welcome home, Dread," said Lord Morbrae, voice thin and cream-smooth. "Come. Tell me your secrets."

He led her through the prison first.

Every Empire outpost had one, and though this one was small and plain compared to the elaborate dungeons below Lord Arkelion's palace in Orline, it was distinctive in one way. Instead of cells, the long, narrow rooms were lined with small, square cages that required the grown adults within to sit hunched. But not all were adults; some were children. Grotesquely thin, bellies swollen, skin red from scratching, lips crusted with blood and vomit.

They watched Eliana as she passed. The newer ones, not so thin or broken, glared viciously, spat through the mesh of their cages. The ones who had been there for a while—filth-encrusted skin, matted hair, gaunt-faced—said nothing at all, staring blankly.

At a turn in the wall, a small child slammed into the door of her cage and gripped the mesh with bony white fingers. Her eyes were furious, the skin around them red and raw.

"Help us!" she shouted, shaking the door. The metal cut into her hands. "Get me out of here! Get me out!"

"Is there a point to showing me all this?" Eliana asked, sounding bored. But her blood raged hot inside her.

May Tameryn the Cunning grant you a swift and painless death, child, she thought.

"I wanted to show you what will happen to you," Lord Morbrae replied, "should you decide to cross me during your stay here."

Then he opened a door into a small, plain room—one chair, one flickering lamp. He held out his hands for her knives. "You may wait inside."

Eliana peered within, raised an unimpressed eyebrow. But her mind raced with panic. She didn't have time to wait in a cell. Remy would tell Simon everything, and they would come for her, guns blazing. They'd shoot her immediately. She needed to tell Lord Morbrae, help him prepare his soldiers to counter the rebels' assault—but not before she had gotten what she wanted from him.

She placed her knives into his waiting hands. "I get an actual room, then? Not a dung-smeared cage?"

Lord Morbrae's smile did not reach his eyes. "Only the best for the Dread of Orline. I hope you're hungry."

When he closed the door, Eliana was left alone and uncertain. She sat on the chair in the middle of the room and waited.

"So. Eliana Ferracora." Lord Morbrae reclined in his chair, brought a glass of wine to his lips. Over the rim of his glass, his eyes watched her, black and unblinking. "I'm listening."

Eliana continued cutting her venison. Blood spilled onto her plate with each press of her knife. They'd kept her in that cell for maybe two hours before calling her into His Lordship's dining room.

She tried not to think of the cage-filled prison, the screaming little girl with the desperate eyes.

She tried not to think of Remy or of Simon. Was he on his way by now? Or would they assume Lord Morbrae would kill her himself and write her off as dead? What would Remy think? Would he be glad to be rid of her?

And what would happen to her mother?

Eliana imagined scraping clean her circling thoughts with the edge of a blade.

"There is a Red Crown compound," she began, bored, "two miles southwest of here. They call it Crown's Hollow." She brought a bite to her lips, chewed, swallowed. Looked up at Lord Morbrae and smiled. "What a delicious meal you've prepared for me. I'm grateful. Rebels don't have much in the way of fine cuisine."

Lord Morbrae's laugh was barely audible. He snapped his fingers. One of the adatrox standing guard around the dining room moved to refill Lord Morbrae's glass.

Eliana watched in silence as Lord Morbrae drank and drank. He snapped his fingers once more. Another glass refilled. He gulped it down like a desert wanderer, then slammed the glass onto the table, curled his lip. Picked up his fork and knife, violently cut his venison, crammed bite after bite into his mouth without pausing to breathe.

At last he stopped, took another gulp of his wine, and sat staring at his plate in disgust. "More meat," he told the nearest adatrox. "Not this." He shoved the platter of venison away. "Something that actually tastes good for once. Can you manage that?"

The adatrox bowed, gave a slight, jerky nod.

Once he'd gone, Lord Morbrae returned his gaze to Eliana, dark eyes heavy and lidded. Red wine stained his lips. "You lie."

A frisson of fear skipped up Eliana's throat. She smirked, incredulous. "I don't. What good would it—"

"If there were a rebel compound two miles from here, we would have destroyed it long ago."

"It's underground. And well guarded."

Lord Morbrae blinked at last.

Ah. Didn't know that, did you? Eliana continued eating, examined the dining room blithely. "Lovely little space you've got here. Nice solid table. Impressive molding work. Did they make it up especially for you?" Fork in hand, she gestured at the nearest wall. "Do they change the art according to each visiting general's tastes?"

"How many?" Lord Morbrae's soft voice was an explosion in the silence.

"Three hundred and sixteen refugees." She took a sip of her own wine. "Fifty-one rebel soldiers. Small bands—anywhere from two to eight rebels—come and go every day. There are ten on patrol in the woods beyond the compound, forming a perimeter. Five roam; five sit in blinds they've constructed in the trees."

"Ammunition and supplies?"

Eliana grabbed a red apple from a gleaming silver bowl on the table-top, took a bite. "Sorry, my friend. I'm afraid I can't offer you more information until I've a guarantee for our safety. Me, my brother, my mother. Otherwise"—she shrugged—"no deal, I'm afraid."

Lord Morbrae's gaze traveled across her mouth as she licked the apple juice from her lips, then to her throat as she swallowed, then down her body. Eliana's mouth felt suddenly dry. That wasn't desire on his face, not the kind she was used to seeing.

It was fascination, raw and ravenous, as though the sight of someone eating an apple was a thing he had never before seen.

"I could kill you right now," he said, his tongue darting out to wet his lips, "if I wanted."

"But you won't. I know so much more than I've told you." She took another bite, made herself watch him as she chewed, despite the apprehension creeping across her skin. "You won't risk losing that information, not now that you know a rebel compound has eluded you for so long. I know the Wolf's plans. A secret mission, beyond the efforts of Red Crown. It could turn the tide of war." She tossed her half-eaten apple onto her plate. "Let me help you, my lord. What I ask for in return is nothing compared to the information I carry."

Lord Morbrae rose to his feet. He stretched, rolled his shoulders, worked his jaw as if rolling out a kink.

Eliana watched, her stomach turning. She leaned back in her chair and picked at her fingernails. "Feeling poorly tonight, my lord?"

He moved across the room, sank into a high-backed red chair beside the crackling fire, and watched her. Shadows masked him, drawing dark shapes across his face.

"I'm still hungry." There was an exhaustion to his voice—and an anger, thin but simmering. "I'm always hungry."

Eliana glanced at the table, heavy with their supper. "Then—"

"Food won't help," he interrupted. "Nothing helps."

A new silence filled the room. Eliana resisted the urge to move, matching Lord Morbrae's stillness.

"Come here," he said at last, holding out his trembling hand.

Eliana forced out a breezy laugh, though her heart pounded with a swift, terrible fear. "My lord, I'm wearing two coats of mud and haven't had the chance to bathe in—"

"Shut your mouth," he bit out, "and get over here."

She waited for as long as she dared, then stood and moved toward him, keeping her gaze on his face. Let him know, with a carefully crafted expression of disdain and boredom, that the thought of what he would do to her in that chair didn't frighten her.

She was the Dread of Orline wasn't she?

But she had never touched one of the Emperor's men.

She settled onto Lord Morbrae's lap and tried to turn her back on the pain in her heart where Harkan's memory lived. But suddenly all she could think of was his laugh, his wide smile, the clomp of his boots on the terrace outside her window. How he had touched her, that first time, with shaking hands. How he had always held her afterward like she was something precious to be kept safe and warm.

Harkan, she thought, fear buzzing in her ears as she placed her palms against Lord Morbrae's chest. *Harkan, Harkan. What am I doing here?*

He had asked her that same question many times, and her answer had always been the same: *surviving*.

Lord Morbrae's legs were long and bony; the buttons of his uniform jacket strained against his protruding belly. How could he possibly still be hungry? He looked to have gained a good ten pounds since they'd sat down.

He shifted in the firelight. Bread crumbs clung to his stained lips.

"I've bedded many people," he said at last, smiling up at her. Bloody scraps of meat were wedged between his teeth; his breath was stale and rancid though they'd only just eaten. "But it never felt good. Not once, Dread. But maybe you…"

He traced his long fingers up and down her arm, found her open collar and toyed with her dirty skin.

"Maybe I what?" Eliana leaned closer, even as her throat clenched with revulsion. She let an inviting smile drift across her face.

"Maybe you can finally do it."

And I will. Slowly, Eliana slipped off the ridiculous frill-sleeved jacket and let it fall to the ground. Beneath her tunic, the pendant bearing the ruined image of King Audric on his flying steed felt itchy and hot against her breastbone. *If this is what it takes—for Remy, for Mother—then this is what it takes.*

Lord Morbrae watched her every movement, his gaze distant and his mouth thin with frustration, as if he'd already decided that whatever kind of experience he craved, he wouldn't find it here.

His hands, though, were tight on her hips. Insistent.

She leaned over him, heart pounding, and let her eyes fall shut. She instructed her mind to detach from her body and tuck itself safely away. It was an excellent skill, one of the first her mother had taught her, and she wasn't half bad at it. Lord Morbrae was a mark, just like any other. She'd get through this as she had many times before.

Except this wasn't like the many times before. And when Lord Morbrae exhaled against her cheek, his breath putrid and strangely cold, Eliana couldn't help it. She flinched away from him. Her eyes flew open.

Two black eyes met her own.

In that moment, it was as though something leaped out of Lord Morbrae's mind and into her own. She felt a charge, as of lightning, reach out for her and grab hold.

She jerked in his arms, and he jerked beneath her.

And suddenly Eliana was no longer in the Venteran outpost.

She stood on the veranda of a palace, overlooking a vast land scattered with snow-dusted hills. Her vision was cloudy; shapes shifted before her eyes as if drawn on the surface of swirling water. She concentrated, fighting for balance. The world cleared somewhat: A city, choked and glittering. Distant neighborhoods spilled over one another, crammed between winding roads paved with white stone. Ivory spires soared to the skies. Sunrise poured rose-gold over a gaping, mountain-sized pit in the earth. Strange lights, like trapped miniature storms, flashed throughout the city streets.

All of it was unfamiliar, and yet Eliana felt a tiny urgent tug at her heart.

Was it unfamiliar?

A movement to her left caught her attention. She turned, somehow, though her body felt detached from everything around her. She couldn't feel the stone of this veranda beneath her feet, yet she could see the world around her plainly, smell a faint scent that reminded her of Orline—river water, city sweat. But the air here was cold, biting.

This place... It wasn't a dream or some delirious vision. At least she didn't think it was.

A figure stood at the stone railing, not far from her, beside a statue of a man reaching for the skies with open arms. There were several such statues on the veranda. Protruding from each of their backs were magnificent wings shaped out of paper-thin colored glass and inlaid with fire-colored stones. Not feathered, these wings, but sculpted from flame and shadow.

Eliana recognized the figures from Remy's tales about the Old World.

Angels?

She must have made a noise. Something changed in the air. The man went horribly still, then whipped his head around to face her.

Shining black hair curled just below his ears. A sleek, dark coat with square shoulders, fastened with brass buttons over his heart, fell cleanly to his feet. His skin was pale, his cheekbones fine, his mouth full. His eyes were blacker even than Lord Morbrae's.

She would recognize him anywhere. His statues stood on every street corner in Orline. Enormous portraits of him, haughty and impossibly beautiful, hung throughout Lord Arkelion's palace.

The Emperor of the Undying.

And, somehow, though she knew him to live half a world away in Celdaria, he was staring right back at her.

─ 21 ─

RIELLE

"When Audric was a boy, I could dismiss his fondness for Armand Dardenne's daughter as harmless. But now...I see the way he watches her when he thinks no one is looking. We must be careful, sister, to discourage them. Ludivine must be queen. Ludivine will be queen."

—Letter written by Lord Dervin Sauvillier
to his sister, Queen Genoveve Courverie
Year 994 of the Second Age

Rielle's favorite room in Baingarde—other than Ludivine's and Audric's rooms—was Queen Genoveve's private parlor.

The queen had many sitting rooms set aside for the receiving of guests, but this was her private space, meant only for her and her family.

"Must we do this?" Evyline muttered, standing board-straight at the parlor door as Rielle peeked around the hallway corners to make sure no one was coming. All was quiet, the air in the castle gone soft for the night. Light from the thin crescent moon filtered through the colored glass in the windows lining this particular corridor. The glass was a northern tradition, intended to bring cheer into a home during the long winter months. Belbrion, the seat of House Sauvillier, featured so much colored glass that it was said to glitter like a jewel-encrusted crown when the sunlight hit.

Satisfied, Rielle returned to the parlor door. "I'm to undergo yet another life-threatening trial tomorrow, Evyline." She looked guile-lessly up at the tall, gray-haired woman. "Would you really deprive me of a few moments of peace, knowing what awaits me in the morning?"

Evyline sighed. "Only a few moments, my lady."

"You worry too much, Evyline."

"I expect that's true, my lady."

Rielle held out her hand, gave Evyline a brilliant smile. "The key?"

Evyline withdrew a small brass key from her jacket pocket and dropped it in Rielle's hand. "I could get banished for this, my lady. Or worse."

"When I'm Sun Queen," Rielle said, "you will be head of the Sun Guard, my close adviser, and the most revered soldier in Celdaria. That's worth a little sneaking around, isn't it?"

Evyline's cheeks flushed, her eyes trained on the wall across from her. "If you insist, my lady."

Rielle inserted the key in the lock. "I won't be ten minutes."

Once inside, Rielle walked to the center of the parlor, sat on a foot-stool, and breathed in slowly. Here, in this quiet, her true nervousness about the next day tickled her insides like birds desperate to be set loose from their cages.

She had read all the books she was supposed to read, said her prayers, studied with Grand Magister Rosier under the watchful eyes of the Archon. Ludivine had worked with the finest tailors in the city to create yet another marvelous costume for the occasion. Visitors had been trailing into the capital all week in preparation for the event.

And perhaps that was it, Rielle thought. It was the people who would be watching her that had stirred up her nerves—many hundreds more than had attended the water trial if Audric was to be believed. It was the Sun Queen banners that winked golden at her from doors and windows as she looked down from Baingarde at the city. She'd seen the banners even at the temples, decorating the libraries, the gardens, the doors outside the acolytes' dormitories. On the fluttering fabric, a crown encircled a blazing sun.

Since the last trial, Rielle had started to understand—to really, truly *feel*—that something was beginning.

She tried to breathe, separate her nervous feelings from her excited ones, and lock the nervous ones away where they could no longer annoy her. She turned her head to the ceiling and gazed at her true reason for coming here.

Queen Genoveve had a soft heart for animals, particularly the gods-beasts of the angelic ages, long died out. Upon marrying King Bastien, she had ordered the ceiling of her parlor painted with an extravagant menagerie of them. There were the fur-crested ice dragons of Borsvall, the firebirds of Kirvaya, the giant white stags of Mazabat, the ferocious krakens of the northern seas, the unicorns of the old angelic lands to the east, the shape-shifting fey-beasts of Astavar.

But Rielle's favorite of the godsbeasts had always been the chavaile—the giant winged horse that the bedtime stories from her childhood had told her lived in the mountains of Celdaria and could fly even faster than the dragons. They hunted game as mountain cats did and were sated for weeks afterward.

Rielle smiled to think of those stories. Hearing them read aloud was one of the only memories she still had of her mother. If she closed her eyes, she could hear Marise Dardenne's voice—low and rich, a voice crafted by God for telling stories.

So her father had said, watching them from beside the fire as Rielle snuggled in her mother's arms, a book of godsbeast tales open on their laps.

Rielle drew in a sharp breath as the memory surfaced. It was one she hadn't remembered before, and yet there it shone in her mind, clear as daylight.

You're welcome, came Corien's voice, kinder than Rielle had ever heard it. *I thought that might comfort you.*

"How did you do that?" she whispered, eyes still closed.

"And now you're talking to yourself."

Rielle's eyes flew open, and she shot to her feet. Beside the windows on the far side of the room, Queen Genoveve rose from a high-backed chaise and considered Rielle with one arched eyebrow.

"My queen!" Rielle hastily curtsied. "I didn't... I didn't see you..." She swallowed, took a deep breath. "I apologize. I would never have intruded, had I known you were resting."

"I wasn't resting. I was thinking. I come here often to think." The queen crossed the room, wrapped in a gray dressing gown hemmed in blue silk. "And you come here often as well, it seems?"

There was no point in pretending. "Only sometimes."

"I should punish you. Or at least your guard. But you are enduring enough punishment as it is, I suppose."

When in the presence of the queen, Rielle often felt herself reduced to the child she had once been, leading Audric and Ludivine on some wild game through Baingarde. The three of them had once burst into the queen's sitting room, shrieking merrily, right as Genoveve was taking tea with visiting dignitaries from Mazabat—and then, not five minutes later, Rielle's father had chased her down, brought her back to her rooms, and shut her away once more.

She had never gotten to know Genoveve as well as Audric or King Bastien. The queen was a Sauvillier from skull to toe, with none of Ludivine's warmth.

"Please, my queen," Rielle managed, "do not punish Evyline. I'm afraid I rather manipulated her into thinking that if she didn't obey me, I would bring the wrath of God down upon her, once I've been named Sun Queen."

Queen Genoveve let out a small, dark laugh. "Rielle, you astound me. These trials are meant to cow you, and yet you make light of them as though they're a child's game."

Rielle hesitated. "If I don't make light of them, my queen, then my fear is liable to overtake me."

The queen inclined her head, then settled on a settee across from Rielle. "Why did you come here tonight?"

Rielle glanced up at the painted bestiary. "I like coming here. The chavaile has always been my favorite. It reminds me of my mother—and the stories she used to tell me."

Queen Genoveve considered her for a long moment. "Are you manipulating me right now, Lady Rielle, as you've done to your poor guard?"

Rielle blinked in surprise. "No, my queen. I'm speaking the truth to you. Perhaps I've been too candid."

"Not at all. In fact, I think this is the most I've ever liked you."

"Oh." Rielle began to laugh.

"Was that so very funny?"

"I apologize, my queen. I'm caught quite off my guard is all. I suppose I need to sleep. My nerves are a tangle."

"It's not that you haven't been a good friend to my son and niece," the queen said after a moment. "It's that you are..." She paused, thinking. "Cunning. Willful and lovely. It's a volatile combination. It unnerves me."

"And now you know I've been keeping secrets from you during all my cunning and willful years."

Queen Genoveve nodded. "And I wonder what others you might have yet to reveal."

Rielle forced herself to meet the queen's thoughtful gaze, one that so matched Audric's that a lump formed in Rielle's throat.

"Come sit beside me." The queen patted the settee's cushion. "We will pray to Saint Grimvald together, that he may bring you success tomorrow."

After a moment's hesitation, Rielle obeyed. For a long while, neither of them spoke. Then Queen Genoveve sighed impatiently and took Rielle's hand in her own.

"A sword forged true with hammer and blade," murmured the queen, in prayer, "flies sure and swift."

"A heart forged in battle and strife," answered Rielle, "cuts deeper than any blade."

"Saint Grimvald the Mighty," continued the queen, "please watch over this child tomorrow as she fights to prove her honor and loyalty in front of my husband, the king, and His Holiness, the Archon." The queen paused. "She is much beloved by my little ones, and I pray for her safety so that they may feel joy upon finishing their day and not despair."

Rielle stared at the queen. "My queen, I...I thank you for that."

The queen kept her eyes closed, but squeezed Rielle's hand gently. "I sometimes forget that, despite everything, you are still only a girl, Rielle. And no girl should have to be without her mother on such a night."

Rielle could no longer speak, her throat tight and hot, but it was enough to sit beside the queen and shut her eyes and imagine that Genoveve's hand was her mother's—alive and unburnt.

They had built her a cage.

Rielle stared out the flap of her tent, her blood roaring in her ears.

In the narrow pass between Mount Crimelle and Mount Peridore, earthshakers had carved out a clean, square pit in the stone-riddled ground, five hundred feet deep. And the metalmasters of the Forge... They had built her a cage inside it.

It was a cube, black and unfriendly, with spiked, groaning insides that churned like clockwork and shifted every few seconds. At any given moment, half the cube's innards were in swift motion. Metal slammed against metal. The hot oiled smell of grinding gears and the sharp tang of the metalmasters' magic—scents that reminded Rielle of her father—drifted up from the pit like invisible curls of smoke.

Somehow, Rielle would have to get from one end of this caged maze to the other without getting crushed or impaled. And all while thousands of spectators watched from the stadium the magisters had erected around the pit's rim.

She swallowed hard, closed her eyes.

"I thought Tal would lose his mind," came a flat voice from behind Rielle, "once he saw what we'd designed for you."

Rielle turned to see Miren Ballastier, Grand Magister of the Forge, and Tal's lover—when they weren't in the middle of one of their legendary fights. In the torchlit glow of the tent, beneath her wild cap of red hair, Miren's pale, freckled skin looked ghostly.

"It's a maze," said Rielle faintly, still not quite believing it.

"It is. And Lady Rielle..." Miren paused, a troubled expression on her face. "I want you to know that I protested against it. It's unfair and cruel. I wouldn't be surprised if the king takes him to task for it, once he finds out—"

"Who? What's cruel?" Rielle barely resisted pleading. She and Miren had never been the best of friends, and now that Tal's long deception had been revealed, Rielle couldn't imagine that would change. "Miren, tell me."

A horn sounded, its lonely wail echoing off the mountain walls. The gathered crowd began to cheer.

"You'll see soon enough," said Miren, before pressing a dry kiss to her forehead. "From Tal," she said simply and then left her alone.

You don't have to do this, Corien reminded her. *You can leave. Right now.*

And do what, then, and go where? Rielle asked irritably. *You're always telling me I don't have to do these things, yet you offer no alternative.*

There was a pause. Then: *You could come to me. And we could begin.*

The shiver that swept up Rielle's body nibbled like tiny, hungry teeth.

We're going to have a discussion, you and I, when this is finished, she thought to him. *I've put it off for too long.*

I quite agree, came his smooth voice.

Unsettled, on edge, Rielle stepped through the flap as the horn sounded for a second time, raised her chin against the glare of sunlight peeking through the mountain pass, and let her cloak fall to the ground.

The crowd's roar rattled Rielle's bones—and she smiled to hear it.

Her outfit, constructed from a dozen charcoal and shining silver fabrics, evoked the armor of Saint Grimvald. Long black gloves stretched past her elbows. A snug jerkin and matching trousers boasted embroidered designs that flattered her curves, and the long tails of her square-shouldered jacket touched the ground. On the jacket's back shone the sigil of the Forge—two black swords crossed on a fiery orange plane. Silver paint streaked her cheeks and eyes; Ludivine had painted her lips a flaming coral to evoke the fires of the Forge.

Eight solemn-faced metalmasters lined the narrow platform stretching toward the pit. She raised her arms to acknowledge the crowd and made her way to the pit's edge—where the Archon stood with a tiny, satisfied smile.

As the door to the cage creaked open, the Archon extended his arm toward it. "You can choose to save them. Or not. What really matters is saving your own skin." He turned to her, blinked twice. "Isn't it?"

Save them. Rielle peered into the cage, and when she saw to whom the Archon was referring, the sudden rise of dread made her stagger.

Three tiny cages rose slowly from the maze's teeming cogs. Inside each stood a child, wailing in fear.

As the crowd began to notice them, shouts of anger and horror arose from the stands.

"Are you mad?" Rielle cried.

"They are orphans from the Low Streets," the Archon explained. "No one will miss them when they're gone. Except, well..." He glanced up at the furious crowd. "*They* might, I suppose."

Understanding sank into Rielle like a slowly twisting blade. The maze was deadly enough as it was. She would have to fight hard to survive it—and to save three children on top of that seemed impossible.

But if she didn't...

She glanced up at the bellowing crowd.

The Archon's smile grew. "Your move, Lady Rielle," he said.

Rielle did not hesitate. She turned, flung off her stiff coat, raced to the waiting door of the cage, and jumped inside.

ELIANA

"The Emperor is a hunter that never tires. A storm that never sleeps. How do we best such a creature? The answer is simple: we cannot. If the entire world turned as one to destroy him, again he would rise—and again and again."

—The Word of the Prophet

"Who are you?"

Eliana startled to hear the Emperor's voice. She'd imagined it before, entertained wild fantasies of storming his palace in Celdaria and slitting his throat before he had the chance to talk her out of it.

Whispered conversations in Lord Arkelion's palace had told her the Emperor's voice could worm its way inside your mind and heart, make you helpless to resist doing whatever he suggested. Which Eliana had long ago decided was nonsense. A voice couldn't control you; anyone who said otherwise was a fool.

But never, in all her blood-soaked daydreams, had Eliana imagined the Emperor's voice to sound quite like this. A purpose lived there, beneath the rich tones—resolute and unmovable, ancient and sly.

She stepped back, stumbled over an imperfection in the terrace stone. "I didn't mean to intrude."

"And yet you did." The Emperor approached, hands behind his back. "I can't see you very well. Can you see me?"

"A little." Her vision swirled and shifted. She felt tempted to rub at the air, as though to clear a fogged window.

"How curious."

"I'll just..." She wanted to turn away and run, but the inexorable blackness of his eyes held her in place. "I'll be going now."

"Oh, I don't think so. No, I think—"

He froze. Expressions she couldn't altogether decipher cascaded across his face: horror, joy, astonishment.

Rage.

"*You,*" he whispered hoarsely, all the loveliness gone from his voice. In its place was a terrible, ragged longing. "It's you."

Eliana met the terrace railing at her back. "What?"

Swiftly he moved closer, reaching for her. "Stay there. Where *are* you?"

A great shudder shook the terrace, throwing Eliana to the side. She pressed her hands against the palace wall to keep herself from falling...

And suddenly, the palace, the city below, the Emperor, were all gone.

The red walls of Lord Morbrae's dining room stood fast and close around her. His slack face stared up at her, eyes clouded and gray.

Like the eyes of an adatrox.

She pushed back from him, fell hard to the floor, scrambled away.

"Who are you?" Lord Morbrae asked, rising jerkily from his chair. Reaching for her, just as the Emperor had done. His voice had been cut in two—part his own, part the Emperor's. "Come here. Come to me."

A blast sounded from outside. Eliana recognized it as the detonation of a bombardier.

Simon.

Remy had told them everything, and now Red Crown was going to destroy this outpost, with her inside it.

Despite herself, she smiled. What a budding rebel her little traitor brother had turned out to be!

The room shook; the dishes on the table rattled, and Lord Morbrae stumbled. Three of the four adatrox stationed around the room hurried out the door, unsheathing their swords. A wineglass fell to the floor and shattered.

Eliana grabbed the biggest shard of glass she could find, leapt to her feet, and lunged for Lord Morbrae. He saw her too late, dodged clumsily. She wondered if the gray clouding his eyes was confusing his sight, then drew the shard's sharp edge across his throat. Blood gushed hot over her hand and onto her clothes. Lord Morbrae made a terrible choking sound, then fell hard to his knees before collapsing.

The remaining adatrox rushed at Eliana. She grabbed a carving knife from the table and met him beside Lord Morbrae's corpse, kneed him in the groin, then plunged the knife into his belly. She ran past him, flew out into the hallway, and ran right into the muzzle of Simon's revolver.

He wore the Wolf's metal mask, but even with his features hidden, she could feel his fury in the air like the charge of lightning.

Another bombardier exploded, this one closer. Simon grabbed her by the arms as something in the ceiling gave way with a creaking groan, pulled her tight against his chest and shielded her between his body and the wall. One of the rafters fell, bringing down stone.

"This way," he muttered, shaking dust from his hood.

She pulled against his grip. "Where's Remy?"

"With Navi. And so help me, I will throw you over my shoulder and carry you out of here if necessary."

"Why not kill me?" She wiped grit from her eyes. "I'm a traitor, aren't I? I thought you'd blow the place to the skies—and me with it."

He laughed bitterly. "If only it were that easy."

Shouts and gunfire sounded from beyond the outpost's walls, and Remy, Eliana assumed, was somewhere in the thick of it. If she didn't cooperate, she might never find him. She shot Simon a glare and swallowed her anger before following him down the hallway.

From behind them came a distant scream, followed by another.

Eliana whirled. Inhaling, she tasted smoke.

The prison.

She ran for it, but only made it a few paces before Simon grabbed her arm.

"Unhand me," she growled.

He did, roughly. "Then don't run away again."

"There are people back there," she said. "Refugees. Prisoners. *Children.* We have to free them."

"We can't."

"*Why?*"

"Because my soldiers have set bombardier charges around the building. When the fire reaches them, they'll detonate. In less than five minutes, this building will no longer be standing."

Eliana felt as though the floor had dropped out from under her. "You're lying."

"I'm not."

"Well, I'm going." She started again for the prison, and this time, when Simon stopped her, she elbowed him in the gut and stomped on his foot, but he didn't release her.

"Let me go!" She struggled, twisting violently. "What do you care if I die trying to save them?"

"As touched as I am by your sudden heroic streak," Simon bit out, "I don't have to explain myself to you. Now, *move.*"

Another bombardier detonated, the closest one yet. A chunk of plaster fell from the ceiling and hit Eliana's head. Pain spiked down her skull; she swayed, tried to move forward, stumbled.

With a curse, Simon caught her, thrust his gun into her hands, and scooped her easily into his arms.

"If someone comes at us," he ordered, "shoot them."

He ran, keeping his head tucked over hers. Clouds of dust, smoke, and grit fogged their way. Eliana coughed against Simon's chest, considered shooting him in the gut right then and there.

But then two adatrox ran out of the shadows. Eliana turned in Simon's arms and fired five times. She was a bad shot even without having been hit in the head, but luck helped at least two of her bullets hit true. The adatrox jerked and fell.

They turned a corner and another, passed a room crackling with flames and another where a glassy-eyed adatrox lay on the threshold, his arm outstretched. Papers marked with muddy boot prints littered the floor.

Then, a shot from behind them—a near-hit. Eliana looked past Simon's shoulder, and her stomach lurched with fear.

Lord Morbrae.

He was *alive*.

He chased them down the corridor, rifle in hand, and though his face, neck, and jacket gleamed with blood, Eliana could see no wound on his throat.

Impossible.

She pointed the revolver past Simon and fired, but nothing happened.

"You used all the goddamned bullets." Simon kicked open a door in their path three times before it gave. Once through, he kicked it back shut. Lord Morbrae fired again; the door's wood splintered at Simon's heels.

He lowered Eliana to the ground. They were out. It had to have been near midday, but clouds and smoke darkened the sky. The outpost's perimeter wall was aflame. Eliana heard screams, shouted commands. Simon pulled her along awkwardly, his arm around her waist as they ran.

Oh, right, Eliana thought, giddy, the pain in her head now completely gone, her limbs strong and steady once more. *I'm supposed to be hurt.* She leaned into Simon's body, let him help her along.

A chorus of high-pitched whines began behind them. The door through which they'd exited burst open. Eliana saw Lord Morbrae search through the smoke, spot them, raise his gun. The whines escalated, shrill and dissonant.

Simon shoved Eliana ahead of him. "Get down!"

She obeyed, skidding down a wet slope into a narrow, swampy ravine. Simon threw himself down after her and covered her body with his own.

The world exploded.

Someone slapped her.

Eliana surged awake with a gasp. "How long?"

"Three seconds," came Simon's impatient reply. "Get up."

She obeyed, then froze. A terrible sound floated down to her from the blackened sky.

Screams.

She climbed the ravine, slipping on the slick wall of mud, and peeked over the rim into chaos. The outpost's main building lay mostly in ruins, debris scattered as far as she could see. And from the ruins came those screams—agonized, beastly.

"The prisoners," Eliana whispered. She looked over at Simon. "Some could still be alive."

"Yes," Simon agreed, "or it could be adatrox or my own soldiers who didn't get out in time."

Eliana lifted herself up by the roots of a watchtower tree. "We should try to help them."

Simon pulled her back down. He began reloading his revolver. "No. We ride north."

"Did you not hear me?" She flung out her arm in the direction of the outpost. "There were children in that prison. They had them in cages—"

"Yes, and if Red Crown had carried out their raid tomorrow as planned, they would have gotten them out. But you ruined that when you ran away. We couldn't risk letting anyone who'd seen you, or heard whatever intelligence you delivered, leave here alive."

Eliana stared at him in horror. "What?"

A shot rang out near the outpost, followed by another. Simon pointed one gloved finger. "Hear that? My soldiers, disposing of the survivors. Listen."

Eliana did, hearing a third shot, then a fourth, a fifth. She reached for the tree roots once more, but Simon pulled her back down and held her close, arms pinned at her sides.

"Listen to them die," he hissed, his mouth hot at her ear behind the cold, hard mesh of his mask. "Their blood is on your hands."

Eliana half-heartedly fought to free herself, but as the shots continued, and the horrible screams abruptly stopped one by one, she subsided.

It will consume you, her mother had warned her.

She breathed past the foul knot of shame burning the back of her tongue.

"We'll add them to your tally, hmm?" Simon's voice was furious. "Do you even remember how many people you've killed, Eliana?"

Eliana nodded, her eyes and mouth dry. She felt shriveled, undone. She closed her eyes. Yes. Yes, she remembered. Including Harkan? He'd be alive now, were it not for trying to protect her.

What had she told Remy?

We can't know for certain.

He could still be alive.

She closed her eyes, clung to the foolish hope to keep from screaming.

"Eighty-seven," she whispered as the gunshots continued. "Eighty-eight. Eighty-nine."

"What did you ask him for?" Simon lowered his hood and pushed back his mask so that it rested in a mess of dirty-blond hair. "Safe passage home for you and Remy? Amnesty? Your mother returned to you, safe and sound?"

Eliana nodded. She felt as though, slowly, all the life inside her were being funneled out.

"And was it worth it? Were their lives worth it?" He jerked his head up at the outpost. "Did you get what you asked for?"

Eliana didn't have the chance to answer, interrupted by galloping hoofbeats. She glanced up, and the sight of a mud-spattered brown horse emerging from the nearby woodlands, Remy sitting on its back behind Navi, knocked the breath out of her.

She met his worried blue gaze and gave him half a smile.

"Simon!" Navi called down to them, a terrible fear on her face. "Crown's Hollow is under attack!"

Simon pushed Eliana ahead of him. "Climb," he snapped. She did, Simon following nimbly. Remy was already dismounting, Navi right after him. Remy stumbled across the mucky ground to bury his face in Eliana's bloodstained shirt. She held on to him automatically, half her mind still back at the outpost with the gunshots.

They'd stopped. So had the screams.

Remy whispered, "Did they hurt you?"

She shook her head, made herself look at him. "No. I'm all right."

Simon grabbed the horse's reins. "What's happened?"

"A squadron of adatrox attacked," Navi explained, "shortly after you'd gone. Patrik got me and Remy out, but just in time. We were the only ones. Simon, they've taken all the exits." Her hood fell back, her eyes haunted. "No one can get out."

Eliana stepped away, detaching herself from Remy. The refugees. Patrik. Hob and his notebook. And tiny Linnet...

Three hundred and sixty-seven, give or take, if no one else had made it out. Plus the ninety-three she'd reached before the guns stopped.

Four hundred and sixty bodies' worth of blood coating her hands a bright, blazing red.

A numb feeling spread out from her chest down her limbs, scouring her veins clean of all reason.

"El, what is it?" Remy asked. "Are you sick?"

But she ignored him. A movement at the corner of her eye grabbed her attention: two Red Crown soldiers, thirty yards away, near the smoking perimeter fence. They were picking through the uniforms of fallen adatrox, pulling out flasks, papers, weapons.

Nearby, grazing among the debris, were two horses. Bridled and saddled, patiently waiting.

Eliana squeezed Remy's shoulders, murmured, "Stay here, quietly," and backed slowly away as Simon and Navi continued their hushed, urgent conversation. Then she turned and ran, ignoring first Navi's cry and then Simon's roar of fury. Mounted the nearest horse, snapped the reins, and bolted.

Two miles southwest of here. She turned the horse that direction. Wet branches snagged her clothes and the horse's legs, carved thin red tracks across her cheeks.

Hoofbeats chased her. When her horse cleared a stretch of trees and broke out onto open ground, she dared to turn around and saw Simon, bearing down hard on his horse as he pursued her. Mask on, cloak flying out behind him like a pair of dark wings.

She leaned lower over her horse and urged him on. "Faster, you stupid beast!"

Then, up ahead—plumes of black smoke churning up to the cloudy sky.

Eliana squinted through the approaching woods, pulling her horse abruptly to a stop. She dismounted, tied the horse to a nearby branch, and crept closer into a cluster of moss-laden gemma trees.

There, perhaps two hundred yards before her, was the stretch of land that covered Crown's Hollow. Smoke churned from five distinct points, flames licking up out of hidden openings carved into the ground. Eliana recognized the one she'd snuck out of with Remy. Had it been only hours before?

Three adatrox stood at every fire, weapons trained on the flames.

A larger group—including a lieutenant with a thick gray band around his left bicep—stood some yards away from the compound, waiting.

They were smoking the rebels out.

They've taken all the exits, Navi had said. *No one can get out.*

Eliana leaned hard on the gemma tree as she realized what must have happened. Somehow, Lord Morbrae had communicated to his soldiers everything Eliana had told him about Crown's Hollow, even though he hadn't left her sight after their conversation at the dining table.

But then, Eliana thought, *I didn't need to be in Celdaria to stand on a terrace with the Emperor, did I?*

Nausea coiled coldly in her belly. Could it be that the Emperor—and his generals, his lieutenants, maybe even all the adatrox—could send messages and visions to and from each other's minds?

How was such a thing possible?

Simon arrived, pulled up his horse at Eliana's side and jumped off. He grabbed her arm. "Are you mad, Dread?"

"I'm sorry, I thought I could help them, I didn't... I wasn't thinking..."

"Indeed you weren't. There's nothing we can do for them now." His voice was flat. "We'll return to Navi and ride north as fast as we can. There's a solid rebel presence in Rinthos. They'll shelter us for a bit."

Eliana grabbed two of the spiked bombardiers strapped to his belt and ran. Simon reached for her; she twisted out of his grip and raced for the gathered adatrox standing patiently behind their lieutenant. Waiting, as the black smoke thickened, for desperate rebels and refugees to come tumbling out, gasping for air.

Her hands tightened around the bombardiers. Her mind was a wreck of noise and blood-soaked images, fanning the flames of rage in her breast until she could feel nothing else, not even a prick of fear as she pulled the bombardiers' caps and burst out of the trees.

Saint Marzana, she prayed as she pushed past the back lines of adatrox and ran into the heart of their orderly squadron. *If you care for the prayers of monsters like me, hear this one.*

The bombardiers vibrated, whining, in her hands. She skidded to a stop, surrounded by shouting, confused adatrox. The lieutenant, at the front of the group, turned. His eyes widened when he saw her. He called out a command. The adatrox nearest her raised their swords; others raised their guns to shoot.

Eliana finished her prayer: *Burn them.*

She threw down the bombardiers, turned, and ran.

This time, when the world exploded, it flung her into the trees. She hit something hard; the back of her body lit up with terrible hot spikes of pain.

Then blackness took her.

— 23 —

RIELLE

"A sword forged true in hammer and flame
Flies sure and swift
A heart forged in battle and strife
Cuts deeper than any blade"

—The Metal Rite
As first uttered by Saint Grimvald the Mighty,
patron saint of Borsvall and metalmasters

The opening of the cage flung Rielle down a smooth chute and onto a tiny platform so small she almost tumbled over the edge. The crowd above let out shouts of dismay.

She swayed, regaining her balance. A blast of heat shot up from below her. Looking down, she saw a churning mass of metal—pulleys hissing, swords flying and fans whirring, large steel plates crashing into one another, staircases folding in on themselves and transforming in the blink of an eye into long ramps slick with oil.

She could not leave this horrible creation without the three children. All her effort in these trials would be for nothing; the people would turn on her.

But it was more than that.

She glanced up through the black bars of the cage to the seething crowds above.

You want them to love you, Corien observed, sounding surprised.

Rielle threw her arms over her head and crossed her forearms, echoing the sigil of the Forge. Cheers erupted from the crowd in response.

Yes, she thought. *I want them to love me.*

Then she turned and ran—not for the opposite corner of the maze, where she thought she glimpsed a door that would lead her to escape. Instead she ran for the child nearest her, his brown face pressed to the bars of his cage.

She jumped over a narrow chasm beside the platform and then started down a set of stairs. Below her feet, each step flattened, vanishing as she ran. She was almost fast enough.

Almost.

Toward the bottom of the stairs, the steps disappeared entirely. She slid down the last stretch, falling forward fast to land, knees first, on a deck of metal grating that careened from side to side. The landing sent spikes of pain up her legs. She clutched the grating, gritting her teeth as her stomach roiled violently.

"Please!" cried the child, not too far off. "This way! Please, my lady!"

She closed her eyes, struggling for breath. She could almost hear Tal's patient voice in her ear: *The empirium is always there. Every moment, every breath, every inch of life you touch. It waits for you.*

Corien remarked softly, *Your teacher is not wrong.*

Rielle set her jaw.

But the empirium does not simply wait for you, Rielle, he continued. *It hungers for you. No one else will ever understand it as you can. It longs for you the way a lover yearns for his mate.*

Rielle snapped open her eyes. The world around her began to shimmer. Her fingers curled. *I hunger for it as well.*

Darling, I know it. Don't resist. Reach out and take it.

She shuddered, heat flooding her limbs.

"Stop," she whispered, reaching out for the churning gears with the edges of her mind.

The deck beneath her jerked, slowing. She slammed her palms

against the grating, tasted its metal tang on her tongue, felt its vibrations up her arms. A gold-tinged wave of energy shot out from her hands, ricocheting through the maze.

"*Stop.*" It was a command.

The deck screeched roughly to a halt. With a choked scream, Rielle lost her grip, fell, then caught herself on the deck's edge at the last second with grasping fingers.

"Here!" the child yelled, below and behind her to the right.

Rielle glanced back over her shoulder, feet dangling. The threads of concentration she'd managed snapped. Silver glinted at the corner of her eye—metalmaster magic?

She followed its trail to a winding set of stairs that flew apart into whirling metal plates. They spun right for her, cutting through the air like spinning knives. Desperation gave her strength; she swung her body once to get momentum, then flung herself through the air to the platform where the child's cage stood.

The metal plates just missed her, slamming into the deck from which she'd hung only seconds before.

Shaking, eyes stinging from sweat and oil, Rielle fumbled with the lock to the child's cage. The near-miss with the flying plates had thrown her; she could hardly see, hardly think.

The child screamed at her, sobbing, "Hurry! Please, hurry!"

"I'm trying!" she snapped and then saw the reason for his terror: His cage was *shrinking.*

In seconds, he would be crushed.

If she got out of here alive, she would tear the Archon's flesh from his bones and relish his every dying scream.

She thrust her palm against the lock with a furious cry. Raw power sizzled up her arm and out of her body, knocking the child off his feet and shattering the lock. The metal scraps of it went flying.

She wrested open the door. "Come on!"

The child flung himself at her and wrapped his arms around her neck.

Overhead, the crowd burst into wild cheers. Beneath the din, Rielle heard a metallic creak and looked up. A small door in the cage's roof was opening. Two metalmasters crouched there, holding their arms out for the boy.

Two more. Rielle shoved him out to safety, not waiting to hear the door shut. The nearest child was wailing for her clear at the other end of the maze.

Between them was a series of shifting corridors made of crashing metal blocks the size of Rielle's body, spears that thrust out at random, stairs that twisted and transformed without pause, paths that twirled on their axes like roasting spits over a fire—too many moving parts to keep track of. Watching them, she felt utterly dwarfed; the thought of saying her prayers, steadying her breathing, felt ludicrous, inadequate.

She'd be crushed. She lacked the control to slip through such a cruelly designed maze. If only she had more time to *think.* She squinted through the wild glinting chaos, her hands shaking.

Don't risk it, came Corien's voice—tense now and unamused. *You are powerful, but you're not immortal.*

I could be, Rielle responded. And that shocked her, made her straighten and blink in surprise. She hadn't meant to say such a thing; the very idea was preposterous. And yet the words had surged up through her body, automatic and instinctive.

Yes, Corien answered pensively. *You could be, I think.*

Rielle shook herself, silencing him. That was a conversation for later.

She wasn't, after all, immortal today.

The platform beneath her shifted. She took a deep breath, dashed forward just as the platform jerked and gave way. She looked back, frantic.

Eyes front, Rielle!

Corien's voice made Rielle whirl just in time. A gigantic metal pendulum swung her way. She flung out her arm. Gears shrieked; a thud sounded, as of a hammer hitting an anvil. The pendulum, now warped and dented, ground to a stop.

Rielle raced on, dodging spears that whistled fast toward her. The path ahead shifted, tossing her off her feet and down a narrow tunnel made of mesh. She landed in a heap, bit down hard on her tongue. Tasting blood, dizzy, she peered through the mesh of the tunnel. It was one of many—a rotating knot of tunnel-shaped cages, long and thin. She crawled, seeking an exit, as the knot of tunnels spun ever faster. They knotted and unknotted like a mass of wriggling snakes. A patch of mesh ahead of her peeled open, creating an exit. She scrambled for it, but wasn't fast enough; the mesh sewed itself shut in the space of a blink. She screamed in rage, nearly slammed her hands against it, stopped herself.

Think, Rielle. If you shatter this trap, you'll fall—and to where?

Eyes shut, struggling to force her mind clear, she found the path she needed. She saw the maze arrange itself, orderly, so that the writhing nest of tunnels trapping her would unfurl and grow still. She saw a path leading out of her tunnel and down to a set of sturdy stairs that would lead her to the second caged child.

The image unfurled in her mind's eye like a map, golden-edged and glimmering, and when she opened her eyes once more, a sea of miniscule brilliant grains winked beneath the shifting veil of the physical world.

Then the world remade itself as she instructed.

Power shot out from her fingers to slither down the mesh of her cage. She felt its progress as a slithering heat under her skin, felt the rough metal beneath the reaching tendrils of her power as if her own hands were touching it. Her eyes drifted shut with pleasure. The knots in her body loosened, then vanished. A shuddering liquid heat cascaded down her limbs, pooled in her belly, shivered down her thighs.

The maze around her shifted, groaning as if in protest. The metalmasters above were fighting for control.

She smiled, sated. *Nice try.*

Just as Rielle had envisioned, the tunnel that trapped her unfolded, docile. Its opening came to rest on a wide platform leading to a set of stairs. She crawled out, stood for a moment to catch her breath. She felt shot full of energy, as if awakening from the best sleep of her life.

She turned her gaze up to the crowd, to the two mountain peaks above that, to the sun beyond.

She bowed low, with an indolent flourish of her hands.

The crowd exploded into cheers, so loud that even from the depth of the pit, Rielle's ears rang from the noise.

Grinning, she bounded up the stairs to the second child's cage. This one was a girl, pale and thin-limbed, her eyes large and dark in her hollow-cheeked face. Peeking out from under a mop of tangled brown hair, she sobbed uncontrollably.

Rielle touched her hand to the cage's lock, felt the euphoric power from a few moments before seep into the metal like a drug.

With a quiet sizzle, the lock collapsed, melted, and dripped silver to the stairs.

Rielle gazed down at the girl, her eyes heavy-lidded.

"It's all right," she said, breathless. "I'm here to save you."

The girl gaped up at her. "Are you the Sun Queen, my lady?"

Rielle held out a hand to her. "I will be soon."

The girl jumped up from her hiding spot and barreled into Rielle's open arms.

But then, with a great, heaving groan, the entire cage rocked beneath them. Rielle swayed, tightened her grip on the child.

A ripple of horrified shouts sounded from the crowd above.

"My lady," whispered the child. She raised a shaking hand to point into the maze below them. "It's falling down."

She was right. Rielle stared, her terror climbing fast as the cage began to move—from the far, bottom corner and the near, top corner,

Swiftly it collapsed, folding in on itself. The horrible grinding racket sounded like all the axes in the world clashing against one another.

And the third child still stood trapped far below.

Above, the creak of a door. Rielle shoved the girl toward it without thinking. "Climb!"

The child clung to her. "You'll die! Come with me, please!"

Rielle caught the child's face in one hand. "Do you really think that I, the Sun Queen, will let such a puny cage be the end of me?"

With a tremulous smile, the girl shook her head.

Rielle returned her smile and pushed her up a long, skinny ladder to the waiting metalmasters. Once they had the child in hand, the floor beneath Rielle gave way.

The fall choked away her scream. She dropped fifty feet and slammed onto one of several rotating poles. They spun out from a center mechanism like spokes of a carriage wheel. She clung to the pole that had broken her fall. She could hardly breathe; her stomach felt bruised from the impact.

But suddenly, even through her exhaustion, Rielle had an idea.

She closed her eyes. *I can do this.*

Corien answered firmly: *You can.*

She let go of the pole, dropping onto a metal plate that had been whizzing through the air only seconds before. At the slam of Rielle's boots, the plate stopped, frozen in midair.

She threw up her hands, felt the simmering hot energy flowing between her and those spinning poles, and made them fly.

They spun out in all directions, so fast any one of them could have cut a man clean in half. Rielle twisted her wrists sharply in the air. The poles slammed to a stop, wedging themselves into the four corners of the cage.

The cage shuddered, its collapse halted. Every piece of metal trembled in place, creaking awfully.

That wouldn't hold for long.

Rielle raced through the air, summoning metal plates from the walls as she ran. They flew to her from the floor, the staircases, the labyrinthine paths crisscrossing the cube. She flung each plate before her, stepped lightly on it, pushed off, and moved on.

Corien let out an admiring laugh. *Marvelous, Rielle. Stunning.*

Pride bloomed in Rielle's chest. With each step on her floating metal path, she felt power gather at her feet. When she landed next to the third child's cage, it blew apart at her touch, leaving the child standing, shivering, in its ruins.

"Come here." Rielle shook her hand impatiently. Every inch of her skin tingled. Distantly, she felt the screaming ache of her muscles. "It's almost over."

"How did you do that?" the child asked, gaping. "You were *flying*."

A series of colossal, metallic crashes exploded around them. Rielle looked up to see the poles wedged in their corners giving way.

But the cage did not continue its collapse.

Instead, it lifted itself into the air, the metal groaning. Rielle grabbed the child, watched the cage's shifting base for an opening, then jumped through it to the ground. She and the child fell hard; the child screamed, clutching his foot. Above them hovered the cage, slowly spinning.

Then it rearranged itself, the metal maze breaking apart, re-forming, *sharpening…*

A storm of blades, ten thousand strong, turned as one and raced toward the lonely spot in the dirt where Rielle and the child crouched.

Rielle stared, panic drumming its way up her throat. Time slowed and quickened, both at once. She could faintly hear Corien shouting at her to do something, to defend herself, to *move*.

But thousands of swords? That was too many. Manipulating a few pieces of the maze was one thing. But this—they darkened the sky. They whistled and roared. They would cut her to pieces—and the child too.

The child grasped her wrist. "May the Queen's light guide us home," he whispered to her, the smile on his face not one of resignation, but of belief.

The Sun Queen's prayer. The Sun Queen's light.

Her light.

Her *power*.

Yes, Corien whispered. *Yes*, *Rielle*.

Rielle pulled the child close, then turned to the swords, closed her eyes, and flung up her arms.

No.

She refused this fate.

No.

She had trials to complete, friends waiting for her, the mystery of a foreign princess's murder to solve.

No.

She had words of love still to speak.

And a voice in her head.

And a hunger, a *craving*, to answer the awakening call of her blood.

No.

Not yet.

She waited in silence, her body trembling. Power stretched out from her fingers, from the sharp turns of her shoulders, from the ends of her hair.

Had it been enough?

She drew a few shallow breaths in the ringing silence, then dared to open her eyes.

A blade hovered before her face. Two more, pointing at each of her eyes. Hundreds. *Thousands*, all held in place by her silent command. They filled the pit, quivering, denied their kill. The air hummed metallic.

Rielle let out an incredulous, tearful breath.

Then she let her arms fall.

The swords dropped flat to the ground, forming a perfect circle around the spot of earth where Rielle knelt with the child. Their fall shook the ground. Their blades pointed away from her; she sat at the center of a scorched metal sun.

Slowly, the world returned to her. She blinked, wiped her eyes clean. A growing surge of voices made her look up.

The people of Celdaria were on their feet. They were screaming her name—a chant, a prayer.

Rielle! Rielle! Rielle!

She raised her face to the sky and showed them her smile.

~ 24 ~

ELIANA

"Something is wrong with Lord Arkelion. He took me into his bed, ordered me to hurt him as he lay naked before me. I did so happily, but his wounds closed almost at once. He roared and writhed and wept. He is ill, perhaps mad. I believe all the Emperor's men to be mad. Every single one."

—Encoded message written by Princess Navana Amaruk of Astavar, delivered to the Red Crown underground

Eliana scrambled upright, gasping, her clothes clinging to her sweat-drenched skin. She had been lying facedown on a mud-crusted blanket. Her hands slipped as she struggled to push herself to a sitting position.

"Remy." She looked wildly about, saw only a black forest lit by a wedge of moon. "Remy!"

"Hush." A gentle hand smoothed the hair back from her forehead. "He's safe, and so are you."

Eliana recognized the voice. "Navi?"

The girl smiled down at her, her gaze worried but kind. "I'm here. You're all right."

Dark clouds shifted meanly across Eliana's vision. She gripped Navi's hand. "Tell me."

"We're three days' ride from Rinthos. You've been drifting in and out for hours. A fever, Simon thinks. Him, Remy, you, and me—we're all alive and safe. Hob is with us as well."

"Hob." Memories of the Empire outpost came rushing back to her: Smoke drifting up from the ground. Running toward the waiting lines of adatrox, two whining bombardiers in her hands.

Only then did Eliana register the searing pain on her back. She winced, and Navi hissed in sympathy.

"Simon and I did the best we could," Navi said, "but the blast caught the entire back of your body. Please, lie down on your stomach."

Eliana obeyed, her vision tilting. The wounds must indeed have been terrible. She'd never suffered from such severe pain hours after an injury.

"The compound," she bit out. "Did they survive? Patrik and...?" She could not make herself say Linnet's name.

Navi sat beside her. "I believe most of the refugees got away, yes. Patrik stayed to help evacuate them to a new site. Hob has come with us to meet a contact in Rinthos who can help with supplies for the survivors. The smoke ruined much of their food. But, Eliana, you saved them. What adatrox you didn't destroy, Simon picked off easily. What you did... I've never seen anything like that."

Eliana lay very still, her cheek pressed to the blanket. Her vision was beginning to settle in the darkness. Remy lay nearby, curled up at the base of a tree. Even as he slept, his brow creased with worry. Beside him sat Simon, arms crossed over his chest, eyes closed. In sleep, he looked almost peaceful. The silver ribbons of his scars shivered like ghosts in the shifting moonlight.

Then Eliana heard footsteps in the woods and tensed.

"It's only Hob," Navi whispered. "He's on watch. Please, try to rest."

"That's unlikely. Where are my knives?" Then she remembered Lord Morbrae confiscating them and groaned. "They're gone, aren't they?"

"Actually, Simon retrieved them from the outpost. Now Remy has them. He won't let any of us touch them."

Eliana let out a tired, relieved laugh. "And now...we go to Rinthos."

"Yes. There, we'll be able to find better medicine for your back than what Hob helped us scrape together." She paused. "I'm sorry to say I think you'll be scarred permanently from it. But you will live."

Eliana closed her eyes. Exhausted tears slid down her cheeks.

"Oh, Eliana." Navi cupped her face with one soft hand. "How can I help you? I feel useless."

"You can't help me. Just leave me be. Please."

For a time, Navi was blessedly quiet. But even in the silence, broken only by the whisper of wind and Hob's occasional steady tread, Eliana could not find her way back to sleep.

She opened her eyes, knowing that she must say *something*, or this dead, black feeling in her chest would rise up and engulf her. "Navi?"

"Yes?"

"I don't know, I...I can't sleep."

"Shall I tell you a story?" There was a smile in Navi's voice.

"You saw things in Lord Arkelion's palace. Didn't you?"

A new stillness fell over them. Navi's voice was careful. "What kind of things?"

Impossible things.

Men with slit throats, somehow walking again.

Men with black eyes, speaking from across a vast ocean.

"Did you ever see...odd behavior from Lord Arkelion?" Eliana asked. "Or from visiting generals?"

"I'm not sure I know what you mean by odd behavior."

But the slightly stilted quality of Navi's voice told Eliana that in fact she did know. "Lord Morbrae. I slit his throat, yet there he was, minutes later, walking once more. His neck was whole. No wound."

"Here," Navi offered. "Water."

Eliana allowed Navi to help her take a few greedy sips from Simon's canteen, then lay back down with a moan.

"And before that," she added. "I was in his lap. I was prepared to pleasure him in exchange for amnesty. I bent to kiss him, and then..."

Eliana's voice had grown so quiet Navi had to bend low to hear.

"And then?" she prompted.

"I saw…a vision," Eliana said. "His eyes locked with mine, and I was taken elsewhere. I was both at the outpost and also across the ocean. I was in Celdaria, in a beautiful city, larger than any I've seen. In Elysium."

Navi's eyes were wide with astonishment. "The Emperor's city?"

"He spoke to me."

"Not the Emperor?"

Eliana nodded once. The pain firing up her legs, back, and skull was so violent it nearly made her sick over Navi's boots.

"Those prisoners," Eliana whispered, squeezing her eyes shut. She was losing her grip on the conversation. Her questions scattered and faded. "At the outpost. They were kept in cages. The fire… They couldn't get out. I heard them screaming."

"Hush now." Navi's hand pressed hers gently. "Think of Crown's Hollow. You saved many lives there."

"I'm a murderer, Navi. Tell me I'm not."

Navi did not reply.

"Ah," Eliana murmured. "A telling silence."

"All I will say," said Navi, "is that you have done the best you could with what was given to you."

"How disappointing. I'd hoped you wouldn't lie to me." Eliana stared bleakly out into the night. Her cheeks were on fire. She pressed them into the cool mud. "He recognized me, you know."

Navi leaned closer. "What? Say that again."

"He recognized me. The Emperor."

Just before Eliana's eyes drifted shut, she saw Simon's own eyes open to watch her.

"He saw my face, and he asked me where I was," she mumbled.

"Eliana?" came Simon's voice, near now, and gentler than she'd ever heard it. Almost asleep, she turned to face it, like turning her face up to the sun.

"Simon." She smiled, fuzzy-headed. "There you are."

"Eliana, say that again. What you told Navi."

"I saw the Emperor. He reached for me. He asked where I was."

"And did you tell him?" One of Simon's hands cupped her cheek, the other, gingerly, the bandaged back of her head. "Eliana, listen to me, this is very important: Did you tell him?"

"No." Her eyes fluttered shut. "I told him nothing."

"Good." Simon helped her settle with her head in his lap. His thumb caressed her forehead. "That's very good. You're all right now. You're all right. Sleep."

Eliana dreamed of death, as she so often did.

She dreamed of everyone's death but her own.

She reigned, a corona of light blazing around her head, over a world of scorched earth.

⭢ 25 ⭠

RIELLE

"I believe us to be lost. How can we fight creatures whose lives stretch before them like infinite roads, who can sift through minds as easily as a child crafts castles on the shore? We have made a mistake, engaging the angels. All our power pales in comparison to that of their ageless minds."

—Surviving journals of Saint Grimvald of Borsvall
September 25, Year 1547 of the First Age

Two nights after the metal trial, Rielle lay in bed, pretending to be asleep for the sake of Evyline, who stood placidly at the door to her rooms.

But her mind raced, and her blood thrummed hot with nerves.

Well? She swallowed hard. She could not delay this moment any longer. *Are you there, Corien? It's time for us to talk.*

Of course I'm here, Rielle, came his voice at once. *I always am.*

She frowned into her pillow. *I don't find that particularly comforting.*

You should. Unlike your other friends, I have no desire to see you killed.

So, we're friends then, you and I?

His response came like a sigh across her skin: *I very much hope so.*

She drew her blanket tighter around her body. *How can I be friends with someone I've never met? Someone I'm not even sure is real?*

A delicate sensation slid down her spine, like the brush of a gentle finger, then faded near the dip of her lower back.

Don't I feel real? came the response.

Rielle shivered. *Are you a spirit? A ghost?*

No.

Then why is it that I can feel you and hear you, but I cannot see you?

It is my own special way of talking to you from afar, my dear. There was a shifting in Rielle's mind, of both sound and sensation, as though Corien were settling himself comfortably beside her. *I can send you my thoughts, and you can send me yours. I can send you how I feel, and I can sense your feelings in return.* He paused. Then, with a tiny smile curling his voice, almost shyly: *I can send you the feeling of how I would like to touch you. And you can do the same back to me if you wish.*

A war was taking place inside Rielle's body, between cold fear and the desire to say at once: *Touch me, then.*

And if I don't wish for you to touch me? she managed to think.

Then I won't. I have been too forward. Forgive me.

Just don't do it again. She paused, her cheeks flaming. *Unless I ask you to.*

Of course. He sounded quietly pleased. *So, you wanted to talk to me. You have questions, I think.*

Many.

That is understandable. Another shift. She had the sense of him sitting on the edge of a divan, leaning forward with his elbows on his knees.

But his face was a blur.

First, she began, *what do you look like?*

I can show you if you'd like. You're already partway there.

Rielle's heart beat faster. *You are sitting on a divan, then? I can see the faint shape of you.*

Indeed. Concentrate on the lines of my body. Try to make them sharper, as if tracing me with a pen.

She obeyed. Slowly, the blurred figure came into focus—a slender, tall, pale man, with fine black hair in shining waves that curled softly at his ears. Fine cheekbones, as if chiseled from white marble. Large eyes of a bright, pale blue. Full lips that stretched into a fond smile when her eyes met his.

"Hello, Rielle," he said, and his voice was no longer simply in her mind. He was there; he was *speaking* to her.

She gasped, blinked, and her concentration broke. Corien disappeared. She was suddenly, terribly alone in her bed, in the dark quiet of her rooms. She struggled to catch her breath, her mouth dry.

Where did you go?

I'm still here, he replied.

I lost you, I— She swallowed. Her skin felt cold and clammy, now that she no longer stood near him.

It's difficult right now for us to communicate as completely as we could. In time, we'll manage it. It requires practice, and—here his voice darkened slightly—*you have so very many things demanding your attention right now.*

The trials.

Yes, among others. There was a tense silence, and then he whispered, *Rielle, may I touch you?*

She drew in a tight breath.

Nothing untoward. I swear it.

Rielle watched the star-spotted night sky beyond her windows. *First, tell me: What are you?*

What am I? He sounded playfully put out. *Dearest, you insult me. I am altogether a person, you know, with an identity and a name.*

But you aren't human. Humans can't talk like this, using only their minds. The night before the metal trial, you showed me a memory. One of my own memories, one I'd forgotten.

Yes, I did.

Corien...that's extraordinary.

I suppose it is, to you.

Humans can't do such things.

That is true.

She waited for him to say more, and when he didn't, she realized he was waiting for her to say what she already knew, what she'd known with increasing certainty for weeks now.

You're an angel.

His response, when it came at last, was toneless: *I am.*

Rielle climbed out of bed, tossing the linens aside. Only when standing did she realize that her nightgown clung to her body, damp with sweat.

"My lady?" inquired Evyline from the door. "Is everything all right?"

"Of course." Rielle could hardly hear herself over the thrum of fear in her veins. "I only need a glass of water."

Somehow, she made it into her bathing room and shut the door behind her. She stumbled to the washbasin, splashed water on her face, then poured herself a glass and let it sit untouched.

She leaned heavily against her vanity's marble countertop, struggling to steady herself. She felt light-headed, detached from her limbs.

Rielle, please sit down. Corien's voice was gentle. *You'll fall and hit your head.*

I wish to stand, she snapped.

Very well. Is there anything I can do to help?

You're lying to me, she managed at last.

You know I'm not.

All the angels are gone. They're in the Deep. The saints banished them there, locked them beyond the Gate.

No gate stands forever, Corien interrupted.

Rielle stalked across the room to stand before the enormous gilded mirror that stood propped up against the far wall. She looked rumpled and terrified, her green eyes bright and wide, her dark hair falling loose from her braid, her nightgown dwarfing her in the grand, tiled room.

Just think what sort of rooms they'll give you once they've made you their beloved Sun Queen, Corien remarked, his voice edged. *A staggering thought, isn't it?*

Stop talking to me.

You don't mean that.

Rielle began to pace. *I think I know my own mind.*

And I know your mind too. Such a spectacular thing it is.

Get out. She stopped midstride, fists clenched at her sides. *Right this moment. Get out of my head, and leave me be.*

They will use you, Rielle, he said at last, urgently now. *They will lift you higher and higher, dress you in jewels and crowns, and when they realize who you really are, what lives inside you, they will spurn you, and you will be left alone—*

"Get out!" she screamed, and when he obeyed, she felt his departure like a thread being tugged out of an infinite canvas until finally snapping free.

The sensation left her feeling unmade. She sat down hard on the edge of her bathing tub.

Evyline barged into the room, sword raised. "My lady! Are you hurt?"

"No." Rielle wiped her eyes with a shaking hand. "Evyline, I think I've had a terrible nightmare. I don't feel quite myself."

Evyline sheathed her sword and hurried forward. "Here, my lady. I'll help you back to bed and send for some tea. And a cinnamon cake, perhaps?"

Rielle leaned heavily into Evyline's broad body. "Perhaps three cakes would do the trick."

"Three cakes are, generally speaking, much more effective than one, my lady."

Rielle's smile was faint and brought prickling tears to her eyes. "Bless you, Evyline. I've taught you well."

Evyline helped Rielle settle back into bed. "I'll return shortly, my lady. I'll send in Dashiell to watch over you."

Rielle nodded and wrapped herself back into her blankets.

The angels are all gone, Rielle told herself, shivering in her bed and staring at the ceiling. If she thought it enough times, perhaps she could make it a real truth, just as she had remade the world of the metal cage into one she could control.

She squeezed her eyes shut and tried not to think about the sweet, lonely ache that lingered against her skin where Corien's touch had once been.

The angels are all gone.

The angels are all gone.

But the prayer did not help.

Rielle couldn't sleep the rest of the night, which left her unfocused and sloppy the next day as her father drove her ruthlessly through her conditioning exercises. And even when she settled into bed the night after, her muscles aching, sleep eluded her.

Corien, apparently, had taken her request quite seriously. She could neither hear nor sense him. Her mind felt hollow as a cave.

Part of her was glad.

But the part of her that lay restlessly in her too-large bed, unsettled and on edge, yearned for company.

And when she thought of his final words to her—*They will spurn you, and you will be left alone*—the hollow of her mind expanded into her heart until all she could feel was a desperate, endless sadness.

"I don't want to be alone," she whispered against her pillow.

She held her breath, waiting. Would Corien answer her? Send her some sort of reassurance?

Five breaths. Ten.

He said nothing.

She flung aside her linens, yanked the heavy plum-and-gold dressing gown from her bedside chair, and marched toward the door to her rooms.

Evyline snapped to attention. "Are we going somewhere, my lady?"

"Indeed we are, Evyline. I need some fresh air."

She considered going straight to Tal and confessing everything to him: Corien, the angels, the frustration blazing hot paths through her body.

But instead Rielle slipped into the darkened castle—seeking solace, craving company.

And recklessly, secretly hoping at each turn of Baingarde's moon-painted corridors, that she would see Corien standing there, with an apology on his lips and a sly kiss for her own.

~ 26 ~

ELIANA

"It is widely believed that the creation of the Gate, which ended the Angelic Wars, began the end of magic as it once was. If the Gate was the beginning of the end, then the Fall of the Blood Queen was the true ending. With her death, the Blood Queen stamped out every remaining spark of ancient power, leaving the world ravaged and dim."

—Foreword to a collection of Venteran children's tales entitled *Stories of a Forgotten Age*

Can you walk?"

Gingerly, Eliana stood and gave Simon a tight nod.

She hoped she was pretending the right amount of pain. Remy squeezed her hand, and she glanced down at him with a smile she tried to make reassuring.

He, of course, would know the truth by the look on her face. If they hadn't healed completely, her wounds from the bombardier blast were now well enough that Eliana could feel no pain, save a dull soreness in her muscles. Over the last few hours of sleep, it seemed, her wounds had closed. Her flesh had repaired itself.

And, Eliana knew, the next time Navi or Simon insisted on changing her bandages, she would have to lie. Or flee. Or be found out.

But found out for what? Was she one of *them*? Whatever Lord

Morbrae was—whatever strangeness gave him his liquid black eyes, the gaunt hunger of his cheeks, the ability to repair a slit throat and walk away whole—was Eliana also such a creature?

A wave of disgust swelled in her throat.

I don't have black eyes.

I have eaten, and I have had lovers. My hunger was sated, and the loving felt good and always has.

But…

But my body was covered with burns. And now, it is not.

She had always known that her body's ability to heal itself faster and more thoroughly than anyone else's was…unusual, to say the least. Impossible and unthinkable. She had, however, always explained it away when she lay awake at night, endlessly worrying. Or when she had first confessed to Remy by cutting open her arm in front of him, only for it to sew itself healed a moment later.

His horrified eyes had lit up with wonder.

"El," he had whispered, "that's some kind of magic."

"Ridiculous," she'd replied, her heart pounding but her voice cool. "Magic does not exist."

"But it did, once. Maybe some of it survived Queen Rielle's Fall."

Eliana had snorted. "Doubtful. That bitch was a lot of things, but she wasn't sloppy. She wouldn't have left us any magic, not even a scrap."

"So how do you explain it, then?"

She had shrugged, grinning. "I won't argue with my body being a wonder. Harkan could tell you that much—"

Remy had clapped his hands over his ears. "Please, spare me."

"I suppose I'm just more resilient than most." She hadn't really believed that inane explanation, even then. But what choice did she have? Any other possibility would be…too much to consider. Preposterous at best and dangerous at worst. And she had given up her hope for miracles years ago.

"Anyway," she had continued, "I hope you won't tell anyone. Not even Mother. Because—"

"Because if anyone found out, they'd use you as a weapon. Even more than the Empire already does."

"Right," she said stiffly after a pause. "Exactly."

He had nodded. "I'm still going to believe it's magic though. I have to."

"Whatever lies you have to tell yourself, Remy, are no business of mine."

But now that Eliana had seen Lord Morbrae, the knowledge of what her body could do—the question of what that meant—sat noxiously inside her.

Am I one of them? she thought, reaching back to scratch her shoulder. *Or will I* become *one of them?*

Out of the corner of her eye, she saw Hob staring at her and remembered to wince as she moved.

"Quickly and quietly," Simon muttered, "slip into the crowd along with everyone else. Stay close."

Together, their ragged group of five slowly moved onto the broad, crowded road that led to the city of Rinthos.

It was a path congested with travelers: Refugees seeking shelter from the wild lands beyond. Small clusters of musicians fiddling baudy traveling songs and singing laments for the dead. A few merchants shilling wares—clothes, medicines, drugs, idols of the Emperor carved out of wood and small enough to wear around one's neck.

Eliana kept her gait stiff, uneven, and her eyes focused straight ahead on the city gates. Adatrox drifted throughout the crowd and patrolled the perimeter wall, but they did not stop anyone from passing through the city gates. Not even the Empire, it seemed, wanted to do the work of clearing out the massive, clogged sprawl that was Rinthos.

It was the perfect place to hide.

It was also, quite possibly, a disastrous place to hide. Surely the Empire knew of what had happened at the outpost, had heard of the girl blowing apart an entire regiment of adatrox and, perhaps, surviving. An adatrox could have seen Simon retrieve her body from the wreckage, flee on horseback with her. Maybe this adatrox had sent a message to Lord Morbrae.

Maybe the general's ashes, blown apart when the outpost detonated, had coalesced back into a solid frame. Maybe he was, at this very moment, stalking their trail.

Eliana counted her breaths until her thoughts stopped spinning.

They had no choice; they had to stop in Rinthos. Hob needed to meet his contact, who would help resupply Patrik, his soldiers, and the now-homeless refugees.

And Eliana, as far as they knew, desperately needed medicine.

As they passed through the outer wall of Rinthos, Eliana glanced up at the overcrowded city towering above her and licked her cracked lips out of sheer uneasiness. An interweaving network of stone paths, wooden bridges, and twisting staircases stretched high above them, connecting apartment to apartment and high road to low road. Not far from the city was the Sea of Bones, which churned between Ventera and the occupied kingdom of Meridian. A thin film of sand coated the crumbling roads, and whenever they passed one of the canals that snaked through the city, the pungent smell of fish and waste was enough to turn Eliana's already restless stomach.

They had been navigating the choked streets of Rinthos for an hour when they finally found Sanctuary's entrance—an unremarkable door at first glance, coated in peeling gray paint and bolted with a broken lock.

But past the door, down a narrow staircase, they emerged into a small, damp room manned by three masked guards. Each towered two heads above even Simon.

The lead guard stopped Simon with a curved blade at his throat.

Simon lowered his hood, then uttered something in a lyrical language Eliana didn't recognize. Not traditional Venteran and not the plain common tongue.

Beside her, Remy sucked in a breath.

Whatever Simon had said must have been the right thing to say. The guards moved aside; one of them unlatched the heavy metal door on the far wall.

Simon inclined his head, then led the way into the dark, low-ceilinged rooms beyond.

Sanctuary.

The smell of the city's infamous gambling pits slapped Eliana like a fetid hand—cooking meat, pipe smoke, scented oils, ale and wine, sweat-stained bodies, the tang of blood.

"What language was that?" Eliana whispered to Remy as they followed Simon inside.

"Old Celdarian," Remy whispered back, his fingers tight around her own.

A chill went down Eliana's back. "The language of the Blood Queen."

"And of the Lightbringer," Navi added.

Eliana glanced at her, resisting the urge to touch the necklace beneath her shirt.

Sanctuary was a cramped and raucous city-within-a-city. Five circular levels, lit by gas lamps at every column support, looked down upon a floor packed with people. They gathered at tables, hands full of cards, or around pits where vicious dogs tore at each other. Men in ragged trousers beat their opponents to a pulp in square wire cages, while onlookers shouted out their wagers and thrust fistfuls of money into the air.

And above, on each of the mezzanines looking down over the fighting pits, the shadows teemed with shapes—couples whispering over their drinks, scantily clad dancers writhing on tabletops. Card players masked in clouds of smoke gathered on cushions surrounding low tables. One man, so corpulent Eliana could not see his eyes within the folds of his skin, shouted out with wet, choking laughter as two men wrestled at his feet. On the third level, a woman so pale that both her skin and hair glowed white in the candlelit gloom held court in a private curtained parlor. A beautiful young man wearing hardly enough to cover himself lounged beside her, muscles shimmering with powder.

They passed the couple and disappeared into a dark, narrow corridor flanked by two hooded figures, their faces hidden. Eliana's fingers itched to grab Arabeth.

A curtain dropped closed behind them, plunging them into silence. Their footsteps disappeared in the corridor's plush carpet. Tiny gas lamps softly lit the way.

"A charming place," Navi observed mildly.

A smirk twitched at Eliana's mouth. "Perhaps we should enter Simon into one of those fights downstairs, win ourselves some coin for your refugees, Hob."

Simon stopped at a door in the wall. "Only if you are my opponent, Dread. We could re-create our first meeting for everyone."

"The one when I would've beaten you, had you not pulled a gun on me?"

"The one when I knocked you soundly on your ass." Then he rapped once on the door. A metal slat in the wood snapped open, and Simon uttered another sentence in Old Celdarian.

At once, the door opened to a quiet chamber lined with silent robed figures. A muscled, middle-aged woman with amber-brown skin rushed out from a side door, straight for Hob. "Thank God you're alive!" She hugged him fiercely, clapped a hand on his back. "We heard about the attack on—"

The woman had seen Navi, and after a moment of frozen shock, she sank to her knees.

"Your Highness," she whispered. "Forgive me. I knew you would be here, and yet seeing you in the flesh—" She looked up at Navi, eyes glittering with tears. "Since hearing of your flight from Astavar, and then seeing the intelligence you sent through Red Crown from Orline... My lady, I prayed every day that the Queen's light would guide you home to us."

Navi helped the woman rise, her own eyes bright. "You are from Astavar?"

"I am, my lady. But Red Crown is my allegiance. I have not seen home since the Empire took Ventera."

"Please, tell me if I can bring back with me any messages for your loved ones."

"I have no loved ones, my lady." The woman set her jaw. "They all came with me to fight for Ventera. I am the only one left."

Navi closed her eyes. "My sister, your courage leaves me without words."

"Well!" The woman sniffed loudly and wiped her eyes. "Lucky for you, my lady, I've enough words for us all. Hob?" She slapped a hand onto his shoulder. Hob grimaced. "I know you need my help, for your Patrik and your wandering rebel babes. And my help you shall have. But first, baths. You all smell like shit."

"Who is this?" Eliana jerked her head at the woman. "Will anyone introduce us, or will we all just stand here and let her ramble on?"

"I know who you are." The woman stepped back from Hob and considered Eliana with narrowed eyes. "You're the Dread of Orline. You ruined the raid. You almost got everyone at Crown's Hollow killed." She looked Eliana up and down, then spat in her face. "My name's Camille. I've got enough paid swords in this place to fill a temple. So don't fuck with me, girl. Or it'll be your end."

Then she stepped back, smiled brightly at everyone, and clapped her hands. Four of the robed figures glided forward.

"We've prepared bathing rooms for you. Please don't talk to me again until you smell better. Oh! Little one." Camille smiled at Remy. "You're a sweet fellow. To whom do you belong?"

Remy lifted his chin and took Eliana's hand. "To my sister."

Camille's face hardened. "Well, that's a shame, isn't it?"

He glared back at her. "Not to me."

Even to Eliana, the smug smile she shot at Camille felt insufferable.

But upon entering the bathing chamber, Eliana's mind caught up with itself, and her happiness died.

Shit.

It was a gorgeously appointed room—walls of white polished stone, dressing screens covered with brocaded fabric in plum and turquoise, cushioned settees piled high with bath linens, baskets of soap, bottles of oils and lotions.

In the center of the space bubbled an enormous circular pool. A fountain stood at its center, featuring a slender statue of Saint Tameryn combing shadows from her hair.

They were to bathe here. Eliana *wanted*, desperately, to bathe. But first Navi would want to change her bandages. She would see Eliana's smooth, unblemished back. Simon and Hob had taken another chamber—*thank God*—but Navi was bad enough.

Eliana released Remy's hand and began backing away from the pool.

"El?" He glanced at her, yawning, then froze. "*Oh.*"

Navi gazed happily at the pool and let out a contented sigh. "God, it'll feel good to remember what it's like to be a proper human again. Eliana, let's change your bandages."

"Here you are, my lady," murmured one of the bustling attendants. She handed Navi a basket of clean white cloths. "The Wolf told us you would need these. We are trained as healers, my lady. Shall we help you?"

"Oh, that would be lovely. Eliana?" Navi frowned when she saw Eliana inching toward the door. "What are you doing?"

"I don't want to change my bandages." Eliana's panic was so complete that she could think of nothing else to say. "They're fine."

Navi's smile was bewildered. "They'll get infected if we don't. It's been hours. Come here."

One of the attendants moved toward Eliana, bowed, then reached out to guide her down the steps toward the pool.

Eliana slapped her away. "Get away from me!"

Navi stared at her. "What in God's name is wrong with you?"

"Don't come any closer."

"Tell me what's wrong. Maybe I can help."

Eliana let out a burst of incredulous laughter. "I need help from no one."

"You're delirious. Your fever has returned."

"Just leave her alone!" Remy cried out.

Before Eliana could move, still frozen with fear, Navi had lunged, spun her around, and pinned her, front first, against one of the room's smooth marble columns. A familiar blade pressed into Eliana's side.

Arabeth, she thought faintly, *you traitor*. She wanted to twist away, but remembered her supposed wounds.

"You're hurting me," she gasped out. "Please, my burns—"

"This knife of yours is my favorite," Navi said tightly. "I couldn't resist swiping it when I had the chance. I'll give it back, perhaps. If you don't make me angry. You're hiding something from me. Tell me what it is."

"Navi, please!" Remy's voice was near tears. "Let her go!"

"Sweet Navi," said Eliana, Navi's cheek so close to her own she could smell the girl's stale breath. "And I thought you wanted us to be friends."

"I do." Navi sounded genuinely sorry. "But if you don't answer me, I'll knock you out and fetch Simon, and *he* will change your bandages, and you won't be able to stop him."

Eliana let out a desperate growl. "Would you like to wager on that?"

"You've been acting strangely for days now. It's not the fever nor your wounds. You're planning something. Another escape? Will you bring death down upon Rinthos like you nearly did on Crown's Hollow?"

"I'm planning nothing."

"Then what is it?"

Eliana realized too late that her eyes were filling with sudden, exhausted tears.

Navi's expression softened. "What are you afraid of?"

"El, don't," Remy warned.

Eliana glanced past Navi at her brother, and then at the attendants waiting frozen nearby. And she realized, with a sick twist deep in her gut, that she wanted this. She wanted to tell someone who could help her sift through her questions—Lord Morbrae's throat, the vision of the Emperor, her own impossible body—and find an answer.

And if she was going to tell someone...better Navi than Simon.

She took a shuddering breath. "Leave us," she said quietly.

Silence. Navi turned to the two attendants. "Do as she commands. Say nothing of this."

They bowed their heads and glided out of the room. Once the doors had closed behind them, Eliana closed her eyes. "All right." She let out a long, slow exhale. "All right."

Remy's tearful voice came out choked. "El, don't. *Please.*"

"I want to."

Navi stepped away and lowered Arabeth, her expression grave. "What is it, Eliana?"

Eliana hesitated, then, still facing the column, shrugged off her jacket. She pulled off her bloodstained tunic to reveal the dirty bandages beneath. Dressed only in her boots and trousers, she whispered, "Take them off, and you'll see."

Navi gently began removing the bandages wrapped around Eliana's torso. When the first bandage gave way, Navi gasped.

Shivering, Eliana leaned her forehead against the wall, crossed her arms over her chest, and waited for Navi to finish. She had never felt more vulnerable in her life.

"Eliana..." Navi traced her fingers over the muscles of Eliana's bare back. "They're gone. Your burns... It's like they were never there. I don't understand."

"You won't tell anyone." She steeled herself and glanced over her shoulder. "Will you?"

After a moment of tense silence, Navi muttered, "Of course I won't tell anyone," and walked away.

Dizzy with relief, Eliana retrieved her tunic and slipped it back on. "If you did tell someone—"

"Then both Red Crown and the Empire would scramble to make you a great weapon, with no regard for your own safety, and that is not a fate I would wish on anyone." Navi's voice hardened. "This war has claimed the lives and bodies of too many women."

Then she turned, thoughtful. "Tell me how it started. Not just this one time, I assume?"

Eliana took a steadying breath. "It's always been like this. When I was small, I thought nothing of it. I'd fall, scrape my leg, and it would heal almost instantly. I figured, ah, well, that's lucky, and moved on. But as I grew older, I realized it was…an unusual thing."

"To put it mildly," Navi said with a troubled smile.

"I told Remy, eventually." Eliana found Remy huddled miserably on one of the cushioned benches beside the pool. She sat beside him, pulled him close. He turned gratefully into her side. "He helped me keep it a secret from our parents, even from Harkan. My friend. My partner." It was the first time she had said Harkan's name since saying goodbye to him on that awful day in Orline. Saying it felt like plucking a physical thing from her heart, leaving a hollow place behind. "I'm sure Harkan noticed—we were too close for him not to—but he never said anything. I don't know why. To respect my decision not to confide in him about it, I suppose." She shook her head. "I did not deserve a friend such as he was."

Navi paced quietly. Then she stopped, staring down at the rippling water.

"You're worried because you saw the same thing happen to Lord Morbrae as has happened to you all your life." Navi looked up, pity on her face. "You're worried that you're one of them."

"But she isn't!" Remy's face flushed angrily. "Their eyes are black. Hers aren't. They're evil, and she isn't."

"I agree, Remy," said Navi, "as someone who has spent too much time among their kind. You are not one of them, Eliana. Your face doesn't hold that same hunger. The air doesn't shift wrongly around your body, as if you don't quite fit in this world."

"What are they, then?" Eliana asked quietly. "What did you see when you lived in the maidensfold?"

Navi sat on a cushioned bench with her shoulders high and tense. "I saw men who glutted themselves and still hungered. Who took lover after lover to their beds and never felt sated. I lay with generals who begged me to carve up their bodies and who threatened to carve up my own if I wouldn't obey—and then, as they writhed beneath me, their flesh healed, and they howled in despair."

Navi drew in a long, slow breath. "Lord Arkelion took quite a liking to me and often summoned me to his rooms. Sometimes, when looking into those black eyes of his, I would see things."

"Like I saw the Emperor," Eliana murmured. "I looked into Lord Morbrae's eyes, and suddenly there he was. And there was Celdaria."

"Yes." Navi looked up, her expression haunted. "Very much like that. When with His Lordship, I saw things I would not understand. Visions. Images. And all of them were of wrath and revenge. Blood-darkened hills. A void that spun me farther and farther away from the light. I would feel these images in my blood after leaving him, like he had infected me with an echo of whatever sickness plagues him. I would return to the maidensfold and keep myself away from the others until the feeling had passed. I was afraid of myself. I feared I would lash out, hurt them."

Navi shook her head. "These men, they are made of a violence I could never have imagined."

"They're not men," Remy said firmly into the silence that followed. "They're angels."

RIELLE

"I have encouraged our young prince to split his time between the House of Light and the Forge, for he must not only study sunlight, but also craft a casting strong enough to contain his considerable power—though he did not seem too keen on the idea of a sword. The boy would rather his casting be some dusty tome as big as his torso."

—Journal of Grand Magister Ardeline Guillory
of the House of Light
Year 983 of the Second Age

The gardens behind Baingarde were Rielle's favorite place in the world. She, Audric, and Ludivine had spent many hours of their childhood running down the hushed dirt paths, crafting secret hideaways in grassy hollows and creeping around the seeing pools that surrounded the royal catacombs.

Rielle smiled, remembering the skipping-stones game the three of them had loved to play. The game was to jump across the seeing pools using the moss-slicked stones as a path. Anyone who fell would be forever haunted by the ghosts of dead kings and queens.

The pools' still black water had always reminded Rielle of unkind mirrors and made her wonder if a secret tunnel existed somewhere beneath the water, into which she might fall and disappear forever.

In that secret world, young Rielle had often thought, *would it be all right to have murdered your mother? Would the people there care at all?*

For an instant she could feel Audric and Ludivine on either side of her. One holding her hand warmly; the other keeping a proper distance away, always, always.

Once her bare feet hit the path that led to the seeing pools, Rielle stopped and inhaled. She imagined the cool night air of the gardens seeping into her lungs and washing her troubled heart clean.

"Are you sure you don't require boots, my lady?" asked Evyline. "There's quite a chill."

Rielle looked back at her guard. "Will you leave me to wander alone for a while? I long for quiet."

Evyline made a small sound of disapproval. "I can be exceptionally quiet, my lady."

Rielle crossed her arms and glared at her.

After a long moment, Evyline sighed. "Very well, my lady. If I hear you yell in distress, I shall come running after you heroically."

"I would expect nothing less from you, dear Evyline."

Then Rielle slipped into the trees, following one of the narrow dirt paths. Soft pine needles littered the ground; dew-glittered ferns brushed the trailing hem of her dressing gown. Centuries before, Queen Katell had planted sorrow trees throughout the gardens of Baingarde in honor of Aryava, her fallen angel lover. Now the ancient trees sprawled low and far across the ground, their knotted black limbs heavy with thick clusters of pale pink flowers.

At last, Rielle emerged near the seeing pools. They stretched dark and tranquil toward the grass-covered mound that served as the entrance to the royal catacombs. Two torches flanked the great stone doors, which were marked with the seven temple sigils.

Rielle knelt at the edge of the closest pool and touched her fingers to her forehead, her temple, and her chest, to her throat, her palm, the nape of her neck, and finally to each of her closed eyes.

May the Queen's light guide you home, she prayed in honor of the fallen saints and the queens and kings who lay resting within the catacombs.

Then she rose to her feet, her dressing gown damp from the dew, and heard a low grunt.

She squinted through the mist rising over the pools and saw Audric on the other side of them, hugged by a cluster of sorrow trees. He wore only trousers and boots, his bare brown torso gleaming with sweat. With Illumenor in hand, he ran through exercise after exercise—cutting the air with the blade, whirling on his feet, dodging imaginary attackers.

The sight of him, lit by the moon from above and the humming sheen of Illumenor from below, was enough to make Rielle lose her breath. His expression was one of utter concentration—brow furrowed, eyes dark and grave.

"Couldn't sleep either?" Rielle called out.

He turned, lowered his sword. A broad smile spread across his face. "I don't sleep much these days."

She made her way toward him along the soft, grassy path between the seeing pools. "And why is that?"

"Oh, I don't know." He sheathed Illumenor, wiped his brow with a cloth. "When dear friends are forced into deadly situations week after week, it tends to keep me up at night."

"Sounds like your friends are more trouble than they're worth."

"Not at all." He stepped toward her, and when the moonlight fell over him, it illuminated the shadows beneath his eyes, the lines of worry about his mouth. "I'd bear a thousand sleepless nights if it meant my friends were safe."

She had to look away from him, her pulse fluttering in her throat. Being near Audric made her earlier loneliness seem more vast and inescapable than ever.

"Tell me," she said lightly, "what does it feel like for you? When you work magic."

His voice was thoughtful. "Like all the pieces of who I am are coming together as they were meant to. Like anything is possible, in that moment, for my focus is that complete and controlled. Like…like a really good stretch."

Rielle immediately pictured Audric in his bed, unclothed and curls tousled, sleepily stretching that long, lean body in a pool of sunlight.

She licked her dry lips, moved past him. At his nearness, the air crackled and stirred, warming her.

"You do have exceptional control," she murmured. "Does it ever… break?"

"I'm not sure I know what you mean."

Of course you don't, she thought irritably. But that wasn't fair. Just because she was on edge, sleepless, and terrified by the thought of where Corien could have gone and what he was doing and if there were other angels and if he would ever come back to her—that didn't give her the excuse to direct her anger at Audric.

He had done nothing wrong. He never did.

"You never do anything wrong," she blurted out, harsher than she'd meant to. *So much for not being angry at Audric.*

"Well, of course I do," he said, laughing. "Shall I remind you of a certain forbidden horse race?"

"I don't mean sneaking out and breaking our parents' rules. I mean, *real* wrong things. You're powerful, and yet do you ever…? Never mind. Of course you don't."

Rielle turned away to sit on the damp ground. "I don't even know what I'm saying," she muttered, wrapping her arms around her middle. "I need to sleep, but I can't. My mind is racing in circles."

After a moment, she looked up to see Audric settling in the grass at her side. He'd thrown his tunic back on, she noticed with deep regret.

"If you try to explain," he said gently, "I'll listen."

For a long time, she stared at her toes curling in the damp grass. She needed to return to her bed, try for some proper rest. Another day of training with her father and poring over books at the House of Night library with Ludivine in preparation for the next trial. She had an appointment with the Archon in the afternoon. He insisted on regular interviews throughout the trials, during which he inquired as to her health, her state of mind, what she'd been eating and drinking, how she'd been sleeping, what her dreams had been like.

If only you knew, Your Holiness.

Audric placed a warm hand on hers. "Rielle, what is it? Tell me."

Slowly, she raised her gaze to his. He was so close she could count the thick dark lashes around his eyes, and she had a sudden vision of herself kissing the tender skin beneath them.

"During the metal trial," she whispered, "when I realized what the Archon had done, that he'd put children in the cage with me"—she swallowed, closed her eyes—"I wanted to hurt him."

"Well, God, Rielle, so did I!" Audric raked a hand through his hair with a slight, hard laugh. "I'd imagine everyone did. Is that what's bothering you? Darling, please don't let that keep you from sleep."

"It's not only that!" Rielle tore a clump of grass from the ground in frustration. "It's...it's so many things."

Even while my mother burned, I was glad to feel the power simmering at my fingers.

Even though I know Corien is an angel, I want him to come back to me.

Even though you belong to Ludivine...I want you for my own.

I want...I want. I crave. I hunger.

"I want so many things," she whispered, "and none of them are very good."

Audric cupped her face in his hand, guided her to look up at him. For a moment they sat frozen, Audric's mouth so close that Rielle could have lifted her chin and met his lips with her own.

Then Audric lowered his hand and looked away.

"We all have darkness inside us, Rielle," he said, his voice rough. "That is what it means to be human."

She shook her head slowly. "I think what it means to be human is that you are able to move past that darkness and do good in the world even so. And you, Audric"—she laughed a little—"I'd wager everything I am that you never experience such thoughts as I do. Sometimes your goodness shines so brightly that I want to devour you. Maybe if I have enough of you, that light you shine will stave off the wickedness that lives inside me."

She rubbed her brow. "I can't believe I'm saying these things. What you must think of me."

"I think of you what I have ever since I've known you." Audric reached for her hand, steadied it between his own. "That I'm glad you are beside me, and that I wish for you to always be."

She dared to look up at him, and when she did, she let out a soft, murmuring sound, leaned closer to him as if pulled by a cord connecting his body to her own. He cupped her face with one hand, let the other trail gentle fingers down her arm. The warmth of his body flooded through her; she shuddered and twisted to move closer to him.

"Audric," she murmured, closing her eyes. She touched her cheek to his, relished the gentle scrape of his jaw.

"If there is wickedness inside you, Rielle," Audric said hoarsely, his lips in her hair, "then I shall treasure it as I do every other part of you."

A soft touch of his fingers against her ribs; another at the back of her neck, sending a tremulous chill down her spine. She melted into him, slipping into his arms as easily as if she belonged there.

But then she remembered Ludivine.

She closed her eyes. "We shouldn't," she whispered, her body screaming at her to stop talking and touch him. "I... Audric, what about Lu?"

Audric moved slightly away from her. Sorrow fell across his face. "I know. You're right, I know."

Rielle propped herself up on her elbows, watching him carefully. "Do you love her?"

"She is dear to me, but...no. Not as I should."

"Then..." She reached for him, turned his face back to hers. Tears of shame rose in her eyes, but she couldn't tear her gaze away from the blazing need in his own. "Maybe just this once? For the memory of it."

He hesitated, glanced back through the trees toward Baingarde.

"The memory," he said slowly, "might make things harder."

"I don't care." She cupped his face in her hands, shook her head. "I want to anyway."

For a moment he was quiet, considering her. Then, a soft smile. His lips against her palm. "My wicked girl," he murmured and lowered his mouth sweetly onto hers.

The kiss was so careful, so gentle, that Rielle's heart ached with tenderness for him. She cried out softly against his mouth and hooked her arms around his neck. At her touch, he shivered and deepened the kiss with a groan. The moment shifted from something cautious, something fragile and slow, to a scorching, helpless need. His hands slid down her body, and she arched up into his touch. When she felt him hard against her leg, she tightened her arms around him and gasped against his cheek.

"Audric," she whispered, closing her eyes. "Yes. Yes, *please.*" She was dizzy with his nearness—his tongue opening her mouth, the soft murmurs of her name, the frantic nibbling gasps against her skin.

He gathered her body against his, fumbled beneath her dressing gown for the thin cotton of her nightgown, cupped her hips in his palms. It was like he couldn't make up his mind where to touch her, and Rielle basked in every moment of his indecision, twisting beneath him, tugging at his shirt to move him where she wanted. She snaked her fingers under his tunic, greedy for the hot, bare skin of his muscled back. He was so warm, so solid and sure. She closed her eyes, pressed her lips to his collarbone. Breathing him in felt like breathing in a summer's day.

"Closer," she murmured, smiling softly against his skin.

He slid a shaking hand up her nightgown, across her bare thigh. He let out a low, broken sound and pressed his forehead to her own, moved his hand up to draw slow circles across her belly, and then slipped lower to settle between her legs. She cried out sharply when he touched her where she most craved it, her body bowing up off the ground and her hands clutching the grass for anchor. The wet earth beneath her swelled, trembled; a soft steaming mist had begun to rise around their bodies. The breeze cooling Rielle's skin sharpened, gusting.

"I can't bear this," she whispered, hooking a leg around his, drawing his hips closer to her own. "Audric, *please*."

He lowered his mouth to her neck, let out an unsteady laugh. "Do you know how long I've wanted you, Rielle?" came his harsh whisper, hot and sweet against the hollow of her throat. "Do you know how long I've—"

A hound let out a baying howl. Then another.

Audric froze, pulled away to stare down at Rielle in dismay. Then he looked over his shoulder, and Rielle felt his body tense.

She propped herself up on her elbows, tugged down her nightgown to hide her bare legs, and when she saw who stood in the trees on the far side of the seeing pools, her stomach knotted with dread.

A man stood in the moonlight, flanked by his hounds: Lord Dervin Sauvillier.

Ludivine's father, staring right at them.

And his face was hard and white with fury.

⭢28⭠

ELIANA

"Though humans and angels were at war for cen-turies, they always had at least one common enemy: marques. The unclean children of traitors who lay with the enemy, their magic was neither of the mind nor the physical world but something else entirely. Were we right to hunt them down? Perhaps not. But we were right to fear them."

—Marked: An Exploration of the
Slaughtered Marque Race
by Varrick Keighley, Venteran scholar

Eliana closed her eyes, weary. "Remy, please don't start this non-sense again."

"Do humans look like they do?" Remy insisted.

"He has these pet theories, you see," Eliana told Navi.

"Their black eyes," he continued. "Everyone talks about them. You can hardly see the white around them, is what I've heard."

Eliana waved a dismissive hand. "Who knows what sorts of drugs the Emperor's generals have access to?"

"Then explain the visions you and Navi had when you were near them. The angels used mind-speak. All the old stories say so."

"And the old stories," Eliana bit out, "are just that. Stories from a world so long past that nobody can remember it, and most intelligent people believe it never existed quite as those stories say." She drew in a breath, more unsteadily than she would have liked. "People look anywhere for comfort during times like ours, Remy. Believe all you want in a world of angels and magic and mind-speak and travelers who can zip from one end of time to another, but please promise me you'll remember it is simply that. A belief. It isn't fact, it isn't proven—"

"And the way your body can heal itself?" Remy interrupted. "Is that belief? Or is it a fact?"

Eliana glared at him but said nothing. For of course he was right. She couldn't ignore the simple truth of her own body.

"Why won't you believe me?" came Remy's voice at last, softer now. "It's the only thing that makes sense after what you've seen, isn't it?"

"Because if the angels are alive and real, then we're well and truly fucked, and there's no point to any of this," Eliana snapped, rising to her feet. "No point to being in this room, no point to searching for Mother."

"No point to the people you've killed and betrayed," Navi finished.

Eliana whirled around to glare at her. "And no point to the years you've wasted as an Empire whore."

"El, stop it!" Remy hissed.

"*Spy* is the word I prefer," said Navi mildly. "It helps me fend off the nightmares."

Eliana stalked a few paces away with her arms crossed. She yearned, suddenly, for Simon to appear, if only so she could throw her knives at something that would fight back and show her no mercy.

"I'm sorry," she muttered, refusing to look at Navi. "I shouldn't have said that."

"No, you shouldn't have," said Navi. "But I accept your apology."

"They might not be angels," Remy admitted, after a moment. "I've never read any stories about angels with solid black eyes. But then, those visions you saw... That can't be nothing."

"If they aren't angels, what are they?" Eliana closed her eyes. "What am I?"

"Maybe," Navi said, after a moment, "you're a marque?"

"Part human, part angel?" Eliana turned back to her with a harsh bark of laughter. "Oh, good. That's better. I am wholly reassured."

"No, I don't think so," Remy mused, chewing on his lip. Excitement lit his eyes, grudgingly warming Eliana's seething black heart. Soon he'd be pacing, lecturing them like a miniature temple scholar. "Marques had markings on their backs where wings might be. And most of them were killed during the Angelic Wars, before Queen Rielle was even born. I think if El was a marque, there'd be some sign of it on her."

A sharp rap at the door made them all jump.

Navi turned at once where she sat. "Simon."

"Not a word to him," Eliana warned. "Or I swear to you, I'll rend—"

"Eliana, would you stop threatening me every five minutes? I told you I won't tell anyone, and I meant it." Navi hesitated, then approached slowly, one hand outstretched. In her palm lay Arabeth. "Take it. Please."

Eliana obeyed, snatching the knife away before Navi could change her mind. With Arabeth held securely in her fingers, some of the churning knots in her chest loosened their grip.

"I would like," Navi said with a small smile, "for things not to be that way between us. I would like us to be friends. For us to trust each other." She paused and looked to Remy. "If there really are angels in the world, as your brother thinks might be the case...we'll need to keep close all the friends we can find. Don't you agree?"

Another, sharper rap on the door. "Ignore me at your peril," came Simon's voice.

"You're an ass!" Eliana shouted over her shoulder.

"I've never claimed not to be," he replied.

Navi laughed softly. "Well? What do you think?"

Eliana shook her head. "I'm not good at having friends."

"I've rather fallen out of practice too. Shall we try to remember how it goes, together?"

"No, don't worry, I'm happy to wait out here forever," came Simon's irritated voice.

Remy burst out giggling, sounding more like a child than he had in long months. It melted the last of Eliana's resolve.

"I will try," she said at last and clasped Navi's hand in her own. "That's all I can promise."

Navi smiled warmly at her. "That is a gift. I thank you for it. Now." She raised her eyebrows at the door. "Shall I let him in?"

"Oh, please, allow me." With that, Eliana marched over to the bathing room door and flung it wide open with a grin—which promptly dropped off her face when she took in the sight of Simon standing there. Linen trousers sat low on his hips, and he wore nothing else, save a dark-blue towel slung over his shoulder. His ash-blond hair was tousled and wild, and his ruined skin… Eliana couldn't stop herself from looking at it. Beyond the layer of dirt coating him, thin silver lines and slender patches of skin shimmering with burn scars snaked across his chest and down his abdomen, slipping beneath the waistband of his trousers.

For a moment, Eliana found herself truly wondering what had happened to him—what had burned him, who had cut him—and what he had been like as a child, before the horrors of the world had found him.

"My, my," he murmured, his blue eyes flashing with unbridled glee. "Never have I seen the Dread struck so speechless. You know how to make a man feel good, I must say."

Eliana's mouth opened and shut, her cheeks flaming. Scrambling to think of something clever to say, her flustered mind could come up with nothing better than "Come to catch a peek at me naked, did you?" She winced.

But Simon only smiled. "Oh, Eliana," he murmured, his voice no longer playful, "I want so much more than simply a peek."

With one last, lingering look, he slipped past her into the bathing room, and Eliana was left standing at the door, alone and unsteady, her hand tingling from the brush of his fingers against her own.

It was a strange thing that had so unbalanced her, beyond her lonely body's reaction to his own. A sensation that sometimes came upon her when Simon was near, and one she couldn't explain. A sense of the familiar.

Like she had felt when standing on the terrace overlooking Celdaria during her vision of the Emperor—an irrational sense of belonging and rightness.

A sense, she thought, dazed and faintly irritated, *of home.*

⊹ 29 ⊹

RIELLE

"I don't know what either of you were thinking, and God knows I don't want you to explain it to me. But, if you need a place to hide or flee, know you can always come to me. Not even His Holiness knows of all the secret places in this city and how many of them belong to me."

—Message from Odo Laroche to Lady Rielle Dardenne
May 24, Year 998 of the Second Age

When Rielle left the House of Night archives the evening after she'd been caught with Audric, her eyes burned from reading far too many books about the physicality of shadows and the life of Saint Tameryn—all so meticulously annotated by Sloane that the sheer size of the woman's notes rivaled the books themselves.

Rielle's shoulders ached; her nerves felt as though they'd been sliced open and left hanging, frayed. She could think of nothing but the haven of her rooms and the fresh cinnamon cake Evyline had promised would be waiting on her bedside table.

But at least now, with the shadow trial in a mere two days' time, the plan that had been brewing in the back of her mind had solidified.

She pulled the archive doors shut behind her, Evyline and two others of her guard flanking her, then turned—and froze.

Ludivine sat in the hallway across from the archives, on an

iron-footed settee fringed with fine dark tassels. Her golden hair fell down her back in waves. The gray gown she wore shimmered beneath a field of elaborate burgundy, dark-blue, and russet embroidery: Sauvillier colors.

Rielle could think of nothing to greet her with except "Oh."

Ludivine stood, a small smile on her face, and held out her hand. "Walk with me, Rielle."

"I don't want to."

Ludivine took Rielle's hand and tucked it through the crook of her arm. "I insist."

Rielle glanced back at Evyline, whose hands rested on her sword.

Evyline nodded grimly. She and the other guards would, of course, stay near.

So Rielle took a deep breath and walked with Ludivine downstairs, through the quiet, dark hallways of the House of Night, until emerging into the central chapel. Dozens of worshippers had gathered throughout the room to pray—at the rims of black marble fountains, on floor cushions and prayer benches. Some knelt at the feet of Saint Tameryn's statue, which stood at the heart of the room. Daggers in hand, she looked up through the open rafters at the deepening violet sky.

At their entrance, everyone in the crowded chapel looked up from their prayers.

The silence was deafening. The whispers were worse.

Rielle planted her heels, determined to walk no farther. "Lu, please don't do this to me."

"Oh, come now," Ludivine murmured. "We're just going for a walk. What's the harm in that?"

So Rielle allowed Ludivine to lead her on through the room. At the feet of Saint Tameryn, Rielle and Ludivine knelt, kissed their fingers, touched the napes of their necks. Ludivine murmured greetings to everyone they passed. Rielle tried to do the same, tried to smile, but her words sounded strangled, and her smile felt like it had been fixed to her face with nails.

Once outside the House of Night, Rielle could no longer contain her frustration.

"Are you going to say nothing to me?" she whispered, as Ludivine guided them through one of the outer temple courtyards. Whistblooms, their pollen glowing a powdery white to match the stars, had begun to open along the paved path. "Will we parade about the city in awkward silence until I faint from the stress? Is that to be my punishment?"

"Calm yourself and act ordinary," said Ludivine under her breath. Then, louder: "Good evening, Lord Talan, Lady Esmeé. Aren't the whistblooms lovely this time of year?"

The courtiers in question bowed their heads, their eyes darting back and forth between Rielle and Ludivine as they murmured brief greetings and glided on through the foliage. Once a few paces away, Rielle heard their furious whispers begin.

Heat crawled up the back of her neck.

"Just a little farther," said Ludivine softly, but it wasn't until they'd passed through the outer courtyards of each of the seven temples that Ludivine finally turned them off the temple roads and onto a narrow side street.

Rielle felt weak with relief once they passed into the shadows of the apartment buildings crowding overhead.

"And that wasn't punishment?" She wiped her face with her sleeve, her hand shaking.

"No," said Ludivine calmly, leading Rielle down the tidy cobbled road. Patches of soft torchlight from brackets in the walls lit the way. The first Grand Magister of the Pyre had, centuries earlier, designed the torches in the temple district to light on their own at nightfall. "If you'd stop panicking for a moment, you would see I'm trying to help you. And please, put up your hood."

"*Help* me?"

"We saw hundreds of people just now," Ludivine said, raising both their hoods to cover their hair. "More importantly, *they* saw *us*. They saw two dear friends, arm in arm, on a leisurely stroll through the gardens. Just as we might have done on any night. Even if seeing us together quells only a fraction of the gossip racing through the city right now, it will be helpful to you, to Audric, and to me."

Ludivine turned them down a set of narrow steps that led to a lower neighborhood. They kept their hoods up and their faces down, avoiding eye contact with passersby. Evyline and her guard followed close behind.

"I don't know if my father will ever quite recover from what he saw," Ludivine muttered, "but I can at least show my support for you, as publicly and as often as I can."

"Why are you doing this?" Rielle watched her feet descend the steps through a film of tears. "You should hate me."

Ludivine blew out an impatient breath. "Rielle, look at me." She stopped them at a quiet landing where the staircase turned sharply right and took both Rielle's hands in her own. "*Look.*"

When Rielle met Ludivine's calm gaze, the terrible twist of pain in her chest robbed her of breath. "I'm sorry," she whispered. "Please, forgive me."

"Answer me this: Do you think I love Audric?"

Rielle blinked, caught off guard. "What? I..."

"Of course I do. We're cousins and dear friends, and I've known him all my life. He's my family. But do I love him like you do? Of course not."

Rielle's mouth dropped open. "I... Lu, what are you talking about?"

"And I know Audric feels the same about me. Do I wish you both had come to me, so we could discuss all of this like civilized people, instead of you rolling about half naked in the gardens for everyone to see? Yes, I very much do."

Rielle would surely die, right there on the stairs. "Lu, I'm so sorry, really. I don't know what came over us."

"Of course you do. You're in love with him, and he's in love with you, and you've been desperate to kiss each other for years now. It was only a matter of time. Do you know how exhausting it's been to sit back and watch the two of you dance around each other?"

"He isn't..." Would the shocks never end? "We're not..."

"Oh, please. It couldn't be more obvious than if you rolled around half naked in the gardens, actually. Oh. Wait."

"Well, sweet saints, Lu!" Rielle rubbed a hand over her forehead. "Why didn't you ever say anything to us? I didn't think... I mean, I *hoped*, but..."

Ludivine's smile was wicked. "Watching you may have been exhausting, but it was also entertaining. I could hardly resist that. Court is dull as toast most of the time."

Rielle threw up her hands. "What, and you would've waited to tell us the truth on the day of your wedding, I suppose?"

"Oh, I would have long before that." Ludivine drew Rielle's arm back through hers and continued down the stairs. "But why ruin my fun? Though I confess," and here Ludivine's voice became quite grave, "I regret my choice not to tell you that I knew sooner. I could have saved us all a lot of trouble. And now..."

"What will happen?" Rielle asked as they walked down another quiet residential street. "Now that your father has seen."

"He will speak to the king, of course," said Ludivine, "and ensure that the betrothal agreement remains intact."

Rielle's throat constricted painfully. "Of course."

"I don't expect he will make life pleasant for you. Neither will my aunt, the queen."

"Have they ever made life especially pleasant for me?"

"A fine point." Ludivine squinted down the darkening road, looking up and down the rows of tall stone houses. "But, truly, Rielle...please don't test anyone, not right now. Not with things so tense and fragile. Wait until my father's temper cools before trying any grand defiant gestures."

Rielle glanced sidelong at Ludivine, her nerves drawn suddenly even tighter. Ludivine couldn't know about the plan she was crafting for the shadow trial, could she? "What do you mean?"

"You know exactly what I mean. Be a proper candidate. Obey the Archon."

"And stay away from Audric?"

Ludivine turned, her face full of pity. "I don't ever want to ask you to do that."

"But I should," Rielle whispered. Her voice felt so thick with sadness that it was difficult to speak. "I've ruined everything, haven't I?"

"As I understand it," Ludivine replied wryly, "kissing involves not just one person, but two. If there is blame to be placed, it isn't only for you to bear."

Rielle followed Ludivine down a thin garden path. A stone archway choked with flowering vines marked the entrance to a tidy square courtyard. Beyond the courtyard stood a wide black door with a brass knob. A tarnished silver plate nailed into the stone above showed crude etchings of a mortar and pestle and a cluster of bundled leaves. Ludivine stopped beneath the archway.

"My darling," she murmured, her gaze soft on Rielle's face, "please don't let your heart grieve. Do you completely wring out my nerves? Yes, every day. But I love you as much as I ever have. And we will find a way to work this out. I will not see you live your life with a broken heart on my account."

Rielle pulled her into an embrace so fierce it knocked back both of their hoods. "Is it possible," she mumbled, "that you've taken me to this strange, dark house in the middle of the city to do away with me?"

Ludivine laughed. "After all those nice things I just said, you have to ruin the moment."

"Perhaps you said all those nice things to get my guard down."

"A fine plan, but alas, this is not as exciting as all that, I'm afraid. I've brought you to Audric's healer." Ludivine ducked out from under the archway and crossed the courtyard. "Audric much prefers him to his father's healers up at Baingarde. He's a good man. Discreet, no-nonsense. And, for all our sakes, I'd like to know that, going forward, your body is protected. Just in case."

Rielle stopped midstride. "You brought me here so I could buy a contraceptive tonic."

"Did you think to buy one for yourself?"

"I..." Rielle flushed once more. "I didn't. I suppose I was still rather caught up in all the..." She gestured helplessly.

"The kissing?" Grinning, Ludivine knocked on the door. "Understandable. That's what friends are for: to do the thinking for you when your own mind's gone fogged."

The door opened, revealing a ruddy-faced older man of middling height and weight, with shaggy brown hair, a slight beard, and piercing blue eyes. He held up a candle, squinting.

"Ah, Lady Sauvillier. Good. And..." He looked to Rielle. His eyebrows raised slightly. "And the honored candidate herself. What a night for me. My name is Garver Randell. Garver is acceptable. Follow me."

Rielle glanced at Ludivine, who hid her smile behind her hand. *No-nonsense indeed.*

He ushered them inside, through a small entryway and into a quiet room lined with shelves of vials, jars, and labeled boxes. Through a door in the far wall, Rielle saw a softly lit staircase and another, smaller room. The sounds of someone sweeping and a child's cheerful humming drifted out to meet them.

"My son's around here somewhere. He'll fetch it for you." Garver found a seat by the crackling fire. "If I have to search through these shelves one more time today, my eyes are bound to pop out of their sockets."

"Here, Father!" A small boy hurried out the lit doorway into the main room, a broom clutched in one hand. "What do you need?"

"A packet of contraceptive powder for Lady Rielle." He glanced back at her. "I'll give you a month's worth. You'll have to come back for more."

Rielle saw the boy's eyes widen at the mention of her name.

"I hope, Garver, that I can count on both you and your son to be discreet in these matters," she said.

"Do you think I'd be in business, Lady Rielle," Garver replied mildly, "if I were in the habit of walking around Âme de la Terre spreading news of what medicines people take?"

"No," Rielle said, with some difficulty, "I suppose not."

Garver's little son had already found the packet in question, packaged it in a small, plain box, and brought it to Rielle.

"Here, my lady." He held up the box, his cheeks bright red. "That'll be five coppers—"

"I'll waive the cost this time," Garver called from the fire. "You did well at the metal trial, Lady Rielle. It's the least I can do."

"We were there," the boy blurted out, seeming ready to burst. His eyes shone. "At the end, with all those swords... My lady, we were screaming for you. Did you hear us shout your name?"

"I heard everyone." Rielle took the box from the boy with a smile. "Thank you for cheering for me. It makes all the difference in the world and helps me not feel so afraid. And, I'm sorry, but I don't think I've yet learned your name."

"It's Simon," said the boy, beaming. He was practically dancing on his toes, quivering with excitement. "My name is Simon."

30

ELIANA

"Hello from home, my love. We celebrated Eliana's twelfth birthday this evening. As I write this, she and Remy are lying on the floor by the fire, bellies full of cake. Eliana is reading aloud from Remy's notebook while he draws a picture of her. His stories really are quite good for a five-year-old. I've enclosed three for you to read. Though we miss you terribly, we are all doing quite well. Eliana stays with me most days, helping me with my mending. She is good with her hands, maybe even better than me."

—Letter from Rozen Ferracora to her husband, Ioseph
May 17, Year 1012 of the Third Age

E liana awoke with a gasp, her hair clinging to her neck and shoulders.

So much for that bath.

"El?" Lying beside her on their shared cot, Remy came awake at once. "What's wrong?"

"Nothing," she mumbled, covering her face with one shaking hand. "Nightmare."

Which was true. Since Red Crown's attack on the Empire's outpost, the same dream had plagued her. It began with the cries of the trapped prisoners. She searched through the smoking ruins for them, shoving past heaps of rubble and digging through piles of ash that grew every time she touched them, until she was swimming through the ash, choking on it, while the prisoners' screams grew ever louder.

Then their screams would change.

They would call out her name.

It was then that she would finally find someone—a hand, cold and stiff from death, reaching out of the ash.

She would pull and pull on the hand, even though she knew what she would find on the other end. But she couldn't stop. She did not deserve to be spared. So she dislodged the person from the sea of ash—and the dream would end as she stared into her mother's death-stricken face.

"What can I do?" Remy scooted closer. "Do you want me to tell you a story?"

"I think I need a walk." The room Camille had given them for the duration of their stay was luxurious, but the air inside it was too still, too close. Eliana felt like a heavy blanket had been wrapped around her and was winding tighter and closer with every passing moment, binding her limbs to her sides.

"I'm sorry," she whispered. She dropped a hasty kiss on Remy's brow, stumbled out of bed and toward the door.

"I love you," came Remy's small, uncertain voice.

"And I love you," Eliana said and left him for the hallway.

Camille's apartments were vast, a labyrinth of bedrooms, parlors, and bathing chambers lined with Astavari artwork she had obtained through the underground markets. If Eliana had had to go far, she might have given up eventually, collapsed in a heap of dream-panic until someone found her in the morning.

She was glad, then, that Navi's room was so close.

Knocking softly on the door, she tried to collect her thoughts. What would she say? And what right did she have to complain to Navi of nightmares after everything she'd done?

I should leave, Eliana thought, still shivering from the lingering awfulness of the dream.

The door opened to reveal Navi, sleep-rumpled and wide-eyed with worry.

"I don't know why I'm here," Eliana began. "I've no right to ask you for anything."

Navi clucked her tongue. "We're friends now, aren't we? And you look terrible."

Navi guided Eliana inside her candlelit room, then sat on her bed and watched as Eliana furiously paced.

"You've had a nightmare," Navi said.

Eliana nodded, her throat tight with tears. "The prisoners at the outpost... I heard them screaming for me. I searched and searched, but I couldn't find them, and then I found...my mother. She was dead." She paused. "They were all dead."

"Haven't you had such nightmares of your victims before?"

The simplicity of the question cut Eliana like one of her own knives. "No. I never allowed it to bother me. I couldn't, or I would never have been able to finish a job. And then where would we all be?"

"None of your family seems very safe right now as it is," Navi pointed out. "Despite everything you've done for them."

Eliana laughed. "You're right. All my work, and Mother's still gone, and Father's still dead, and Remy and I are at the mercy of people I used to hunt. And Harkan..." *We can't know for certain. He could still be alive.*

She dragged a hand through her hair. "What's the point, then, of any of it?"

Harkan had asked a similar question, the day of Quill's execution: *God help us. El, what are we doing?* It felt to Eliana as though years and years had passed between that day and this one. She felt every one of them digging hotly into her shoulders like grasping fingers.

Navi was quiet for a long time. "Perhaps if nothing else, what's happened has taught you that there is more to life—and even to war—than simply staying alive. Perhaps this is the point." She rose and pressed a gentle palm to Eliana's chest. "That you are beginning to awaken and remember your humanity."

Eliana shoved Navi away with a harsh laugh. "That assumes too much of me."

"You are very unkind to yourself."

"Wouldn't you be?"

Navi inclined her head. "Perhaps."

"I am unkind to the bone. It's all I'm capable of."

"I don't believe that. I don't think you do either."

"I have to believe it! Otherwise—"

Eliana fell silent. A terrible hissing panic simmered just underneath her skin. Her breaths came fast and shallow.

"Eliana." Navi took her hands. "Please, sit. Breathe."

But Eliana moved away from her. "It sounds silly, but...I have always imagined a monster dwelling inside me instead of a heart. And that's why it was so easy for me to kill, to hunt." She backed against the far wall. She angrily wiped her eyes, glared up at the ceiling. "That monster is the reason why I liked being the Dread. I told myself that. I started to believe it too."

"Monsters do not weep for the dead," Navi said, "and they do not regret."

But this was no comfort. Eliana shook her head, the room a blur of shadows and shuddering candlelight. "If I am not a monster," she whispered, "then what excuse do I have for the things I've done?"

"Eliana, look at me."

She obeyed, realizing that she had slid to the carpeted floor and that Navi was now crouched before her, holding her hands.

"We are all of us dark creatures," Navi said, "but if we linger in those shadows, we'll be lost. Instead we must seek the light when we can, and that's just what you're doing. I see it happening."

"You believe too easily," Eliana muttered.

"And you don't believe enough."

"Belief doesn't keep you alive."

"But, given time, it can win wars."

Eliana's breath was running away from her. A hard heat felt ready to burst from her chest. "I don't agree with you."

"You don't have to."

"But I want to. I used to be like you. Like Harkan." Harkan, *God.* She scoffed, wiped her eyes. "My fucking hands won't stop shaking. I can't stay like this, or I'll get killed, and then we'll never find Mother—"

Words failed her. She could hardly breathe past the fear spiraling wildly through her body. She wrapped her arms around her legs, leaned her forehead on her knees.

Then, warmth, and a hand drawing slow circles between her shoulder blades. Like Harkan used to do when she had trouble sleeping. Like her mother had done when Eliana couldn't eat for missing her father. Together they had sat in the dying candlelight of their quiet house, waiting night after night for the sound of his steps in the hallway.

"Navi," Eliana whispered, fists clenched. "I don't know how to do this."

"Do what?"

Seek the light.

Fight a hopeless war.

Believe.

She didn't answer. After a few moments, Navi shifted, opening her arms, and Eliana moved into her embrace without thinking. She burrowed into Navi's front and closed her eyes, listened to the steady beat of Navi's heart and the in and out of Navi's lungs.

Slowly the tension knitting her muscles into knots began to loosen.

"Tell me about your mother," Navi said.

Her mother. Eliana closed her eyes.

A memory surfaced, swift and painful: her mother's arms around her, Eliana nestled in her lap as Rozen guided her tiny fingers across the face of her necklace.

"You've always loved this ugly old thing," Rozen had told her, "ever since the day we found it. You loved it so much you finally stopped screaming at me and let me sleep through the night. As long as you were holding it, you would sleep for hours."

Eliana had giggled, blushing at the thought. She had traced her fingers across the necklace's rough surface. "What does it mean?"

"It's an etching of the Lightbringer. Do you remember that story?"

"He was a great king," Eliana had whispered, eyes wide as she traced over the sweeping arcs of the horse's wings and the blacked-out figure on its back. "And this... What was it called?"

Eliana had looked up at her mother, wrinkling her nose.

Rozen had laughed. "A godsbeast. Back when the world was very, very young, such creatures roamed the skies and the waters and the great, green earth. This one was called a—"

"Chavaile," Eliana had answered, beaming. "I remember now." She brought the necklace to her lips and kissed the horse on its nose. "That's my favorite one."

In Navi's arms, Eliana shook her head. Grief lanced her through the heart. "I can't. Not her. I..."

She remembered Linnet's forlorn cry: *Mama?*

If she'd only known what would happen, she would have never gone hunting for the Wolf. She would have climbed into her mother's bed and held her close, every night. She would have moved only to gut the people who dared try to steal Rozen away.

"All right." Navi stroked her hair. "Tell me about Harkan, then."

"Well. He wasn't my only lover, but he was the best. Except for this woman Alys, who worked in the Brightwater red rooms. God, she made me black out a few times—"

"No, Eliana," Navi chided gently. "Tell me something real."

For a long time, Eliana didn't speak. Instead, she let the rhythm of Navi's fingers caressing her scalp coax her breathing slow and quiet.

"Why are you helping me?" Eliana asked at last.

"Because I have nightmares too," Navi answered. "And I'm glad for the company."

Eliana hesitated, then found Navi's hand and gripped it tight.

"Something real," she said. "Harkan dreamed of us all someday escaping to Astavar. He was going to teach me how to grow tomatoes and make me wear a straw hat."

Navi's laughter shocked Eliana into a smile. She squeezed Navi's fingers, closed her eyes, and spoke of Harkan until sleep claimed them.

Morning came. They'd moved to Navi's bed during the night, and though at first Eliana lay in the soft tangle of Navi's sleepy limbs with a feeling of rare and utter contentment, that did not last long.

All too soon she remembered: *There is still a war. Astavar still may fall. Mother is still missing. And I...*

She slipped out of bed, glanced once more at Navi's still form, then the room.

I am still...whatever I am. Angel? Human? Marque?

Monster?

A dark pocket opened inside her, all doubt and meanness, slowly pushing away the quiet peace the night had brought. She made for the kitchen. She would eat, she decided, and stretch, then find Simon and demand they spend the morning sparring.

Storming down the dimly lit corridor, she grinned to imagine her fists slamming into Simon's chest. He'd give her a good knock or two, but she'd bounce back. He would dodge her blades; she'd catch him on the arm, make him curse her—

Eliana rounded a corner and ran into Camille.

The woman scowled in greeting. "Dread."

Eliana pushed past her. "Camille. I was just—"

But Camille stopped her, hand on her wrist.

Eliana's head snapped around to glare at her. "Unhand me at once."

"Or what?" Camille looked her up and down with a sneer. "You'll kill me, as you've killed so many others?"

Eliana reached for a cutting reply and found none. Sudden exhaustion stretched from her shoulders to her toes; the previous night's peace bled out with her breathing.

"I've no desire to kill you," she said at last, dully.

Camille watched her through narrowed eyes. "Where's your brother?"

"Sleeping."

"Why aren't you?"

Eliana shrugged. "Bad dreams."

After a long moment, Camille released her. "I thought you'd strike me, for touching you."

"There are others I'd prefer to strike more."

Camille nodded and glanced down the shadowed corridor. All was quiet. "I've this girl who works for me," she began slowly. "Laenys is her name. She came up from the Vespers. The islands have fallen into despair. There's no work, little food. She got out, came here. A hard worker, Laenys. She never complained."

"And you're telling me this why?"

Camille watched her for a moment longer. "I've heard many things about you, Dread. That you're a pet of the Empire, for one."

Eliana laughed and looked away, eyes burning. "Typically pets are cherished, aren't they?" She needed to get some food in her body, flush out the treacherous stormy feeling in her chest.

"And," Camille went on, "that you're invincible."

Eliana looked at her sharply. "And now you'd like to test the truth of that rumor, is that it? Slice me open and see what happens?"

"No. I've got a job for you if you'll take it."

"I'm rather in the middle of the last job I accepted," Eliana reminded her. "Simon wouldn't appreciate you poaching me."

"And what if my job could get you to your mother sooner than Simon can?"

Eliana's hand flew to Arabeth at her hip. "Careful, Camille," she said softly. "This is dangerous ground you're treading on."

"Laenys was taken a few days ago. I want you to find out who took her and get her back."

Taken. *Just like Mother?* Eliana stiffened, her heart pounding. "What happened to her?"

"I don't know." Camille's mouth thinned. "They come in the night. They come every seven days. They're called Fidelia. That's the word I've heard used. People whisper it like they used to speak of the Empire before the invasion."

"What is it, then? A splinter faction of Red Crown?"

"I've only heard rumors." A flicker of uncertainty moved across Camille's face. "You'll think it's nonsense."

"I won't. Speak."

"People say that Fidelia..." Camille dragged a hand through her short black hair. "They're angel lovers, I've heard. They believe the Emperor and his generals are not men, but angels. They hunt to serve them, that they may be raised to glory once the world is conquered and the angels rule all." She scoffed. "It's daft, I know, but isn't everything these days?"

Horror dropped cold down Eliana's spine. Could Remy actually be right?

Camille continued. "We didn't realize for some time that people were disappearing. Rinthos is so crowded that someone can go missing for days before you even realize they're gone. At first they only took one. Then a few. Then many. People started noticing. And yet it won't stop." Camille drew in a slight shaky breath. "Every seven days, girls are disappearing. And women too. Grown, young, rich, poor. Mostly poor." Her voice acquired a bitter edge. "No one misses them, you see."

Eliana could keep quiet no longer. "My mother was taken, just like that. Back in Orline."

Camille nodded grimly. "So I've heard. It's been a week since the last taking. People have been whispering about it all morning, up above."

Eliana thought quickly. "Is there a pattern to the disappearances? A place from which more girls are taken than others?"

"Laenys vanished from below, on the fighting floor. A week ago now. We were coming back from the market, and we turned a corner. I felt something—a movement, a coldness—and turned around, and..."

"And she was gone?"

Camille looked away, fists curled at her sides and eyes bright. "I don't understand it. Why only girls? Where are they taking them?"

The same questions I asked myself weeks ago, Eliana thought, *back in Orline.*

"I don't know," Eliana said, fingers curling at her side around an invisible dagger. *Fidelia.* She would carve the word across their foreheads, right into the bone. "But I'm going to find out. And I'm going to make them pay."

Camille watched her from the shadows. "If I help sneak you out past Simon, you'll do it? Tonight is the seventh day. Night will fall, and by morning, more girls will be gone."

"Then once night falls," Eliana said with a loving caress of Arabeth's hilt, "I'll go hunting."

31

RIELLE

"I fear no darkness
I fear no night
I ask the shadows
To aid my fight"

—The Shadow Rite
As first uttered by Saint Tameryn the Cunning,
patron saint of Astavar and shadowcasters

R ielle stood in the middle of the Flats, the first horn blast of the shadow trial ringing in her ears.

Wooden stands, draped with the black and blue colors of the House of Night, created a vast circle around where she stood alone in the whispering tall grass, cloaked and hooded.

Waiting.

Twelve platforms around the circle's perimeter towered high above the ground. A shadowcaster stood solemn and dark on each one, faces masked and castings in hand.

The horn's second call wailed across the Flats.

Rielle stepped free of her cloak, let it fall to the ground.

The gathered crowd lost its collective mind. Their cheers exploded, and they rose as one to stamp their feet and shout her name. Rielle threw up her arms to acknowledge them, and their cries became a roar.

She had been worried that, given the current gossip, the reception might be different for this trial.

But on the contrary—the people of Âme de la Terre now seemed to adore her even more.

She knelt in the direction of the House of Night, to say a quick prayer to Saint Tameryn, and could not hide her grin.

Ludivine had truly outdone herself with this costume. The gown's snug black-velvet bodice was backless, scandalously low in front. The neckline dipped between her breasts and nearly reached her navel. Fine netting made of swirling ebony lace, so subtle it looked even from up close like a veil of shadows rather than fabric, shimmered across her exposed skin and held the dress in place. Floating around her legs when she moved was a gorgeous skirt of countless black, midnight-blue, and silver layers—silk, chiffon, Astavari lace. Ludivine had painted tiny silver stars across Rielle's cheeks and brow, rimmed her eyes with kohl.

She was night itself reborn on the earth, a queen swathed in shadows.

And the best part was yet to come.

As one, the shadowcasters lifted their gloved hands to the sky, their castings in hand.

Rielle stood with her head bowed, arms flung out behind her like rigid wings. Her blood ran wild inside her.

This is what I was made for. The thought arose as naturally as breathing. She flexed her fingers, felt power gathering hot in her palms. No, not hot—*vital*. Her power was not an intangible thing, a trick of the mind. It was the power of the world itself—and all that lived inside it.

And only I, she thought, *can tell it what to do.*

A stirring at the back of her mind. Familiar and delighted.

She stiffened. *Corien?*

The horn blasted a third and final time.

The shadowcasters began.

Spirals of darkness shot hissing from their castings like snakes, then fanned out across the sky to form a dome of shadows. Darkness fell over the grass. Only a few scattered holes in the dome allowed in columns of sunlight, illuminating the Flats so the crowd could see.

Their jubilant cries turned to jeers.

Rielle felt courage rise swift and undaunted in her breast. In this place, she was their hero and the shadowcasters the enemy.

With the dome in place above, the shadowcasters made their next move. They lowered their castings to point right at Rielle—and unleashed their monsters.

Rielle's courage vanished as quickly as it had arrived.

The magic that lived in the veins of shadowcasters gave them the power to imbue darkness with physicality, with heft and a cunning, voracious will. The shadows rushing at Rielle across the plain carved new roads in the ground. The shadows took the shapes of horned black leopards and winged wolves, bears with spiked spines and great hawks that breathed dark fire. With each running step, they sucked the air out of the Flats until Rielle was forced to stagger, gasping, to her knees.

A hawk reached her first, swooping low over her head. Cold ruffled the ends of her hair, frosted her scalp. She sucked in gasp after greedy gasp, but the air was growing thin, brittle. The hawk latched to her neck, squeezing with hard, thin feathers that sliced lines into her skin. The spike-spined bear skidded to a stop at her feet. A massive scaled paw struck her across the face and knocked her to the ground.

And she did nothing.

Head reeling, she let them come.

Sweet saints, she thought frantically, *I hope this works.*

The winged wolf pounced, baying, onto her chest. Once it touched her, the wolf morphed into a shapeless veil that wrapped around her head and mouth, until she had to claw at her own face in order to breathe. Her nails pierced her skin, drawing blood. Shreds of shadow fell away at her touch, misshapen and muttering, before dissolving into the ground and re-forming into a buzzing flock of arrows. Cold fear slammed into her chest. *The metal trial.* Some shadowcaster's joke, she supposed.

The falling shower of arrows pierced her like needles, scalp to ankle. They rose up, vibrating with angry intent, then fell on her again. And again. And again.

She squeezed her eyes shut, dripping with sweat and rivulets of her own blood, and let the shadow-beasts swarm upon her, let them pinch and grasp and choke. A chittering black rat forced its way inside her mouth. She gagged on the freezing wriggle of its body, fought the urge to vomit when the rat dissolved and spread through her blood in a surge of cold.

Tears leaked out of her eyes. Her body vibrated with the need to fight.

But she stayed sprawled across the ground, inert and helpless. Distantly she heard the crowd yell for her, their cries growing hysterical with fear.

You have something planned, Corien remarked, curious. *Do tell.*

Can't you tell? she managed, though even her thoughts came ragged and breathless.

I could, yes. But I feel like being surprised.

You'll see soon enough.

He beamed at her. She saw a flicker of a pale, handsome face before her closed eyelids. *You're happy to see me.*

She let out a small, tearful laugh. *I thought you'd left me for good.*

Never, Rielle. Soft lips brushed against her brow; a hand cupped her face, guiding her up. *Never.*

She turned her face to him, safe in the haven of her thoughts. The tearing shadows, the screaming crowd, the plan she'd engineered— they all fell away. There was only Corien and her own body and the power writhing for release inside her.

His mouth brushed against hers, slow and chaste. His hand trailed the length of her spine, drawing her up from the cold ground.

Now, he said, his voice tight and hoarse. *Get up. Make him sorry.*

Him. The Archon.

You cheated, she thought, smiling. *I thought you wanted to be surprised.*

I cannot resist you, he replied. *Not you or your phenomenal mind.*

Rielle's eyes flew open. She drew as deep a breath as she could. Then she reached her hands across the muddy ground, cracked her eyes open to look at the columns of sunlight breaking through the dome above.

"With the dawn I rise," she prayed. Then, curling her fingers into the dirt, "With the day, I *blaze.*"

In one brilliant instant, every ray of sun in sight dropped from the sky and raced across the ground like bolts of lightning to her fingers.

She gathered the light between her hands, ravenous for its burn, delighted at how it sizzled against her skin. Her eyes saw and did not see, glazed over with a hunger that made her chest hum with need. She blinked; the world was gilded through with countless waves of shimmering gold.

Her breath caught in her throat. *The empirium.*

She blinked again. The world darkened.

She pressed her palms together, then slammed them down against the earth.

A blinding blast rocketed out from where she knelt in the dirt, tearing through the shadowcasters' monsters. The shadowcasters themselves toppled from their platforms. The dome overhead vanished. Sizzling, black shreds of shadow cascaded to the ground.

When the darkness cleared, Rielle stood alone, her skin bloodied, her beautiful gown torn to shreds, but her back straight and her head held high.

And she *shone.*

A wave of shock tore through the crowd. The ground beneath Rielle's feet vibrated from the sheer weight of their cries, their stamping feet, their pounding fists.

Rielle! they cried. *Rielle! Rielle!*

And then, another roar, dwarfing the first: *Sun Queen! Sun Queen!*

Ludivine's tailors had spent hours sewing tiny mirrors into Rielle's gown, into the layers of her skirt, along the ribbons tied in her hair and through the lace lying limp against her sweat-soaked skin.

And now, Rielle had not only summoned sunlight to destroy her enemies and shatter the darkness.

She had drawn it up her body, trapped it glittering in her mirrors. Hundreds of shifting sunbursts lined her arms and legs and hair, shimmering between her breasts and along the ripped hems of her gown.

It was a look inspired by the armor of the Lightbringer himself.

And she was the Sun Queen: radiant and unstoppable.

She spun in a circle, her torn skirts flying, and called every dead scrap of shadow to her. Her power slithered across the ground like seeking tongues. She spun her hands through the air, crafting a shape from the shadows as a sculptor would from his clay, then turned sharply on her heel and sent her creation flying straight at the Archon.

It was a dragon—half the height of the Archon's tower in the High Temple. Its sharp-tipped wings spanned one hundred feet. Inside its jaws wriggled a nest of black snakes. And its hide shimmered not with scales but with the wailing forms of all the conquered beasts the shadowcasters had sent flying at Rielle.

They served the dragon. And now the dragon served her.

Screams of terror and delight exploded from the crowd.

The shadowcasters staggered to their feet, fumbling to find their castings, shouting for help.

The Archon rose to stand at the edge of his box, empty-handed and defenseless.

Rielle ripped her hands back through the air.

The dragon froze, its teeth snapping before the Archon's face. Its heavy wings flapped with loud, low booms like distant drums.

Rielle cocked her head. Flicked her fingers.

The dragon opened its jaws wide. Seven hooded snakes, shifting with each gust of wind, rose out of its mouth to taste the Archon's papery skin with their tongues.

I could kill him, thought Rielle. *Right now. I could do it.*

You could, Corien agreed. *But will you?*

The ground shifted. The dragon's weight pulled at her fingertips. The earth underfoot and the air above and the light glossing her skin waited, tense.

What would she ask of them?

Whatever the demand, they would obey.

It would obey.

The empirium. Rielle shuddered. Pleasure spilled down her front in tingling waves, raising every fine hair on her body. *It waits for me.*

Grasp it. Corien's voice came urgent and hot at her ear. *Take it for your own. No one else can do this but you. Do you know what you could accomplish, Rielle? The answers you could find, the worlds you could build—*

Then, a flash of golden color, followed by green: Ludivine's hair. Audric's cloak. They were rushing down the set of stairs from the royal box. Rielle thought, in fact, that she heard them calling for her, even across the Flats and through the noise of the crowd.

She blinked, stepped back, lowered her arm. The dragon, waiting above, shifted.

Don't listen to them, Corien hissed. *They won't be your friends for much longer. Don't you see? They don't understand, and they never will. Kill him.* Make *them understand.*

Not like this, she thought at last with a regretful pang—and a swell of relief. *Not now.*

She lowered her aching arm and clenched her fist. With a gust of cold wind and a low, tired groan, the dragon snuffed out.

Rielle sank to her knees, braced herself against the ground with shaking hands.

A vision flashed across her sight, watery and unclear:

Corien. Near. And angry.

He stalked toward her, yanked her body up roughly against his own.

Is this really what you want? he murmured. She blinked, and he was gone, though she could still feel his tight grip. She blinked again; he returned, his furious gaze on her lips.

They are what you want? He jerked his head behind him, at the flood of figures rushing toward her across the Flats.

Corien made her look at him. He wound his fingers in her hair, pulled her head gently back so that her throat was bared. His lips ghosted across her skin.

They are nothing, he told her, his voice rich and low. *And you are everything. What must I do to make you understand that?*

For a moment, Rielle closed her eyes and gave herself up to his dream-grip, caught in the shifting soft place between the solid reality of the Flats and wherever in the world it was that Corien truly stood.

Then she turned her face away and closed her eyes.

Let go of me, she whispered.

He did, at once. The vision faded, and all that was left of him was an echo of his touch on her arms and a dark voice sneering in her mind:

I will not always be this patient, Rielle.

That made her bristle. She opened her eyes and watched the approaching crowd. *You will do as I tell you,* she replied—and then tried not to think too hard about the coy shiver that grazed its claws across her skin when Corien did not answer.

⇀ 32 ↼

ELIANA

"It was while passing through Rinthos from the east-ern coast that my daughter disappeared. I'd heard of these vanishings. Even out in the wild, there are ripples. I thought, surely, that won't happen to us. Haven't we endured enough? But these girl-snatchers, they have no hearts, no pity. No souls. I've heard rumors of what is done to them, these missing girls, and I hope my daughter is safely dead."

—Collection of stories written by refugees
in occupied Ventera
Curated by Hob Cavaserra

Later that night, Eliana waited until she heard the slight knock from Camille on the door to her room, then slipped out from underneath Remy's arm, snatched her daggers from the floor, and stepped into the hallway.

Camille waited, her face drawn and tense. "Are you ready?"

"I'm here, aren't I? Lead the way."

They moved silently toward the front entrance. Eliana slid Arabeth into the holster at her hip, slipped Whistler into the one under her left sleeve and Nox into her left boot, then tucked Tuora and Tempest into the inner pockets of her jacket.

At the door that led back out into Sanctuary, Camille stopped her.

"I can't afford to lose any more of my people. You get in trouble out there tonight, you're on your own."

Eliana nodded once. "And if I don't come back?"

Camille's expression softened slightly. "I'll give your brother your message. Don't worry, Dread."

"I never worry if I can help it," Eliana replied smoothly, then slipped out the door and listened to Camille close and lock it behind her.

She crept down the carpeted corridor and onto Sanctuary's broad third-floor mezzanine. Immediately, the stench of the world outside Camille's apartments overwhelmed Eliana—the hot reek of dirty bodies, spilled ale, plates of food left out to sour. At half past nine, Sanctuary crawled with hundreds of souls seeking distraction from the world above, and the night had only just begun.

Two women brawled in one of the fighting cages. A raucous game of cards had taken over half the second floor, onlookers shouting out their wagers as the players rolled dice in clouds of smoke. Between two pillars in a dark corner, two half-naked figures writhed against the wall.

Eliana made a pass through the entire third level, which housed dozens of other apartments besides Camille's. On the fourth level, red-curtained doors lined with beaded fringe led the way to a brothel, out of which floated the sounds of shrill music and unrestrained laughter. Eliana's bile rose at the coy gazes of the children with collars around their necks, the keening distant cries that bordered the line between pleasure and pain.

She hurried through the fifth level, then back down to the second and first. There, the noise of the fighting pits—punches, cheers, shouted obscenities—drowned out all quieter conversation. Eliana could not move without brushing up against a stranger. Hot drops of sweat from the cages and from the yelling spectators above scattered across her arms.

If Fidelia wants to snatch girls unseen, Eliana thought, *this is the place to do it.*

She made straight for the bar and slapped three coppers onto the slimy bar top. "The best ale you've got."

The barkeep curled his lip. "We don't have any good ale."

Eliana smiled, flicking her jacket aside to show him Tuora's gleaming blade. "Find me some. Quickly."

The barkeep sighed and rolled his eyes. But he did as she asked, sliding a dirty tin mug of ale down the countertop with a disdainful flick of his wrist. She caught the mug, tossed him another copper because she was feeling generous, and moved away.

Eliana brought the mug to her lips as she walked. After the first sip, her mouth puckered in disgust. The barkeep hadn't lied; the drink tasted like piss.

She slid into a narrow wooden booth against the far wall, the backs of the benches high and private.

Already an hour had passed since she'd left Camille's apartments, and for all the woman's talk about fear of Fidelia running rampant in Rinthos, Eliana had seen nothing noteworthy. The shadowed booth was as fine a place as any to sit and observe, unremarkable and unnoticed, until she had become as much a part of the room as the ancient, grimy furniture.

Sometimes, she thought, *the hunter must not prowl, but rather wait. And watch.*

She slid low in her seat, propped her boots up on the table. It felt good to be working again, to settle in and watch the dirty cogs of Sanctuary turn around her. Since her bombardier attack, she had felt unlike herself, shaken loose and off-balance. But this...this was familiar.

It was a good spot: she could still see the bar, the fighting pits, and at least one of the entrances to Sanctuary, though not the one they'd come through two days before. She imagined there must be all manner of rat holes leading in and out of such a vile nest. Twenty feet away, a brown-skinned woman brooded over her cup. Two tables away and to the left, a group of men and one pale woman with a head of wild black braids howled with laughter.

To Eliana's right: an ebony-skinned man and a freckled woman, finishing off bowls of stew. One of the fights had ended. A singing crowd raised the bloody winner to their shoulders and began an impromptu parade.

Eliana took another sip from her drink, eyes roving about the crowded dark room over the rim of her mug—then froze.

She blinked a few times as if trying to clear her vision of a speck. A sudden, heavy pressure pinned her to the bench, making her head spin. A feeling of wrongness filled the air, a faint sour scent, like someone had lashed a whip of ill intent through the room.

Hard chills surged through her body.

She remembered that feeling, that scent, from Orline—from the night she had tried to save the abducted child, and from the night her mother had disappeared. It was more violent now, the feeling. Closer. Urgent. She gripped the table's edge, fighting the desire to lay her head on the table. The world teetered, knocked askew.

Beneath the table, Eliana found Arabeth and felt a little better as her fingers wrapped around the dagger's hilt.

The chill across her shoulders became a sharp pang of warning.

She forced up her gaze.

The woman who'd been sitting alone, frowning over her drink, was gone. Her ale lay spilled on the tabletop, dripping onto the ground. Her mug rolled to a stop under the chair in which she had been sitting.

But she could have simply left the table.

Mouth dry, heart pounding, Eliana quickly ran back over the path of people she had been observing only a few seconds earlier, before the world had changed.

The woman with the black braids was gone. The man who had been sitting next to her slapped her empty chair, wiping tears from his eyes as one of the drinkers vomited.

And the man and woman who had been finishing off their stew— the man now sat alone, his head in his bowl as he slurped up the last drops of his meal. The woman's bowl hit the ground and shattered; the man looked up, frowning in bewilderment, then craned his neck to peer through the crowd.

Three women, all gone in a matter of seconds.

Three women, gone like her mother.

Eliana licked her lips, her blood hot and humming. She unsheathed Arabeth and rose to her feet.

They were here. Fidelia.

They come in the night. They come every seven days.

Eliana rose, slipped through the crowd as quickly as possible without drawing attention, scanned the room. She let her eyes unfocus.

There.

To her right, a dark, hooded figure moved swiftly across the room. Eliana thought she saw another person at its side. The woman who had been drinking alone? But as soon as Eliana tried to focus on that particular shape, her vision tilted.

She leaned hard against a nearby pillar—sticky and caked with filth—as a wave of nausea ripped through her. She gritted her teeth, pushing through it. The figure had been moving toward the eastern wall. If she didn't move quickly, she'd lose the trail.

A hand caught her wrist. "Going somewhere?"

Eliana turned to glare at Simon. "Let me go, or I'll lose them."

"Who?" Beside Simon, Navi peered out from under her hood. "What's happening?"

"One moment these women were there, *right there* in front of me, and the next—" Eliana staggered against Simon as the sick feeling returned. He caught her around the waist, kept her from falling. "God, that's annoying," she bit out, tears smarting in her eyes. "I can't think for two seconds without feeling sick. What are these people doing to me?"

Simon peered closely at her face. "Who? Someone's hurting you?"

"Fidelia." She leaned against the solid length of his torso, suddenly glad he was there. If he hadn't come, she would have been a pile on the floor. "Camille said they take women, and girls, just like the people in Orline. At least, I think they're all the same. Angel-worshippers, Camille said. Every seven days. I was going to help her find this girl who worked for her. Then...they came. They're here. They took three women in a matter of seconds. I don't understand it."

Simon's piercing blue gaze was intent on her face. "You said they're doing something to you. Explain."

She struggled weakly to break free of him. "Too much to explain, have to find them."

"Wrong. We're going back to Camille's, and after I dismember her for sending you out here, I'm locking you in the safest room I can find, possibly forever."

"Touch her," she mumbled, "and I'll dismember *you*." It was becoming increasingly difficult to organize her thoughts. "What are you two doing here together, even?" She took unsteady step after unsteady step, frowning at the floor.

"Navi and I met outside your room," Simon said. "We discovered you gone, and she insisted on coming with me to find you."

"Why were you both there?" Eliana brought a hand to her throbbing temple. "That's rather odd, isn't it?"

"Well, *I* wanted to look in on you, make sure you'd managed to sleep," Navi said, her voice light. "Simon?" She looked guilelessly up at him. "Why were *you* at Eliana's door in the middle of the night?"

Simon's mouth thinned. "This is not the time for—"

"Not a chance in the Deep that I'm leaving here without finding Fidelia," Eliana muttered, "and slitting throat after throat until they tell me where my mother is."

"A charming image. Now, *walk*."

Eliana dug deep for strength and pulled free of Simon's grip. Without him holding her up, the world turned upside down. She collapsed at once, but Simon caught her before she could hit the ground.

"What's wrong with her?" came Navi's worried voice.

"Eliana?" Simon's hand cupped her cheek. "What does it feel like, what's happening to you? If you don't tell me, I can't help you."

She took three long, shallow breaths to quell the sick feeling rising in her throat, then glared up at him with watery eyes. "This is the first real lead I've had since leaving Orline," she said through gritted teeth. "I'm not going to give it up. Don't make me hurt you, Simon. I'm not keen to."

He quirked an eyebrow. "Aren't you?"

"God, do you ever shut up?" She tried to shove past him, but Navi was the one to stop her that time.

"Eliana, stop this," she said quietly. "Let's go back. It isn't safe out here."

"But I can find my mother," Eliana insisted, "and all the others who have been taken." She glanced at Simon. "Including people from Red Crown."

"Unimportant," Simon said. "Our priority is getting Navi to Astavar. Once that's done, I'll help you find your mother. As we agreed."

"Or I could go find her *right now*. By the time we get to Astavar, it could be too late."

"A risk you knew when you accepted my offer."

"Why do you care about me staying with you, anyway? If it's a fighter you want, Camille has dozens of sellswords to pick from."

The words said, Eliana's mind began to clear, cutting through her muddled senses. *Why does he care indeed?* When she looked back at Simon, his carefully implacable face told her the truth: she'd hit upon a nerve.

"What is it about me," she said quietly, taking one step toward him, then another, "that makes you want to keep me close?"

Navi looked curiously back and forth between them. Simon opened his mouth, hesitated.

Then a voice rattled from the shadows underneath the nearby staircase: "Because you're special, Eliana Ferracora. And he wants you for his own. Just as I do."

Eliana's mouth went dry at the sound of that voice. She knew it, though now it rasped rather than purred.

A slim figure came into the light, wearing a tattered black uniform and frayed crimson cloak made nearly unrecognizable by the caked mud and bloodstains marring the once-fine fabric.

"Rahzavel," Eliana whispered in horror. Even Simon seemed dumbstruck. "You're *alive*."

The assassin grinned, his pale face marked with a long, swollen scar that ran down from his temple, bissected his face, and disappeared into his collar. His white hair hung in matted clumps.

"Alive," he agreed, "and so very excited to kill you."

Then he ripped his sword from the sheath at his waist, raised it with a horrible hungry cry, and swung hard for Eliana's neck.

⭢ 33 ⭠

RIELLE

"I'd hoped the recent news wouldn't reach you for sev-
eral more days. It is true, however, about Prince Audric
and the Dardenne girl. I'm sorry I couldn't tell you in
person. Stay in Belbrion, guard the north. Patience,
my son. All will be as it should, and soon."

—Letter from Lord Dervin Sauvillier to his son, Merovec
May 30, Year 998 of the Second Age

The doors to King Bastien's council hall banged open.

Rielle shot to her feet. She had been tensely waiting in a hard, uncomfortable chair for a solid hour under the equally tense eyes of her guard. During that hour she had prayed for the hasty arrival of the king, so they could get the inevitable explosion over with.

Now, however, with the king storming to his seat—the Archon, the queen, her father, every member of the Magisterial Council, and Lord Dervin Sauvillier accompanying him—Rielle passionately wished she could return to her lonely chair and sit there for the rest of the day, unbothered.

At least Audric and Ludivine had come in as well, standing at opposite ends of the table.

"Lady Rielle," began the king, his voice tight as he stood behind the enormous Privy Council table, "I have no idea where to begin."

"Well," said Lord Dervin, the words bursting out of him in a razor-thin voice, "perhaps we can start by discussing Lady Rielle's willful abuse of power during her latest trial. Or else, her flagrant disregard for the sanctity of our children's engagement—"

"Lord Dervin," the king snapped, "when I want you to speak, I will ask you to do so."

The man fell silent with a curt nod.

King Bastien glared at the table for a long moment, then turned his angry gaze onto Rielle.

It's just King Bastien. She made herself meet his eyes, reminding herself over and over that this man was not only a king. He was also Audric's father. She had grown up running through the halls of his home, shared a bed with his son and niece when they were all too young for it to be thought ill of.

"What," he began quietly, "were you thinking out there?"

She hesitated, reminded herself to keep her voice clear and calm. "The truth, my king?"

"Yes, Lady Rielle. Please, for the love of God, tell me the truth."

"I wanted to show the people what I am capable of. We've already discussed how important that is, have we not? That they think well of me, that they see my power out in the open and also see that it is nothing to fear."

The king's expression remained implacable. "Continue."

"It seemed to me that the best way to show everyone that I am not only succeeding in the trials, but actually growing stronger because of them, was to demonstrate my ability to manipulate two elements simultaneously." She resolved to look at neither Sloane, who sat rigid and pale at the council table, nor Tal, whose urgent gaze she could feel like the quiet pull of panic.

"What you're saying, Lady Rielle," said Queen Genoveve, her expression caught between amusement and something darker, "is that you wanted to show off."

Well, they've got you pegged, haven't they?

Corien's soft laughter pricked goose bumps from Rielle's flesh.

"And to demonstrate that my control is remarkable enough that a deadly threat can hover mere inches from someone," Rielle answered, glancing at the Archon, "and I can ensure no harm befalls them, even so."

The queen raised her eyebrows. "Remarkable?"

"I think my power is deserving of the word, don't you?"

Tense silence reigned. Rielle glanced at Tal; he nodded at her with a small smile.

Her heart was a drum, steady and triumphant. "As for showing off… I think any human who can still work magic in this world understands the urge to embrace that gift and let it shine for all to see."

"I do not understand that urge." Rafiel Duval, Grand Magister of the Firmament, brown-skinned with black braids, sat with impeccable posture beside Tal. He wore windsinger robes of sky blue and storm gray. "Power does not exist to be flaunted. It exists to be tamed."

"We disagree, then, Magister Duval. Now that I am free to use my power as I see fit, it feels stronger and healthier than ever."

"You mean, now that you may use your power as the king sees fit." Ludivine turned imploring eyes to Rielle. "Don't you, Rielle?"

Rielle flushed, realizing her mistake.

Not a mistake, Corien said quickly. *You said what you really think, my dear.*

"Forgive me, my queen, my king." Rielle bowed her head. "Lady Ludivine is right. Of course I misspoke."

The king sat heavily in his chair. "And the creature you created. The dragon. What of that?"

"I think we can all agree," Audric began, "that Lady Rielle demonstrated incredible control—"

"Hold your tongue, Audric," said the king. "Lady Rielle can defend herself."

"But, darling, don't you remember?" Queen Genoveve's cold gaze did not match the sweetness of her voice. "Our son has a hard time keeping his tongue to himself when Lady Rielle is near."

A burning flush climbed up Rielle's body. The Archon turned a delicate cough into his sleeve.

Audric was the first to speak, his voice low and furious. "Mother, do you really want to have that conversation right now?"

"Well, I certainly don't," the king answered with a sharp look at his wife. Then he glanced past her. "My apologies, Ludivine."

Ludivine gave him a warm smile. "It is nothing, Uncle. A mistake made during fraught times." Then she came to Rielle and gently took her hand before turning back to the council table. "I bear no grudge against Lady Rielle." She extended her other hand to Audric, who approached after a moment's hesitation. "Nor do I bear a grudge against my cousin, the prince."

Lord Dervin's mouth twisted as he took in the sight of the three of them standing united before the king.

"Were you going to kill me?"

Rielle startled to hear the Archon's mild voice. "I...I beg your pardon, Your Holiness?"

His unblinking smile crept inside her like a nightmare. "I could feel it, you know. I could feel the empirium moving inside that dragon as it licked my face. It was angry at me." He cocked his head, considering her. "*You* were angry at me. For those children, I know."

Was this a challenge? Rielle's hackles rose. "Yes, I was angry. I wanted to frighten you."

Lord Dervin threw up his hands. "My king, is this the talk of someone we can trust to stand beside our children, much less parade about recklessly in front of thousands of people?"

"Frighten me you did," the Archon continued, ignoring the outburst and leaning forward across the table. A new light glinted in his eyes. "I didn't think you would kill me. Not yet. But I wondered how far you'd go."

Not yet. A thrill skipped down Rielle's body. She could not look away from the Archon's narrow, bright gaze. Those eyes seemed to see everything inside her—the power even now leaping high in her blood, the presence of Corien sitting pensive in her mind, and the truth.

That truth was this: a dark kernel of regret stewed inside her, and if she could go back and live the trial over again, that hard black knot might just be enough to change her mind. To not stay the dragon's claws and instead let it feed.

The Archon's smile grew, as if he could see Rielle's thoughts plainly on her face.

A sharp knock on the great hall doors disrupted the agitated silence, and when a page entered, Rielle relaxed slightly, glad for the distraction. Audric stood near, arms tense at his sides. She wanted to turn in to him, to hide her face in the warmth of his chest. She didn't want to hide there forever, just for a while. Was it so wrong to wish for that?

"Father?" Audric's voice carried a new note of worry. "What is it?"

Rielle glanced up at the king. He held a small, curled slip of paper—a message from the royal aviary—and on his face was a stark absence of expression. He had retreated somewhere; he did not want to be reading this note in front of an audience.

"Three attacks," he said flatly, "along the border. Castle d'Avitaine. The Castle of the Three Towers. Castle Barberac." He paused, his mouth in a hard line. "Seventy-three Celdarian soldiers have been killed. Six—two from each post—survived and fled south to the nearest villages."

"My God." Queen Genoveve's hand went to her throat. "Did their reports include what attacked them? Or who?"

"'It came during the night,'" read the king. "'It came without sound and without warning.'"

An eerie silence bled through the room.

King Bastien stopped reading. Audric snatched the note from his hands.

"Audric—" snapped the king.

"'I'd turn in the dark,'" Audric continued reading, "'and another would fall. White as bone their faces were, and still, like they'd been caught in the middle of a scream.'"

The king stormed around the table, ripped the note from Audric's hands, and crumpled it in his fist. "These northern posts are bitter and cold. A pale face is no strange thing."

Audric watched him gravely. "Two survivors from each post can be no coincidence."

"Can't it? Don't start raving at me about your mad theories, Audric."

"The signs have been clear for some time now." Audric ignored his father and addressed the entire table. "The longer we wait to face them head on, the deadlier the consequences will become."

"Signs!" Bastien laughed harshly. "Storms and revolutions in distant lands, soldiers being killed on a border between unfriendly nations. Yes, indeed." His voice took an unfamiliar, sarcastic turn. "I've never heard of such things happening. Truly, we are at the brink of some magical undoing."

"And what about Lady Rielle? You cannot look at her performance in the trials and call it anything but extraordinary."

"He has a point," said Tal quietly. "I've worked with Rielle for years, and the prophecy—"

"Magister Belounnon," King Bastien snapped, "until I have asked for your opinion, you will take care to remain silent in my presence."

Tal met the king's gaze with only a little flare of defiance, but it was enough to make Rielle's heart swell with love for him.

"Yes, my king," Tal replied.

"The prophecy," King Bastien continued, looking around at all of them, "cannot even be dependably interpreted. How many official translations of Aryava's words exist? Twenty? Twenty-five?"

"Thirty-four," replied the Archon at once, "though the differences between some are minimal."

"But even a single word can mean the difference between a

prophecy"—the king shot a dark look at Audric—"and an entertaining story that no learned man takes seriously."

Magister Duval's eyebrows shot up. "Your Majesty, this is rather bold of you to say, in front of the entire council and the Archon himself."

"All of whom answer to me, I'll remind you." Bastien stalked away to stand before the windows and look out at the setting sun. When at last he turned back around, he looked weary but resolute. "I apologize for my outburst, Your Holiness. I do not think the prophecy a mere story, nor do I think the intelligence of you and your magisters to be anything less than exceptional."

The Archon inclined his head. "You are most gracious, my king."

"I'll speak no more of this tonight. Armand?"

Rielle's father rose from his chair and joined his king. At the doors, he glanced back once at Rielle, and she saw a flicker of concern in his gray eyes.

The look frightened her.

Ever since the trials had begun, with Rielle's life imperiled every week, her father had kept himself closed off from her, even more than usual. She saw him only during their mornings at the obstacle course, and sometimes in the halls of Baingarde. Encircled by her guards, she would greet him politely, and he would return the sentiment with a mere nod.

And so even the smallest change in expression on that hard face was of note.

Something about the message from the north, and the king's reaction, had pricked at the inconquerable Lord Commander Dardenne.

As the council rose with rustlings and murmurs, Audric turned to Rielle, then glanced at Ludivine. "We must speak in private," he said quietly. "Now."

"Audric, my love?" Queen Genoveve extended her hand toward him. Her brocaded gray gown caught the red light of the setting sun and cast strange, harsh lines across her face. "Come with me. Your uncle and I thought we could all enjoy some tea together."

"So you can scold me again and speak ill of Lady Rielle?" Audric said it loudly enough for everyone still in the room to hear. "I have far better things to do."

Then he threw his mother a swift, angry look and left the hall.

Rielle nearly burst out laughing at the affronted expression on Queen Genoveve's face, but before she could, Ludivine took her firmly by the elbow and rushed her out of the hall.

Only once in the familiar quiet of Audric's rooms did Rielle's nervous laughter finally escape. She collapsed on her favorite chaise by the window, a shabby old thing so comfortable that she forbade Audric from ordering another.

Ludivine sank into her own favorite chair by the fire. "I don't see what's so funny, Rielle."

"What *isn't* funny? The fact that Audric insulted his mother in front of the entire council? Or that your father looked like he was trying to make me drop dead using only the force of his stare?"

Or that even as the king scolded me, she thought a little wildly, *I was talking to an angel in my head?*

"Please don't make light of my father's anger," Ludivine said. "It won't serve any of us well."

"And then," Rielle continued, "there's the fact that Audric and I nearly... Well." She flushed, losing her nerve. "And yet here we all are, acting as if nothing has happened!"

Audric tensed. "Rielle, can we please not talk about that right now? I know you and Ludivine have discussed it, but there are political ramifications of any changes made to the agreement between our families."

"No." Rielle set her jaw. "I insist we talk about it, this very night. It's unfair to all of us until we do."

Into the silence that followed, Ludivine spoke gently. "She's right, Audric."

Audric leaned heavily against his desk.

"If I could give up my crown and my duty," he said, "and leave this place behind, with only you at my side..." He glanced at Rielle. The quiet anguish on his face seized her heart. "I would do it in an instant, with Lu's blessing."

"Abandon your birthright? Leave your country without an heir?" Rielle scoffed, tears standing hot in her eyes. "You'd never dare."

"You're wrong!" He stormed away from them to face the starlit windows, his shoulders high and tense. "I'd do it for you. Sometimes I think I'd betray everything I hold dear for the chance to—"

His voice broke; he fell silent. Rielle turned away, arms tightly crossed over her front. Audric's servants had prepared his fire for the night. The crackling flames and popping wood were the only sounds in the room for several long minutes.

Then Ludivine cleared her throat. "There's no need to give up anything, you know. Not the crown, and not each other. You would just need to be...discreet." She smoothed her skirts. "I could help you, as needed."

Rielle stared at her. Ludivine had taken her to Garver Randell for a contraceptive tonic, yes, but to hear her suggest such a thing so plainly, as if they were all merely discussing the weather, left Rielle without words.

Audric laughed in astonishment. "Lu, are you suggesting what I think you're suggesting?"

"That you be together?" Ludivine raised an eyebrow. "Yes. In secret, of course, but soon. And as often as possible, so I'm spared the agony of your tortured pining." She leaned back in her chair, closed her eyes. "It's exhausting to witness. I've reached my limit."

Heart racing, not daring to look at Audric, Rielle breathed, "I can't believe you're actually saying this."

"Why not? I've told you both how I feel about the situation." Ludivine smiled, eyes still closed. "Or do you doubt my word?"

"No, it's not that, it's just—" The images crowding Rielle's mind made a delighted heat climb up her cheeks. "Wouldn't you be embarrassed?"

"That my dearest friends could be happier than they've ever been? Why would that embarrass me?"

"Maybe 'embarrass' isn't the right word." Rielle did look at Audric, then. Half in shadow, he frowned at the floor.

"If we're discovered," he said at last, "even if we explained that you knew and approved, it could be humiliating for all of us, but especially for you."

"Oh, is that what could happen?" said Ludivine blandly. "I hadn't realized."

Rielle let out a rush of nervous laughter. "We would just have to... not be discovered."

Audric scrubbed a hand over his face. "It's not as simple as that."

"Of course it is." Ludivine watched him fondly. "We'll be careful, and you'll... Well, Audric, you'll have to get good at lying somehow."

"And your family? What about them? If my mother finds out? Or your father? He'll be studying us closely now."

"I can handle my family."

For a long time, Audric stared at the crackling flames.

"We can't," he said at last, his voice heavy. "Something is happening in Borsvall. The attacks on the border, that report I read... House Sauvillier is our strongest defense against whatever might come south. While we sort out what's happening, we need your father and his soldiers to remain loyal to the crown. And they surely will not if they discover that Rielle and I are having an affair."

Rielle struggled to speak past a rising despair. "But, Audric—"

"What did you tell my father, weeks ago? Enough lies have been told, enough secrets kept?" He glanced at her. "This is not how I want us to begin."

"And I don't care how we begin," she protested, stepping toward him, "as long as we *do*."

In the blazing silence, Audric's gaze dropped to her lips and then away.

"Perhaps," Ludivine said after a moment, "you can simply wait a while. Until the danger at the border has passed and my father's temper has cooled."

Rielle threw up her hands. "And then what? He'll suddenly be happy when we tell him what will happen next? Sorry, Lord Dervin, but your daughter won't be queen after all?"

"No, he won't be happy," replied Ludivine evenly, "but he won't be as angry."

"And the kingdom will hopefully be stable, then, and safe," finished Audric. "Whatever attacked our border will have been found out and vanquished." He took a deep breath, dragged a hand through his curls.

Rielle moved to stand before him. She refused to touch him, though her body ached to.

"Is this really what you want?" she whispered.

"What I want?" He smiled sadly, moved as if to touch her, then drew back. "Of course not. But it's what we must do, Rielle."

He has the eyes of a cow, Corien sneered. *Soft and unthinking.*

Rielle's wrath rose swift and hot. *And you have the tongue of a serpent. Cruel and repellent.*

Corien retreated, a sulky bend to his presence.

"Rielle, I'm sorry," Ludivine murmured, rising from her chair. "But I think Audric's right. This is the wisest—"

"Lu, I'm thankful for your selflessness and for your friendship," Rielle said tightly, a terrible pain lodged in her throat, "but I think I need to be alone."

Then she tore herself away from Audric and left the room.

— 34 —
ELIANA

*"Because of your generosity and teaching, my lord, it
will take more than a fall from a tower to kill me. One
more day, and I will have them."*

—Message written by the Invictus assassin Rahzavel
to His Holy Majesty, the Emperor of the Undying

E liana staggered back to avoid Rahzavel's flying sword, stumbled
over a chair, and fell hard into Navi's arms.

Simon lunged in front of them, his own sword raised to strike. The
two blades crashed together and caught.

"Navi, get her out of here!" Simon bellowed over his shoulder, just
before Rahzavel let out a harsh scream and swung his sword around
to free himself. Simon stumbled against a pillar, kicked a chair into
Rahzavel's path.

Navi grabbed Eliana's wrist, and together they raced into the
crowd. Bystanders had noticed the fight and hovered nearby. Navi
wove through them, shoving at bodies twice her size when they didn't
move fast enough.

"Eliana!" Rahzavel called after them, his words punctuated by
grunts and the clashes of blades. "You can't run from me! I'm like you,
don't you see? I can't be killed!"

Fear was a fantastic energizer; Eliana's head cleared with every
step. Soon she was the one dragging Navi after her.

"In here," she gasped, turning Navi into the maze of the fighting pits. Narrow paths separated each cage from the next; a turn past one cage, then another, and they were in the thick of the brawls. A bare-chested fighter threw his opponent against the wire wall to Eliana's right. The noise was tremendous, the crowd a seething mass on all sides.

"Back to the apartments," Navi cried. "We'll be safe there!"

"If a fall wouldn't kill him," Eliana replied, "then we'll never be safe from him again, not until he's dead."

I'm like you! I can't be killed!

But he was wrong, wasn't he? She could be killed. She wasn't completely invincible. If he stuck her through the heart with a sword, she would die just like any beast that bleeds.

And him... His fall off the maidensfold tower in Orline must have been a lucky one. He'd hit the water at just the right angle, avoided the rocks scattering the river. The Emperor had fed him a regimen of drugs, conditioned his mind and body over the years to withstand impossible abuse.

"Could he be an angel?" Navi shouted over the din.

Eliana grimaced. "Knowing our luck?"

They emerged from the pits onto the open floor. Eliana ran for a set of twisting iron stairs nearby. As she reached for the railing, a body flew out of the crowd and slammed into her side, knocking both her and Navi to the floor.

Eliana pushed herself up, head spinning. "Navi?"

She lay unconscious two feet away, beside the inert body that had hit them. She must have hit her head against the bottom stair. Eliana crawled toward her.

A sword struck her across her back once, then twice. Blazing pain ripped through her body. She screamed, tightened her grip on Arabeth, turned, caught Rahzavel's sword with her dagger.

He leered down at her, pressing hard against their joined blades until she was nearly flat on the floor. Her bleeding back was a twisting plane of fire.

"Hello again." His voice rattled; his ravaged face stretched into a madman's grin. He stomped down hard on her thigh, then on her ribs. As she screamed, blinking away starbursts of pain, he raised his sword with wild eyes. She plunged Arabeth into the top of his foot, then rolled out from under him right as his sword slammed into the ground.

Navi shook herself awake, then looked in horror at something past Eliana's shoulder. "Watch out!"

Eliana turned, ducked in time to avoid Rahzavel's sword. The tip of the blade caught her cheek. Blood spurted hot across her face and arms. She thrust out with Arabeth; he bashed it out of her hand with his sword. She spun out a hard kick at his chest; he grabbed her leg, twisted, slammed her to the ground.

Before his fall, he would have fought her in silence, every movement swift and calculated.

Now he laughed, yelped playfully when one of her daggers caught his skin, clucked his tongue when she missed. A tight crowd had gathered around them, boxing them in with pumping fists and wordless, rhythmic cries hungry for violence.

Eliana grabbed a carving knife from a nearby table, whirled to throw it at him. He knocked it easily aside. She found another one, turned.

She dropped the knife. It clattered useless to the ground. Swaying on her feet, she reached out for support, found nothing, fell to her hands and knees.

Fidelia.

Fog blackened her vision. The nausea returned, sweeping through her with startling violence.

"Look at her!" Rahzavel cried, dancing gleefully around her prone form. "The famous Dread of Orline!"

The crowd responded with a chorus of jeers.

"Eliana, get up!" Navi frantically tugged on her arms. Eliana tried to stand; her limbs gave out, and she crashed to the floor.

"They're here." Her stomach wrung itself into a knot. The world spun, tilting right then left. Whoever or whatever was pinning her down, it was wrong. It didn't fit; it didn't belong here.

"Run," she gasped out, groping for Navi's hand. "They'll find you."

"Who will?" Navi's voice was full of panicked tears.

A furious cry behind them made Eliana blearily turn.

Simon dropped down from the stairs above, crashing feet first into Rahzavel. The assassin dropped hard, then rolled away with a feral peal of laughter and sprang back to his feet. Simon advanced ruthlessly on him, his scarred face ferocious with anger.

Then, turning to block one of Rahzavel's thrusts, Simon glanced over and found Eliana on the floor. Their gazes locked.

The world seemed to stop. Eliana's breath caught in her aching chest.

They had been here before—not in the fighting pits of Sanctuary, but in a similar moment of danger and flight.

Of separation.

The certainty of that—like suddenly recalling a lyric long forgotten—opened an unfamiliar chasm in her heart.

A flicker of some unnameable sadness shook Simon's face. Did he feel it too?

"Run!" he roared at her.

Reality returned. Time spun forward, blistering and unkind.

Eliana shoved her way into the crowd. She heard Navi yell her name, heard a harsh cry, hoped it wasn't Simon. She searched for another set of stairs that would take her back to the third floor. She would get Remy and leave. They would run as fast as they could, for as far as they could. She would shave their heads; they would get new clothes. They could make it to Astavar like that, disguised and unrecognizable.

She made it to the second floor before Navi caught up with her.

The girl grabbed her arm, yanked her back hard. Eliana spun around, pressed Whistler to Navi's throat.

"I'm getting my brother and leaving," she spat, "and if you try to stop me, Navi, I swear I will gut you."

The world spun and wouldn't stop. Eliana dropped Whistler, sagged against Navi's body.

"Eliana?" Navi sank to the floor with her. "Get up, please!"

Eliana gasped for breath, her voice choking in her throat. She tried to dislodge herself from Navi's arms, crawl away, but she couldn't move.

Then Navi disappeared.

A gloved hand came over Eliana's mouth, pressing a reeking cloth to her face. She struggled, her scream muffled. Another hand caught the back of her skull, forcing her harder against the cloth.

As her vision dimmed, she saw a black-clothed figure—hood drawn, mask on—gathering an unconscious Navi into his arms.

The wrongness in the air swallowed Eliana whole. She wanted to be sick again, but the pressure bearing down on her throat prevented it.

A voice at her ear whispered, "And when the Gate fell, He found me in the chaos, pointed to my thirsting heart, and said, 'You I shall deliver into the glory of the new world,' and I wept at his feet and was remade."

Then Eliana slipped into a narrow pit, where the fading world around her jolted sharply before folding her away into nothingness.

35

RIELLE

"The mountain falls under my fists
The sea dries at my touch
The flame dies on my tongue
The night howls with my anger
The light darkens in my shadow
The earth fades beneath my feet
I do not break or bend
I cannot be silenced
I am everywhere"

—The Wind Rite
As first uttered by Saint Ghovan the Fearless,
patron saint of Ventera and windsingers

R ielle sat on a throne in the center of a dark room.
A narrow light illuminated her from above. Beyond lay a vastness of shifting shadows. She sensed that pieces of a world just beyond her reach were rearranging themselves, whispering to one another how best to play tricks on the foolish lit-up queen who thought she was something.

The throne beneath her was made of knobs and ridges that bit into her thighs. A voice whispered to her, *Look.*

"At what?" Rielle peered through the darkness. Doing so made her dizzy. "I see nothing."

Look closer.

Rielle obeyed. Days passed. Her eyes burned; she did not sleep. Voices whispered from a distant realm.

She rose from her throne. Desperate unseen hands grasped at the hem of her cloak. She tasted a sour ancient rot on her tongue.

"There is nothing here," she insisted. Time had shredded her voice.

Keep going.

She walked for centuries. The whispering voices grew bold. They became a conversation, then a din. They spoke in an unfamiliar language, but still she understood what every word meant and that all were spoken for her:

Maker.

Queen.

Liberty.

Rielle.

At last, she saw a spot of light in the distance and cried out. Was this finally the end? She had tired of walking alone. She wanted no more of these voices calling for her, of sensing the nearness of others, but not being able to find them.

When the light came into full view, she saw it was one she already knew—the illuminated throne.

And now she understood why it had hurt her to sit upon it.

It was made of bones.

Exhausted, elated, she sank down onto it. She clutched the throne's smooth white arms and knew them for the bones of those who had once tried to cage her.

"What is this place?" Rielle demanded. "I deserve an answer."

Shadows slithered around the bright solid wall of her throne, then coldly across her cheeks, her breasts, the curve of her scalp. She closed her eyes; her mouth fell open to receive a kiss.

The shadows became a man.

"This is where we have lived for an age," he whispered. He pressed his lips to the curve of her ear. "And where we will soon no longer be if you have the nerve for it."

"Corien," she breathed. "I don't understand what you mean."

He inhaled deeply. His mouth moved against her cheek. "Don't make me beg."

Rielle brushed her lips along the line of his jaw. "What if I want to make you beg?" she whispered. "What if I want you at my mercy?"

"Then I shall happily obey." He moved one white palm down her body, across the flat of her stomach. His knuckles grazed the tops of her thighs, and she leaned back to make room for him—

Rielle awoke with a choked gasp, her fingers already working between her legs. Three quick strokes, and she came apart, quietly pulsing around her hand. She turned her face into her pillow, seeking relief for her flaming cheeks, but the pillow was drenched in her sweat.

She sat up, her body trembling. Eyes squeezed shut, stomach in knots, chest tight around her heart. Fear chasing pleasure, pleasure chasing shame.

Then she realized how strange it was that she would have woken up in such a state, and Evyline would have said nothing.

"Evyline?" Her voice sounded like it had been run through with razors. "Evyline, are you—"

Something hard struck the back of her head.

She crashed to the floor. Pain throbbed through her skull and coursed through her body in waves. Cheek pressed against the plush carpet, she found the prone form of Evyline across the room.

Hands yanked her up from the floor. A dark heavy cloth came around her eyes. Someone tied it behind her head, too tightly, then fisted a hand in her hair, pried open her mouth, and forced a bitter liquid inside. She choked, tried to spit it up. Her attacker clamped her mouth shut. She was forced to swallow, coughing up as much as she could. Her nose burned; her eyes watered behind the blindfold.

People were talking above her head. Whispered instructions,

distorted and monstrous. Bizarrely, she was upside down. She could feel her head lolling and large arms cruel around her body.

Wake up!

How strange that anyone would tell her to wake up. She *was* awake; she had simply been poisoned. She tried to speak, made a terrible inarticulate noise. A gloved hand struck her hard on the temple. She hardly felt it. She was a girl made of fog.

"Don't kill her," came a voice. Rielle thought it sounded familiar, but the poison was clogging her ears and her brain and every pore of her skin. "I want her to feel it when she dies."

It was very cold, wherever they had gone. Cold and howling.

Strong hands pinned Rielle's arms behind her back. Her teeth were chattering; her nightgown was nothing against the wind. Under her bare feet was frigid, rocky ground.

For God's sake, Rielle, wake up!

"I am awake," she managed to mumble.

"Not for long." A thin, nearby voice whispered, "I'm sorry to say you won't be able to save yourself this time."

The blindfold was ripped from her eyes, and her mind exploded with fear. She blinked into sheer brilliant white: snowcapped mountains. Sky and a fine mist of clouds. A cliff's edge.

Oh, God.

"All hail the Sun Queen," whispered that mocking voice, and then the hands holding her arms flung her off the mountain to her death.

The wind punched her helpless body through the air as she fell.

She had no chance to scream—and no breath for it. Freezing wind slammed up her nose and mouth.

Save yourself! Corien's voice was frantic.

She was in the world, falling through the mountains, and she was also on the ground before her throne in that hollow dream realm. Corien scooped her limp body into his arms and tried to breathe life back into her.

Fight this! Fight it!

She knew he was right. She could fight this.

She forced open her eyes; the cold pulled thick streams of tears down her face.

I do not bend or break, she prayed. *I cannot be silenced.*

But the poison had formed an immovable wall between her body and the empirium. She reached for its power and found nothing.

She knew, then, that she was going to die.

No, you're not! Corien cried. *God, Rielle, no, please!*

Beside the throne, his face raw with grief, Corien cradled her body against his chest. The endless dark world around him sent up wailing, terrified screams.

A rush of swirling cold gusted up from below Rielle, spraying her with snow. A spinning ocean of gray peaks sped toward her.

When she closed her eyes, she saw Audric and Ludivine, and her heart clenched painfully with despair, and she wished, and she *wished*—

She slammed to a stop so sudden that it knocked the wind out of her.

But she felt no pain.

And she was rising.

A creature beneath her let out a piercing cry, part hawk, part horse, part...some unearthly, lonesome thing that sent a pang of longing through Rielle's heart.

She finally let herself understand the truth:

A chavaile—a *godsbeast*—had caught her midair and was now climbing up through the sky with Rielle nestled safely on its back between two massive black wings.

Stunned, still gasping for breath, she finished her prayer in the brilliant light of the morning sun:

I do not break or bend.

I cannot be silenced.

I am everywhere.

36

ELIANA

"We are the ones he calls at night
We are the vessels of his might
We speak the word that he has prayed
Upon his wings, our souls remade"

—The initiation pledge of the cult Fidelia

The world was a flat gray box, and Eliana lived inside it.
A floor, a wall, a ceiling. No windows. A metal door with a thin slot cut out near the bottom—and a narrow strip of light underneath it the only light source.

The air filled with faint, distant screams.

Slowly, she sat up and realized she was wearing plain white trousers with a matching tunic. Her feet were bare; the floor was cold and hard. Her knives…her knives were gone. As was her necklace.

A cell. She was in a cell.

She drew her knees to her chest, held her aching head in her hands.

Memories returned to her: Rahzavel grinning down at her, the shadowed rafters of Sanctuary arching high overhead. Simon crashing down from the stairs. Running with Navi, the world lurching around her with every step. Remy. She needed to get to Remy.

Her breath came thin and quick. She remembered, she remembered…

A hand over her mouth, poisonous fumes shooting up her nose.

Three women gone in three seconds.

Fidelia.

With a wild cry, she surged to her feet and slammed against the door—over and over, throwing her left side into each blow until her head spun and her teeth hurt. She would be bruised, but only for a little while. Might as well keep going, then, right?

"Who are you?" She pounded her fists raw, kicked her toes bloody. "Release me! Show me your fucking face!"

And then, she remembered one last thing: her mother. Her mother could be in this place.

She threw herself against the door with renewed fervor. "Mother? Mother, I'm here! Someone answer me! Answer me!"

But even her body had its limits. She screamed until her voice gave out. She crumpled to the floor, clapped exhausted palms against the door until she could no longer hold up her arms, then dragged herself to the corner of the cell and folded her body into a tight ball.

Eyes fixed on the bright line of white below the door, she waited.

She woke up when she heard Navi screaming.

Scrambling upright, she called out hoarsely, "I'm here! Navi, I'm here!" She crouched at the door, ear pressed to the metal, fingers flexed and ready.

Silence.

She held her breath. Had it been a dream?

The screams began again—heart-punching, shattered sounds like something being forcibly unmade. At first wordless, and then, minutes or hours later, Navi began to beg for an end.

"Kill me!" The screams became desperate shrieks. "Kill me!"

Inhuman roars joined the chorus, carved into pieces as if issued from many mouths.

Women?

Girls?

Beasts?

Eliana retreated to her corner, light-headed, hands clamped over her ears. She was not the Dread in this place. She forgot everything but the awful truth of Navi's screams and her own vulnerable, trembling body. She was a rat in this cell, and the catcher would come for her soon. The stupid animal part of her brain told her so. Faster than she had ever believed possible, it rose up to stomp out all of her training and left her shaking with fear in the dark.

Would they torture her for information and then feed her to a pit of animals?

What information did they want?

Red Crown?

Navi?

God, what they might have already learned from her...

Eliana paced. Movement made the fear feel smaller. She practiced slicing through the air with the tray that had brought food she dared not touch.

"I shall name you Arabeth the Second," she told the tray and then laughed and told herself to stop talking to trays right this instant. If she lost her mind so soon into imprisonment, it would be an insult to her mother's training.

"Arabeth," said a voice behind her, sonorous but warped and faintly amused. "A fine name for a weapon."

Eliana whirled and threw the tray at the shadowed shape that stood against the far wall. A woman, Eliana thought, tall and thin and... transparent.

The tray shot through the woman's body, hit the wall, clattered to the floor.

Cursing, Eliana staggered back as far as the cell allowed. "What are you? Show yourself!"

The woman obeyed, drifting forward until she knelt at Eliana's feet. She was a colorless distortion in the air. Shimmering, thread-thin lights outlined robes, a full mouth, and a mass of hair that fell to her hips.

"It's true, then," the woman murmured, reaching out to touch Eliana's hand.

Eliana's vision jolted, then blackened. She swayed on her feet, braced her hands against her knees, fought against unconsciousness.

"You don't belong here," she managed. "You feel wrong."

"I know," said the woman, a great sadness in her eyes. "I'm sorry for that. You will get used to it, if it's any comfort."

"You're Fidelia. Get the *fuck* away from me."

"I am certainly not Fidelia."

Eliana pressed her fingers to her temples. "I felt this sickness in Sanctuary, right before you took me. And the night you took my mother and when you took those girls from the slums—"

"I did none of this, my queen. The Prophet does not snatch girls from their beds, and neither do I."

Eliana squinted at the woman, breathing thinly through the ill feeling churning in her gut. "What did you call me?"

"There have been rumors for months that Simon found you at last," the woman continued, her voice thrumming with excitement, "but I did not let myself believe it until now. Now, I see your face, I hear you speak, I feel you breathe, and I know."

The woman floated nearer, cupped Eliana's face in her hand. Eliana felt nothing at her touch except for a fresh wave of nausea. She squeezed her eyes shut and sank to the floor.

"I'm going to be sick," she moaned.

"Forgive me, my queen." The woman moved quickly away. "I should not have touched you. It is difficult for humans to adjust."

"Who are you, *what* are you, and why are you calling me that?"

The woman bowed her head. "I am forgetting myself. If you only knew how long we've been waiting for this day...but then, you will know soon enough."

Eliana looked up as the woman stretched to her full, translucent height—eight feet, at least. Her elongated limbs reminded Eliana uncomfortably of a spider.

"I am Zahra," the woman said, "and I am a wraith. And you are Eliana Ferracora, the Dread of Orline, the last of House Courverie, daughter of the Lightbringer, heir to the throne of Saint Katell, the true queen of Celdaria, and..." Zahra spread her long arms wide. Her dark smile was full of joy. "You are the One Who Rises. The Furyborn Child. You are the Sun Queen, Eliana, and I have come to bring you home."

37

RIELLE

"Katell's writings show that, out of all the godsbeasts, she most favored the chavaile. Perhaps due to its similarity to the white mare that carried her into battle against the angels. Perhaps because its wings reminded her of her beloved Aryava and brought her comfort after his death."

—A Chronicle of the Godsbeasts
by Raliquand d'Orseau, First Guild of Scholars

T he chavaile did not stop until Rielle began to heave on its back. They touched down on a small rocky cliff dotted with stubby tufts of grass and sheltered by boulders as big around as King Bastien's carriage. Rielle slid to the ground and managed to crawl a few paces away before violently emptying her stomach.

After, hollowed out, she dragged herself toward the rocks, seeking shelter from the wind. Every movement sent shocks of pain through her body. The poison had done fine work; she felt as though she'd been hammered up and down every muscle and bone. She hoped she had gotten it all out—and not too late.

Then, lumbering hoofbeats approached.

She looked up. The chavaile had crept close. Bigger even than her father's largest warhorses, with an elegant arched neck, a long unkempt black mane, and bright, intelligent eyes, it behaved like a horse—and yet it did not. Its nostrils flared as it sniffed the air around her; its ears pricked forward curiously.

But then it cocked its head to the side, as a human might when trying to understand something new. There was an ancient weight to its presence that Rielle had felt surrounding no other living creature.

"Hello." She reached out feebly with one shaking arm. "You've always been my favorite."

A sharp blast of mountain wind slammed into her. She collapsed, shivering.

Beyond her closed eyelids, the light shifted. Then, at the sound of movement, she opened her eyes and watched blearily as the chavaile lowered itself to the ground between her body and the open sky. It extended one of its enormous feathered wings—it must have been at least twenty feet long—and gently scooped her close to its body.

Wedged between a shell of gray, black-tipped feathers and the warm swell of the chavaile's belly, Rielle breathed. The beast's coat was impossibly soft, speckled gray as a storming sky.

"Are you real?" she whispered, placing her hand against its stomach. "Where did you come from?"

In response, the chavaile settled its wing more securely around Rielle's body, then tucked its head underneath its wing. Rielle felt the hot press of its muzzle against her back, followed by a warm breath of air as it let out a contented grunt.

It was a strange nest, but too cozy to resist; Rielle fell into a fitful half sleep. Her shapeless dreams burned black.

When she woke, her mind was clear and the chavaile was watching her.

So. She hadn't been hallucinating.

She remained still, comfortable and warm beneath the canopy of its wing, and stared up at it.

"I thought all the godsbeasts were dead," she said at last. Hesitant, she placed her hand on the chavaile's muzzle. "Why did you save me?"

Its nostrils flared hot between her fingers. She stroked the long, flat plane of its face, the swirling tufts of hair between its wide black eyes.

"I wonder if you have a name."

The chavaile whickered softly and pushed its nose into Rielle's palm.

"Well," she said, beaming, "then I'll have to give you one."

And that was when she remembered:

That thin voice, right before she'd fallen. No, not fallen. Right before she'd been *pushed*.

She remembered it now, and she knew to whom it belonged.

"Will you take me home?" she asked. "I need to kill a man."

The chavaile watched her, motionless.

"It's all right," she added quickly. "He deserves it. He tried to kill me."

The chavaile grunted and rose to its feet. The chill hit Rielle hard, but she ignored it, climbed up a boulder with teeth chattering, and slipped onto the chavaile's back.

The chavaile looked back at her, ears pricked.

"Well?" Rielle wound her fingers through its wild black mane. "How do I get you to go?"

At once the beast launched into a gallop, snapped open its wings, and leapt off the mountain into the sky.

They approached Baingarde fast from the north, soaring low over the treetops covering Mount Cibelline, and then circled around the castle to the broad stone yard in front. It was full of people: Rielle's father and the city guard, her own guard, pages and stable hands hurrying horses to their riders. Her father shouted instructions; a team of four mounted soldiers took off for the yard's southern gates.

He was organizing search parties, she realized with a swell of satisfaction.

There was Audric, swinging up onto his stallion, and there was Ludivine, reaching up to touch his arm, and there—

Ah. There he was, the sniveling little shit.

The rage that had been boiling in Rielle's heart erupted.

She tugged gently on the chavaile's mane and shifted her weight, turning the beast left and down. Its wings flattened against its sides as it dove. She lowered her body against its neck, closed her eyes. The wind raced past her, and she tugged the power from it like plucking a fiddle's strings. When the chavaile landed, the crowd scrambling to part around it with cries of horror, Rielle did not wait for the beast to stop before jumping to the ground.

She stormed across the yard, thrust her palm in front of her. The wind snapped rigid in her hand like an executioner's noose. Her prey watched her approach in disbelief, cowering and white-faced. She flicked her wrist. The noose of wind caught the man around his neck. Still a good twenty feet away from him, she slammed shut the massive twin doors of Baingarde's front entrance, then pinned Lord Dervin Sauvillier against the closed doors—and squeezed.

He gasped for breath, clawing at the invisible hand closing around his throat. Rielle watched him with a hard grin, raising her hand higher. Lord Dervin's body slid up the doors until he hung some ten feet off the ground, feet kicking wildly.

"Lady Rielle," he croaked, his face reddening, "what—*why*—?"

"Shut your mouth, you filthy coward," Rielle snapped. "You know why."

Audric ran to her. "Rielle, what are you doing?"

"Stop!" Ludivine threw herself in front of the doors, reaching in vain for her father's feet. "Rielle, you'll kill him!"

"He tried to kill me." Rielle squeezed her fingers closer together. Lord Dervin squirmed, gagging. "He drugged me, brought me up into the mountains, threw me off a cliff. I'm merely returning the favor."

Dimly, she heard soft cries of shock among the gathered crowd.

Ludivine turned, mouth open in disbelief. "You're lying."

"Tell her, Lord Dervin."

When the man did not reply, Rielle took two furious steps forward and clenched her hand into nearly a complete fist. "Tell your daughter the truth," she shouted, "or I will execute you for your crime right here, right now!"

Eyes bulging, face gone a deep, vivid purple, Lord Dervin at last gasped out, "It's true. I tried to kill her."

Ludivine's hands flew to her mouth. Dismayed exclamations rippled through the crowd.

And still Rielle did not move. Her lungs were afire, the hand that held the noose shook white-hot, and a fringe of bright gold swirled around the edge of her vision.

Kill him, screamed her heart.

Kill him, roared her furious blood.

Kill him, whispered Corien.

Audric stepped between her and the doors, took her empty hand in his.

"Rielle, look at me." His voice was quiet but firm. "I need you to look, please."

Rielle shook her head and snarled, "He tried to kill me."

"I know. And believe me, he will be punished for it. I will see to it myself."

She blinked at that. Her vision cleared; her blood cooled. Reluctantly she tore her wild eyes from her would-be murderer and looked to Audric instead.

"Please, darling." Audric gave her a tight smile. "Listen to my voice, and let him go. If you kill him right here, in front of everyone..."

Rielle knew he was right. Abruptly she turned away, letting her hand fall. Lord Dervin slid to the ground with a choked cry.

"Call for the healers!" Ludivine cried, gathering her father up in her arms as best she could.

"For...you," Lord Dervin said, his voice a wheezing rasp. He touched her face. "I did it...for you. Ludivine."

Her skin humming with furious energy, Rielle turned away to scan the gaping crowd. When she found who she was looking for, watching her in amazement from the center of the yard, she approached him at once.

"Your Holiness." She bowed, then spoke loudly enough that everyone gathered could hear. "I wonder if you might accompany me to the Firmament? I would like to pray to Saint Ghovan, and to the wind for sparing my life, and I can't think of anyone else I'd rather have for company."

The chavaile joined her, tossing its head.

The Archon could not stop staring up at the creature, his face gone deathly pale. "I don't understand," he muttered. "All the godsbeasts are dead. Lady Rielle, how did you do this?"

It was a question she had herself been wondering. "I was going to die," she answered honestly, "and I asked the empirium to save me. I had been drugged and could not use my power, so..."

"So the empirium...sent you this?" The Archon gestured helplessly at the chavaile. It snorted and bumped Rielle's shoulder with its nose.

For the first time since Rielle had known him, the Archon seemed rather at a loss.

"Shall we?" She offered him her arm. "To the Firmament?"

Without a word, the Archon took it, and as they proceeded across the crowded yard, he said quietly, "Be careful, Lady Rielle. This is no longer a matter of trials and costumes." He glanced back at the chavaile, which followed them at a distance. The awestruck crowd crept as close as they dared. Some ran away in a panic, shouting warnings. "The empirium has helped you today, but it may not always do so. It is my duty to test you. I do not wish to see you consumed."

"Don't you?"

The Archon did not respond to the tease in her voice, and when

Rielle glanced over at him, she saw a new expression on his face, drawn and thoughtful, that sent a thrill through her body. She couldn't decipher the sensation.

Fear?

Corien's voice came crooning: *Or appetite?*

⤙ 38 ⤚

ELIANA

"Not all angels are alike, and not all worship at the Emperor's feet. There are those who have taken pity on us and believe the Emperor's actions to be cruel and unjust. They remain bodiless and are considered traitors to their kind, all in order to ally with humans—descendants of those long-ago saints who once drove the angels into the Deep."

—*The Word of the Prophet*

E liana sank to the floor with a tiny dark laugh and rubbed the heels of her palms against her eyes.

"I don't have time to sit around listening to...whatever this is. And whatever you are." Eliana struggled to her feet and moved to the door. She was hallucinating. She was talking to a hallucination.

"My name is Zahra," said the wraith.

"Right."

"Rozen is not here."

Eliana turned. A slow, panicked feeling unfurled in her chest. She kept her face blank. "Who's Rozen?"

"The woman you think is your mother but truly is not."

"Do you know a way out of here?" Hallucination or not, if she could use it to escape, she would.

"Yes."

"Then either show it to me or fuck right off, would you please?"

Zahra raised one floating eyebrow. "This is not how I had imagined you would be."

"Sorry to disappoint." Eliana resumed pounding on the door with angry clenched fists.

The wraith appeared between her body and the door. Eliana's fists flew through the wraith's torso. Her balance tilted, her vision phased in and out of focus. She backed quickly away.

"What *is* that? Every time you come near me—"

"You feel ill." Zahra nodded sadly. "It is a common human affliction when in the company of wraiths. You'll get used to it, over time. Others have. Though you seem to be affected far more than most. Unsurprising, given your ancestry. Your sensitivity to changes in the empirium is undoubtedly tremendous."

Eliana glared at the floor. "Get me out of here."

"Wait a moment."

"Get me *out*—"

The wraith rose to her full height once more, her black eyes flashing. "We can't leave yet. We must wait first until the shift change is complete, and second for you to calm down, so I can be assured you won't do something rash and endanger yourself." Zahra exhaled sharply, considering her. "Simon's message was accurate. When you're angry, you very much resemble your mother. How unsettling."

Eliana shook her head. "This is quite an elaborate delusion."

Zahra raised one amused eyebrow. "I assure you, your mind is quite sound."

"You know Simon, do you?"

"I do. Though, only through messages passed through the underground. I serve the Prophet, and so does he."

"The Prophet this, the Prophet that," Eliana muttered, rubbing her temples. "Who is this man, and why does everyone fawn over him so? What does he want, anyway? There has to be more to him than simply some noble selfless desire to save the world from tyranny. And how long has he been around? Is there one Prophet or many?"

"You certainly have many questions. I don't blame you." Zahra drifted to the door, cocked her head. Listening? "But perhaps we'll wait until a bit later for a Red Crown history lesson."

"You're Red Crown?"

"Obviously. As I said, I serve the Prophet."

Eliana longed to punch something. "What are we waiting for exactly? I promise I won't act rashly. Is that what you want to hear, my imaginary little friend? All my rashness has fled, I swear it."

Zahra's black mouth thinned. "No matter how long I spend among humans, I sometimes forget that I must actually put voice to my thoughts for you to understand."

"As opposed to?"

"When I speak to my own kin," Zahra explained, "I have no need for words."

"Wait, you..." Could Remy have been right? Were the old stories true after all? "You mean mind-speak."

Zahra inclined her head.

Eliana's blood ran cold. Suddenly the idea of conversing with her own hallucination no longer amused her. "You're an angel."

"Once, I was. But no longer."

"Well," said Eliana, retrieving her tray from the floor, "if I hadn't already decided to mistrust you, I certainly do now."

"I understand that compulsion. Our two races have not always been friendly."

"What is it you want with me?"

"To take you home," Zahra said patiently, "as I told you before."

"To Orline? Why?"

"Not Orline. Celdaria. We cannot go immediately there, of course, but—"

"I've never even been to Celdaria," Eliana snapped, though her

336

stomach tightened unpleasantly at the name of the far eastern king-dom. Her vision of the Emperor returned to her, as though it had been carved into her mind and coated with dust, and now a sharp wind had uncovered it.

"You have, once," Zahra argued. "My queen, you were born there."

"Ah, I see. Of course I was."

Zahra frowned. "You're mocking me."

"Tell me what you want me to know, and I'll say yes to it all, and I'll believe what you want, as long as you get me out of this cell and help me find Navi."

"I'm afraid I can't do that."

"But you just said—"

"Princess Navana is not our priority. Nor, I must add, is Rozen Ferracora. You, Eliana, are all that matters—to Red Crown, to the Prophet, to all enemies of the Empire."

"If you don't help me rescue Navi and then help me search for my mother, I will make every last second of your life a miserable and agonized one."

"I doubt that," said Zahra, "as you will die long before I will."

Eliana froze. "Is that a threat?"

"It is a fact. You are a human. I was once an angel, and now I am forever trapped as this." She reached down with long-fingered hands, picked wistfully at her robes. "I will live long past the age when the last human walks the earth. And yet, if given the chance to step backward in time, I would make the same choice."

Eliana narrowed her eyes. "What choice is that?"

"I would choose to stay in this form—stripped of all physicality—rather than be resurrected. What so many of my kin have done is abhorrent."

At Eliana's blank expression, Zahra sighed. "Am I to assume from the look on your face that you, the Sun Queen, are unfamiliar with the stories of how the world once was?"

"I know the stories," Eliana bit out impatiently. "My brother won't shut up about them."

Zahra's expression softened into something like pity. "Simon sent word about him as well. Remy, yes?"

Tears rose hot and sudden in Eliana's eyes. "Don't you dare say his name."

Zahra reached for her, then closed her hand and floated back. "I wish I could touch you and give you comfort, my queen. That is the thing I miss most of all about my body."

Eliana looked to the ceiling, willing her eyes dry. "You may call me Eliana. Nothing else."

"As you wish, Eliana. But whatever name I use, it does not change the truth. You are my queen, and I serve you with great joy."

"Then," Eliana said through her teeth, "get me out of here."

"I have always intended to do so," Zahra said patiently, gesturing at the door. "The shift change is underway. In five minutes, once the new guards have settled into their posts, it will be safe to move. Believe me, my queen, I would not keep you here longer than absolutely necessary."

"I will start pounding on this door and ruin our supposed escape if you don't open it this instant."

"And here I thought all your rashness had fled."

"I'm not joking, whoever you are."

"Zahra."

"Yes, right."

"Anyway, feel free to pound on the door all you like," said Zahra, folding her vaporous arms smugly across her chest. "No one will hear you."

Eliana narrowed her eyes. "And why wouldn't they?"

"Though I may no longer look like an angel, and though my mind is not what it once was, I can still use it. And right now I am using it to make the vermin of Fidelia forget you are here."

Eliana's heart pounded hard in her ears. "You mean…you're hiding me."

"As best I can, yes." Zahra hesitated. "Though once Semyaza finds us, that will change. Wraiths are not strong enough to deceive other wraiths."

"Semyaza?"

"He serves this faction of Fidelia. He helps them hunt, disguises them, and distracts their prey. It was him you sensed in Sanctuary." Zahra turned up her nose. "You'll find, Eliana, that not all wraiths are as enlightened as I am."

"What does he want? Why is he helping them?"

"Semyaza hopes that if he serves the Empire loyally, then once the Emperor has found the Sun Queen and bound her to him, Semyaza will be resurrected. He will have earned a body at last."

Eliana shook her head, stepping away from Zahra. "I don't understand what you're saying. Resurrected?"

"It would be easier to show you, Eliana. If you'll permit me to take hold of your mind?" She tilted her head toward the door. "We have just enough time for it."

"Take hold of my mind. Like the Emperor did?"

"What?" The drifting tendrils of Zahra's hair and robes went rigid. "You have spoken with the Emperor?"

"At an outpost several days ago, I was...I was with Lord Morbrae. He looked at me, and something changed. I saw the Emperor. I was in Celdaria somehow. I couldn't see anything very well, but I could see enough. And the Emperor, he found me standing there, and he... he *knew* me. I don't know if he was happy or furious to see me. And I don't know which is worse."

Zahra closed her eyes. "Simon did not send word of this. Oh, he has seen you. He knows, then, that you are alive."

"Why does the Emperor care who I am or that I'm alive?"

The wraith's huge, dark eyes were terribly sad.

"May I show you, Eliana?" Zahra whispered. "Forgive me, but it will be easier for me than words." She shook her head, sank to the floor. "This is a shock. This is an awful blow."

Eliana crouched before her. "You swear to me that my mother isn't here?"

Zahra peeked out from behind her hair. "Yes. Simon's instructions were to send word if any of us found her. But I have not."

"Wait." Eliana's body drew tight as a bowstring. "He knew that Fidelia took her?"

Zahra nodded miserably. "We were all told to look out for her."

So. Simon had known. He had *known* who had taken her mother— and, Eliana suspected, he had known Fidelia was behind the other abductions too.

And he had not done a thing about it. He had led her across the country on this wild quest without so much as a whisper of the truth.

She gripped her knees, hard, and stared at the stained stone floor of her cell.

I will kill him for this.

"You may show me what you want to show me," she said, her voice trembling with barely contained fury, "as long as you then help me find Navi before we leave this place. Do we have a bargain?"

Zahra nodded. "Yes, Eliana. I pledge this to you."

Eliana gave her a grim nod. "Then do it. Quickly."

Without warning, Zahra collapsed into a twisting cloud of light and shadow. Her new shape resembled great, jagged black wings.

Then she rushed at Eliana and disappeared.

And Eliana opened her eyes—and she *saw.*

Unlike when she had seen the Emperor, this vision was all too clear.

There was no fog blocking her sight. She felt the steaming hard ground beneath her feet. The air was close, rippling with heat; her nostrils burned from the ash darkening the air.

Movement at the corner of her eye made her turn. A woman stood watching her, tall and ebony-skinned, wearing a suit of tarnished platinum armor. Her thick white hair fell in braids past her hips, and gold paint rimmed her dark eyes. Massive wings of shifting light and shadow spanned out from her back.

"Zahra?" Eliana whispered.

Even Zahra's small nod was magnificent. "As I was during the Angelic Wars. Before the Gate. Before the long curse of the Deep and the loss of my body." Then she pointed. "Look, Eliana."

Eliana squinted across the fire-ribboned plain, and images rushed at her like the horrors of a nightmare:

A woman stood on a distant flat plinth. She raised her arms and carved a blinding door from the sky.

A castle flashed white, then fell, and from the abyss around it rushed a wave of ruin. There was a cry of pain and fear, a chorus of thousands—*millions*—and then silence.

The screams of a woman in a bloodied bed.

A baby, held tightly in the arms of a boy. Eliana peered over the boy's shoulder, and she knew as she stared at the infant that the face looking back up at her was her own. Then she turned to see the boy, and—

A vastness of black, filled with screams too alien to belong to either human or animal. There was a light on the horizon and a figure standing beside it. Eliana cried out, crushed by the lonely weight of this place, and ran toward the light—

She was back on the firelit plain, watching a woman kneel beside a dismembered, blood-soaked corpse. The woman's back was to Eliana. She wore a suit of black armor and a crimson cloak. The woman moved pale hands over the corpse, knitting across skull and collarbone, down chest and across severed hips. The air around the corpse shimmered, shifting, and then the woman sat back, calm, and the corpse jerked, gasped, and staggered to his feet. He was no longer a corpse. His skin was whole and new, his limbs intact. He took a few unsteady steps before falling to his knees. He looked down at his body and then threw out his arms and shouted to the skies—with joy, with relief, with fury.

The woman rose, smooth and silent, to her feet.

"You're working faster now," said the man beside her, whom Eliana had not noticed before. "Well done." He drew the woman into an embrace, and Eliana stood frozen in horror as their faces came into view.

The woman was dark-haired and unspeakably beautiful, with a face so pale and faultless it could have been carved from porcelain—save for the shadows stretching dark beneath her green eyes and the small, hungry smile curling her mouth.

Eliana brought shaking fingers to her own lips.

My mouth, she thought and then touched the brittle ends of her own tangled dark hair. *My hair.*

And the man standing beside this woman—blue-eyed instead of black but with the same lovely pale face and untroubled poise that graced the painted portraits in Lord Arkelion's palace. Black hair, mud-caked cloak, a bloodstained sword at his belt. He guided the woman's mouth to his, and she clung to him as if their kiss was the only reason she remained standing.

The Emperor.

Eliana frantically backed away, tripped over another corpse, fell to the ground hard.

The world shifted, darkened.

She blinked.

She had returned to her cell, and Zahra hovered quietly in front of her—a mere distortion of the air once more, ephemeral and wingless.

"Please breathe, Eliana," Zahra urged gently. "I know it is a great deal to understand."

Eliana gasped for breath, tears streaming down her face. Her skull felt too heavy for her body. Her skin still felt flushed from the battle-field's flames.

"That was him," she croaked. "That was the Emperor. But..."

"That was the Emperor before he called himself the Emperor.

When his name was simply Corien. He was the first of us to escape. And I am sorry that he was."

Remy was right. The thought kept circling through Eliana's mind. *They're angels. The Emperor, his generals, Lord Arkelion, Lord Morbrae. Remy was right.*

"And the woman," she whispered. "I know her face."

"I would imagine so." Zahra touched Eliana's hands, and Eliana felt nothing. "For it is your own, is it not?"

"Partly. More beautiful. More..."

"More unkind." Zahra offered a small smile. "You have a kind face, Eliana, though you try to make it not so."

Eliana crossed her arms and shut her eyes. "That's why he recognized me. The Emperor. *Corien.*"

Zahra was silent.

"What were they doing?" Eliana asked. "That *body.*"

"What he failed to accomplish with your mother before her Fall ruined all their work," Zahra said, "and what he hopes to finish with you. Resurrection. Our return—and our revenge."

"Our. The angels?"

"Yes, Eliana."

When Eliana opened her eyes once more, her body felt caught on a high, hot wind—floating, untethered.

"I hope you are lying to me," she said at last. "Please tell me you're a hallucination. I won't be angry, I swear it."

Zahra bowed her head. "I wish I could."

"I am the daughter of the Blood Queen." Her voice came out hollow, heavy. "Daughter of the Kingsbane."

"You are."

"I don't believe you."

"That is understandable. It does not, however, change the truth."

Eliana stared at the floor through a furious fog of tears. "How did I get here, then? If I was born back then, to *her*, and now I'm here... How?"

"That, I'm afraid, is not my story to tell."

Eliana laughed wearily. "Of course."

"Eliana, I'm not being coy—"

Eliana waved Zahra silent. She waited until her tears had dried, until she felt she could stand, until she could almost believe the story she told herself—that this was indeed a hallucination, some horrible dream brought on by whatever Fidelia had used to knock her unconscious.

Zahra said quietly at the door, "It's time to leave."

Eliana rose to her feet, wiped her face on her sleeve, and said to Zahra, "Then get me out of here. I have things to do."

❧ 39 ❧

RIELLE

"I worry about Tal. I've always worried about him for reasons I couldn't name, and now I understand why: because he has lived a lie for years, for the sake of this girl, and now is suffering for it. I would never say this to him, but I write it here or else it will burst from my tongue: I hate her for doing this to him. Yes, she was only a child when it all began. But after that, as she grew and learned? What then? What stayed her tongue? Fear? Or malice?"

—Journal of Miren Ballastier, Grand Magister of the Forge
June 8, Year 998 of the Second Age

When the doors to the Council Hall opened, Rielle rose from her chair and steeled herself.

She did not expect her father to enter and hurry straight toward her, his face pale.

Rielle's guards formed a tight circle around her.

"Sorry, Lord Commander," said Evyline, her hands hovering above the hilt of her sword. "I can't let you past."

"Let him past," ordered King Bastien, the Archon and the Magisterial Council filing in behind him.

As soon as the guards stepped aside, Rielle's father hurried over and gathered her close.

"Oh, my darling girl," he whispered against the top of her head.

Rielle's shock was so great that tears sprang to her eyes before she could draw a full breath. "Papa?"

"I'm sorry. I'm so sorry."

Rielle's thoughts had scattered at the touch of her father's hands. How long had it been since he had held her like this? Years.

She clutched his jacket, burying her face in the scratchy, stiff fabric. All at once, she was four years old again, and her mother was still alive, and nothing had happened except a few unexplained odd incidents: candles extinguishing themselves, an overflowing sink, a crack appearing in the kitchen floor beneath Rielle's small, tantrum-throwing body.

All at once, she was four years old again, and her father still loved her.

"Papa," she whispered, "I was so frightened."

"I know." He wiped her tears with callused fingers. The implacable Lord Commander of the Celdarian army was gone, and in his place was a mere aging father. "He won't hurt you again."

King Bastien, standing before the council table, cleared his throat. "Lady Rielle."

She turned to face the king, but her father remained at her side, and despite everything, a part of Rielle's heart she had thought long dead swelled with joy.

"Yes, my king." She curtsied. "I must apologize for my treatment of Lord Dervin."

"No, indeed you must not." The king's face was grave. "Lord Dervin has been found guilty of attempted assassination and is being sent home to Belbrion, under house arrest for the remainder of his days. He and his accomplices will never again set foot in this castle."

Rielle immediately looked past the king to Queen Genoveve, rigid in her chair, and then to Ludivine, who sat in the corner with her hands held tightly in her lap. Audric stood behind her, his hand on her shoulder.

When Ludivine's red-rimmed eyes met her own, Rielle had to look away.

"I…I don't know what to say, my king," she said quietly. "I cannot be glad for it, and yet I must thank you."

But you are glad for it, Corien murmured. *In fact, you wish you'd kept going, don't you? You wish you'd squeezed your fist closed, popped his head right off.*

I don't.

His voice was low and angry: *Don't lie to me, Rielle.*

She flinched at the sound; it came like a sharp slap.

King Bastien's smile was tight but genuine. "I am glad you are safe, Lady Rielle," he said, taking his chair. "Now, the Archon has an additional piece of news for you."

The Archon rose from his seat. Rielle looked at once to Tal, who was trying unsuccessfully to hide his smile.

Beside him, Sloane scowled and elbowed him in the ribs.

"Lady Rielle," the Archon began, "it is the unanimous decision of the Magisterial Council, including myself, that, given recent events, we shall forgo the remaining two trials and now begin the canonization process."

Rielle stared at him, silence gathering around her in thick spools until she at last managed to say, "But…what does that mean?"

"This means, Lady Rielle, that you have demonstrated tremendous control and power throughout your trials thus far—"

"And that," interrupted Grand Magister Duval with a broad grin, "by surviving a fall off a mountain and arriving back home not only alive but with a flying godsbeast, you have more than fulfilled the requirements of the wind trial."

The Archon sniffed. "In short, Lady Rielle, in the eyes of the Church, you are indeed and inarguably the Sun Queen as foretold by the angel Aryava, and therefore will be accorded all protections and privileges that are due you as a symbol of the Church and the protector of Celdaria."

As Rielle listened to him speak, her heart pounded harder and faster until it felt ready to burst from her chest.

No more trials.

No more training.

No more dark rooms or hiding herself away.

All of this, and a kingdom full of people—a *world* full of people—cheering her on.

But would that be enough? Were five trials—four if she counted shadow and sun as one—and a fall off a mountain sufficient to claim her crown?

Some people would be satisfied with that, but not all.

Some would insist she fight the only remaining element she had not faced.

Fire.

She glanced at Tal, saw him watching her carefully. A thrill of her oldest, deepest terror raced across her skin.

Tal nodded, his mouth in a grim line but his gaze soft.

"...of course," the Archon was saying, "I must still discuss what has happened with the other churches of the world. But stories of your trials have already spread so far and so quickly that I doubt I will have trouble convincing them of what and *who* you are. You will visit them, if you must, to prove yourself. Or they will come here, and we will show them that any doubts they may have are baseless."

Beside Rielle, her father bristled. "Must she be paraded around like a prize horse?"

But Rielle hardly heard them.

She could hear only her mother:

Rielle, darling, please help your father put the fire out.

Rielle, it's time for bed.

Rielle, I'm not going to ask you again!

She opened her eyes. Breathing in, she smelled the smoke of her parents' house crumbling to ashes, heard the horrible choked sounds of her father sobbing over his wife's body.

Corien's words were gentle: *You are not your mother. The flames, if you face them, will not hurt you.*

Rielle's breath snagged on tears she would not allow to fall. *Hurting myself is not what I'm afraid of.*

The Archon was addressing Rielle's father. "I cannot say what the other churches will require of her. But rest assured, Lord Commander, that whatever they request will have to go through me before it so much as touches your daughter's hem."

"This also means, Lady Rielle," said King Bastien, "that once you are anointed Sun Queen, you will take on not only the privileges of the position but also the responsibilities. You understand what this means."

Rielle shook her head. "No. I don't agree to this."

"I beg your pardon?" asked the king.

"I'll accept your generous offer regarding the wind trial, my king," she said. "I survived my fall; I've suffered the wind's wrath. Fine. But"—she looked to Tal, imploring—"I must complete the fire trial."

The Archon frowned. "But, Lady Rielle, we have decided that is not necessary."

"Forgive me, Your Holiness," interrupted Tal, "but Lady Rielle is right." He gave her a small smile, then addressed the king. "Some in the world will be satisfied with four trials and a fall off a mountain. But not all. Some will insist Rielle fight the only element she has not yet faced. And that is fire."

Rielle blinked, startled. *Did you tell him what to say?*

I nudged him that way, Corien replied. *Your teacher has a remarkably open mind, easier to slip into than most.*

Please, don't. Rielle swallowed hard against a sudden tilt of fear. *Not him. Not any of them.*

Corien fell silent. Then, his voice coy and curling: *Shall I tell you what secrets I sensed in that pretty blond head of his?*

"Is this what you want, Rielle?"

The entire room was staring at her. It took her a moment to realize that Audric had spoken. She gathered her scattered mind.

"It is," she replied. "Not only to show the world that I have mastered every element but also because…my mother died in a fire. Of my own creation."

To her left, her father tensed. She reached for his hand, her heart in her throat.

After a moment, he curled his fingers around her own.

The part of Rielle that had come alive when her father embraced her now grew wings and took to the skies.

"I would like," she said, "to prove to myself, and to my father, that I am no longer that girl of ashes and ruin. I am stronger than she was. I am stronger than any flame that burns."

That evening, Rielle skipped dinner and instead paced through her rooms.

"Are you sure you don't want something to eat, my lady?" asked Evyline from her post by the door.

"I'm quite sure, Evyline, thank you."

Evyline glanced out at the terrace. "Do you think your beastly friend will be with us for long, my lady?"

Rielle grinned to see the chavaile there, sleeping curled up on the dusk-lit stone terrace as happily as a cat.

A very large, very horse-like cat.

"I don't know the ways of godsbeasts," she told Evyline. "But I certainly hope she stays."

Evyline tugged at her collar uneasily. "Do you think, if I asked, she would let me pet her?"

"Why, Evyline, I've never seen you so bashful."

A knock on the door interrupted them.

"Lady Ludivine here to see Lady Rielle," called out Dashiell from the corridor.

All joy vanished from Rielle's heart. "Please let her in, Evyline."

Evyline looked dubious but obeyed, her hand on her sword.

Ludivine entered, looking utterly wrung out—her hair a mess, her face red and swollen.

"Hello." She could not meet Rielle's eyes. "I wanted to see if you were all right."

"Well, I'm alive," Rielle said shortly—then winced. "Sorry. I'm fine. Just resting."

Ludivine nodded slowly, sitting on one of the hearthside chairs. "I see." A terrible silence filled the room.

At last, Rielle blew out a breath and took the seat opposite Ludivine. "Lu, I don't know what you want me to say or do right now, but I won't apologize for—"

"I don't want you to apologize," Ludivine snapped. Then she scrubbed her hand over her face and sighed. "Do I wish you hadn't tried to kill my father? Yes. Do I wish he hadn't been sent home?" She paused. "No. I'm glad of it. I'm so furious with him I can hardly think straight."

She shook her head, staring into the fire. Then she moved to kneel before Rielle, gathered Rielle's hands in hers.

"Am I glad you are alive?" Ludivine whispered. "Oh, my darling." She pulled Rielle down into an awkward hug. "I love you so much I feel I might break from it. I'm so glad you're all right."

Rielle helped Ludivine rise and walked her to the bed. She drew back the covers and helped Ludivine lie down, then snuggled close beside her. Resting her cheek against Ludivine's shoulder, she let Ludivine cry herself out, and when at last Ludivine stopped, Rielle looked up with a smile.

"You'd better not wipe your nose in my hair."

Ludivine let out a shaky laugh. "Can I stay here tonight?"

"I insist that you do."

Another knock on the door: "Prince Audric to see Lady Rielle."

"Let him in," said Ludivine and Rielle at once.

Audric entered, then hesitated when he saw Rielle and Ludivine in bed. "I can come back later."

"Don't you dare." Ludivine patted the pillows. "Come. We're having a party."

Audric approached cautiously. "Are you crying, Lu?"

"Yes, she is," answered Rielle, "and if you don't hurry up and get over here, she'll start all over again, and you'll feel terrible about it."

Audric rubbed a hand through his hair. "Is this really the wisest thing to do? I mean, considering…"

"Audric, calm down, there's not anything wrong in it. I almost died today. I thought I'd never see either of you again, and I'd like my friends near tonight. Come lie down with us." She sat up, extended a hand to him. "Like when we were little?"

His expression as he took her hand was unbearably fond. "We're not little anymore."

"Pretend it for me. We used to play pretend all the time. Remember?"

Ludivine laughed. "I recall a certain prince obsessed with pretending he was a horse day and night, running down the halls on all fours and banging up his knees."

Audric settled in the bed beside Rielle, above the blankets. Disappointment nettled her, but she bit her tongue to keep from teasing him. She would be satisfied with his nearness and the solid heat of his body.

"I was a very good horse, I thought," said Audric. "I had the neigh down and everything."

"There was a particular day," Rielle added, "when you tucked one of your mother's scarves into your trousers and pretended it was your tail."

Evyline's cough sounded suspiciously like it was meant to cover laughter.

"Go on," said Audric, stretching out on the bed with a happy sigh. "Keep embarrassing me. I don't mind."

Beside Rielle, hidden from view by the bed linens, Audric touched his hand to hers. She wrapped her fingers around his, warmth rushing sweetly down her body, and felt herself dangerously close to moving right where she shouldn't.

—◆◆—

"You should have visited me sooner."

Rielle tried not to scowl. Garver Randell had done that enough for the both of them. "It was rather a busy day yesterday," she said dryly, "what with the attempted murder and all. Besides, I saw the king's healer right away."

"That man's an idiot. Why do you think Audric comes to me instead?" Garver screwed a lid onto the jar and shoved it across the table at her. "Take a spoonful four times a day until it's gone. Waspfog is a nasty poison. You'll feel queasiness for days, can't do anything about it, but this will help."

"How much do I owe you for it?"

"Only this: next time you're poisoned or almost murdered or stabbed or strangled or—"

"I get the point."

"Yes, well, next time, don't wait a night before coming to see me." Garver heaved himself up from his chair with a tired grunt. "Prompt, *proper* care conducted by healers who are not idiots can make the difference between life and death. Even for Sun Queens."

With his back turned, Rielle rolled her eyes.

"I heard that," he said mildly.

Rielle grinned, then looked out the open door to the courtyard, where Audric was showing Garver's little son, Simon, how the chavaile liked to be petted. Beyond the courtyard, people crowded at Garver's front gate, gaping at the prince and the godsbeast, probably wondering why this boy was special enough to get an audience with the creature.

"It's funny," she murmured, watching tensely as Simon reached for the chavaile's neck with his eyes squeezed shut.

But the chavaile only closed her eyes and leaned into his touch.

Garver had started to sweep. "Hmm? What's funny?"

"Atheria doesn't usually like it when people touch her."

"Who in God's name is Atheria?"

"The chavaile. Do you like the name?"

"Whatever her name is, I'd rather not have her stomping up my flowers."

"Besides me," Rielle said, "Atheria only lets two people touch her. Audric, and now..." She smiled as the beast nibbled at Simon's hair. The boy went perfectly still and stood wide-eyed while Audric shook with silent laughter. "And now, it seems, your son is the second."

~40~

ELIANA

"Tender lost lambs will wander into our fold, dumb
and blind, driven by His call. Gather them close. Teach
them His word. Remake them as He demands. Punish
those who defy Him, for they are truly lost."

—*The First Book of Fidelia*

When the door opened, Eliana hurried out into the brightly lit corridor.

A male guard stood just outside, staring blankly at the wall. A ring of keys dangled from his hand.

Eliana found the two keys Zahra had described—one a plain and dirty brass, the other thin and silver—and removed them from his ring. It was as Zahra had said: the soldier didn't move or even blink.

She stepped back, watching his face.

The corner of his mouth twitched.

According to Zahra, a proper angel would be able to influence the man's mind for as long as necessary. But, as a bodiless wraith, Zahra could only affect him for seconds at a time. And even then, she'd told Eliana bitterly, her ability remained unpredictable and easily drained.

The man's hand moved, as if in sleep. He blinked. His body shifted.

"Go." His mouth moved, but Zahra's voice emerged. "Hurry."

The man would awaken—and soon.

Keys in hand, Eliana ran down the deserted hallway in her bare feet. Metallic doors lined the gray stone walls.

She found the alcove that Zahra had told her about—the entrance to a supply closet—and pressed her body flat against the wall. Eyes watering after so long in darkness, she squinted up at the buzzing yellow lights lining the ceiling—and waited.

A minute passed. Then Zahra drifted into the alcove.

"Through here—quickly," she whispered, gesturing at the closet door. "I'm sorry, Eliana. I wish my protection was as strong as you deserve. But the Fall damaged so many things, including the minds of wraiths."

"Don't apologize. You're doing fine." Eliana used the brass key to open the closet door and hurried inside. The space was long and narrow, lined with shelves crammed with tied bundles, packs of food, boxes labeled with unfamiliar lettering.

She crouched, searching the lower shelves. "I don't recognize that writing."

"One of the old angelic languages," Zahra explained. "To be initiated into Fidelia, you must learn all five."

"And those lights outside, in the hallway. I've never seen anything like them."

"Galvanized energy. One of the Emperor's many experiments. Have you found them?"

"Not yet. Wait." Eliana opened a wooden crate with metal clasps. Inside was an array of weaponry and gear, including her own. Whistler, Nox, Tuora, Tempest. Only her beloved Arabeth was missing—lost forever, she supposed, on the filthy floors of Sanctuary. She strapped her holsters to her legs, her arms, her waist, sheathed the knives, and straightened with a sigh.

Zahra watched, a smile rippling across her face. "Better?"

"Much."

"Before we go." Zahra pointed at another shelf. "This is yours, I believe?"

Her necklace. Eliana's heart lifted to see its battered brass face—though now the sight of those familiar lines reminded her of Zahra's words: *the daughter of the Lightbringer.* Did she believe such a wild story? And if it was true, how much of the truth, if any, had Rozen known?

And could she even still call Rozen her mother? And Remy her brother, Ioseph her father?

A fist of sorrow seized her heart, but she shoved away her questions. None of them mattered if she couldn't first escape this place.

She settled the chain around her neck and said to Zahra, "Lead the way."

They returned to the corridor, keeping to the shadows.

"Here," Zahra said at last, drifting to a stop outside one of the metal doors. Black numbers reading 36 had been stamped on its surface.

Eliana's pulse jumped as she fumbled with the long silver key and let herself inside.

"Navi?" she whispered, once she had pulled the door shut. "Don't be afraid."

The air in Navi's cell was stale and squalid—waste and sweat and something acrid and medicinal that made Eliana's tongue tingle. She saw a small pile against the far wall, rushed over, hesitated, then took Navi gently by the shoulders and turned her over.

Hovering beside her, Zahra made a soft noise of pity.

"Oh, Navi," Eliana breathed, unable to hide her shock.

Navi's head had been shaved, and her skin was a mosaic of pain—ugly dark bruises, angry red wounds, thin black markings with numbered figures beside them, as if Navi had been labeled with instructions for some malevolent seamstress. At Eliana's touch, Navi moaned, her swollen face crumpling with pain.

Eliana whispered, "What have they done to her?"

"Their work is abominable," Zahra said, her voice low and furious. "I have tried to stop them when I can, but without giving away my presence to Semyaza, there is only so much I can do."

Questions gathered angrily on Eliana's tongue, but she would ask them later. She heaved Navi's body off the ground and slung the girl's limp arm around her shoulders. "Show me the way out of here."

"I cannot hide you again," Zahra whispered, wringing her smoky hands together. "I used the last strength I had on that soldier in the corridor."

Navi mumbled something pained against Eliana's shoulder.

"How long until your strength returns?" Eliana asked.

Zahra looked away, as if ashamed. "I cannot say. My queen, I swear to you, I wasn't always so weak."

"We'll just have to escape like normal people. Let's go."

They left Navi's cell and hurried down a maze of corridors, the strange galvanized lights humming overhead. Zahra drifted ahead, then hurried back in time to warn Eliana of approaching Fidelia soldiers.

Eliana crouched with Navi in the shadows of a small alcove, her hand gently over Navi's mouth. The soldiers passed, carrying a dead-eyed woman on a canvas stretcher. Bulbous dark growths marred her body.

Eliana's stomach turned.

"It's clear," Zahra whispered and led the way once more.

Gritting her teeth against the persistent nausea of Zahra's nearness, Eliana followed. When they exited the compound into a flat dirt yard bordered by tall stone walls, they took cover behind crates piled high with stinking wrapped heaps that she suspected were bodies. Night stretched vast above the compound, with faint blue at the horizon.

"Are we on a mountain?" Eliana whispered.

"Yes," answered Zahra, "and not far from the northern border of Ventera."

That explained the cold and the wind. "How far from Rinthos?"

"Four days' ride."

Eliana whipped her head around to stare at the wraith. "Four *days*? How long have we been here?"

"A week."

Eliana closed her eyes, fighting back a swell of panic. Eleven days since their capture. Eleven days away from Remy, and no idea of where he might now be.

Navi moaned quietly, her head lolling against Eliana's shoulder. "Eliana?"

"We're going to have to run soon," Eliana said quietly. "Can you wake up for me, Navi?"

Zahra uttered a hissed curse.

Eliana tensed. "What is it?"

"Semyaza is here." Zahra jerked her head at the perimeter wall. "He was supposed to be out on tonight's hunt. He must have realized you were gone or sensed my own presence."

Eliana squinted across the yard, seeing nothing—but then, a disturbance rippled in the air. There was a shift, a flicker of a dark shape. A man, but taller and longer-limbed than a human.

Fear dried out her mouth. "What do we do?"

"I'll take care of Semyaza," Zahra said, her voice hard—and, Eliana thought, rather delighted. "You'll hear a loud crash when I hit him and see a slant in the air. Run for the gate on the eastern wall. Run until you can't anymore, then hide in the forest. I'll find you, if Semyaza doesn't trap me first."

"Trap you?"

"I'll explain later."

"But the guards." Eliana gestured at the Fidelia guards patrolling the yard. "I can't fight off all of them, especially not with Navi."

"What we need," Zahra mused, "is a diversion."

The western wall exploded.

Eliana ducked low over Navi as stone and wood went flying across the yard, then peered through the clouds of dust to see that a thirty-foot section of the wall was now gone.

Zahra stretched to her full height. "Well," she said cheerfully, "that will work."

Then she zipped out into the chaos and disappeared.

Eliana waited, wiping sweat from her forehead.

A low boom rattled the yard, as of two winds colliding. Fifty yards away and ten feet above the ground, a patch of light shifted and warped, swirling like a whirlpool's mouth.

Zahra had found Semyaza.

Eliana hefted Navi back to her feet and slapped her across the face. Her drug-clouded eyes snapped open, and Eliana was pleased to see a spark of anger inside them.

"We have to run, now," Eliana told her, "or we'll die."

Navi nodded, set her jaw.

"Hold on to me." Eliana turned, Navi's arm once more slung around her shoulders, and ran into the yard. Beside her, Navi's breathing came labored and thin. In the bedlam of dust and shouting soldiers, no one saw them—until they had almost reached the abandoned eastern gate.

A Fidelia soldier jumped down from the gate's watchtower, a crude revolver in hand and a belt of ammunition strapped to his torso.

Eliana skidded to a halt.

The Fidelia soldier smiled kindly.

"There, now, lambs," he said, gesturing with his gun, "you've gotten turned around in all this ruckus."

Eliana watched him approach, saw him glance at the knives she had strapped to her body. His gaze hardened; his smile remained.

"Poor lambs." His gun still pointed at Eliana's chest, he brushed a lock of matted hair out of her eyes and clucked his tongue. "So lost, so young."

A shift in the darkness behind him was Eliana's cue. She lowered her eyes to the ground, nodded forlornly.

"We didn't mean to do wrong," she whispered—and then heard the familiar sound of Arabeth finding a home in someone's heart.

She looked up as the Fidelia soldier grunted, gaped down at

Arabeth's jagged blade protruding from his chest, coughed up a pool of dark blood.

Behind him stood the Wolf, mask in place.

Eliana's exhausted body nearly buckled with relief. Despite everything, she said, "Thank you."

Simon wiped Arabeth clean on his cloak and handed it to her. "I'll trade you."

Eliana complied, shifting Navi into Simon's arms. They hurried together out of the yard and into the night, down a rocky slope cluttered with flat pale stones that crumbled underfoot.

"Remy?" she asked.

"Safe and hidden." Simon's mask glinted, moon-colored. "We're going to him now."

And when we get there, Eliana thought, tightening her grip on Arabeth as she ran, *we will speak alone, with my blade at your throat.*

RIELLE

"No one can be sure of Audric the Lightbringer's last words, but in the days before the Fall, whispers trav-eled fast across the world. His last words, the whispers said, were for his murderer: 'I love you, Rielle.'"

—The Last Days of the Golden King
author unknown

Three days. Rielle dragged herself up to her rooms long after the sun had set. *Three days until the fire trial.*

And then...what?

"My lady," chided Evyline from the door, "you really must try to get more sleep, at least until the trials are over."

"You're right, Evyline," Rielle replied. "It's only that when you're soon to be thrown into a death pit of flames, you find yourself wanting to study your prayers as much as you can."

"Prayers are well and good, my lady, but sleep is better. You can neither pray nor fight fire if you're exhausted."

Rielle, yawning, untied her braid and shook her hair free. "I'm inclined to agree. My father, however, is not."

After checking to make sure Atheria had taken her usual nighttime post on the terrace, Rielle stumbled into her bathing rooms.

And froze, suddenly and wholly awake.

Audric sat on a settee by the far window. His hair was a mess of curls, as though he'd been running his fingers through it for hours. He stood to face her, hands clenched at his sides.

He gave her a tight smile. "Hello," he said quietly.

Rielle stepped back into her bedroom. "Evyline," she called over her shoulder, "I hope you don't mind, but I wonder if you might give me some time alone."

"My lady, it isn't safe—"

"I'm quite safe with Atheria on my terrace."

As if on cue, the chavaile snorted from beyond the curtains.

"Grant me this wish, would you please?"

"Just tonight," Evyline said sternly, after a moment. "The least I can do, I suppose, after everything you've been through."

"That's right." Rielle ushered her out as kindly as she could manage. "Good night, Evyline, and thank you for your vigilance."

"Of course, my lady."

Rielle shut the door, locked it, took a breath to brace herself. When she turned around, Audric was standing in the middle of the room, looking rather abashed.

"I'm sorry for sneaking in," he said, "but I wanted to see you. I won't make a habit of it, I promise."

"Maybe you should," Rielle teased—but her voice came out shaky.

Audric's dark gaze searched her own, then fell to the floor.

A flurry of nerves danced up her breastbone. "Did you want to talk to me about something?"

"Yes, it's—" Now his voice was the unsteady one. He cleared his throat. "I'm afraid, though, that I shouldn't. That I'm a fool for coming here tonight."

"You know you can tell me anything."

"I know."

"Then talk to me." She reached for him. "What is it?"

He brought her hand to his lips. "Rielle," he whispered against her skin, "Rielle, Rielle..."

"You're frightening me. Say something other than my name. Say something real."

"Something real." He laughed a little and stepped away from her. "It's just…"

When he fell silent again, Rielle thought she might scream. "Audric, if you don't start talking this instant—"

"You understand what all of this means, don't you?" He gestured at the castle around them. "I will be king someday, and you will be the Sun Queen."

"Well, not if the fire trial—"

"Oh, Rielle. You'll conquer that trial as you have all the others. You'll be glorious, and then…" He dragged a hand through his hair, turned away, then back to her. "Then you will serve me, and if I have to send you into battle to save the kingdom, I will do it. That is the Sun Queen's foretold purpose: to defend and protect. And I cannot stray from that simply because I love you."

His voice caught on the last words.

Rielle approached slowly, her heart pounding. She touched his arm, and when he looked down at her, his eyes warm and troubled, she cradled his cheek in her hand.

He leaned in to her touch, cupped her hand in his, and kissed her palm. "I know I shouldn't touch you," he said, his voice rough. "We decided it. We had good reasons. But, God help me, I've been able to think of little else since that day in the gardens."

Rielle moved closer to him, drawing his hand down to her waist. "Remember, Ludivine doesn't care. She wants us to."

"It's not Lu or her family. Not anymore. Now I'm wondering…" He leaned his forehead against hers, closed his eyes. "If only I could stop loving you."

"What are you saying?"

"As Sun Queen, you will be sacred to our people, Rielle. A symbol longed for and prayed for since the dawn of our age."

"Let's not call me that unless it actually happens. I'm nervous enough as it is."

"The Archon will bless you in front of the entire city. I cannot interfere with that. I cannot tarnish it."

She stepped back from him. "Are you saying taking me into your bed would tarnish me somehow?"

He looked at her helplessly. "I don't know how to both love you and be the person who sends you to war."

She crossed her arms over her chest. "Are you just now realizing that could happen? What did you think the trials were for, exactly?"

He turned away, eyes bright.

She followed him. "Audric, I want you to listen to this, for I will only say it once."

He looked up at the change in her voice.

"If you ever sent me into battle," she said, "I would go gladly, and I would burn our enemies to ashes. But I would not do it for you—or because of the prophecy. I would do it because this is my home too. And if you tried to keep me near you for love of me, you would fail."

He stared at her, the air between them snapping taut and furious. She lifted her chin and dared him silently to defy her.

But he didn't. Instead he strode toward her and caught her mouth hungrily with his.

She gasped into his kiss, stumbling back from the force of it. He steadied her, hands at her hips, and moved with her until she stood pressed between the wall and his body. She opened her mouth to him, wound her fingers through his hair.

His hands were everywhere—first cradling her face, then cupping her hips to pull her closer against his body. When he trailed his lips down her neck, and lower, kissing along the neckline of her gown, Rielle arched her body up into his.

The fire popped and hissed.

"Yes," she whispered, tugging up his shirt to find bare skin. "*Yes.*"

His voice was a low rumble. "Yes what, darling? Tell me where to touch you."

"Where you did before. Please, Audric."

He moved back to her mouth as he gathered up her skirts, then slid his palm across her thighs. At the first touch of his hand on her belly, Rielle jerked against him with a gasp.

"Spread your legs for me, Rielle," he murmured, his voice shaking at her ear. "I've got you."

She complied, and when his hand found her, stroking softly between her legs, she cried out and clutched his shirt in her fists.

The wall at her back trembled.

He slid one finger inside her, his thumb still stroking her. "Every night since that day," he whispered against her mouth, "I've dreamed of this. I wake with your name on my lips."

No matter how Rielle moved, she could not get enough of him. She dug her fingernails into the small of his back, pulling him closer. "Faster, Audric. Harder, *please*."

He obeyed. "Like this?"

"Yes, *yes*." She felt herself stretch around his fingers; he had added another, thrusting faster. "Like that, oh, God—" She let out a sound she had never made, a low, throaty groan that shook her to her toes.

"That's it." Audric kissed her temple, her hair. His voice was full of wonder. "That's it, Rielle."

She clung to him, ground her hips against his hand until the tingling wave that had been building deep inside her crested, sweeping across her skin and down her spine. She jerked against him, gave a sharp cry, and shattered.

The room shook around them.

The lit candles across the room sparked, jagged flames leaping inches into the air. The hearth fire snapped; embers scattered across the carpet. The walls quivered for a few seconds, as if caught in a small quake, then fell silent.

"What was that?" Audric whispered.

"It was me." Rielle closed her eyes, her cheeks flaming. "I'm sorry."

"You?"

"We shouldn't have done that. Let me go, please."

He released her, and she moved away unsteadily, straightening her gown. She could think only of her father's voice, so many years ago:

You might lose control one day, hurt him.

The last thing Audric needs is someone like you hovering about.

"You should go," she said, folding her arms over her chest.

Audric was quiet for a moment. "I will, of course, if that's what you want. But first, would you tell me what happened?"

"Four trials, and I was fine. I made it through; I felt stronger than ever before. And now? A few moments with you, and I make the room fall apart."

"Nothing's fallen apart. Rielle, it was only a little tremor."

She whirled on him. "Only a little tremor? And what if we had kept on? What if I had lost control? What if the floor had cracked open beneath our feet? My father was right. He could see it before I did."

"What did he see?"

"That I love you!" she burst out, tears splitting her voice. "That for all my years of work, every night alone, every prayer… It's undone when I'm with you. You touch me and I burn, and I could take everything burning down with me!"

"Rielle, look at me." Audric took hold of her hands so gently that she began to cry in earnest.

"I'll hurt you," she whispered.

His eyes were steady and warm on her face. "You won't."

"If anything happened to you because of me, I couldn't bear it, Audric. I won't do it. I'll be alone forever if I must."

"No, no, not you." He tenderly turned her face up to his, feathered soft kisses across her cheeks. "You deserve only happiness. Not a cold bed and an empty room."

She closed her eyes at his touch. "I'm too dangerous."

"You're just my kind of dangerous."

"This isn't a joke, Audric. This is your life—and mine."

"And my life is pale without you in it." His hands cupped her face. "I'm not afraid of you, Rielle. I trust you, and I want you."

Rielle leaned into his chest, breathed him in—his sun-warmed skin, the cotton of his tunic.

"What if I asked you," she said at last, "to kiss me again?"

"I would kiss you all night and never tire of it."

She pulled back to look up at him. "And if I asked you to take me to bed?"

"Then I would take you there," he said, "and not rest until you'd had your fill of me."

"That's just what I want." She kissed the triangle of skin above his collar and whispered, "I want you to fill me."

She stretched onto her toes to kiss him before he could reply, and when his arms came feverishly around her, she grinned against his mouth and let out a delighted laugh.

"Bed," she whispered, pulling him blindly toward it.

He backed her up against one of the bedposts, his mouth never leaving hers. He kissed her as if the air inside her was what he needed to survive. She put her hands behind her, against the post to brace herself, and arched toward him.

"Yes," he said breathlessly, fumbling with the line of buttons down the front of her gown. He slid the bodice down her torso so that it pooled around her waist. Her breasts fell free, and he lowered his mouth to them at once, groaning against her skin.

Rielle twisted beneath him until she could bear the ache between her legs no longer. "I need you," she gasped, clutching his shoulders. "Please, Audric."

He pulled his tunic over his head, then undid his belt, kicked off his boots. He moved her toward the bed, sucking gently on her bottom lip. Together they tugged on her gown until it fell to the floor.

Audric murmured, "My God, Rielle, you're beautiful," and helped her down onto the pile of blankets strewn across the bed. His hands traced the curves of her breasts, her waist, her hips. He kissed each of her bruises from the shadow trial, murmuring her name against her skin more lovingly than any prayer.

When his hips settled on hers at last, Rielle barely managed to stifle her scream. He threaded his fingers through her own, pressed her hands gently back against the pillows. At each shift of his hips, a new wave of pleasure surged inside her.

Shaking beneath the hard, warm lines of his body, she said desperately, "Audric, *please*."

"Wait." He kissed the curve of her chin, pulled slightly away. "Wait a moment."

"No, *now*."

"Before we do this—"

She heard the cautious note in his voice and understood. "I'm taking a tonic for it." She tenderly touched his face. "Please don't worry."

He nodded, lowered his mouth to hers, murmured, "I love you, Rielle," and entered her in one smooth movement.

She cried out, bucking against him. She felt impossibly, deliciously full and touched his face with a breathless laugh.

"Are you all right?" he whispered.

"Fine." She clutched his arms, smiling up at him. "Don't leave."

"Never. I'm sorry—"

"No. Don't be sorry. I'm fine." She touched two fingers to his lips, let out a shaky laugh. "I'm more than fine."

He grinned, kissed the soft skin beneath her eyes, and began to move inside her. Rielle gasped, arching up against him.

"Look at me," he urged her quietly, and when she locked eyes with him, the focused devotion on his face made her heart swell. "I'm right here, and I love you. I love you, I love you."

"Kiss me," she whispered, trembling.

He obeyed, his mouth warm and slow on hers, echoing the gentle thrusts of his hips.

"Should I stop?" He kissed along her jawline. The soft scrape of his teeth sent delicate chills across her skin. She closed her eyes and shifted beneath him. Pleasure swelled slowly up her body, warm and unhurried.

"Don't stop," she murmured. "Not ever."

"Rielle. *Rielle.*" He moved a bit harder against her, his voice darkening. "Tell me what you want, and I'll do it."

She twisted in his gentle grip with a sigh. "I want to hear what you want. That is my wish."

"I want to make you come apart in my arms. I want you to forget your fear, your worries, whatever darkness haunts your thoughts." He slid one hand down her body to their joined hips, stroked between her legs.

She cursed, slammed her palm against the bed, fumbling for an anchor. His hand found hers, steadied it in his own.

"What else do you want?" she murmured, gazing up at him. She moved her hips against his own.

"I—" His voice broke. He shook his head, shuddering as she slid a hand up his arm. She brought his hand to her mouth, kissed his palm.

"You want to make me scream."

He made a small, choked sound. His hips jerked sharply.

"God, yes," he groaned.

"Faster, then." She touched his lips with her thumb. When he took it in his mouth, his eyes drifting shut, she shivered and smiled and hooked her leg around his. She could have watched him like this forever—losing himself in her, coming unraveled in her arms. "Please, Audric."

Even as he obeyed, his gentleness astounded her. His hand released hers to cradle her face, then slid down to caress her breasts. The sweet ache of him inside her drew shuddering waves across her skin. She arched up into his touch, clutched the blankets in her fists.

She let out a frantic little sob. "Audric, *please*—"

He murmured into the hollow of her throat, his hands shaking around her, "Yes, Rielle, *yes*, that's it." The rough longing in his voice set her afire. When she slid her hands into his hair and tugged hard on his curls, he cried out against her neck, and the desperate, utterly male sound was her undoing, sending her spiraling up and up, until she fell back against the bed, pulsing golden with pleasure. She clung to him, helpless and limp, her vision a buzzing haze, and stroked his hair as his hips slowed.

And with the solid weight of Audric above her—his lips in her hair and his voice hoarse with love, her own body feeling blissfully boneless—Rielle watched the sparking bright flames around her room with no fear in her heart and thought nothing of Corien at all.

⊸ 42 ⊷
ELIANA

*"Have you ever seen the Wolf? Talked to him? The man's
got a bad light in his eyes. You look at his face for half
a minute, you see he's been ripped apart and sewn back
together more times than anyone ought to have been."*

—Interrogation of an unnamed Red Crown
defector, preceding execution

S imon brought them to a Red Crown safe house deep in a pine
wood at the base of a cliff—a small log cabin, draped in moss and
cloaked by a tangled thicket of trees.

As soon as Eliana stepped inside, she heard a soft cry and looked
around in time to see Remy jump off a chair by a tiny stove. When she
knelt to catch him, his hug nearly knocked her over.

"Stop leaving me behind," he whispered into her hair. "El, I woke
up, and you were *gone.*"

She closed her eyes, pressed her palms against the delicate bones of
his back. He'd grown thinner since leaving Orline.

Then, as he wiped his cheeks on her shirt, she remembered Zahra's
words: *The woman you think is your mother but truly is not.*

The boy she thought was her brother but—

Remy pulled away from her, face splotchy and tear-streaked, and
gave her a brave smile. "Hob taught me how to use the stove. I'll make
you some supper."

And Eliana decided at once that Zahra was wrong, even if the wraith had been speaking the truth. Even if Ioseph, Rozen, and Remy Ferracora were not hers through blood, they were hers at heart, always, and if anyone tried to tell her differently, she would send them crashing to their knees at her feet.

She dried Remy's cheeks with her thumbs. "Only if you make some for yourself too."

As he hurried away toward the stove, Eliana found Hob himself at the far side of the room, settling Navi into a small bed.

"Is Camille safe?" she asked.

"When we left her, she and her people were alive and well," Hob replied. "Simon sent that Invictus assassin limping off into the night."

Eliana's stomach dropped. "Rahzavel. Simon didn't kill him?"

"Unfortunately, no."

She closed her eyes. "He won't rest until he finds me."

"Well, at least he's not here now. You can thank Simon for that."

Eliana refused to acknowledge that or the man in question. "Why are you here? What about Patrik?"

"Simon took some blows in that fight. I wanted to help him get the boy to safety." Hob smiled at Remy. "He's good company, your brother."

On her cot, Navi shifted with a moan. Hob wrung out a rag in a pail of water and draped it over Navi's forehead.

"Have you seen this before?" Eliana asked him. "What's been done to her?"

Hob's face was tight with anger. "No. I don't know what this is, and I'm not sure I care to." He drew a quilt up to Navi's chin, tucked it around her body. "Camille requested I ask after Laenys. The girl, her missing attendant. She was taken by Fidelia as well?"

Laenys. She had completely forgotten to look for the girl.

Eliana shook her head, hoping Hob couldn't see the truth on her face. "There wasn't time to look for her. I'm sorry."

"Do you know what they were doing there? Fidelia. Did you find out why they steal girls?"

"I don't, but the sounds I heard while in my cell—"

"It's all right. You don't need to tell me, Dread." The word had no venom in it, only a heavy sadness. "You should rest. When Simon returns, you'll be leaving soon after."

Simon.

Eliana turned, searching the room for him—but he was gone.

She barely restrained herself from flinging Arabeth at the wall. "Where did he go?"

"To meet a contact at the border who will help you across the Narrow Sea to Astavar," Hob said.

Eliana began unstrapping the knives from her body. "Do you have clothes for me? Something other than prison garb."

"You're not leaving again?" Remy asked quickly.

She gave him a small smile. "Not leaving. I just want to sit outside, get some air after being cooped up in a cell for a week."

And so she could see Simon before the others—and not let him past until she'd gotten the answers she deserved.

Zahra arrived two hours later, appearing without warning at Eliana's side.

Eliana spat out a curse and jumped up from the tree stump she'd been sitting on.

The wraith's black smile was barely visible in the shadowed trees. "Hello, my queen. I mean...Eliana."

"Next time," Eliana hissed, returning to her seat, "give me some warning before you just pop into the air like that."

"I am overjoyed to see you as well, especially since we parted in such a dire moment."

Eliana sighed sharply. "Yes. Thank you for that."

"For what?"

Despite her irritation, Eliana smirked. "You're going to make me say it, aren't you?"

"I did risk much by engaging Semyaza," Zahra pointed out. "Though I would do it again, and happily, to serve you."

"Thank you, Zahra," said Eliana with a sweep of her hand, "for battling Semyaza so Navi and I could escape. Your loyalty and bravery are to be commended."

Zahra's form shimmered with pleasure. "You sounded very regal just then, Eliana. Blood will out, as they say."

"I don't want to talk about my blood," Eliana snapped.

"As you wish." Zahra paused. "It will, however, have to be discussed eventually."

Eliana looked away into the trees. "And if I don't believe what you claim?"

"You forget I was in your mind, back in your cell," Zahra said gently. "I think you've known for some time that something was misaligned in your past. That you aren't like those around you. There is the matter of your body's ability to heal itself, for one."

Eliana whirled on her. "Listen to me right now, wraith. You may have the power to enter my mind, but you will not do so again unless at some point in the future I demand it of you. And until then, you will not even once mention the Blood Queen or the Lightbringer or whatever person it is you think I am. Is that understood?"

Zahra bowed her head. "Of course, Eliana. I will respect your wishes."

"Thank you."

They sat in silence for a long time, the woods quiet and dark around them.

"Do you know what they did to Navi?" Eliana asked at last.

"I wish I didn't," Zahra replied. "Throughout the long years since the Blood Queen's Fall, the Emperor has undertaken many experiments in an attempt to achieve resurrection without her. Medicines, drugs, surgical procedures, manipulation of what he calls genetics."

"What is that?"

"Put simply, it is the basic life structure of any living creature. Not the empirium—not even the Emperor can touch that, much to his despair—but it is effective nonetheless."

Eliana shook her head. "And he uses it for...what?"

"He is creating things," Zahra murmured, "with the help of healers who exchange their skills for their families' safety. He is creating creatures that aren't quite human or animal. They are called crawlers. They are monsters, Eliana. *Mutations* is the word I've heard used by the Empire physicians. And an army of them is bound for Astavar."

Eliana stared at Zahra, her mouth gone dry. "I don't understand. They have a whole army of adatrox, an army that's devoured the world. Why this too?"

"There are many ways to strike fear into the hearts of those you have conquered," Zahra said gravely. "The continued existence of Red Crown eats away at the Emperor, as does the resistance of Astavar. He is creative. He will think up new horrors for every day that any human walks free, until there is no fight left in you."

"And only women, only girls?" Eliana's stomach turned. "Why? If it's an army he wants, why not abduct a bunch of hulking men?"

"That, I don't know."

"And that was what happened to Navi? She was being turned into...?" She couldn't finish the question.

"By the state of her, it looks to me as if she has only gone through the early stages. Not transformation, but that will come soon—"

Zahra fell silent, then whispered, "Simon is near."

Eliana tensed. "Is he alone?"

"Yes." The air around Zahra suddenly felt charged. "He has run afoul of angels."

Eliana drew Arabeth and surged to her feet. "You said he was alone."

"He is. But..." And then Zahra closed her eyes, shuddered, and made a low sound of pain. "How does he bear it? I never knew..."

"How does he bear *what?*" Eliana scanned the trees.

"His mind bears many scars," Zahra whispered, her eyes still closed. "Deep ones. How they must hurt him."

"What kind of scars? Explain to me, with real, ordinary words."

"Someone has hurt him. Badly. Again and again. I can feel it as he approaches. I'm not trying to invade his thoughts, Eliana. But when someone's mind has been abused so thoroughly, a wraith cannot help but feel it."

Zahra zipped around to hover behind Eliana.

"Beware of him," she whispered. "He is almost here. I can hide you if you wish. I've regained enough strength for a few seconds."

"Beware of him *why?*"

"A man with such scars cannot be fully trusted, for those wounds hide his full truth, even from a creature such as I am."

Eliana narrowed her eyes. "You mean, you *can't* read his thoughts?"

Zahra shook her head. "I know he's near, that he lives in pain he shares with no one. But I can see no more than that. Eliana, I'd no idea Simon was such a man. I would never have trusted his word... Oh, please, let me hide you from him."

"No." Eliana caught a flicker of movement in the trees. Her heart kicked wildly. "I will speak to him."

"He won't be able to see me," Zahra whispered. "You are the only human who can."

That surprised her. "Why?"

"No one else has enough power for it. Since the Fall, all your eyes have been shut to the empirium—"

"What are you doing out here?" Simon emerged from the trees, lowered his hood, and removed his mask. "You should be resting."

Shaking her nerves free of Zahra's hovering fear, Eliana stalked toward him. "I was waiting for you."

He stopped, watching her approach. "Oh? To what do I owe the pleasure of a private meeting with the Dread of Orline?"

She marched past him into the trees. When her shoulder brushed his arm, the touch shot through her, shoulder to belly, like a hot arrow. "Come with me."

"An illicit encounter in the dark, dark woods," he murmured, following her. "My most secret dreams have come to life."

She kept silent until they had gone a few hundred yards from the safe house. Then she stopped, facing away from him, arms rigid at her sides.

"The building where I was held captive by Fidelia," she began, her voice tight. "What was it?"

"Laboratories," he answered at once.

She turned, steeling herself. "For experimentation on the captured women."

"Yes."

"Where they are turned into crawlers, thanks to the Emperor's study of genetics."

A flicker of surprise moved across Simon's face. "You have spoken to someone. Who?"

Beside Eliana, Zahra muttered low, "Someone who will protect her at all costs."

Simon unsheathed the sword at his belt. "Who's there? Step away from her, or I'll gut you."

So Zahra was right. He couldn't see the wraith, but he could hear her.

"I did speak with someone," Eliana replied. "Someone who told me you knew about Fidelia all along. You knew who they were, what they were doing. You knew they took my mother, and you knew where to look for her. She wasn't in the laboratories where I was kept, but she is somewhere else—and I'm sure you know, being the mighty Wolf, exactly where across the country Fidelia can be found. And yet instead of telling me any of this, you dragged me through the wild and kept me in the dark, knowing all the while what was happening to her."

Simon stood frozen, his sword still in the air.

"Your silence," Eliana said, fury rising fast in her chest, "is all the confirmation I need."

"I did what I was ordered to do," he said, his voice made of stone.

She let out a scornful sound. "The mighty Prophet's orders, I suppose."

"The Prophet sees much and guides my every step."

She turned away, too angry to speak.

"If you slice at him," Zahra said quietly, "I won't try to stop you. I'll make sure to hide the noise from the others."

"I don't want to hurt him," Eliana said. "Not yet."

Simon's voice was tight with frustration. "Who are you talking to?"

Zahra rounded on him, an eight-foot tall echo of the woman she had once been. "If you continue to upset my queen," she boomed, vibrating with anger, "I will strike you down where you stand."

"Who is this?" Simon spat. "Show yourself."

"Your eyes are not worthy of me, Wolf."

Simon stilled, his expression clearing. "Zahra. The wraith who's been spying for us."

Zahra let out a sharp laugh. "I spy not for you but for my queen."

"She keeps calling me that," Eliana whispered. "She says…" She let out a shaky burst of laughter.

Behind her, Simon sheathed his sword. She heard him approach her, slowly.

"She says you are the Sun Queen," he said, his voice very low.

She looked back at him. The shadows drew new scars across his face, but his eyes were clear and sharp, even in the dim light, and in them, she saw a spark of something—pity, she thought, and a burning conviction.

"She says you are the One Who Rises," he continued, "the Furyborn Child. She says you are the daughter of the Lightbringer and that she will do anything to protect you." He hesitated, the muscles in his jaw working. "She isn't the only one."

"Tell me the truth, then, if you care so much about me." Eliana's voice came out a hard whisper. "Tell me no more lies."

"A few months ago," he said, moving through the trees, "I heard of a bounty hunter called the Dread of Orline. A girl, the rumors said, who had racked up an impressive number of kills. One of the highest in the Empire, in fact." He stopped, turned back to Eliana. "A girl who was invincible."

Eliana watched him, waiting. Her body felt so tense she feared it might snap.

"A silly enough rumor to dismiss, at first," he continued, "but I kept hearing it, again and again, and when I told the Prophet, I was ordered to investigate. I would go to Orline, find this Dread, and observe her. And if it was nothing, I would bring Princess Navana north, as was my original mission. But the rumors were indeed true. I knew you, Eliana, as soon as I saw your face."

His voice took on a rough quality that filled Eliana with a slow-creeping fear. What he was saying...whether it was madness or not, he believed it.

"How could you have possibly known me for anyone?" she asked. "We'd never met before that night in Orline, and—"

"I knew your parents," Simon interrupted quietly. "I see them on your face as clearly as I see the sun rise at dawn."

She stepped away from him, the truth settling slowly in her mind. "It was never about me helping you bring Navi to Astavar. You didn't need me for that."

"No. When I found you, my mission to bring Navi home became secondary to keeping you safe. Everything," he said, moving urgently toward her, "is secondary to keeping you safe. Navi's life. My life. Red Crown."

She stared at him in horror. Zahra murmured close to her ear, "He isn't wrong in this, Eliana. We may not trust him altogether, but this, at least, is the real truth."

Simon shot an irritated glance Zahra's way.

"It's not my fault your human eyes aren't strong enough to see me," Zahra said archly. "There's no need to scowl."

"I don't understand," Eliana whispered. "This is ludicrous."

Simon stopped just short of touching her. "Why do you think your body can do what it does? You've been lying to yourself about it for years, and I understand why, but it's time to face the truth."

She lifted her chin, fumbling for speech. "I've just been lucky is all."

"You don't believe that." He did reach for her then, his touch on her cheek so gentle it was a mere whisper of warmth. "It's your power, Eliana. The power you inherited from your mother. It's fighting to awaken at last. And when it does—"

A scream pierced the night, followed by Remy's voice: "El, he's here!"

Glass crashed against stone.

A brilliant orange light flared to life through the trees, illuminating the awful truth:

The safe house was on fire.

A familiar figure stood before it, staring out into the trees with a flaming torch in one hand.

Simon swore.

"Tick, tock, tick, tock!" crowed Rahzavel. "We're all waiting for you, Dread! Come out and play!"

RIELLE

"Marzana wandered the bitterly cold Kirvayan tundra in search of solace. She dared not touch anyone for fear of burning them and wandered alone for long months until stumbling upon a fresh green woodland tucked inside a canyon of ice. A fire burned in its heart, and as Marzana warmed her feet, a red-eyed firebird emerged blazing from the flames, and Marzana was not afraid."

—*The Book of the Saints*

After Tal's acolytes removed her blindfold, Rielle stepped out of her tent and onto a stone platform, a cloak of feathers draped around her shoulders.

A wall of sound slammed into her—cheers, cries of her name, ringing handbells. For Rielle's final costume, Ludivine had drawn inspiration from Saint Marzana's firebird. A scarlet jumpsuit embroidered with golden flames clung to her curves. From her shoulders spilled a dramatic ten-foot-long cloak fashioned to look like trailing wings. Feathers of brilliant violet, vermilion, and amber covered the cloak from clasp to hem. Ludivine had gathered her hair into a high feathered knot, dusted her hair with gold, and painted her cheeks with crimson swirls.

Rielle drew in a long breath, scanning her surroundings.

They'd brought her to a narrow valley between the grassy foothills north of Mount Sorenne, to the east of the city. Stands for spectators had been erected along the rocky ridges that terraced the slopes, but most of the crowd stood on foot, crowding behind safety railings for a better view. Flashes of gold winked at her from all sides: Sun Queen banners, pendants, sun-shaped play castings waved by screaming children.

At the end of the platform, stairs led down into an enormous circular maze of wood and stone. The Archon stood at the top of the stairs—as did Sloane, red-eyed and shaking.

And holding Tal's bronze shield.

Terror swept through Rielle like a physical force. "Sloane? Why do you have Tal's casting?"

"He's in the maze," Sloane replied, her voice hoarse. "Bound—and waiting for you."

"Before you accuse me of anything," the Archon said, "it was Magister Belounnon's idea, not mine."

Rielle felt suddenly and impossibly small beneath her heavy cloak. "I don't understand."

"He thought it would help you," Sloane said, "if you were forced to face death by fire once more, as you did the day your mother died. You can save him, as you couldn't save her." Sloane's tears spilled over. "He said, tell her it's all right to be afraid, but her fear will not triumph this time. Tell her she is stronger than any flame that burns."

The doors at the bottom of the stairs opened, revealing a narrow dirt path between twelve-foot wooden walls.

Rielle stared at the path in dismay, the crowd's cries ringing in her ears.

"You will find Magister Belounnon in the maze's heart," the Archon explained, pointing at a structure in the distant center of the maze. "Each dead end you meet will result in his acolytes setting fire to a section of the maze that surrounds him."

The world fell away, leaving Rielle adrift. She glared at the Archon. "How could you let this happen?"

The Archon's face was grave. "Magister Belounnon insisted on it."

"Then you should have stopped him!"

A horn blasted from one of the stands overhead.

Rielle nearly lunged at the man. "At least let me bring him his casting!"

"He requested that his casting remain with his sister," the Archon replied.

The horn blasted a second time. Across the maze, hissing snakes of fire sprang to life along random stretches of wall.

Rielle ripped off her cloak and flung it to the ground. Feathers went flying; her palms blazed hot as she advanced on the Archon.

"If he dies," she ground out, "I will flay every inch of skin from your body."

The Archon did not flinch. "If he dies, Lady Rielle, you will have no one to blame but yourself. The maze will burn quickly. I suggest you run."

A third horn blast. Rielle threw a desperate look at Sloane, then raced down the stairs and into the maze.

— 44 —

ELIANA

"They called her the Dread, not knowing that beneath the mask and cloak and painted-on smile, she was simply a girl. A girl with a heart that burned for blood."

—*The Terrible Tale of the Deadly Dark Dread*
by Remy Ferracora

E liana grabbed Arabeth and Whistler, then lunged forward only to be yanked back by her left arm.

She whirled on Simon. "Let go of me!"

"No." He held her fast. "Leave them."

"Are you mad? That's my brother!"

"And his life is nothing compared to yours." Simon glanced once at the safe house. Eliana thought she saw the ghost of regret in his eyes. "Let's go."

Eliana twisted savagely in his grip. "I'll kill you!"

"I don't think you will." He pulled her closer. "You're intrigued by what I've said. You want to know more."

She spat at his face. Simon chuckled.

"You are so like her," he muttered darkly.

"I am like myself," she hissed, "and no one else."

She kicked his knee, swiped Whistler across his stomach, but he dodged quickly enough to miss the worst of it. She broke free and ran;

he caught her once more. Panic was making her sloppy. She heard terrified cries from the safe house and shouted a furious curse.

"That's it." Simon struggled to hold on to her, chuckled breathlessly. "Rage at me, Eliana. Fight me. I'm keeping you from your brother. I'm keeping him in pain."

"Let me go!"

"You can't ignore your destiny forever. Let it rise, let the anger come. *Wake up.*"

She snarled, "I warned you," then kneed him ruthlessly in the groin.

He dropped her, staggering.

She turned and ran.

"Zahra!" she called.

"Right here," answered Zahra, rushing through the trees at her side. Her form flickered, wavering. "I'll hide you from him for as long as I can."

Together they raced out of the trees and past Rahzavel, who stood looking out at the forest with wild eyes. Eliana froze at the safe house door. Flames crawled up the roof; the trees on either side crackled with fire. She ripped off her jacket, wrapped it around her hand, and reached for the front door just as the rafters overhead crumbled. She jumped back, coughing.

"Here!" Zahra beckoned from a few yards away. A wooden door was set into the ground, draped with moss and covered with piles of rocks—a basement so well blocked that Remy and the others wouldn't be able to get out from inside.

Eliana raced over, started frantically pushing away rocks. "Tell me what's happening!"

Zahra peered around the house. "Simon has engaged your attacker. Who is this man?"

"Rahzavel." Eliana ripped a sheet of moss from the door's hinges.

Zahra hummed in disapproval. "He is Invictus."

"Yes." The door was jammed. She braced her foot against the frame and yanked hard. "I can't open it!"

"El?" A voice sounded from beyond the door. "Is that you?"

"I'm here! The door is stuck!" Eliana pulled hard, every muscle in her body straining. "Push from the inside, when I say, you and Hob. Ready?"

Hob's voice came faintly. "Ready!"

"One...two...three!"

She yanked at the door with all her strength, and it finally gave way. She flung it aside, reached down for Remy. Hob pushed him up and then Navi right after—all of them coughing, their faces streaked black from smoke. Remy clung to Eliana's side; Hob hefted Navi over his shoulder, his expression grim.

He looked to Eliana. "What now?"

"We must go at once," Zahra warned, her form shimmering. "Simon is nearly finished, and then Rahzavel will find us. My strength will fail at any moment."

Hob's eyes widened. "Who said that?"

Eliana turned, squinting through the smoke. Zahra was right: Simon was gravely hurt, holding his side. Rahzavel knocked away his sword, kicked his wound. Simon cried out in agony, knees buckling, and collapsed. Rahzavel stood over him, a crazed grin splitting his cheeks.

Eliana set her jaw against the hot swell of shame in her heart and turned away. "Then we'll go north, toward the Narrow Sea."

"But we can't!" Remy tugged on her arm. "He'll kill Simon!"

"And he won't kill us." Eliana glanced at Hob, who nodded once.

"Let's go," she said and hurried into the woods, holding Remy tightly by the hand. She saw him look back once, his eyes bright with tears, but did not allow herself to do the same.

45

RIELLE

"My students, please know this: I chose to give up my casting and bind myself inside my own maze. I did it for two simple reasons: I trust Rielle Dardenne, and I love her."

—Letter written by Grand Magister Taliesin
Belounnon
to the acolytes of the Pyre
June 19, Year 998 of the Second Age

O nce Rielle stepped inside the maze, the crowd's cheering dimmed.

The doors slammed shut behind her.

She kept running down the path, dry grasses crunching beneath her feet.

The maze will burn quickly.

Already, she could smell smoke. But coming from where?

She climbed the nearest wall and had almost reached the top when a hard knot of fire shot down from the stands. It slammed against the wood, knocking her back to the ground. Head spinning, she watched flames spread along the wall.

No climbing, then.

She pushed herself to her feet and ran. The structure containing Tal was in the dead center of the maze. She reached a fork in the path—three routes. Left, right, continuing center. She thought quickly. If she'd been mapping the maze correctly, the path on the right would bring her to the maze's outermost wall—and a dead end. Center would keep her running around the maze's rim.

She turned left, heard a faint burst of cheers from the distant crowd above.

She smiled in relief. Left had been the right choice.

She raced down a corridor of walls capped in roaring flames. Wood snapped, showering embers across her path. Bile rose in her throat, along with a smoky black flavor that twisted her stomach. For weeks after her mother's death, the taste of ash had lingered on her tongue.

Ahead: a door in the wall to her left, which should lead to the maze's center.

She ducked through the door, turned right, raced down the path, then turned left—and skidded to a halt.

A stone wall blocked her path.

Outside the maze, the horn blasted once more.

Rielle looked up just as three knots of flame arced through the sky. Their impact crashed through the maze like fists against glass.

The crowd cried out in awe.

Tal.

Rielle turned and ran back the way she had come, the pressure of tears building behind her eyes. When she turned the corner, the path before her erupted into flames.

She screamed, raised an arm to shield her face, and stumbled back against the wall.

Rielle, where's your mother?

Rielle, what did you do?

She bent over, hands on her knees, and made herself breathe until the memory of her father's frantic voice faded.

Corien? She reached out with her mind, cautious. He had said not a word to her since she'd taken Audric into her bed, and she had not dared speak to him. But the angry flames devouring the path before her made her feel shrunken, brittle. Too much heat, and she would crack.

She squeezed her eyes shut. She had worked with Tal for years, had manipulated torches, candles, hearth fires. But these flames were different—wild and vindictive. She could hardly breathe, the heat stealing away her air.

Are you there? Corien, please, help me.

Another horn blast.

She looked up as three more arcs of fire shot across the sky.

"No!" she screamed. The crowd's cries echoed her own.

She turned to face the fire blocking her way, fear punching a sob from her throat. She flung out her hands without thinking.

The fire parted, clearing a charred path for about twenty feet in front of her, and then collapsed. The fire re-formed.

Her hands shook. She wiped the sweat from her eyes. She couldn't think, couldn't find the empirium, not with these flames crowding her, not with Tal trapped somewhere behind her.

But she had to. Somehow, somehow…

She sank to her knees, watching bleary-eyed as the flames climbed. The twin biting scents of smoke and firebrand magic carved sour ruts down her throat.

Rielle, make it stop!

Rielle, she's still inside!

She closed her eyes, crouched, ready to run. What had Tal always taught her? Prayer steadies the mind.

Fleet-seeming fire, she prayed, *blaze not with fury or abandon.*

She glared up through her lashes at the nearing flames. She let her eyes unfocus, breathing in and out with each familiar word.

The world shimmered gold.

Unless, she finished, *I command you to.*

She pushed off the ground and ran, shoving all her rage and grief ahead of her like a wave. The fire broke at her approach, flames peeling away up the walls to let her through. She heard them collapsing back down as she fled, felt the snap of flames against her heels. Turned a corner, and another, ducked under a doorway and came out in a circular clearing.

Seven identical doors surrounded her, including the one through which she'd entered. Despair swelled within her. Which way?

The sky was filling with smoke. As she knelt, closing her eyes, she heard more fire erupt behind her—to the left, then the right. Sparks scattered across the ground.

She dug her fingers into the dirt, imagined that every bead of sweat sliding down her body could seep into the earth, race off through the veins of rock in the ground like buzzing beacons.

She saw it in her mind's eye: Gold knots zipping lightning-quick through the deep dense dark, seeking fire. Seeking Tal.

Warmth suffused her, but not from the fire.

From the empirium.

She felt it rise from the ground, called by her desperation. Heat bloomed up her arms and legs, unfurled in her belly, raced up her spine, and burrowed into the base of her skull.

When she opened her eyes, the world blazed gold. One door—second to her right—shone brighter than the rest. From down that golden path came the faraway sound of a man calling her name.

She blinked. The gold faded, and the world was itself again.

She launched herself off the ground, ran through the door, followed the path to the right, then right again, then left. Climbing flames surrounded her on all sides. Above the roar of fire and the crashes of the collapsing maze, she heard the crowd cheering and pushed herself faster. Flames chased her over a caved-in wall. She dropped and rolled, leapt up, kept running.

Another fork. She took the left path. Not fifty yards later, she hit a wall of stone.

The horn blasted; the fire arced overhead.

Then, three crashes. Very near. The wall just beside Rielle rumbled and groaned.

She whirled to follow the sound, then raced back to the fork, took the right path instead. Ran for a full minute at top speed, her side cramping. Dodged a buckling wall, shielded her face from a cascade of sparks. She could hear it now—a larger, roaring fire, straight ahead past a pile of smoking rubble that had once been a wall.

She climbed through it, kicking aside planks of charred wood, then emerged into a circular yard pockmarked with blackened craters. From the craters snapped trails of fire, and in the center of the yard, surrounded by rubble and walls of flame, stood a familiar building.

It was a narrow, three-storied house, not as grand as one might expect for the commander of the royal army. Painted gray in honor of his metalmaster heritage and forest-green in honor of the family he served.

So he had said. But Rielle's mother had told Rielle the truth— no-nonsense Armand Dardenne had ordered his house painted green because that was the color of his daughter's eyes.

All clarity left Rielle in a flood of dread.

It was her parents' house, re-created in the center of the maze. And it was on fire.

Rielle, what did you do?

She's dead! Oh, God! Help us! Someone help us!

But then Armand Dardenne had come to his senses. He had stared at Rielle over the red, ruined wreck of his wife's body, watched her frantic sobs with an expression of abject contempt until everything Rielle had known about her father had disappeared. His face had closed to her, never to be opened again. He had lowered Marise Dardenne's body to the ground, picked up his shivering daughter, and hurried her through the tunnels below the castle to the Pyre and Tal's bedroom.

Tal, sleep-rumpled and only nineteen years old, had opened his door, taken one look at Rielle's face, and held out his arms to her.

Help us, her father had said, his voice carved hollow. *Help her. Don't let them take her from me.*

"Rielle!"

Tal's distant shout shook her. She took two halting steps forward, gazing up at the burning house.

"I can't," she whispered, a sharp, ill heat flaring throughout her body. "No, no, no."

Then, with a groan, the front face of the house began to collapse.

A choked scream rang out—her own name, quickly silenced.

Rielle ran around the house, searching through the smoke for the back door. It was there, just as she remembered it. She kicked the blackened wood; it gave way easily. She raced over the threshold into a world of black smoke and leaping orange flames. How strange it was to see the rooms just as they should have been—but empty now. No furniture, no art on the walls. Only flames and a noxious smell that coated her every breath with darkness.

She hid her face. "Tal? Where are you?"

"Here!" His voice was faint. "In the parlor!"

She stumbled down the main hallway and to the door of her mother's parlor. The wall was buckling; overhead, the rafters creaked and groaned.

She shoved her weight against the door. It didn't budge. She slammed into it again and again, her throat tightening, her vision a luster of tears.

Outside, three monstrous crashes hit the ground. The house rattled, windows shattering. More fire from the acolytes?

She cried out in frustration, then heard a loud snap and scrambled out of the way right before the ceiling above her collapsed.

The door, wedged loose, fell out of its frame.

"Tal?" She crawled to the door, the floor blazing hot under her palms. Dragged a hand across her face to clear the grit from her eyes, looked inside the parlor past billowing waves of heat.

Tal.

He was there, wrists and ankles bound, trapped in the far corner by a shattered window. Glass sparkled across the floor. Rafters and chunks of plaster from the collapsed ceiling separated them, as did a roaring ribbon of fire.

"Tal!" She clung to the doorframe. "Answer me! Come on, get up! We have to leave!"

"I can't move," he called out to her. His voice was ravaged, wheezing. "The ceiling fell on my legs!"

She sagged to the floor.

"Douse the flames, Rielle!" He coughed violently. "Just as we practiced!"

As if it were that simple. Just a prayer, just a lesson.

The sound of the flames roaring between them was turning her stomach inside out. She couldn't think past them to remember her prayers, much less find the empirium.

Rielle, save her!

Rielle, please! Do it, now! Oh, God...

She fell to her hands and knees, stomach heaving.

Papa, I'm sorry! I can't stop it! Mama! Mama, run!

"I can't," she gasped. "I can't stop it."

"You can do this, Rielle," Tal was calling to her. "Listen to my voice! I trust you!"

From elsewhere in the house came a massive groan. The floor shook. Rielle looked back, down the smoke-filled hallway to see the second floor collapse. Her bedroom, her father's study, her mother's music room. New flames roared up the walls. A great gaping hole in the roof revealed a smoke-stained sky.

"Rielle, listen—" Tal's voice disappeared into a fit of coughing.

"Tal?"

He didn't respond.

"Tal!" She rose on shaking legs, searched through the inferno for a path through, and found one—small and shrinking.

She ran for it, diving through the flames and slamming to the floor on the other side. A few feet away, Tal lay under a ceiling beam, his face sallow and slick with sweat.

She crawled to him, head ringing from her wild leap. The fire's heat pressed down on her back like a hand determined to bury her.

"Tal, I'm here. Tal?" She helped him sit, slapped his cheeks until his bloodshot eyes fluttered open.

He smiled up at her. "There you are." His hand fumbled for hers. "I knew you'd find me."

"We're trapped, I can't... I can't carry you. Please get up."

He gasped for air, shaking his head. "You can put the fire out."

"Tal, I..." Her tears dropped onto his neck. *Papa, I can't make it stop!* "If I try, I'll just make it worse. You know I will."

"What I know is that you were only a child. And that now..." He touched her cheek. "Now, you are a queen."

His eyes began to flutter shut.

"Tal? No! Tal!" She looked helplessly at the encroaching flames, tried reaching for the empirium with a weak thrust of her hand. "Move! Leave us alone, *please!*"

Another rafter collapsed, not five feet from them. Rielle ducked her head over Tal's body, breathless.

Then she heard Tal's voice, faint at her ear: "Burn steady and burn true. Burn clean and burn bright."

The Fire Rite. She closed her eyes.

"Burn steady and burn true," she repeated, her voice cracking. "Burn clean..."

His hand tightened around hers. "...and burn bright. Again, Rielle."

"Burn steady and burn true."

"Think," he whispered, "of the ones you love."

"Burn clean and burn bright."

The ones I love.

Ludivine. Tal.

Audric.

Fresh warmth touched her fingers, her toes.

From overhead came Atheria's piercing cry—part horse, part hawk. A distracted part of Rielle's mind recalled the discarded firebird cloak. Her vision flooded with a thousand shades of summer.

"Burn steady," she whispered.

"And burn true," Tal finished, his voice a mere thread.

"Burn clean." She opened her eyes to a room of soft gold. Gold fire, gold ashes, golden shimmering Tal. "And burn bright."

She blinked. She inhaled.

The gold shifted, gathering in twisting knots that hovered, waiting.

Rielle breathed out. Hot points of energy surged away from her fingertips, like needles stabbing their way out of her skin. The gold flooding the room careened away in spinning whorls of light.

All at once, the heat crowding her vanished.

She blinked, gulped down a breath as if surfacing from water.

The world returned to her, dull and ordinary.

Except for the thousands of feathers floating down from the rafters, gusting along the walls, coating the ruined floor. Everywhere that flames had been, now there danced among the diminishing curls of smoke long needlepoint feathers of tangerine and gold, violet and vermilion. Firebird colors.

"Rielle..." Tal swept his arm across the floor. Feathers flew up at his touch before drifting back down to rest lightly among the piles of simmering embers.

He looked up at her, wonder turning his face soft. "How did you do this?"

She retrieved a feather of a particularly brilliant red and watched with a thrill of delight as the fine downy barbs flickered at her touch.

"I don't know," she whispered, caught between exhaustion and the most perfect joy she had ever felt. "I think—"

But the words died on her lips. For at that moment, a familiar touch scraped down her spine.

Corien? She looked through the house, her grip tightening on Tal. *Are you there?*

Silence was his answer. But she was not fooled. She sensed his nearness like a familiar shape in the dark.

Distant horns blasted—staccato, frantic. Warnings. With the flames gone, Rielle could hear the crowd's terrified screams.

Oh, God.

"What is it?" Tal searched her face. "Rielle, say something."

And thus, Corien murmured, *we begin.*

Rielle touched her mouth, chasing the sensation of lips brushing against her own.

With a small smile, she whispered, "He's here."

46

ELIANA

"Dearest brothers and sisters, please do not grieve my absence. Know that I was of sound mind when I left for Ventera. As the youngest of five, I have often felt dim in the shadow of your brilliant light. Now, it is my turn to shine. In the belly of the beast, I will serve Red Crown's cause of justice and freedom and strive to earn your admiration. May the Queen's light guide us all home."

—Letter from Princess Navana Amaruk of Astavar
to her siblings
December 13, Year 1014 of the Third Age

They moved through the cold forest for hours—all through the night and into the next day.

The ground became rockier the farther north they went, soft earth giving way to pale sand. The trees were strange here, short and spindly, with brittle leaves that hissed spitefully in the wind. Long, misshapen barrows crowned with crumbling stones snaked through the forest like veins.

"These trees reek of death," Hob whispered as they crouched near one such mound. "I'll be glad to leave them behind."

Eliana agreed—but where to go after this? Simon's contact, their path across the Narrow Sea, was now lost to them.

They stopped at last to rest, huddling beneath a moss-draped over-hang on the side of a slight hill. Navi had lost much of her color, her skin slick with sweat. They settled her on the ground, piled leaves atop her shivering body.

She raised one feeble hand. "Eliana?"

Eliana took it, settled beside her. "I'm here. You're all right. We're going to be fine now."

Navi smiled weakly. "Don't lie to me."

"Fine. We're quite likely all doomed."

"That's better."

Remy wedged himself against Eliana's other side, his arms crossed over his chest. He had spoken not a word since leaving Simon behind.

Eliana glanced at Hob. "Do you know who Simon could have been talking to? The contact he went to meet."

Hob pulled a few wrapped pieces of food from his pockets—dried meat, hard rolls, all he'd managed to grab before fleeing the fire—and passed them around. "No. According to Simon, I am not high-ranked enough an ally to be privy to such information."

"There must be smugglers that cross the Narrow Sea."

"A few. But we haven't the money for that." Hob yanked a berry off a nearby bush, chewed it, spat it out. "Rotberries. This forest is useless."

"Can we go back to Rinthos? Ask Camille for help?"

"I don't think Navi would survive the trip. If we can get to the port of Skoszia without someone seeing us and killing us on the spot, I can send a message to Camille from a place there, but it will take time."

"That's time we don't have."

"We left him." Remy shifted to look up at Eliana. "We left him to die with Rahzavel."

"Yes, we did," said Eliana, refusing to meet his eyes. "He would have wanted us to."

"That doesn't make it right."

"Hey, you know what?" She slid her arm around Remy's shoulders.

"I have something to tell you. I wish I could show you, but I can't. You too, Hob."

Hob raised an eyebrow. "Don't talk to me like I'm a child."

"I met a friend," Eliana said, "in the laboratories where they held me and Navi. Her name is Zahra, and…she's here with us. Right now."

Some of the sadness left Remy's face. "Really? How? Where?"

Hob was staring at her. "Have you lost your mind?"

"This is no joke, Hob," said Zahra.

Hob's arm shot out to shield both Eliana and Remy. "Who's there? Who said that?"

"Who are you?" Remy looked around wonderingly. "Can you show me what you look like?"

"My name is Zahra, little one." Zahra swooped down to Remy's eye level, her chin in her hands. "What a darling thing you are. Your mind is as wide open as the sky."

Remy cautiously waved his hand around. "You're very close, aren't you?"

"Indeed."

"Eliana," Hob muttered, "what is this?"

Remy hugged his knees to his chest. "Are you a wraith?"

Zahra blinked in surprise. "What is this child, who knows so much of the world?" Her expression turned tender. "Oh, sweet one. You are a dreamer, a teller of tales. I see that now. You ache for magic and for all those golden giants of the past."

Remy flushed with pleasure. "Before the invasion," he said eagerly, "people stole books from the temples, so they wouldn't be destroyed. I buy them whenever I can and read them all."

"Hang on." Eliana pulled back to frown at him. "You mean you used to sneak around Orline buying books in the underground market?"

"Do you think I learned everything I know just from rolling dough at the bakery?"

"Well, I—" She shook her head, astonished.

"Oh, I do like you." Zahra draped an arm across Remy's shoulders with a smile. "A curious mind and a pure heart both in one."

Hob flung his gloves to the ground. "Can someone tell me what a wraith is?"

"Don't move," a male voice warned from the shadows before them. "Or I'll tell my archers to let their arrows fly."

Eliana froze as shapes shifted in the undergrowth—five soldiers, ten, gathering close with bows raised and arrows nocked.

Zahra shot up to her full height, dark eyes flashing. "Eliana, forgive me. I was distracted; I didn't hear them!"

One of the archers jerked their arrow to the side, seeking Zahra— and of course finding nothing.

"You've a fifth in your party?" asked the first man. He approached Eliana, no bow in his hand but a long curved sword at his hip. His hood hid his face from view.

"Do you see five people here?" Eliana glared up at him. "Your eyes fail you, I'm afraid."

"But my ears do not." The man stopped, considering Navi's shorn head. "You escaped from Fidelia."

Eliana tensed. "Perhaps."

"Malik?" Navi moaned, struggling to push herself up. "Is that you?"

"Navi?" The man flung off his hood and fell to his knees at her feet. "Sweet saints." He gathered Navi against his chest before Eliana could stop him, pressed a tender kiss to her head. "Simon said you were alive, but I didn't believe it. I couldn't let myself."

Navi clung to him, her gaunt face free of pain for the first time since they'd escaped the laboratories. "Eliana," she murmured, "please don't be afraid. We're safe now."

"I'll be the judge of that." Eliana moved in front of Remy and reached under her singed jacket for Arabeth. "Who are you?"

Malik turned, his brown cheeks wet with tears, his eyes large and dark, his jaw strong. The resemblance, now that Eliana knew to look for it, was obvious.

"I am Malik Amaruk," he said, wiping his face. "I am Navi's brother—and a prince of Astavar."

Later that afternoon, after Malik and his scouts had shared a proper meal with them, Eliana stood with Malik on the edge of a cliff over-looking the Narrow Sea. Across the black channel lay a line of white cliffs: Astavar—and freedom.

Eliana made herself look at it and imagine the fresh green country beyond the border, even though doing so opened old wounds in her heart.

Harkan, she thought, *you should be here.*

"So there are monsters on those boats," Malik murmured. On the far horizon, black specks moved steadily west against the darkening sky. The Empire fleet.

"They're called crawlers," Eliana told him.

Down the coast, a small flotilla of Empire warships waited at the port of Skoszia. The faint shapes of adatrox bustled back and forth along the docks, moving supplies and weapons. Hanging high on the warships' masts, the Emperor's colors of black, red, and gold snapped in the wind.

The Emperor. *Corien*, Zahra had called him.

Eliana's mouth thinned. That was not something she would allow herself to think about just yet. "So we have to make it across the sea without anyone on those ships seeing us."

"Yes." Malik pointed behind them, farther west along the coast. "There's a small smuggler's ship two miles away, in a small cove aban-doned by the Empire. The ship crosses at nightfall, and its crew will take us with them. Simon and I arranged it before..." Again Malik glanced at her. "Well."

"Before I abandoned him to save my own ass?"

"I wasn't going to say it quite like that."

"No need to hold your tongue around me, prince." Eliana stared out at the water, trying not to remember Simon's cries of pain. "I know what I've done."

"I would've done the same, you know."

"No need to comfort me either."

Malik inclined his head. "Once we're across, you'll be taken to the capital. There are tunnels below the palace. My fathers will hide all of you there, and I'll join the army at the beach."

"To fight?" Eliana couldn't hide the scorn in her voice.

Malik said mildly, "You think we can't win."

"I know you can't."

"And what should we do? Sit on the shores of our country and let the Empire slaughter us without raising a single sword?"

"Your people excel at sitting and not raising a single sword."

Malik regarded Eliana calmly. "All of Astavar grieved with you the day Ventera fell."

"Your grief means nothing to me."

"We saved our own asses. Isn't that how you said it? How are we so different, then?"

"Simon is a murderer. A soldier. He knew what he was getting into when he joined Red Crown. A country, though, is full of innocents." Eliana glared at the sea. "Don't try to compare yourself to me or your country to mine. You'll come up short."

"My lord!" A scout hurried up the cliffside path to whisper something in Malik's ear.

Malik turned to Eliana, eyebrows raised. "It seems Simon is alive."

The world beneath her feet floated away. "What? But Rahzavel—"

"Has taken him captive, apparently. They are on one of the warships bound for Astavar."

"Which one?" When the scout hesitated, Eliana grabbed her arm. "Which *one?*"

"I can't say," the scout replied. "Our contact on the smuggler's ship saw them board, but couldn't recall which ship. They all look the same, he said."

Eliana snorted. "And these are the people we're entrusting our lives to?"

"Not many smugglers remain who dare to cross the Narrow Sea," Malik pointed out. "We're lucky we could find anyone at all."

"What are you thinking, my queen?" Zahra murmured at Eliana's ear.

Eliana stared hard at the ships down the coast.

"I'm thinking," she said slowly, "that we won't be going with the others when they leave."

Zahra nodded. "You're thinking we must save Simon."

A warm wave of relief swept through Eliana's body. "Yes."

"Because you feel guilty for leaving him?"

Yes. Because not even he deserves death at Rahzavel's hands. Because he gave his life to allow us escape.

Because I couldn't save Harkan. But I can, perhaps, save Simon.

"Because he has answers I want," she replied.

Zahra gave her a pointed look and tapped her own ghostly temple. "Remember…angel."

"Not anymore, you aren't." Eliana turned to face Malik. "You'll get my brother to Astavar—and Hob as well." She glanced at Hob. "Unless you wish to return to Patrik?"

"I won't leave Navi or the boy," Hob said quietly, his eyes bright but his jaw set. "I'll find Patrik later. Sometimes our work for the rebellion requires us to live apart. He will understand."

An ache swelled beneath Eliana's ribs.

Sometimes, Rozen Ferracora had told her, when their training had first begun, *your work will take you away from home for days at a time. Remember this: I will always love you when you return. No matter what you have done.*

She clutched her necklace so hard that the corroded rim bit into her palm. "Well, Malik?"

"For the girl who saved my sister and showed her such kindness?" Malik bowed his head. "I would do anything."

"Remy won't forgive me for leaving without saying goodbye."

"Yes, I will."

Eliana turned to find Remy standing behind her, his face pinched and grave. "If you can save him, El," he said quietly, "you should do it."

A horn blasted from down the coast; across the gathered warships, torches flared to life.

"Night comes," Zahra murmured. "We must go."

"And so must we." Malik turned, whistled softly. His scouts gathered, breaking camp in efficient silence.

Eliana pulled Remy to her, and together they found Hob helping Navi to her feet at the trees' edge. "You'll watch over him?"

"He won't leave my sight," Hob said. "Neither of them will."

"Eliana," whispered Navi, reaching for her. "You'll save him. I know it."

Eliana moved toward her, Remy still at her side, and kissed her brow. "I will try."

"I know what you are. The wraith thought it would comfort me to know."

"*What?*" Eliana glared at Zahra.

"Don't be angry with her. It was a kindness." Navi kissed Eliana's hand, pressed it to her cheek. "If anyone can save him, you can."

Remy stared. "What is she talking about?"

"Navi," Eliana said quickly, "all of that is childish nonsense—lies that people craving comfort tell themselves."

"You don't believe that," Navi murmured.

Eliana's necklace felt suddenly too heavy around her neck. "I don't know what to believe."

Zahra smiled. "Then you are on the right path."

Eliana ducked to kiss Remy's cheek, whispered, "I love you," and cupped his face in her hands, memorizing every line and curve.

"Save him," he told her, his voice wobbly, and before Eliana could change her mind, she turned and ran down the cliff toward the darkening sea.

47

RIELLE

*"My dreams are strange of late. I fear... My darling
daughter, please forgive me. I am sorry. I am so sorry."*

—Letter from Lord Dervin Sauvillier
to Lady Ludivine Sauvillier
June 19, Year 998 of the Second Age

R ielle glanced back at Tal only once.

"Stay here," she commanded, then ran out of the house, ignoring his shouts. She felt a twinge of guilt at leaving him pinned under the rafter and hoped it wouldn't hurt him irreparably, but at least there he was out of harm's way.

He also wouldn't be able to interfere.

She raced out of the maze, aiming for the nearest hills and the spectator stands. The acolytes' fire had ravaged much of the maze; her path out was clear, though clogged with smoking rubble.

At last she emerged into the foothills—and chaos.

Half the stands stood in ruins, bedraggled banners in the colors of House Courverie flying ragged in an unnatural gale. The sharp alpine scent of windsinger magic stung Rielle's nose.

Dozens of bodies lay strewn across the ground. Thousands had come to see her trial, and now they scattered across the valley like upset ants. The air was clogged with screams, wails of pain, the crash of elemental magic.

On one of the ridges that lined the hills, she scanned the scene with a pounding heart. She could make no sense of what she saw—people running with children in their arms, elementals in scattered duels. Who was the attacker here? Borsvall?

Every sense pulled taut as she searched for some sign of him. Corien, *here*, no longer a dream. The very idea seemed impossible.

And yet—

She straightened, her skin tingling. A sharp twinge of satisfaction that was not her own plucked a song across her ribs.

Come find me, Rielle.

"Protect the king!" shouted a familiar voice. She whirled, saw her father and a company of soldiers herding King Bastien away to safety. Others, led by her father's first lieutenant, hurried Queen Genoveve away in the opposite direction.

Audric. Ludivine. But she saw no trace of them.

She moved to join her father, then heard a furious shout.

A uniformed soldier—not one of her father's—raced along a ridge, nocked his arrow, let it fly into the belly of the queen's horse. It screamed and fell; the others nearby panicked, rearing up wild-eyed.

"Get her to safety!" bellowed the first lieutenant, shoving the queen behind one of his soldiers.

The uniformed archer shot another arrow, just before Sloane, long black coat flying, jumped down from a collapsed viewing stand. She knocked the arrow out of the sky with her twin obsidian daggers, then thrust them at the archer. A pair of shadowed wolves burst from her blades and tackled the man, jaws open wide. One latched onto his throat, the other his belly.

Rielle ran to him, joining Sloane in time to see the man's clouded eyes flicker, as if a shadow had passed through his mind. The wolves flinched away and dissolved. The archer's body jerked once; his neck snapped. His gray eyes cleared to an ordinary brown.

"What was that?" Sloane muttered, wiping the sweat from her face. "Did you see that?"

"I did," said Rielle, a slow understanding creeping through her. *Corien?*

Hmm? He sounded entirely satisfied. *What is it, my dear?*

"These are Sauvillier colors." She touched the man's collar. "Why would Lord Dervin's men attack like this?"

Something slammed into the ground, shaking the hills.

"I don't understand," Sloane snapped, a thread of desperate fear in her voice. "We're their own people!"

What a tragedy it all is, Corien mused. *If only there was a way to stop it.*

"He's doing it," Rielle whispered. "He's controlling them."

Sloane stared at her. "What? Who is?"

If you want to stop this, you will come to me. Now.

A chill shook her. *Where are you?*

Come find me, my marvelous girl. Or I will kill them all where they stand.

Sizzling booms of magic and the agonized cries of soldiers ripped the air of the foothills to shreds. Rielle started to run.

Sloane grabbed her arm. "No, wait! Tell me what's happening!"

Rielle knocked the flat of her palm against Sloane's chest and sent her flying back twenty yards into a clump of grass.

She turned and ran, tears smarting her eyes, but there was no time for guilt. She tore up the hill's rocky slope, along a series of cliffs overlooking the still-burning maze.

The earth bucked beneath her feet, sending her flying. She landed hard, turned to see an armored Sauvillier woman wrench her ax from the ground. An earthshaker.

The woman stared at Rielle with a face made of stone. Her eyes were an unseeing gray. The woman's mouth twitched; Rielle recognized that smile.

"Come find me, Rielle," the woman croaked, raising her ax once more.

Rielle flicked her wrist. The earth rose up like a cresting wave, then opened up and swallowed the woman. A terrified scream rang out, then fell silent.

Getting closer, Corien whispered.

She turned, following the trail of his voice along the cliffs. She ran past dueling soldiers, gathered churning knots of wind in her hands and knocked them all aside. An arrow shot past her, barely a miss.

Then she heard a familiar voice cry out, "Lady Rielle!"

She whirled, saw a group of people huddled against a rocky out-cropping, young Simon Randell and his father among them. Fifty yards away, a dozen Sauvillier metalmasters advanced on them, palms outstretched, flinging an endless cyclone of blades.

And Audric stood between them and his people, Illumenor casting a brilliant shield of light around them.

But the metalmasters were fast, and their weapons faster. The blades tore themselves into smaller pieces as they flew, spinning so fast between their casters' hands and Audric's wall of sunlight that they became a storm of sparks and steel. They bore down on him, relentless, ricocheting off his blazing shield again and again.

Audric's heels sank into the ground beneath the pressure. He low-ered his head and let out a furious roar of pain. Light scattered across the ground like fallen stars.

From behind Rielle came a terrified cry: "Save him!"

Ludivine.

Rielle whistled for Atheria, power rushing down her limbs to pool in her palms. Atheria dropped from the sky, raced low across the clifftops.

Turning, Rielle whipped her arm in a circle. The metalmasters flew back from her, their weapons crashing to the ground.

She spun back to Audric, thrust out her palm. A blast of wind slammed into him, sent him flying back through the air right as Atheria passed by the cliff's edge. The chavaile maneuvered sharply to catch him, then climbed back into the sky.

"Rielle, no!" Audric reached back for her as Atheria carried him away to safety. "Rielle!"

What a delightful development, Corien crowed. *I would say how noble of you that was, Rielle, but we both know the truth, don't we?*

Rielle raced past the people Audric had been protecting and threw herself into the knot of metalmasters. They'd recovered, retrieved their weapons. Their eyes gray and clouded, they lunged at her. Daggers came flying. She pivoted, dodged them. An angry tongue of metallic-tasting magic wrapped around her foot, yanking her down. She slammed her palms to the ground; tremors cracked the earth open. The metalmasters stumbled, and she leapt up, ducked under a chain's angry lash, then thrust her forearm at the group and watched them fly. Some skidded off the cliff's edge.

She turned, searching wildly for Ludivine, found her and Garver Randell helping the survivors down a cliffside path.

"Lu! Over here!"

Ludivine looked up, hair mussed and cheeks bloodstained. Their eyes locked; Ludivine smiled breathlessly at her.

Then, an enormous metal-tipped hammer spun across the space between them, slammed Ludivine in the gut, and knocked her screaming over the cliff's edge.

Furious instinct took over Rielle's body. She spun on her heel, punched the air so hard that the metalmaster who'd thrown the hammer flew back one hundred yards. His skidding body carved a furrow into the ground before slamming into the mountainside.

Rielle stumbled to the cliff's edge, searching the ruins of the maze far below for signs of Ludivine's body—and finding nothing. The smoke was too thick, the distance too great. Shock swept through her in waves. She clung to the rock, her vision rolling.

"Lady Rielle," said Garver Randell, approaching carefully up the cliffside path. He extended his hand, Simon watching wide-eyed behind him. "Please, my lady. Come with us."

Oh, my darling girl. Corien's voice was as gentle as it ever had been. *Let me comfort you.*

Rielle stood, pushing Garver's hand away. She turned, unsteady, and gazed through tear-filled eyes across the hilltops.

Where? Her thoughts felt sluggish. *I can't... Corien, she's...*

Follow the sound of my voice.

She did, running first slowly and then frantically. A terrible clouded grief yawned inside her, threatening to swallow her whole, but beneath even that was the pulsing *need*—to see Corien, to know that he was real.

To stop him from doing anything worse.

His trail led her into a cave beneath a large hill. She ran through a nest of cramped stone passages, the walls trembling on either side as the fight behind her continued.

At last, she rounded a corner into a circular cave. Tree roots snaked up the walls. A small opening in the center of the ceiling gave her a glimpse of the sky.

King Bastien rose from a boulder against the wall. Lord Dervin sat on the floor. Gray clouds clogged each man's eyes.

At the sound of footsteps, Rielle turned to see her father walking toward her out of the shadows.

She hurried toward him at once. "Papa, you're all right!"

"You found me." Her father's mouth curled into a slow smile. "Well done."

Rielle froze. He extended his hand, gray eyes unblinking on her face. She brushed past him, searching the room's shadows.

"Manipulating my father's mind," she declared, "is not the way to win my heart."

"Shall I release him, then?" murmured a voice.

She whirled at the sound. A column of still black watched her from the corner. Her mouth went dry; her heart skipped up her throat.

"Release all of them," she ordered.

"As you wish."

A ripple shifted through the room. Lord Dervin looked around in confusion, his eyes clearing.

King Bastien shot to his feet. "What is the meaning of this? Why are we all here?" He glared at Rielle's father. "Armand?"

"I don't know, my king."

At the touch of her father's hands, Rielle turned to face him. "Papa, I'm so sorry."

"Are you hurt?" He smoothed back her hair. "What's happening here?"

"Rielle is leaving you, I'm afraid."

Rielle turned—and there he was.

Corien.

He moved slowly across the room, light-blue eyes fixed on her face. Tall and slender, hands held carefully behind his back, sleek dark coat buttoned at his shoulder and trailing to the floor. Pale face, cheekbones high and elegant, a full mouth that curved with delight at the sight of her.

Rielle's breath came high and thin. Her dreams, as vivid as they had been, had not done him justice.

"My God, Rielle," he murmured, his hungry gaze raking down her body. "I didn't think it possible, but you are even more exquisite now than you are in my mind."

Her father stiffened with fury at her side. "Rielle, you know this man?"

"Who are you?" King Bastien stepped forward, a furious expression on his face. "Why have you brought us here?"

Corien took one step closer to Rielle, then another. His eyes never left her face. "I wanted to make sure Rielle didn't run from me. And you won't, will you? Not with all these very important men so danger-ously close to me."

"You won't hurt them." She shook her head, her voice cracking. "I forbid it."

"Queen of my heart," murmured Corien, putting a gloved hand to his chest, "my greatest wish is to please you. But you must promise to leave this place with me, tonight, or I'm sorry to say you will force my hand."

Panic and craving waged a war in her chest. "But I can't, I need more time."

"More time? For what? To be poked and prodded, studied by lech-erous magisters and ordered around by an idiotic king too frightened to face the truth?"

Lord Dervin stared at his hands. "I never meant for this to happen."

Corien laughed. "As if you could have stopped it!"

"Rielle, who is this man," her father demanded, "and why does he talk to you this way?"

"He's an angel," Rielle bit out.

Corien's eyes flared with displeasure, even as his smile grew.

King Bastien drew his sword. So did Rielle's father, shoving her behind him.

"That's impossible." King Bastien looked as though someone had kicked him in the gut. "The Gate is strong. It was meant to hold for—"

"For a long time," Corien snapped. "Not forever. Rielle, it's time to go. Unless you'd like me to demonstrate firsthand what I'm capable of?"

Rielle swallowed hard and moved toward him, her power itching to touch him even as her mind screamed to stay put—but her father threw out his arm and stopped her.

"You will stay away from my daughter, whatever you are," he said, "or I will—"

"Do what? Kill me?" Corien chuckled. "My dear man, I'd like to see you try."

Rielle's father didn't hesitate. He lunged at Corien, raised his sword to strike. Then his body jerked, his eyes clouded over, and his sword crashed to the ground.

"No!" Rielle ran to him.

He looked at her, head tilted unnaturally to the side, and struck her hard across the face.

Rielle staggered to the cave wall. When she touched her lip, her fingers came away red.

"Interesting," said Corien calmly. "I only told him to stop you. *His* mind was the one that chose to strike you." He turned to her, and she could feel through their connection a twinge of genuine sadness. "Could your father be angry at you for something? I thought you two had put that mess behind you."

Rielle glared at him. "Release him, or I will destroy you."

"If you try, they'll be dead before I hit the ground."

Tears gathered in her eyes. "I thought you..."

"That I loved you?" Corien's face softened. "Child, I love you more than I can say. I'm doing this for you. If you don't leave them, they will stifle, shame, and punish you for daring to breach the walls they are building around you."

He approached her slowly. "They will use every memory you share with them—every sweet feeling, every kind moment—to wring out all the power they can from that miraculous body of yours. And they won't stop, or even consider sparing you, because they will be too afraid of what faces them. If you hesitate, they will remind you of their supposed love for you and chain you with it until you back down and do as you're told."

He now stood so close she could smell the clean coldness of his skin, a spice of scent on his clothes. He cupped her cheek in one gloved hand. Heat blazed through her body, her power firing so completely alive at his touch that she felt fevered.

Helplessly she turned into his palm.

"Yes," Corien lowered his head to whisper against her ear, "even him."

Audric.

"You're wrong." She desperately hoped it was true. "He loves me, and he always will."

Corien's pity caressed her mind. "Who told you that? The rat?"

And as he said the words, an image came to her, shoved violently across the plane of her thoughts:

Audric, crying out in pain on Atheria's back. The chavaile landed on a grassy plateau seconds before Audric hit the ground. He dropped Illumenor, clutched his head in his hands. His eyes flickered from a brilliant, stormy gray to brown and back to gray.

The image vanished, and though Rielle couldn't know if it was real or imagined, it was enough. Rage erupted in her heart. "You will not touch him," she growled.

Corien stepped back from her. "Rielle, wait—"

She rounded on him, thrust out her palm, screamed, "Get away from me!" and let her power fly.

Not the wind, not the earth or the shadows lining the room.

This power was more than that and all of it and none of it.

Simply, it was this:

The empirium, raw and blinding.

At Rielle's feet, the unseen fabric of the world split open and detonated. A wave of light, a savage shudder.

Not far, but far enough.

When the aftershock dimmed, Rielle was on the floor. Her head spun. She looked down at her palms; they were covered in blood.

Her own?

She blinked.

Yes. The pain surfaced in sharp, jagged waves.

And Corien?

She looked around, dizzy, heard a horrible, keening sound, and found him crawling away from her, his clothes burned to ashes, and his *body*...

The blast had burned him.

He was an unmade creature, red and ravaged and glistening. He howled in pain, dragging himself across the cave floor toward an opening that led back to the hills.

"Don't look at me!" he screamed at her, his words slurring. "Not like this! Not like this..."

She could see not a single recognizable feature on his face. But his agony, his shame—his *anger*—vibrated through her mind.

When she looked up again, he was gone.

Then a low cry sounded from across the cave—her father, struggling to breathe. And beyond him, King Bastien, Lord Dervin...

Still, still, both of them *still*. Not burnt, as Corien had been, but rigid. The light gone from their glassy eyes, their faces frozen in shock.

Rielle tried to rise, crashed back to her knees. "Papa?" She crawled to him, turned his face to her.

He gulped down air, his eyes dim.

"I'm here." She touched his face; his cheeks were wet with tears. "It's all right. He's gone, and I'm here. We just need... Oh, God." She turned to the cave passage down which she'd come, screamed her voice raw. "I need a healer! Someone, please, help us! Garver!"

"I...remember."

"Papa? What is it?" She held his hands against her cheek. "You remember what?"

"'By the...moon...'" He gulped emptily at the air. "'By...the...'"

"Mama's lullaby?"

He gave her a shaky smile. "'By...'"

"'By the moon,'" she finished, singing unsteadily, "'by the moon, that's where you'll find me.'"

He nodded, closed his eyes. Tears slipped down his cheeks and into his neatly trimmed beard. A ghost of a smile touched his mouth.

"'We'll pray to the stars,'" she continued, a mere whisper, "'and ask them to set us free. By the moon...'"

He shuddered once, his hands falling slack in hers.

She closed her eyes, pressed her face against his fingers. If she finished the lullaby, if she didn't look, then it wasn't really happening.

"'By the moon,'" she whispered, "'by the moon, that's where you'll find me. We'll hold hands, just you and me...'"

She could no longer speak. She curled up beside him, pressed her face into his side, and lay there shivering and alone.

A familiar cry pierced the air outside the chamber, shaking Rielle from her grief.

A gust of wind followed by stamping hooves announced Atheria's arrival, just beyond the door through which Corien had crawled.

She sat up, her heart pounding. *Audric*. What would she tell him?

He rushed through the door an instant later, windblown and frantic. "Rielle?"

"Here," she croaked. She tried to go to him, but her legs wouldn't work. She instead watched with mounting dread as Audric hurried to her, then faltered with a sharp cry—and then stared in horror at his father's frozen face.

Rielle at last found the strength to rise.

"I tried to stop him," she whispered, approaching him slowly. "I'm sorry, I...I burned him. He's terribly wounded, but..." She gestured at the floor, where the smears of Corien's bloody body marked his exit. "It wasn't enough. Audric, I'm so sorry."

"Who? Who did you burn?"

"His name is Corien," she managed. "He's an angel, Audric. He turned the Sauvillier men against us... And Ludivine..."

Despair crushed her, left her choked with tears, and that was good, that was true and real, for when Audric turned to her, saw the blood dripping down her fingers and the mark of her father's hand across her cheek, his shocked expression shattered, and he gathered her tightly in his arms.

"Thank God you're all right," he whispered into her hair, his voice thick. "Rielle, I thought I'd lost you."

She wrapped her arms around him, shook her head against his chest. "Never. *Never.*"

You lie, Corien's voice whispered, thin with pain. *Even now, you lie to him.*

She felt Audric's shoulders shake under her hands and helped him sink to the floor.

"It's all right," she whispered as he wept against her neck. She took comfort from knowing that at least this one small fact was not a lie, and the truest thing she knew in this place of death: "I'm here, Audric, and I love you."

← 48 ←

ELIANA

"In these dark times, not even the light of the Sun Queen is as powerful as the light waiting inside our deepest hearts, if we only have the courage to look for it."

—*The Word of the Prophet*

"Hurry up," Eliana whispered, crouching behind a stack of crates marked with the Empire's winged emblem. The dock was slick beneath her feet, the frigid air sour and salty. "They're disembarking."

Zahra sighed irritably. "I'm trying. There's a lot going on here, you know. Wait..."

Eliana tensed. "Did you find him?"

"Perhaps. Stay here." Zahra disappeared into the night.

Eliana watched two uniformed adatrox patrol the deck of the ship to her right. A distant boom sounded from far across the water. She peered around the crates, down the narrow pier, and out to sea. Another boom snapped like an approaching thunderclap, and then another, each accompanied by distant flares of light against the starlit sky.

The main fleet, steadily moving toward Astavar, had begun to fire its guns.

"Come on, come *on*," Eliana muttered.

"The far ship," Zahra said, appearing so suddenly that Eliana jumped. "The sleek black one. Smaller than the others, with a thick hull. That's where they are."

Eliana let out a slow breath. "That might be a general's boat. Ready?"

Zahra put a shifting dark hand on Eliana's wrist. "Remember what I told you about my limited power since the Fall. I will only be able to mask your presence for a few minutes, at the most, before needing to rest again."

Uneasy, Eliana nodded. "Save it for when we're actually on the ship. I can get there unseen on my own."

She closed her eyes, said a quick prayer to Saint Tameryn that she would hide Remy and the others on the smuggler's boat—and that they would reach Astavar before the fleet did.

"May the Queen's light guide them home," Zahra murmured.

Eliana shot her a look.

Zahra shook back her hair. "What, I can't pray to you now that we're friends?"

Eliana rolled her eyes, then darted out from behind the crates and followed the docks to the farthest pier, keeping to the shadows.

Suddenly Zahra moaned, "Oh no."

"What?" Eliana crouched beside a railing draped with netting and wiped her brow. "Wait, where's the ship?"

"Out there." Zahra pointed at a black ship slicing out across the water.

"Oh, sweet *saints*," Eliana hissed, "can nothing in this world be easy?"

She made sure her knives were secure, then dove into the freezing water.

"Hurry," Zahra cried above the choppy waves. "They're speeding up!"

Eliana kicked desperately, her teeth chattering, then threw herself at the ship's hull and grabbed a black line hanging down from the deck. At her grip, it came loose from its knot, sliding fast, and she plunged back into the sea. But she held tight and pulled herself along the rope's length until she reached the ship once more. Muscles burning from her frantic swim, she climbed.

"I insist upon hiding you now," Zahra whispered, floating nervously around her.

Eliana glanced up at the deck. "Not yet."

An adatrox leaned over the steel deck railing, peering down at the taut, swinging line. Before he could raise his weapon, Eliana launched herself over the railing, grabbed Nox from her boot, and plunged it into his stomach. She clamped her hand over his mouth, then staggered with him to the railing and shoved him over the side.

From down the deck came footsteps, approaching fast.

"Now?" Zahra asked.

Eliana hated to waste the precious few minutes Zahra would give her, but capture was not an option. "Now."

"Follow me closely." Zahra sped along the port-side deck, the world shifting in her wake. As long as Eliana stayed safe in that distorted space, no one could see her—though someone would see the trail of seawater she left behind soon enough. They passed adatrox staring blankly outside closed doors, patrolling side by side along the deck rails.

Zahra beckoned at a door ahead on their right. An adatrox stood beside it, revolver in hand.

Eliana flattened herself against the wall, hoping the shadows would hide her. Zahra moved away, then disappeared. Two seconds later, the adatrox stiffened, his already vacant eyes turning even glassier.

Eliana hurried over, glancing behind her as she ran. With Zahra occupied, she felt horribly exposed.

"The fat silver one," Zahra whispered, through the adatrox's mouth—the voice part wraith, part man.

Eliana grabbed the fat silver key from the ring at his belt, unlocked the door, and let herself inside. She waited just beyond the door for Zahra to drift through the wall and join her.

Zahra shuddered. "Never enter an adatrox's mind if you can help it, Eliana. Nasty place."

"I'll try to remember that." A vacant hallway stretched to either side. Moonlight pouring through the round portholes in the wall was the only illumination. "Where do we go?"

With one long arm, Zahra pointed down the narrow, dark stairwell in front of them. "He has him below."

Rahzavel. Eliana hurried down the stairs.

At the bottom, Zahra buckled over with a gasp.

Eliana hid against the wall, looked quickly up and down the stairs. "What is it?"

"Simon's in great pain," Zahra muttered. "Hurry."

Heart pounding, following Zahra's whispered instructions, Eliana raced through a maze of corridors, staying in the wraith's wake to avoid the adatrox bustling from cabin to cabin. It was unbearably dark and close belowdecks, even with flickering gas lamps screwed into the walls.

At last Zahra brought her to a solid metal door cloaked in shadows.

"In here," Zahra whispered.

Eliana stared at the door's handle, fear pounding hard against her breastbone. Arabeth in one hand, she held her breath and turned the handle.

The door opened easily.

"That seems ominous," Zahra whispered.

Eliana stepped inside and closed the door behind them. It was a small room, dark and choked with hissing pipes.

And in the center of it, lit by a single hanging gas lamp, was Simon.

Eliana faltered at the sight of him. He had been bound with black rope to a pole that spanned from floor to ceiling, his arms wrenched cruelly behind him. His torso was bare and blood-spattered, the scarred flesh torn to pieces from new wounds. *Carvings.*

"Simon," she whispered, moving slowly to stand before him. His head hung low, his eyes closed. The thought that he might already be dead brought a terrible sadness crashing down upon her, so unexpected that the shock of it made her throat ache. "Please be alive."

His head jerked up at the sound of her voice. "Eliana?"

She saw his eyes and recoiled. They were bloodshot and yellowed, the brilliant blue irises turned dull and cloudy. She smoothed her thumb across one of the few patches of skin not covered with blood.

"You're going to owe me so much after this." Her voice came out shaky. "Do you know how cold that water is?"

"No. *No!*" Simon struggled against the ropes. "Get out of here, run!"

Beside Eliana, Zahra shifted in surprise. "Look out!"

Eliana whirled to see Rahzavel emerge from the shadows, a thin sword in each hand. "Hello, Eliana," he crooned. "Welcome to the end of your story."

"Why didn't I sense him?" Zahra whispered, her voice tight with anger under the hissing of the pipes. Then her form stiffened. "The Emperor's touch is heavy upon him. We must leave, my queen, before Corien finds you."

"Eliana, leave me!" Simon howled, yanking hard at his bindings.

"I'm not going anywhere." Eliana watched Rahzavel approach, noticed the red sprays across his face and how his dark uniform glistened with blood—Simon's blood, she assumed.

"How right you are," said Rahzavel. "You know, don't you, that if you try to kill me, you'll fail, and if you make even one move at me—*one fucking move!*—then I'll kill you first and make him watch." He pointed his sword at Simon and grinned. "Either way, your little rescue mission will be for nothing."

"Eliana, please, run!" Simon cried.

Rahzavel batted his eyelashes, whimpering. "Leave me! Oh, my darling, darling Eliana, save yourself!"

"Eliana," whispered Zahra, floating tensely beside her.

"Shut up," Eliana snapped, eyes trained on Rahzavel's lithe form, watching how he moved, gauging the weight of his swords and the size of the room.

"No, I don't think I will shut up, thank you." Rahzavel sauntered around Simon. "In fact, I think I'd like to tell you a story. It's about a bounty hunter who thought she was invincible, but really she was just a fool bitch who got lucky one too many times."

"God, I'm sick of listening to you," Eliana ground out, her body itching to move.

Then, a thought came to her. She looked to Zahra, raised an eyebrow.

"My queen," Zahra murmured, "if I do this, I may not have the strength for anything else."

"Do it, *now*."

The wraith shot toward Rahzavel and dove straight into his smiling mouth.

Rahzavel staggered back, choking. He dropped his swords and clutched his face, stumbled back against a knot of piping.

"What is this?" His warped voice shook with the weight of Zahra's anger. He clawed at his clothes, at his hair. "What is it, Dread? What have you done? What's inside me? A *wraith*?"

Eliana stormed over, grabbed his shirt in her fist, and slammed him to the floor.

"I'm afraid, Rahzavel," she replied, straddling his chest and wedging Arabeth's jagged blade against his throat, "that this is the end of your story."

Then she slashed open his throat, rose calmly to her feet, and left him choking where he'd fallen. Zahra drifted up from his body and clapped her hands together as if wiping them clean. A few seconds later all was silent—until two explosions shook the world.

The ship shuddered and moaned. From outside came the shouts of adatrox, the frantic clap of boots against the decks.

Eliana froze. "What was that?"

Zahra cocked her head, listening. Then her face darkened, an ink-blot dropped into gray waters.

"It has begun," she whispered. "The fleet has engaged Astavar."

Eliana ran to Simon, started cutting at the ropes that bound him.

"I told you to leave," Simon rasped as she worked. "You didn't listen to me."

"Does that surprise you?" She came around to cut the last two ropes. When he fell free, she tried to hold him up, bear his weight as best she could, but she was exhausted, and it had been too long since a proper meal. Her knees buckled; she sank with him to the floor, swearing under her breath.

"All right," she said, trying to slide out from under him, but his body was a deadweight, pinning her to the floor. "Come on, get up. We have to get off this boat and make it to shore while everyone's shooting at each other. Doesn't that sound fun?"

He didn't answer her. He was laughing—looking up at her from his spot on her lap and *laughing* at her.

"Oh, Eliana." Dull tears slid out of his eyes. "If only you knew. There are so many stories I need to tell you."

"I'm sure that's true, but can we do it later?" She shoved at him again, but he was shaking with laughter now and wouldn't budge.

"I've seen this before." Zahra pointed at his eyes. "During the invasion. Poison gas."

"You're saying he's blind?"

"For now. Sometimes the eyes repair themselves. Other times…"

"Wonderful. That makes everything easier. Simon?" She slapped him lightly on the cheek. "If you don't move, I'm going to get angry."

"Do it," Simon whispered. "Get angry for me. Sweet, sweet Eliana." He raised a trembling hand to her face, smoothed his thumb across her cheek. "It's just what I want."

"I'm hardly sweet," she protested with a slightly nervous laugh. They ought to be moving, but she could not tear herself away from him.

"I can't see you very well," he said. "A blur of color, shadows for eyes, but I know your face even so. I'd know it anywhere."

"You're speaking nonsense. Do you know that?"

"I didn't tell him anything," Simon whispered urgently. "I would never. *Never*. Not about you. He could have cut on me until the end of time. He could have whispered in my ears until he killed me from the inside out." He laughed again, but it sounded horribly sad. "It wouldn't matter. I'd never tell him about you."

She watched him struggle to his knees, dig for something in his trouser pocket.

"Where is it?" he whispered.

The ship shuddered once more. Rapid gunfire sounded from above; a horrible scraping sound shrieked along the hull.

"Simon, we have to go."

"Where is it?" He yelled the question, a sob tearing his voice in two. "I lost it; I *lost* you!"

Then, with a small cry, he pulled a filthy rag from his pocket and held it out for Eliana to see.

"This," he murmured, "belongs to you."

She stared at the rag, at a loss. Was his mind breaking at last?

Hovering at Eliana's elbow, Zahra shook her head. "I cannot see inside him. His thoughts are tangled with storms."

"I tried to hold on to you." Simon fumbled to fold the rag into her fingers. Then he lifted their joined hands to his lips and kissed her knuckles. "But I couldn't. The thread was too strong for me. I was too young for it. And then your mother…"

"My mother." *The Blood Queen.* If she believed that. Did she believe it? Tears gathered in her eyes. They didn't have time for this, but if she moved away, the moment would snap, and she might never find it again. "Simon, what are you saying?"

"We are the only two left, Eliana. You and me. The only two who lived there."

She ducked down to look at his face. "Where did we live? Tell me."

"Celdaria." He drew in a shuddering breath. "I tried to hold on to you, but time tore you away from me. We were only supposed to go to Borsvall. They were going to hide us from him."

All the air left her lungs. Her mind raced. "From who? Corien?"

"He'll never touch you. I lost you once, but I won't ever again."

She kept her hands folded around the little scrap of rag. Out of all things, she couldn't move past one tiny question: "But, what is *this*?"

He looked down at the rag cupped in her palms and smiled.

"Your blanket." The sorrow in his voice pierced her heart. "She wrapped you up in it, and when the thread ripped you out of my arms, it tore. I've kept this piece with me because it reminds me…of everything. Of home. We were so small, Eliana. And then I brought us here, and ruined everything. I failed you. I failed everyone!"

An explosion detonated; the ship rocked, heaving them both to the side.

"Eliana," Zahra said tightly.

"I know." Eliana cupped Simon's face, looked into his ruined eyes. "We're going to run now, and I can't carry you. You have to help me. Just like you did before, in—" Her voice caught. Her necklace felt too sharp and cold beneath her shirt. "In Celdaria. Right?"

He nodded, then heaved himself to his feet. She propped him up against her side, slung her arm around his shoulder. Zahra leading the way, they limped out into the corridor and up the narrow stairs. Another explosion sounded, knocking them against the wall. Eliana hissed at the slam of Simon's hard weight.

"Just give me a moment," he said, his face tight with pain, "and then I'll walk on my own."

"I'm sorry, I know you're hurt."

"Don't apologize to me, Eliana. Not ever."

When they stepped outside onto the main deck, Eliana stopped cold.

A broad bay flanked with tall, jagged rocks and scattered with small icebergs stretched before them. Two lines of ships faced each other across a narrow expanse of black water choked with flaming wreckage. Beyond the water, crowded with soldiers, a white beach hugged a cluster of night-shrouded hills.

Astavar.

She stepped out from under Simon's arm, made sure he could stand. "Zahra? Can you hide us?"

Zahra shook her head, mouth in a frustrated line. Her form faded, then flickered back whole. "I don't think so, my queen."

Eliana exhaled. "Perfect."

"Stay close to me, step where I fly. I'll find the best path I can for you."

"We survived the end of the world, you and I," Simon murmured, squeezing Eliana's fingers. His breath puffed in the air. "We'll survive this too."

A chill seized her at his words. Then she tightened her grip on his hand, and they ran.

RIELLE

"Onto this bleak and unknown path
Born from loss and paved with wrath
Cast down your heart and light the way
From darkest night to brightest day"

—"The Song of Saint Katell"
unknown composer

R ielle stepped inside the Hall of Saints, her heart racing.
This was wrong.

To be in this room, wearing a glittering gown, with Bastien's body not yet interred in the catacombs, with the kingdom grieving their dead and the loss of their king—it felt thoughtless, even cruel, for this to be the day that the Archon crowned her Sun Queen.

It would have felt cruel even if she hadn't been the one to kill them all.

But the Archon had insisted upon it.

"Saint Katell's writings require that the Sun Queen, when she comes, be crowned on a solstice," he had explained to her the day after the fire trial massacre, her ears still ringing with the sounds of death. "We timed your trials for precisely this reason. You know this, Lady Rielle."

She'd closed her eyes. A mistake. Every time she did so, she saw Ludivine falling to her death. After days of searching the maze's smoking rubble, they hadn't even been able to find her body.

"Yes, I know," Rielle managed, her voice thick, "but perhaps, given recent events, the Church could—"

"No." The Archon searched her face. She wondered what he would find. Did he look into her eyes and see what her father had always seen? The soul of a murderer?

"Now more than ever, Lady Rielle," the Archon had said, "our people need hope. We cannot wait until the winter solstice to crown you. Celdarians need their Sun Queen to help them through the days to come."

And what hope, she wanted to ask, *can they possibly find in a killer such as me?*

In the Hall of Saints, Rielle closed her eyes to fight back tears. Were it not for her, Corien would not have invaded the fire trial. The Sauvillier soldiers he'd entrapped would be at home in the north, and those innocents who had died in the hillside skirmish would be alive.

Ludivine. Papa. King Bastien. Lord Dervin.

The names cycled constantly through her mind, nicking away at the crumbling shell of her heart.

Ludivine.

The final count, according to the Lord of Letters's report, was fifty-eight dead. Their blood now coated her hands, and she could not reveal the truth about why. Not yet. Not ever. Maybe, if Ludivine were still alive, Rielle would have dared confess to her.

Ludivine, she thought, despairing, *I'm so sorry.*

She opened her eyes to the waiting crowd, managed a solemn smile. The entirety of King Bastien's court and the city's elite had gathered inside the hall. Outside Baingarde, a throng of citizens waited in the stone yard at the castle's entrance. At midday, after the Archon's blessing, the solstice bells would ring.

Rielle looked ahead at the gold-plated altar, shining under the light of a thousand candles. The Archon waited for her in his formal robes.

Behind him, in the rafters, stood a choir of temple acolytes singing "The Song of Saint Katell."

She took a deep breath and began the long walk toward him, leaving her guards standing at the doors.

Weeks ago, she had made this same journey, frightened and uncertain beneath the stern eyes of the saints. On that day the hall had been mostly empty, and her walk had been lined with guards prepared to kill her.

But today the crowded room watched her progress with shining eyes. Reverent whispers rippled through them as she passed.

Ludivine had, apparently, commissioned the gown without Rielle's knowledge. Ludivine's red-eyed servants had brought it to Rielle three days before for final adjustments. She had taken one look at the gown and barely managed to send the servants away in time before losing her composure.

It was a vision in pale Astavari lace. The wide neckline left her shoulders bare. Long, airy sleeves fell to the floor, trailing beside the train of her skirt. A shimmering iridescent lining clung to her torso, shining through the lace's fine weave. The effect made her look as though she had been dipped in liquid sunlight. Ludivine's servants had begged permission to weave fine golden ribbons through the dark fall of her hair and paint glittering amber swirls around her eyes.

"Lady Ludivine would want us to take care of you," the eldest of them had said, her mouth trembling, "and make you resplendent as the sun, my lady. And so we shall."

But, walking through the hall, Rielle cared nothing for the gown, nor the murmurs of appreciation from the people she passed. Her fingers itched to clutch the necklace at her throat.

Instead, she found Audric sitting beside his father's empty throne, and took comfort from the weary warmth of his eyes.

He'd given the necklace to her that morning, knocking at her door when she was still bleary-eyed from yet another sleepless night.

"For you," he had said simply and folded the necklace into her hand. He'd kissed her knuckles and the inside of her wrist, closed his eyes, and let his mouth linger against her skin.

Standing a few feet away with her gaze resolutely on the wall, Evyline had cleared her throat.

"Audric," Rielle had said, her voice breaking, "must I do this thing? With our fathers not even given proper rites—"

"Today, the sun will shine long and bright." He'd touched her face, his own worn with grief. "But not as bright as you. Please, Rielle. Our people need to see you."

Now, a smooth white-gold sun sat on a delicate chain between her collarbones. Its broad rays fanned out in gilded leaves thin as butterfly wings, and when Rielle knelt before the Archon, the light fell upon it and sent a sunburst flying across the ceiling.

The Archon placed a hand heavy with rings on her bowed head.

"The Gate will fall," he began, the familiar words of Aryava's prophecy bringing a hush to the room. The choir's voices softened. "The angels will return and bring ruin to the world. You will know this time by the rise of two human Queens—one of blood, and one of light. One with the power to save the world. One with the power to destroy it. Two Queens will rise. They will carry the power of the Seven. They will carry your fate in their hands. Two Queens will rise."

One of blood.

One of light.

Rielle stared at her clasped hands, longed to scrub them clean. Her clammy skin itched. She had a vision of herself peeling it away to reveal the roiling black truth of what lay beneath.

The Archon stepped back from her. "Lady Rielle Dardenne, you have passed the trials set before you by the Church and withstood great danger in doing so. This kingdom has watched you carefully over the past few weeks, and your power is unlike anything we have seen. Tell us, then, Lady Rielle: Which Queen are you?"

One of blood.

One of blood.

Rielle met the Archon's eyes. "I am the Queen of Light, Your Holiness. And I will serve Celdaria proudly until the end of my days."

The Archon smiled and extended his hand. "Then rise, Lady Rielle, and let us begin—"

A cry from the back of the hall interrupted him, followed by another, then a third. A clamor of astonishment and fear filled the room.

The Archon's face paled, his eyes fixed on something behind Rielle. He took a step back, reaching for his chair.

Audric shot to his feet, his hand around his mother's. Queen Genoveve's soft cry came out shattered.

Rielle turned, dread plugging her lungs. Was it Corien? Had he come ready to shout the truth of what she was for all to hear?

It was not Corien.

Ludivine, barefoot, hair a tumble of gold, stepped out of the crowd.

She clutched a tattered cloak at her throat and hips; beneath it she wore nothing. Her skin was ashen, but whole. She was alive... She was *alive*.

Rielle made a choked sound, swaying where she stood.

Ludivine climbed the altar steps, caught Rielle's hands with one of her own. Her touch was warm, familiar. She turned to face the room.

Out loud, Ludivine's shaking voice rose above the crowd's stunned voices. "I know this is startling, even frightening. Please forgive me."

Inside Rielle's mind, Ludivine whispered, *I'm so sorry you had to find out like this. Please, trust me. We must be careful.*

Rielle's shock crashed painfully through her body as if she'd been struck across her shoulders. Ludivine's iron grip kept her standing.

"I don't know how to explain it to you," Ludivine continued. "The last things I remember are a fog. Lady Rielle fighting a group of metal-masters. Rogues from House Sauvillier. My own father's house." Ludivine's voice trailed off, heavy with sadness.

We must convince them, all of them.

"Lu?" Rielle whispered, shaking.

It's all right. Please, my darling, don't fear me.

"I remember a weapon striking me in the stomach," Ludivine went on. "I remember...I remember falling."

Suddenly Audric was there beside them. He unclasped his long dress cloak and wrapped it around Ludivine's shoulders. Rielle was glad for the solid warmth of his body, anchoring her to her own breath, her own wildly pounding heart. This was not, then, a dream.

Not a dream. Ludivine's thoughts came gently. *It is the truth, at last. But they cannot know it. None of them.*

"You all thought I had died," said Ludivine, reaching for Audric's hand. Gingerly, he took it. "I thought I had too. But then I felt a power rise up beneath the earth and breathe life back into me. I felt a familiar touch, and I looked round for Lady Rielle, but she wasn't there. Her power, however...that was all around me. It lingered from her trial. It gave me back my body—and my life."

Trust me.

Rielle's thoughts raced. Trust her? Trust *who*? What was this creature? This was not Ludivine; this was an impostor.

You're wrong. It is me, truly. Please. If you ever loved me, you'll trust me. Just for a little while. Then I'll explain everything.

Rielle could hardly breathe. Her tears gathered fast. *I didn't bring you back. I don't understand.*

But you will. Soon. I promise.

"We have always known that the Sun Queen, when she came, would protect our kingdom from those who wish harm upon us." Ludivine's voice shook with emotion. "But now she is here, and her power is even greater than we have believed. She not only carries the power of the Seven, as the prophecy foretold."

Ludivine knelt at the hem of Rielle's glittering train. "She carries the power to bring life to that which has died."

Trust me. Quickly. In Rielle's mind, Ludivine stood firm. *They must believe me. They must accept this now, or all is ruined.*

"Rielle, is this true?" Audric murmured, his face awash with confusion and a trace of fear. "Did you do this?"

Fighting the urge to collapse, Rielle placed her hand on Ludivine's bowed head. "I'm sorry all of you had to find out like this," she said, echoing Ludivine's words. She lifted her eyes to the crowd, summoning a serenity to her face that she did not feel. Her mind raced through its shock to find words, any words, that would make sense. "The trials have deepened my power in ways I could not expect, but I did not want to raise any hopes before I was sure it would work. Before I could be sure that I had indeed brought our Lady Ludivine back to us."

Good. Ludivine's relief came as a caress. *Very good.*

"I only wish..." Rielle's voice failed her. "I only wish I were powerful enough to save everyone we lost that day."

Audric's gentle touch at the small of her back kept her standing, but she could not look at him. She didn't trust her face to hide what she needed it to.

Ludivine smiled up at her. "You saved me, Lady Rielle, as you did all of us here today. You faced a great evil, right here in our beloved city, and vanquished it. Your power is a marvel, and we owe you our lives."

Then Ludivine kissed Rielle's hand, and as Rielle watched through a humming veil of astonishment, the nearest in the crowd sank to their knees. Others followed, and still more, until the entire room, hundreds strong, had knelt before her.

"Long live the Sun Queen!" Ludivine's jubilant voice rang out, and others immediately took up the call. Midday sunlight streamed through the high windows to paint their tearful faces gold. Lower in the city, the solstice bells of the House of Light began to chime.

Looking out over the crowd, Rielle noticed a small handful of people in the room not repeating Ludivine's cry.

They knelt, the same as the rest, but watched Rielle with faces of silent stone.

A shiver of worry climbed up her body, but she had more pressing matters to consider first.

She squeezed Ludivine's hand. She hoped it hurt.

You're an angel, she thought, suddenly and viciously angry. *You lied to me.*

And you lied to Audric about his father's death, Ludivine answered, a note of sadness in her voice. *We are well-suited for each other. Now, keep smiling.*

~ 50 ~

ELIANA

"Whatever tomorrow may bring, the world will remem-
ber this as the day Astavar stood its ground against
a great evil and fought for its fallen sister kingdoms
until there was no more fight to give."

—Speech from Tavik and Eri Amaruk,
kings of Astavar, to their army
August 16, Year 1018 of the Third Age

E liana jumped off the ship and into the lifeboat, landed hard on
her knees, then used Tuora and Tempest to hack through the
boat's load lines.

Once they were free, she grabbed the oars and started rowing.
Gunfire struck the water on either side of them. Adatrox crowded the
ship's railing, guns sparking with every shot.

Eliana ducked as a bullet shot past her ear and yanked Simon down
by his collar. Cannon fire slammed into the water nearby, rocking the
boat and splashing them with a frigid spray.

At Simon's hissed curse, Eliana spared a glance for his bloodied
torso. She had grabbed him a jacket and sword from one of the adatrox
she'd slain while securing their boat, but a jacket and sword would do
him no good if she couldn't get him to a healer—and fast.

Once out of the adatroxes' firing range, Eliana passed the oars to
Simon. "Can you row? Just for a minute."

"I'll row for as long as you need me to," he replied.

She hurried to the front of the boat, crouched beside Simon, and scanned the water ahead.

"Maybe five hundred more yards," she said, "through these icebergs, and then I think I see a path to shore."

"You see a path of *what*, exactly?"

"Ice. Some rocks too."

"Ah. No problem at all, for a newly blinded man to skip across the water on such a path."

She couldn't help a smile. "I'll help you. So will Zahra."

"Eliana?" Zahra's stricken voice made Eliana turn. "Something's happening."

"What?" Eliana squinted across the black water. The Empire fleet—thirty vessels, most of them massive warships—were moving into a long line along the thinning ice. "What are they doing?"

"Describe it to me," Simon said.

"They're gathering beside the ice in a line, one right after the other, their prows facing north." Eliana couldn't make sense of the maneuver. "It's like they're making a barrier between the ice and the open water. A blockade?"

"And they've stopped firing," Zahra observed.

With a scraping thud, the lifeboat rammed into a low slab of ice. Eliana climbed out at once and held the boat fast, Zahra floating beside her.

"Climb out over here," Eliana instructed.

Simon fumbled to find the stolen adatrox sword and obeyed, slowly feeling his way out of the boat. Eliana guided him across the ice, then over a narrow gap of dark water to another huge slab.

Simon looked out at the fleet with reddened eyes. "Why have they stopped firing?"

"I don't know, but we should take advantage of it and hurry."

But then, just as Zahra let out a sharp cry of despair, a low horn blasted across the water. As one, entire sections of the warships' hulls fell open and slammed down onto the ice. A wave of darkness tumbled out and started galloping madly for shore. Discordant, shrill cries filled the air—howls, half-formed words, screams of fury.

Eliana's blood ran colder than the ice now quaking under her feet. She knew those sounds, from her time in the Fidelia labs.

"What is that?" Simon tensed beside her. "Eliana, tell me what's happening."

"Crawlers!" Zahra shoved through Eliana's shoulders. "We must go, my queen!"

But Eliana stood frozen. She watched the creatures barreling toward them across the ice. They moved so *quickly*, half running, half crawling, their limbs turning unnaturally with every stride.

"Fidelia," Eliana whispered, taking two unsteady steps back. It was just as Zahra had said: Fidelia had turned the stolen women of Ventera into monsters.

Zahra stretched to her fullest, darkest height and roared, "Run!"

Eliana spun, slid and fell, hit her jaw on the ice. She scrambled back to her feet, found Simon, grabbed his hand.

"Can you see at all?" she cried over the approaching din. Alarm bells rang across the Astavari ships. Their cannon fire resumed, blasting a dozen new holes in the ice before the encroaching wave of crawlers.

"Just run," Simon shouted at her. "And don't look back!"

He tried to shake her off, but she held fast. "I'm not leaving you here!"

"I'll keep up, now move!"

She turned and ran, Simon on her heels. Zahra flew ahead of them across the ice, seeking the safest path.

"Left!" she cried, directing them around a thin patch of ice. "Jump!"

Eliana threw herself off a ridge of ice and onto another slab a few feet away.

"Simon, here!" she cried over her shoulder. "Follow my voice!"

He jumped onto the ice beside her. It rocked violently, sent them both sliding. Eliana stabbed Arabeth into the ice and grabbed Simon's shirt with her other hand. His weight yanked hard on her muscles. She cried out in pain, clung to her dagger with every ounce of strength she possessed.

Simon scrabbled up the ice beside her, tipping the ice level once more. A dark shape flew over their heads, landing hard a few feet away.

Eliana looked up in horror as a stream of crawlers raced by. Their heads were human enough—but misshapen and approaching bestial—with sharpened teeth spilling out of broken jaws. Faded scraps of clothing clung to their bodies, and the patches of skin Eliana could see were spotted with scales, patches of scraggly dark fur. They sniffed the air like hounds. Thick, pointed fingernails stabbed the ice.

All those women, snatched while they slept, taken from their beds and their homes and their loved ones, and made into *this*.

It was an unthinkable fate—and the one awaiting her mother if she couldn't find her in time.

Two crawlers slammed into the ice, then spun around and raced right for Eliana.

Zahra cried out, her form flickering out of sight. "This way!"

Eliana turned and ran. On all sides, a sea of howling crawlers raced for the shore. Cannon fire hit the ice. The impact blew the pursuing crawlers behind them into pieces.

Ears ringing, Eliana turned. Simon? Still there, his sword out and ready, his hair frosted with ice. Eliana followed Zahra's shimmering path over a shifting, dark gap between icebergs, along a ridge of icy rocks, across a long, flat stretch of frozen white.

Then, Zahra's form shuddered and disappeared.

Eliana stumbled, her ears ringing with panic.

"Keep running!" Simon shouted.

"Zahra?" Eliana cried. "Where are you?"

The wraith swooped alongside her, a faint distortion in the air. "I'm sorry, my queen. I can barely hold myself together!"

"Go to the fleet, tell them we're out here!" Another blast exploded just ahead of them. Eliana skidded to a halt, shoved Simon to the ground. Shards of ice and bodies went flying. Fiery sparks rained down upon them. "And for God's sake, tell them to stop firing at us!"

Zahra fled.

Eliana looked back over Simon's head to see a group of four crawlers crouching on an icy ridge a few feet away.

One of them, hair a dark matted mess, pawed the ice with a bulbous hand.

"Simon," Eliana muttered, "get to your feet, slowly."

He obeyed. Together they took a few slow steps back.

Then the lead crawler let out a baying howl. The four of them leapt across the water, teeth bared. They moved like roaches—fast, erratic. Simon brought his sword down hard on the neck of one; its head flew off into the water. Another slammed into him, knocking him flat.

A third reared up, nails bared. Eliana ducked the blow, then stabbed it in the stomach. As it fell, she yanked Arabeth free and whirled, flung the dagger between the shoulder blades of the creature hissing on Simon's chest. It roared in pain and fell to the ground.

Eliana turned, reached for Whistler. But the fourth crawler with the tangled dark hair was nowhere to be found.

Eliana raced over to Simon, yanked Arabeth from the crawler's twitching body, and kept running.

"This way!" she called, but Simon was already behind her, his breath labored in the air. "Are you all right?"

"Splendid," came his strained reply.

Crawlers scrambled across the ice on all sides. Hundreds, Eliana thought. Maybe thousands.

Gunfire split the air in two, followed by terrified human cries. She looked to the west. Some of the creatures had made it ashore. They slithered onto the beach from the water like sea monsters come to ground. The Astavari army engaged them with revolvers and swords, but the crawlers kept coming.

A shadow fell over her as they ran. She looked up. They'd reached the Astavari fleet—small, elegant ships, each mast a hundred feet in the air. Crawlers swarmed the nearest one, tearing sails from their masts and tackling Astavari soldiers to the decks.

"Almost there," she shouted over the sounds of death and gunfire, howls and snapping wood. "Stay with me, Simon!"

They slid down the sharp incline of an iceberg and ran out onto a long, flat slab, now past the Astavari fleet and only a few hundreds yards from the shore. Simon's knees buckled. He cried out in pain.

A brutal weight slammed into them from behind, knocking them both far across the ice.

Eliana's vision faded, then flared back to life. She looked up, woozy.

A crawler had Simon pinned to the ice. It was the crawler from before, with those piles of matted dark hair. Its teeth—*her* teeth—gnashed just above his throat. He twisted away from her, punched her square in the jaw. She cried out, a garbled, familiar word that Eliana recognized as a Venteran curse.

Eliana jumped onto the crawler. She knocked her aside with one monstrous arm. Eliana sprang back to her feet just as Simon rolled away and sliced his sword across the crawler's side.

The crawler screamed in agony, clutching her wound. Her hand was bulbous, malformed, and covered in oozing sores. Eliana saw the same markings that now stained Navi's body and felt a rush of pity.

As she hesitated, the crawler looked up—and Eliana at last saw her bruised face in full view.

A thousand memories flew at Eliana in the span of a few seconds:

Sitting beside Rozen at home, Remy in her lap. Rozen holding open a book of children's stories so that Eliana could read them aloud to her baby brother—stories of the seven saints and the animals that carried them into battle against the angels.

Rozen, finding Eliana sobbing in her bed in the middle of the night. The invasion had taken their kingdom, and her father had not come home.

Rozen teaching Eliana how to fight, how to lie, how to kill.

Now, standing half alive on the ice, Eliana looked for Rozen Ferracora in the crawler's disfigured face, the angry world howling around her.

"Mother?" She placed the hand gripping Arabeth against her chest. A dull roar filled her ears, pulsing with the beat of her heart. "It's me. It's...Eliana."

The crawler blinked, croaked something unintelligible. Then she snarled and lunged for Eliana.

Simon crashed into the creature, wrestled her to the ground, raised his sword.

"Wait!" Eliana cried. "Don't hurt her!"

But then the crawler twisted out of Simon's grip, struck him across the face.

Simon fell, his sword flying across the ice and into the water. The crawler pounced with bared teeth. Her fist, run through with metal spikes rimmed in infected flesh, punched the ground beside Simon's face.

"Eliana!" Simon roared, dodging her. "Get out of here!"

But Eliana was already moving.

She ran, tears muddling her vision, and just when the crawler reared back to strike Simon with a killing blow, Eliana plunged Arabeth into her stomach.

Blood gushed out over her hand. The crawler jerked, choked, slid off Simon and onto the ice.

Eliana sank to her knees at the crawler's side and watched as her last breaths seized her. With each harsh inhale, intelligence returned to her darkening eyes.

"I know that knife," she gasped, her words broken, rattling, hardly comprehensible. But Eliana heard the threads of a familiar voice buried inside and was no longer afraid. "I know that face."

Rozen brought a shaking hand to Eliana's cheek, her own skin rough with scaly sores.

"Finish it," Rozen pleaded, a wet cough seizing her. "Please...sweet girl."

Eliana brushed a kiss across her swollen, fevered forehead and whispered through her tears, "I love you."

Then she sank Arabeth into the side of Rozen's throat and watched the light leave her bloodshot eyes.

Eliana's head buzzed. Her breath came fast and thin. The world rolled away from her, then surged back and clawed away her air.

An immense rage was building inside her—hotter and blacker than any vicious urge that had ever sent her flying into a fight.

The battlefield roared around her, a symphony of explosions and agonized cries. Fire arced overhead—bombardiers, ignited and ready to explode, soaring for the beach. Crawlers surged out of the water, dragging Astavari soldiers under.

"Eliana," Simon said, very near, "we have to move."

His voice, firm but exceedingly gentle, was the thing that broke her. She screamed.

The world screamed with her.

For a moment—brief but wild and impossible to understand—Eliana saw everything:

The ice, sky, and water flared to life, and she saw it all for what it was: a veil, nothing more. A covering hiding something incredible and divine.

Time slowed.

She saw herself, and Simon, both of them shivering and bloodied. She saw the beach being swarmed by monsters and the prows of the Empire fleet carving through the ice. She heard the Astavari soldiers' cries for help, and she thought she heard Prince Malik Amaruk shouting orders for those fighting on the beach. She thought she heard Remy, hidden in Navi's castle, whisper, "Eliana, please be all right."

And she thought she heard a voice drift across the ocean to tell her, *I felt that, Eliana. You can't hide from me now.*

Unseeing and all-seeing, Eliana stared at the exploding, frigid world around her.

Icy fingers of grief closed around her throat.

It will consume you. Her mother's voice. A memory now and nothing more.

She dropped to her knees. Shoved Simon's hands away, uttered a wordless protest.

I will not be consumed.

Then she slammed her fists hard against the ice and buckled over, struggling to breathe.

The noises of the battle around her fell away. She existed in a cocoon—the water lapping at the ice, the ice hot with her mother's blood, the blood slick on her clenched palms.

The water rumbled, shifting. The ice cracked open. Rozen's body slid into the water and disappeared. A dim percussive noise struck the air. Bright lights flashed—angry and too many.

A muffled shout pulled her out of whatever place she'd gone.

She blinked. Blinked again.

Simon pulled her to her feet. "You're burning up. Come on, let's move. God, Eliana, what did you do?"

She didn't answer, didn't *know* the answer. A charged feeling tugged at her hands, nipped across her skin.

They plunged into frigid, knee-high water. She watched her feet wade through a black ocean thick with chunks of ice, felt her boots slide through mud.

"Eliana, stop!"

She stood on shifting sand, water lapping at her toes. *The shore.*

"Look at me!" Simon was shouting at her, but the field of light beyond her eyes was too bright, too terrible. She squinted her eyes shut and turned into him. Her body could no longer hold itself up. She sagged to the ground, and Simon went with her, holding her in his arms. The wind howled around them, whipping ice and sand against her skin.

"What's happening?" she murmured. A brutal coughing fit seized her. Every bone in her body ached, every muscle burned.

A cold hand smoothed the hair back from her forehead. "Look at what you're doing, Eliana. I need you to open your eyes for me, come on."

She forced open her eyes and looked out to sea.

Lightning flashed, three new strikes every second, painting the battlefield a fevered silver. They blasted apart the crawlers still swimming to shore; icebergs erupted into flame. Roiling dark waves crashed against the Empire fleet. A savage wind whipped sails from their masts, stirred the sea into whirlpools that sucked the warships underwater and snapped them in two.

"You have to stop it," Simon shouted over the wind.

"Am I doing this?" she murmured, then realized she wasn't breathing, that the storm had sucked all the air from her lungs. Her gasp hurt, cleaved her chest in two.

Simon's hands cupped her face, steadying her. "Please, Eliana, look at me, look into my eyes."

She did, sobs she didn't intend to release tearing out of her throat. "I killed her. I couldn't save her!"

"I know." He wiped the grit from her face. "And I'm sorry. But you have to stop this now, or you'll kill us all."

She shook her head, realizing through the frantic roar of her despair that somehow she was doing this, that the world was echoing her own rage. Zahra was right, and so was Simon. There was an impossible *thing* living inside her. She had always thought it a monster of her own creation, forged by the violence she had done to survive.

But the truth was this: It was a monster given to her by her mother. The Blood Queen. The Kingsbane. A traitor and a liar.

And Eliana decided, in that moment, to hate her.

"I don't know how to stop it," she cried. Her fingers blazed along with the storm; the feeling revolted her. She watched ships being torn apart, soldiers swimming for their lives. Black waves surged toward the shore.

"Just hold on to me," Simon whispered, cradling her against his chest. "Hold on to me and think of Remy. Think of Navi." He pressed his cold cheek to her forehead. "Think of home."

Home. And what was home to her now? Orline? Or Celdaria?

With the storm raging, she could remember neither place.

Instead she listened to Simon's wild heartbeat, imagined Remy's voice reading her a story before sleep, and breathed.

⟶51⟵

RIELLE

"Wind and water
Fire and shadow
Metal and earth and light above—
Hear our prayer on this day of death
Take in hand our fallen friend
To be born anew, through you
And begin again
In the eyes of the Seven, we pray"

—Traditional Celdarian funeral rite

Hours after the Archon's blessing, near the midnight hour, Rielle brought Audric to Ludivine's rooms.

Ludivine rose from a hearthside chair with a cautious smile. "Good, you've come."

Audric pulled the door shut behind them with a snap. "Rielle told me what you are."

Ludivine's face fell. She glanced at Rielle. "What else did she tell you?"

"Isn't that enough?"

Her eyes filled with tears. "Please don't be afraid of me. I want only to help you. That's all I've ever wanted."

Audric softened. "All right. Help me, then. Help us understand."

Ludivine's gaze settled on Rielle, infinitely tender. "I came to protect Rielle. The moment she was born, I felt her. We all did."

"All?"

"The other angels?" Rielle said, her chest clenching.

Ludivine nodded miserably. "Yes, the other angels. I've been trying to protect you as best I can for years now."

Audric dragged both hands through his hair. "I don't understand. You're Ludivine. You're my cousin. We've known you since you were small. I was there the day you were born, for God's sake. You've always been...you."

"Yes." Ludivine's smile was sad. "And no. Do you remember when I...when Ludivine had that terrible fever a few years ago?"

"You were sixteen years old," Rielle remembered. She sank onto a bench by the fire. "We waited outside your door all night with Queen Genoveve and your father, hoping you'd get through it."

"Yes. Well." Ludivine drew a deep breath, squaring her shoulders. "I didn't. That is, she didn't. Ludivine Sauvillier died that night. And I took her place."

Audric turned away and moved swiftly across the room. "This is some kind of trick."

It's not a trick, Ludivine's voice cried out in Rielle's mind. *Tell him!*

"It's not a trick," Rielle whispered, and she believed it, though the horrible truth of it sat like a weight on her lungs. "How could you keep the truth from us for so long? If you love us as you claim to—"

"I wanted to!" Ludivine's eyes were bright with tears. "Every day, I wanted to. But I thought it would be best not to. I thought it would protect you. I thought..." Ludivine shook her head, gestured helplessly. "I wanted you both to be spared from all of this for as long as possible."

"Protect us from what?" Audric asked, his voice fraying. "You're dancing around the point. Speak clearly—and quickly."

Ludivine breathed in and out, clenching her fists. When she spoke once more, it was with a sense of tired finality. "The Gate is falling."

The room fell into silence.

"The further it weakens," Ludivine said after a moment, "the more we will see the shocks. Tidal waves, terrible quakes, other disasters I cannot predict. And when the Gate falls at last, the angels will return, just as Aryava said. Imagine a door being battered constantly from one side by hands that will never tire. That is the Gate, and the hands are those of my kindred, locked beyond it."

"Trapped in the Deep." Audric sat unsteadily on a chair by the wall, far from them both.

"Yes. In the Deep." A small, strange shadow moved across Ludivine's face; an echo of it rippled inside Rielle's mind, like a shift during sleep.

"How many of you are there?" he asked.

"Millions."

"I meant here. In this world. If you came here, then others must have as well."

Rielle stiffened. Without thinking, her mind reached out to him: *Corien? Are you there?*

He did not answer. He had been silent since the day she burned him.

Ludivine looked quickly to Rielle. "Yes. I was not the first. And I was not the last. With every passing day, cracks widen in the Gate's structure. Not all angels are strong enough to escape. The Gate is strong and well-made. Escaping its gravity is difficult; one crack opens, and another one repairs itself. But enough angels are managing to break through that it will soon be a problem for you. Dozens right now. Soon? Hundreds."

"You weren't the first." Rielle lifted her eyes slowly to Ludivine. "Who was?"

"He is very strong," said Ludivine quietly. "The strongest of us left alive since the Angelic Wars. It took him centuries to escape, but he did it. I slipped out in his wake, along with a few others, before the Gate resealed. I've watched over Rielle, in one form or another, for thirteen years, as did he. His name is Corien."

Thirteen years. *Since I was five years old*, Rielle thought. A field of flames flashed before her eyes. A crumbling house. Her father, falling to his knees.

She decided she would go see him after this conversation. She would wake him up, bring him hot cocoa, keep him talking until the sun rose and she no longer felt so afraid.

Then her mind caught up with the truth: his bed would be empty.

"The day your mother died, Rielle," Ludivine said, pity in her voice, "we felt your power erupt. Corien came for you soon after, and I did as well. Only...I am quite young. My mind is nothing compared to his. It takes nearly everything I am to protect you from even some of his thoughts."

"And why do you?" Rielle bristled at the careful compassion in Ludivine's voice. "Why do you want to help me or any of us? Don't you want revenge for being trapped in the Deep for centuries?"

"No," Ludivine said simply. "Humans and angels were at war. I don't blame you for the actions your ancestors took to save themselves. You are innocent."

Ludivine reached for Rielle, but Rielle flinched away, and Ludivine withdrew at once.

"Corien, however, desires revenge above all else," Ludivine said quietly, "and it isn't fair that you should suffer for it. I will do what I can to stop him because it's the right thing to do."

"Really?" Rielle raised an eyebrow, determined to remain unmoved at the sight of Ludivine's tear-filled eyes. "How noble of you."

Ludivine's expression crumpled. "My dear, I'm sorry I'm not a stronger ally. I know it is difficult for you. I feel it every time he speaks to you."

"Corien—the angel from the attack?" Audric looked first to Ludivine, and then to Rielle. "What does she mean, Rielle? He speaks to you?"

Rielle's panic rose swiftly. *He will be furious when he finds out.*

No, he won't, came Ludivine's firm reply. *He loves you.*

But for how long?

Forever. He will love you forever.

"Months ago," Rielle began, her voice unsteady, "on the day of the Chase, I heard a voice in my mind."

Don't tell him everything, Ludivine suggested. *Spare him the worst of it.*

The worst of it: That dark vastness, the throne made of bones. Corien's name on her lips as she awoke lonely in her bed, and the ghost of his hands on her skin.

Rielle swallowed, shame burning tears from her eyes. "He visits me in dreams—and sometimes when I'm awake. He talked to me during the trials. He tells me..."

Go on, Ludivine urged gently.

Rielle touched her temples, swallowing hard.

Audric knelt before her. "What does he tell you? How can I help?"

She met Audric's steady dark eyes through a haze of tears. "He wants me," she whispered. "I don't know what for. He wants me to go to him. He says he won't always be so patient. He tried to make me leave with him, the day of the fire trial. I wouldn't. I burned him, but...I can't say if that will stop him."

"It won't," Ludivine said, "but he won't recover from that for some time."

Rielle threw her a dark look. "So you say."

Ludivine looked as though she'd been slapped. "You don't trust me anymore."

"I should think that much would be obvious by now. And anyway, can you blame me for that?"

"I understand. I'll have to earn back your trust." Ludivine nodded, pressed her lips tightly together. "I can do that. I *will* do that."

"My God." Audric's worried expression tore Rielle's heart in two. "Rielle...why didn't you ever say anything about any of this?"

"I was frightened. I didn't know what you'd think of me."

He cradled her face in his hands, catching her tears on his thumbs. "I could have helped you."

"I hate him," she whispered, and it was true. But it was not the whole truth, and she despised herself for it. "And I don't know how to be rid of him."

"We will find a way," Ludivine said, coming to sit beside her.

"Have you been in her mind as well?" Audric asked sharply. "Like him?"

Ludivine met his eyes. "Yes. For three years now, though I have been near her for much longer."

"And does Corien know about you? That you're here, in Ludivine's body, protecting Rielle from him?"

Ludivine nodded. "He does."

"And I would imagine," Audric observed, "that he isn't too happy about you working against him?"

"He considers me a traitor to my kind." Ludivine squared her jaw. "A title I am happy to bear if it keeps Rielle safe."

Audric glanced at Rielle. "You said you've been looking after her for years. And then you mentioned your…Ludivine's fever. You mentioned…" He looked slightly ill. "Taking her place."

"Ah. Yes." Ludivine stood. "When we were locked away in the Deep, we lost our bodies and existed only as our thoughts." She said it matter-of-factly, as though being stripped of one's body were a small thing. "Once Corien and I escaped that place, we were able to take possession of human bodies that had been recently…vacated."

Rielle's stomach churned. She stepped away from Ludivine, trying to keep her mind as numb and clear as possible. If she thought too closely about Ludivine—*her* Ludivine—long dead, and her body now possessed by this *other* Ludivine, this *creature*, she felt dizzy and frantic, like she was hurtling toward a cliff's edge.

"Sweet saints," Audric whispered. "You mean you possessed these bodies and now live inside them, controlling them."

Ludivine nodded. "Essentially."

"Can you do this…forever?"

"Once I took hold of this body, it stopped growing, and it will remain like this as long as I am inside it."

"Even if you fall to your death," Audric whispered, a sad smile on his face.

"Even if I fall to my death."

He shook his head. "I don't know what to say to you right now. I can't decide which I feel more deeply—anger or fear or, quite frankly, fascination." He glared up at her. "You shouldn't have lied to us for so long. We deserved better than that."

Ludivine nodded. "I know. You're right. I was only..." She hesitated, with a sad smile. "I was afraid of losing you."

"We were not yours to have," Audric replied sharply.

Ludivine let out a soft sob. She reached for their hands, and when they did not pull away, the look of relief on her face was so profound that Rielle had to avert her eyes.

"Please know," Ludivine said, "that the things we have shared, these last few years, are real and precious to me. I've lived at your sides since you were small, I've watched you grow, and I grieved deeply when Ludivine died. It was of great comfort to me that I could bring her back to you, even in a small way. And, my darlings," she whispered, "please do not doubt that I love you. In my long lifetime, I have never loved anything or anyone as I do the two of you."

"I cannot say the same to you." Audric laughed harshly. "I don't even know what to call you. Do you have an angelic name?"

"Ludivine. I beg you to call me Ludivine. My angelic name is no longer relevant—and not a word I care for. I know I don't deserve to ask that of you, but it is who I am, she is who I have become—"

"Please." Audric cut her off. "No more of that, not right now. I need... I have to think about this."

She nodded, smiled bravely. "Of course. I understand."

Please don't shut me out, Ludivine thought to Rielle. *The world depends on it, but more than that, I cannot bear—*

Don't be afraid. Rielle tried to send her a feeling of love, faint as it was—and even though she wasn't sure Ludivine deserved it. But she could no longer bear the weight of Ludivine's quiet despair without offering her a slight ray of hope. *You will not lose us as easily as that.*

"I should tell you," Ludivine added quietly, "that though I am not much more than a child in your terms, and not as powerful as Corien, I am a good deal stronger than most of our kind. The majority cannot take hold of a human body like this, at least not with such... effectiveness."

For that, she thought to Rielle, *they would need help.*

Rielle stared at her, the realization seeping into her slowly and leaving room for little else. *They will need...me.*

One week later, Rielle stood before the floor-length mirror in her rooms, adjusting the heavy black folds of her gown.

Outside, a star-scattered lavender sky faded to a cloudless night. Atheria stood solemnly on the terrace, looking down at the city. Soon the temple bells would ring, and the procession of King Bastien's body up the streets of Âme de la Terre would begin.

Ludivine emerged from the bathing rooms, golden hair in a crown of braids around her head. Her own mourning gown, like Rielle's, fastened high at the throat.

"Are you ready?" Ludivine asked, tugging on her gloves.

Rielle stared at her reflection. Shadows hugged her eyes. Two weeks had passed since the fire trial, and she hadn't slept more than three or four hours every night since. Lord Dervin's body had been sent home to Belbrion for his son, Merovec Sauvillier, to attend to. And mere hours earlier, Rielle had watched her own father's body burn on a mountaintop pyre. It had always been a wish of his, for his body to return to the empirium as his wife's had.

Rielle watched Ludivine move about the room, tidying up the mess of combs, pins, and smoothing creams. It was such a familiar ritual that Rielle felt tears rise once more to her eyes.

"I thought I was done crying," she said with a hollow laugh. "I suppose I'm not."

Ludivine paused at the window, her slender body framed in twilight. Frozen forever at sixteen—what a strange and terrible thing.

And not a secret any of them would be able to hide forever.

"I wish I could help you," Ludivine said, and Rielle felt the truth of it brush against her mind. "I wish so many things."

"Just because I don't trust you right now doesn't mean I don't love you. I wish I didn't, and maybe I shouldn't after what you've done, but I still do nevertheless." Rielle turned away from the hope shining on Ludivine's face. "There. I've wanted to say that for days, and now I've said it."

A soft knock on the door. Evyline entered with a delicate cough. "My lady? Prince Audric is here to see you."

Rielle's heart jumped with nerves. Since the trial, Audric had been so occupied with meetings, funerals, and caring for his mother that she had barely seen him. And whenever she did, she faced him with a new fear: that he would sense the lies spinning in her heart and turn her away forever.

But as he entered the room, meticulous in mourning black, all of that flew out of her mind. If she looked tired, he looked far worse—his skin sallow and drawn, his eyes red from exhaustion. His grief trailed him like shadows.

She went to him at once, and without a word he opened his arms to her.

"I've missed you," he whispered, his voice muffled in her hair. "Would it be awful of me if I asked you to my bed tonight?"

For a moment, she could think only of his arms around her. She smiled against his shoulder. "I was about to ask you the same thing."

"My light and my life." He bent low to kiss her softly.

"Is everything ready below?" Ludivine asked.

"Our escort is waiting for us." Audric paused, then released Rielle and, hesitating, held out his hand to Ludivine. "But before we go down, I need to talk to you for a moment. To both of you."

Rielle stiffened.

Don't worry. Ludivine took Audric's hand. *He knows nothing. And he never will. I'll see to it.*

"It's this...all of this. Corien. The Gate and the angels. And you, Lu." Audric released Ludivine's hand with a tight smile. "It's a lot to wrap my mind around. And now, with Father gone—" His voice caught. "Mother will be the one to lead us to war, when it comes, and we're to help her with that, Rielle—you and me. And Lu, we won't tell anyone what you are, of course, but you will also be instrumental as we move through these next months and years. The knowledge you have about your kind will be invaluable."

Ludivine nodded. "Of course."

Audric considered her. "Can you really be so eager to turn against your own people?"

"They are not my people," Ludivine said. "Not anymore. You are my people." She looked to them both, her face open and fierce. "I am loyal to you and no one else."

Rielle glanced at Audric. Their gazes locked, and she didn't need Ludivine's power to understand what he was thinking: He was still wary of Ludivine, just as Rielle was. But what choice did they have but to trust her?

"Mother will need advisers," Audric continued after a moment, and we will be her closest ones. We must fortify our borders, reach out to the rest of the continent. Find out what they know—and what they don't."

"And we must travel to the Gate," Rielle finished, "and assess the damage for ourselves."

Audric nodded. "Tal and Sloane will accompany us. Tal insisted upon it. And where Tal goes..."

"Sloane follows." Ludivine clasped her hands in her lap. "She wouldn't want him to have all the fun after all."

The forced note of cheer in her voice seemed to shake them all.

Audric's gaze dropped to the floor. "There's one more thing. If we are to do this, together, then we must have no more secrets. If you hear murmurings from the other angels, Ludivine, I want to know. And when Corien comes"—Audric took Rielle's hand in his—"I need you to tell me, darling, when it happens. If he forces himself on you again, I need to know. What he says, what he does. Any clues as to where he is, who he might be with, what his plans are... Any of that could be helpful to us. When he moves against us, I want to be ready. And you are the closest link to him we have."

Rielle nodded, unable to speak. It was unbearable, how little he suspected her of lies. He raised her hand to his lips, kissed her clenched fingers.

"I'm sorry," he said, his voice tight with anger. "I wish I didn't have to ask this of you."

"Don't be sorry." She tried for an encouraging smile. "I'm the Sun Queen, aren't I? This is what I do."

"You're only half right, my love. You protect me and my kingdom, but we also protect you."

Below, throughout the city, the temple bells struck nine o'clock. In half an hour, the procession would begin.

"Shall we go down?" Ludivine stood a little apart from them, a careful smile on her face. "We don't want to be late."

"Promise me, first." Audric held out his hand to her. "If we're going to do this, we'll do it together. All of us."

Ludivine hesitated, then took his hand.

Rielle joined them, swallowing against the guilt wedged hot in her throat. "I promise," she said and kissed his cheek. "No more secrets."

"No more lies," Ludivine added.

"Together, then," Audric said and escorted them downstairs.

Hooded citizens lined the streets of Âme de la Terre, carrying candles in tiny brass cups. Hanging from every door and window, mourning lamps flickered softly.

The procession moved slowly up the city—first across the bridges over the lake, then the cramped lower streets, and at last the smooth paved roads of the temple district. The youngest acolytes from each temple led the way, scattering white petals. Seven windsingers guided King Bastien's silk-draped stretcher slowly through the city on a gentle cloud of air. The king's hands lay folded at his waist, his face peaceful.

Queen Genoveve followed behind them, her arm hooked through Audric's. From behind her, at Ludivine's side, Rielle saw how heavily the queen leaned against her son.

At the castle gates, only the royal party was allowed to proceed. Mourners crowded silently at the line of guards that barred their way. Rielle looked back once, saw the mass of bowed heads and bobbing candles winding like black rivers down the mountain to the city's outer wall and the Flats beyond. They filled every road, lined every temple garden.

Some, Rielle noticed, looked not at the king, but at her. Did they wonder how so many had fallen, even with the mighty Sun Queen there to defend them?

Did they fear what that meant for the days ahead?

Rielle turned away from the scattered stony eyes upon her, heart clenched with worry.

What are they thinking? She clutched Ludivine's hand. *The ones staring.*

They wonder many things, Ludivine replied.

They wonder why I was able to save you but not their loved ones who died at the trial. And not their king.

Ludivine was quiet for a moment, then squeezed Rielle's fingers.

Don't think about that now. Be here, with me and with Audric. We both owe Bastien that much.

The procession entered the gardens behind Baingarde. Sorrow trees glowed pink throughout the shadowed green canopy. The seeing pools stood black and still.

At the mouth of the catacombs, Queen Genoveve stepped away from Audric and took her place before the great stone doors. She knelt, touched her fingers to her heart, her temple and throat, her palm, forehead, the nape of her neck, and the lids of her eyes. She rose to her feet as acolytes rolled open the doors and began to sing.

Saint Katell had sung the same ancient lament over Aryava's body, and the queen's shredded voice tore on every word—but she stood tall and unbroken as her husband's body passed beside her into the shadows.

It was then, as Bastien's body faded into the blackness of the catacombs, that Rielle felt the wind kiss her skin.

Her power swelled gently against her bones—a wave building on a rumbling sea.

She looked, shivering, through the trees to the east, where the mountains surrounding the capital stood darkest. Ludivine's hand tightened around her fingers, but she barely noticed.

It might have just been the wind she had heard, she supposed.

Or it might have been a whisper, calling her name.

ELIANA

*"I saw the storm she pulled down from the sky, how
it set the Empire monsters afire and tore their ships in
two. I saw her storm, and I fell to my knees and wept.
For I knew it as sure as the bones in my body: the Sun
Queen had come at last."*

—Collection of stories written by soldiers in the free
kingdom of Astavar
Curated by Hob Cavaserra

Eliana awoke quietly from a hard sleep.

Above her, a vaulted, violet-colored ceiling painted with silver stars.

Beneath her, a comfortable bed. Piled pillows and cool linens.

Beside her—

"Simon," she whispered. He sat in a simple wooden chair at her bedside, his head in his hands. At the sound of her voice he looked up, and across his battered face flickered a softness she had never seen him wear.

"Hello there." He pressed the back of his hand against her forehead. "You've cooled a bit more. That's good."

Then she remembered:

The storm raging black and brilliant over the crashing sea.

Simon holding her on the beach, his own body trembling with exhaustion. *You're burning up. Look at me, Eliana.*

You have to stop it, or you'll kill us all.

"No," Eliana whispered, her face crumpling. "No, no, no."

"Listen to me." Simon gathered her hands in his. "You saved us. You saved *everyone*. Astavar still stands free. The Empire fleet has been destroyed. You did that, Eliana, and should be proud of it."

She blinked back tears, struggling to breathe. "How long?"

"Three days. I've kept you fed as well as I could."

"Remy?"

"Asleep." He looked over his shoulder.

Eliana peered past him, found Remy sleeping peacefully on a pile of blankets by a blazing hearth. His mouth hung open as he snored.

She let out a tiny, tired laugh. "Navi?"

"Resting and well. The kings' healers think that Fidelia had not begun their experiments, only the preparations."

"And you?" She inspected his stitched-up torso, the bruises coloring his face, the redness rimming his eyes. "Oh, Simon, your eyes..."

"Don't fret. They're healing nicely. And anyway, I've had worse."

She believed that without question but nevertheless sat up, ignoring his protests. Someone had dressed her in a simple, dark nightgown. Her body ached, but it was whole and healthy, and she hated it bitterly. One monster walks away unhurt while the other takes every scar for himself?

She swung her bare legs over the side of the bed and scooted close to Simon, her knees bumping against his. She reached for his face, hesitated. He watched her so intently she almost lost her nerve.

Almost.

She drew her fingers softly through his hair, down his cheek, across his jaw. She avoided the worst of his wounds, and yet still wondered if this was too much—an intrusion, a selfish one.

But she couldn't resist touching him. She searched the tired lines of his face for the frightened little boy Zahra had shown her, and when her thumb brushed against his mouth, they both shivered.

"Am I hurting you?" she whispered.

He closed his eyes, leaned into her touch. "No," he said hoarsely, "and if you ever did, I'd bear it gladly."

"We fought well together out there."

"We did."

"I'm sorry you're hurt." Her chest tightened at the raw longing on his face, and she wondered when it last was that someone had touched him with any sort of kindness. "I wish I could take it from you."

"Eliana...please." He caught her hand gently and opened his eyes. "Don't pity me. When I can, I take the blows meant for you." He gathered something from the table beside her bed, folded it into her hands. "You are my queen, and my life is yours. It has been since the day you were born."

She stared down at the necklace resting in her palms. "This was hers, wasn't it? The Blood Queen. Mother said she found it on the street, but... Did she know?"

"Did Rozen Ferracora know who you really are? I doubt it."

She settled the chain around her neck once more and breathed a bit more easily with its weight between her breasts.

"So you believe me now?" he asked.

She avoided looking at him. "About what?"

"That you are who I say you are."

"What would it mean if it was true?"

"It would mean that you had inherited the power of the Blood Queen. That you are without doubt the only person capable of destroying the Empire. And that soon everyone in the world will know that Rielle's daughter lives—and want you for their own."

"Oh, is that all?" A tremor shook her voice.

"You won't have to do this alone," Simon said urgently. "I won't ever leave your side, Eliana. And whatever I can do to keep you safe, I will do it."

"Because I'm...your queen." The words sounded hollow and ridiculous to her ears.

"Yes. And because…" He paused. "Because you are the best chance to save us all."

She rose, moved past him to pace unsteadily through the tiny candlelit alcove surrounding her bed.

"I suppose I can't deny it anymore, can I? After…" She waved one of her hands in the air.

"After your storm?"

Her storm. She closed her eyes, her mouth souring as she remembered the wildness of lightning and ocean scorching her fingertips, how she'd felt not at all herself and no longer in control of her own body.

She never wanted to feel that way again.

She watched Remy's chest rise and fall. "Tell me about the night I saw."

"What night?"

"You told me about it, I think, on Rahzavel's boat." She turned to him, losing her breath for a moment at the sheer unwavering focus on his face. "Zahra slipped into my mind, showed me a vision of it. There was a little boy, holding a baby. You showed me the bit of my blanket."

"It was the night you were born," Simon said at once. "Your mother—Rielle—decided to send us away, keep you out of Corien's hands. I was her only chance to do so. She wrapped you in a blanket, put you in my arms, told me to take you north to Borsvall. We would seek asylum there."

Her hand moved to her necklace. "And this?"

"A gift from King Ilmaire of Borsvall. She placed it around your neck, tucked it into your blanket. It was meant to be a message for him, I think."

Eliana nodded slowly. She had heard various versions of the Blood Queen's Fall from Remy over the years, all of them much grander than this one. The thought made her sad, which angered her. She didn't want to feel sad about the woman whose unholy blood festered in her veins.

"And then she died."

"And then she died. Her last act in this world was saving you."

Scoffing, Eliana looked at the ceiling. "I'm not sure she did a good job of that. And I still don't understand how we ended up here, over a thousand years later."

Your mother—Rielle—decided to send us away.

I was her only chance to do so.

She walked back to Simon slowly. "*You* sent us away. You mentioned a thread, that it was too strong for you to hold onto me." Heart pounding, mind racing, she sank onto the edge of her bed. "You're a marque."

Simon's eyes glittered, watching her. "I was, long ago."

"But Remy said marques have wings on their backs from birth, like a brand. I've seen your back—"

"The force of Rielle's death threw the entire world out of alignment. Many things do not look as they once did. And whatever proof was left on my flesh, the Prophet made sure to eradicate it."

The darkness in his voice made Eliana bristle. "Who is this man, anyway? The Prophet. What did he do to you?"

Simon touched her cheek with the backs of his fingers. "My queen worries for me. Be still, my wicked black heart."

"As your queen," she interrupted, her voice only a little unsteady, "I could have you hanged for touching me without my consent. Isn't that right?"

He lowered his hand at once, but Eliana caught it and pressed his palm against her cheek. "I could also order you to stay as close as I please."

His eyes never leaving hers, he knelt at her feet. "As my queen commands, so shall I obey."

"Your life is mine," she whispered, sliding his hand down her face and throat, coming to rest against her necklace. Through the thin fabric of her nightgown, his fingers burned her skin.

"To do with as you will, Eliana," he said softly. "Then, now, and always."

With her free hand she reached for him. "Come here," she said, drawing him up to meet her. So near to him, she could think of nothing else—not her mother or this world of war and black-eyed angels or the storm still tingling under her skin. His fingers brushed against the dip of her waist, and she closed her eyes, grief and desire twining sharply up her spine.

"Please, Simon." She breathed in and slowly out. Her eyes burned, her tears near and precarious. It had been too long since she had been held, since she had come apart at the touch of another's hands, and suddenly she craved that release so ferociously that her head spun. "If it wouldn't hurt you too much—"

"I don't care about that." He slid his hands into her hair, and the careful caress made her shiver. "I care about nothing else but you."

She moved into him, clutching his shirt to pull him closer. The heat of him beneath her palms cleared her tired mind, sharpened the aching edges of her body. "Is there another room nearby?"

His thumbs touched her cheeks, reverent and feather-soft. But his eyes blazed. "Mine is just down the hall—"

"Ah! There you are."

Eliana jumped back as Zahra emerged from the rafters overhead.

Simon hissed out a curse and glared up at the ceiling. "Wraith, can you not enter and exit rooms through the doors, like everyone else does?"

"What would that matter, since you wouldn't be able to see me even if I did?" Zahra floated down to sit beside Eliana. "Anyway, my way is so much more *fun*."

Simon stormed off, dragging a hand through his hair.

Eliana tore her eyes away from him with no small effort, heat blooming in her cheeks. "Zahra. It's good to see you."

Zahra raised an eyebrow, her inkblot mouth curving. "Is it, my queen?"

"Of course it is." She brushed her fingers through Zahra's wrist. "I'm grateful for your help out there."

"I know you are," replied Zahra, beaming. "I've brought a message for you from Prince Malik. He's coming up with his fathers shortly, to thank you for what you did and to begin discussing…what comes next."

Zahra's eyes flickered to Simon.

"And what is that?" Eliana followed the wraith's gaze to where Simon stood half in shadow, watching the fire. "What comes next?"

Remy sat up, a blanket clutched around his shoulders and his cheek pink from sleep. "We fight him," he said simply. "We fight the Emperor." He looked up at Simon. "Right?"

Simon's mouth quirked. "Something like that."

Eliana watched Remy smile with an ache in her heart. He looked so like Rozen. Same sharp little nose, same bright eyes. She would have to tell him—and soon:

Our mother is dead, and I'm the one who killed her.

She would lose him the moment the words left her lips.

Remy saw her dismay before she could hide it. He left his blankets at once and squished himself on the bed beside her.

"It's all right, El," he told her, taking her hand. "No matter what happens, no matter what they say, you're still mine."

Eliana glared at Simon. "What did you tell him?"

"Navi told me who you are," said Remy, jutting out his chin. "She said I could handle it, and I can."

Eliana brushed a hand across his wild dark bangs. "Remy, this story of theirs… It could be nothing. It might not even be true."

"Think about it," he said. "Your body could heal itself, and we never knew why. But it was because all that power was trapped sleeping inside you, and it didn't have anything to do, so instead it fixed you up whenever it could. It makes perfect sense."

Simon chuckled. "An interesting way to describe it."

Triumphant, Remy grinned at her. "I knew you were special, El. I've always known that."

"God, Remy." She rubbed her face. "Please stop—"

"Let him speak if he wants to," Simon said. "Especially since he's right."

"But if he's right, I'm what, exactly?" She threw up her hands. "A general? A freak?"

"A savior," Simon answered. "A symbol. A queen."

"But I don't know how to do this!" Her voice was turning desperate. Good. She *felt* desperate. "How to fight the Emperor? I wouldn't know where to begin."

Or if I even want to try.

Fighting to save friends and allies was one thing. But fighting for the world was not a task she appreciated having dropped in her lap.

Zahra looked curiously at her. She knew the wraith could sense what she was thinking, and she didn't care.

"I'll help you," Simon said, still watching the fire. "You won't be alone in this. Not for a moment."

She stiffened. "What if you fail me?"

"I won't."

"What if *I* fail?"

"Then we're doomed even more completely than we already were. But at least we'll have tried, hmm?"

"Tell me this, then," Eliana said, "if you're so confident: Will I be like her?"

The fire painted Simon's piercing blue gaze a flickering amber. "Like your mother?"

Beside her, Remy flinched.

"Like the Blood Queen," Eliana said sharply.

"Will you be like her? That's a question I can't answer. Only time can do so. And you."

"I was afraid you'd say that."

At the bitter note in her voice, Simon turned and watched her for a long moment. When he spoke again, it was gentle. "I'll tell Malik to wait a few hours before your meeting with the kings. You can rest, talk with Remy. I'll send for food."

She shook her head, cutting him off. She couldn't talk to Remy, not yet. And hours of waiting would make the inevitable feel even worse than it already did.

"Food, yes," she said, "and lots of it. But after that…bring the kings to me." Then she rose to her feet and told the first lie of her new life: "I'm ready to begin."

ELEMENTS IN THE
EMPIRIUM TRILOGY

———◇———

In Celdaria, Rielle's kingdom, the Church is the official religious body. Citizens worship in seven elemental temples that stand in each Celdarian city. Temples range from simple altars in a single, small room to the elaborate, lavish temples of the capital city, Âme de la Terre. Similar religious institutions exist in nations around the world of Avitas. In Eliana's time, most elemental temples have been destroyed by the Undying Empire, and few people still believe in the Old World stories about magic, the saints, and the Gate.

ELEMENT	ELEMENTAL NAME	SIGIL	TEMPLE	COLORS
sun	sunspinner		The House of Light	gold and white
air	windsinger		The Firmament	sky blue and dark gray
fire	firebrand		The Pyre	scarlet and gold
shadow	shadowcaster		The House of Night	deep blue and black
water	waterworker		The Baths	slate blue and sea foam
metal	metalmaster		The Forge	charcoal and fiery orange
earth	earthshaker		The Holdfast	umber and light green

SAINT	PATRON SAINT OF	CASTING	ASSOCIATED ANIMAL
Saint Katell the Magnificent	Celdaria	sword	white mare
Saint Ghovan the Fearless	Ventera	arrow	imperial eagle
Saint Marzana the Brilliant	Kirvaya	shield	firebird
Saint Tameryn the Cunning	Astavar	dagger	black leopard
Saint Nerida the Radiant	Meridian	trident	kraken
Saint Grimvald the Mighty	Borsvall	hammer	ice dragon
Saint Tokazi the Steadfast	Mazabat	staff	giant stag

ACKNOWLEDGMENTS

———◇———

Fourteen years ago, I had an idea for a book and decided I wanted to be a writer.

Fourteen years is a long time, and there are many people I need to thank for helping me realize my dream and helping *Furyborn* become the book it is today.

First, to Diana Fox, who pulled my original *Furyborn* query from the slush pile, generously (and gently) explained to me just how much work I needed to do, and helped me get started in this industry. To you, Diana, I am forever grateful.

To my editor, Annie Berger, who is an absolute delight to work with—patient, insightful, fearless. Thank you for going on this journey with me.

To my agent, Victoria Marini: Your enthusiasm keeps me inspired; your sheer ferocity keeps me feeling safe and sane. I'm honored to call you my agent—and my friend.

To the entire team at Sourcebooks Fire—including production editor Elizabeth Boyer, editorial manager Annette Pollert-Morgan, copy editor Diane Dannenfeldt, Alex Yeadon, Katy Lynch, Beth Oleniczak, Margaret Coffee, Sarah Kasman, Kate Prosswimmer, Heidi

Weiland, Valerie Pierce, and Stephanie Graham—thank you all for embracing me and *Furyborn* with such passion and excitement.

To Michelle McAvoy, Nicole Hower, and David Curtis, who made *Furyborn* look so beautiful, inside and out. Thank you.

This book used to be about three times longer and took up two massive three-ring notebooks. There are actually people in my life who read that whole thing and still talk to me. Thank you to Erica Kaufman, Beth Keswani, Starr Hoffman, Ashley Cox, and Cheryl Cicero. More thanks to others who read this book in crucial bits and pieces over the years: Kait Nolan, Susan Bischoff, Justin Parente, Kendra Highley, Gabi Estes, Britney Cossey, and Amy Gideon.

To Jonathan Thompson—the Lysol to my Monica, the Simon (Tam, not Randell) to my River, the Brit-Brit to my Cate: thank you for always believing in me.

To my sweet stepsister, Ashley Mitchell, who put together the first official fantasy cast list for this book, years and years ago. I still have that Word document, and I will never stop loving it (or you!).

To Brittany Cicero: You read the first draft of the first version of *Furyborn*, week after week, chapter by chapter, as I hovered over your shoulder, watching your face for every miniscule reaction. I love you. This book would not exist without you.

To Michelle Schusterman: You read the first draft of *this* version of *Furyborn* as I wrote it, day after day, chapter by chapter. I could not have conquered this wild monster without you by my side. Thank you, forever.

To Diya Mishra: I'm not sure anyone else in this world gets this book as completely as you do. You are my brilliant Slytherin witch-queen, my fellow shipper-in-crime, my soul-sister, and I'm so glad *Winterspell* brought us together.

To Alison Cherry, whose marvelous brain made this book so much better than it was, and who has talked me down from too many anxious, self-doubting cliffs to count—thank you, friend, for being mine.

To Lindsay Eagar (for constantly inspiring me, and for your wild, unstoppable heart), Heidi Schulz (for Marky Mark and for being one of the best humans I know), Lindsay Ribar (for that walk in the woods), Sarah Maas (for ballet and *Alien(s)* and your generous notes), Sara Raasch (for our wintry dual launch party and for *your* generous notes), Lauren Magaziner (for your love and support and writing dates), Isaiah Campbell (ditto!), Ally Watkins (for always checking in on me, and for your gentle heart), Katie Locke (for your notes, insight, writing dates, and encouragement), Mackenzi Lee (for your fierce friendship), and Kayla Olson (for Cheez-Its, for our spots at that perfect table, for always cheering me on)—thank you.

More huge thanks and hugs from afar: Emma Trevayne, Kat Catmull, Stefan Bachmann, Megan McCafferty, Sammy Bina, Anna-Marie McLemore, Sarah Enni, Caitie Flum, Adam Silvera, Leigh Bardugo, Corey Ann Haydu, Nova Ren Suma, Anne Ursu, Phoebe North, Serena Lawless, Shveta Thakrar, Laini Taylor, Sarah Fine, Amie Kaufman, Brooks Sherman, Anica Rissi, Navah Wolfe, Cat Scully, Shannon Messenger, Nikki Loftin, CJ Redwine, Eugene Meyers, Ellen Wright, Jay Kristoff, Zoraida Cordova—you have all supported and inspired me in countless ways over the years, and I can't wait to see what the future holds for each and every one of you.

To my family: Y'all have put up with a lot from me over the years. You read those giant three-ring binders. You listened to me fret about getting an agent. You never once stopped telling me I could achieve my dreams. Anna, Drew, Dad, Mom—I love all of you so, so much.

Lastly, I'll thank you, intrepid readers, for welcoming this book—and these characters I so love—into your hearts.

READ ON FOR A SNEAK PEEK
AT BOOK TWO IN THE EPIC
EMPIRIUM TRILOGY:

KINGSBANE

A TRAVELER
AND A STRANGER

*"The dangers of threading through time are many,
but one often overlooked is the danger it poses for the
traveler. The mind is fragile, and time is pitiless. Even
powerful marques have lost themselves to the ravages
of their temporal experiments. Perhaps it is best, then,
that over the course of recorded history, only a few hundred beings have ever possessed this power, and that,
now, most of them are dead."*

—*Meditations on Time*
by Basara Oboro, renowned Mazabatian scholar

W hen Simon awoke, he was alone.
　　　He lay flat on his back on a scrubby, brown plain veined
with brown rocks and white ribbons of ice. The sky above him was
the color of slate, choked with sweeping clouds that reminded him of
waves, and from them fell thin spirals of snow.

For a few moments he lay there, hardly breathing, the snow collecting
on his lashes, and then the memories of the last hours returned to him.

Queen Rielle, giving birth to her child.

Simon's father, his mind no longer his own, throwing himself off
her tower.

Rielle thrusting her infant daughter into Simon's arms, her face
worn, her eyes wild and bright gold.

You're strong, Simon. I know you can do this.

Threads glowing at his fingertips—*his* threads, the first ones he had ever summoned on his own, without his father's guidance, and they were strong and solid. They would carry both him and the child in his arms to safety.

But then…

The queen, behind him in her rooms, fighting the angel named Corien. Her voice, distorted and godly. A brilliant light, exploding outward from where she knelt on the floor, knocking Simon's threads askew and summoning forth new ones—dark and violent, overtaking the others. Threads of time, more volatile than threads of space, and more cunning.

He'd tightened his arms around the screaming child, wound his fingers in the blanket her mother had wrapped around her, and then, a rush of black sound, a roar of something vast and ancient approaching.

Simon surged upright with a gasp, choking on tears, and looked down at his arms.

They were empty.

The only thing left of the princess was a torn piece of her blanket— slightly singed at the edges from the cold burn of time.

He understood at once what had happened.

He understood the immensity of his failure.

But perhaps there was still hope. He could use his power, travel back to that moment on the terrace with the baby in his arms. He could move faster, get them both away to safety before Queen Rielle died.

He pushed himself to his knees, raised his skinny arms into the frigid air. His right hand still clutched the child's blanket. He refused to let it go. It was possible to summon threads with a cloth in his fist, and if he released the blanket, something terrible would happen. The certainty of that tightened in his chest like a screw.

He closed his eyes, his breaths coming shaky and fast, and remembered the words from his books:

The empirium lies within every living thing, and every living thing is of the empirium.

Its power connects not only flesh to bone, root to earth, stars to sky, but also road to road, city to city.

Moment to moment.

But no matter how many times he recited the familiar sentences, the threads did not come.

His body remained dark and quiet, the marque magic with which he had been born, the power he had come to love and understand with his father's patient tutelage in their little shop in Âme de la Terre, was gone.

He opened his eyes, staring at the stretch of barren, rocky land before him. White peaks beyond. A black sky. The air held nothing of magic inside it. It was pale, tasteless. Flat where it had once thrummed with vitality.

Something was wrong in this place. It felt unmade and clouded. Scarred. Scraped raw.

Once, his marque blood—part human, part angel—had allowed him to touch the empirium.

Now, he could feel nothing of that ancient power. Not even an echo of it remained, not a hint of sound or light to follow.

It was as if the empirium had never existed.

He could not travel home. He could travel nowhere his own two feet could not take him.

Alone, shivering on a vast plateau in a land he did not know, in a time that was not his own, Simon buried his face in the scrap of cloth and wept.

He lay curled in the dirt for hours, and then days, snow drawing a thin carpet across his body.

His mind was empty, hollowed out from his aching tears. Instinct told him he needed to find shelter. If he lay for much longer in the bitter cold, he would die.

But dying seemed a pleasant enough thought. It would provide him an escape from the terrible tide of loneliness that had begun to sweep through him.

He didn't know where he was, or *when* he was. He could have been thrown back to a time when there were only angels living in Avitas, and no humans. He could have been flung into the far future, when there were no flesh-and-blood creatures left alive, the world abandoned to its empty old age.

Wherever he was, whenever he was, he didn't care to find out. He cared about nothing. He was nothing, and he was nowhere.

He pressed the scrap of blanket to his nose and mouth, breathing in the faint, clean scent of the child it had once held.

He knew the scent would soon dissipate.

But for now, it smelled of home.

A voice woke him—faint but clear.

Simon, you have to move.

He cracked open his eyes, which was difficult, for they had nearly frozen shut.

The world was thick and white; he lay half-buried in a fresh drift of snow. He couldn't feel his fingers or toes.

"Get up."

The voice was close to him, and familiar enough to light a weak spark of curiosity in his dying mind.

An age passed before he found the strength to raise his body from the ground.

"On your feet," said the voice.

Simon squinted through the snow and saw a figure standing nearby, wrapped thick with furs.

He tried to speak, but his voice had disappeared.

"Rise," the figure instructed. "Stand up."

Simon obeyed, though he didn't want to. He wanted to tuck himself back into his snow bed and let it take him the rest of the way to death.

But he rose to his feet nevertheless, took two stumbling steps forward through snow that reached his knees. He nearly fell, but this person, whoever it was, caught him. Their gloved hands were strong. He peered into the folds of furs over their face, but could see nothing that told him who they were.

They wrapped an arm around Simon, bolstering him against their side, and turned into the wind.

"We have to walk now," they said, their voice muffled in the furs and the snow, but still somehow familiar, though Simon's mind couldn't place it. "There's shelter. It's far, but you'll make it."

I will. Simon agreed with their words. They slipped into his mind, firm but gentle, and gave him the strength to move his legs. A sharp gust of wind sliced across his face, stealing his breath. He turned into the furs of the person beside him, seeking warmth in their body.

He wanted to live. Suddenly, passionately, he wanted to live. He craved warmth and food. He clutched the baby's blanket in his trembling, half-frozen fingers.

"Who are you?" he asked, finally able to speak.

The person's arm was a firm weight around his shoulders, their gait steady even in the snow. For a strange moment, so strange it left him feeling unbalanced and not quite within his own body, it seemed to Simon that perhaps this person was not even truly there.

But they answered him nevertheless.

"You may call me the Prophet," they said, "and I need your help."

ABOUT THE AUTHOR

———◇———

Claire Legrand used to be a musician until she realized she couldn't stop thinking about the stories in her head. Now she is a librarian and the *New York Times* bestselling author of several novels for children and teens, including the Edgar Award–nominated *Some Kind of Happiness* and *The Cavendish Home for Boys and Girls*. A Texas native, Claire currently lives in central New Jersey.